MW00908405

# MYTHIC

Jae Lynne Davies

*Enjoy the read!*

*♡ Jae Lynne Davies*

This is a work of fiction. Names, characters, places, and incidents are products of the author's imagination or are used fictitiously and are not to be construed as real. Any resemblance to actual events, locales, organizations, or persons, living or dead, is entirely coincidental.

**Mythic**

A Shadow Bay Publishing Book/E book

Copyright© 2011 Jae Lynne Davies
Cover Artist: Stella Price
Interior text design: Stacee Sierra

All rights reserved. No part of this book may be used or reproduced electronically or in print without written permission, except in the case of brief quotations embodied in reviews.

# Acknowledgements

I'd like to take a moment to thank the people who've played a role, regardless of how small, in the creation of this novel.

Thank you to my husband Wayne and our two wonderful children whose support, encouragement, and understanding allowed me to complete this novel through dinners and weekends. I love you all more than words could ever say.

To Nonnie, I think I might owe you a box of red pens. Thanks for being the first brave soul to take a peek and for not being afraid to suggest corrections.

To my girls, Sandy, Mar, Kat, and Kerri, for listening when I wanted to send characters into the black hole of literary nothingness.

Last but not least, thanks to Pat, Ryan, Jordan, and Kyle for your weapons expertise and willingness to read for accuracy.

# PROLOGUE

*America – 1756*

War. The new world discovered by Christopher Columbus less than three hundred years ago, was locked in bloodshed. The gruesome battle over territory ensured the victor ownership over grounds the current residents called home. Although horrendous, the war was a minor problem compared to the one that plagued a particular family—Vincenzo and Grace Marino, and their daughter Gianna.

At only two human years old, the young vampire's senses were comparable to those of a human child roughly nine or ten years of age. Considering her infancy, the girl's advanced speech and literacy capabilities, hinted she was unique. The problem was that someone informed the wrong party of the anomaly or abomination, as she'd been defined.

The evidence proving the child's existence wasn't concrete and for now, it was speculation. The fact that the child lived was a miracle alone, but only those who were close to the family agreed, while others within their species shunned the toddler and her family for fear that she was cursed, a work of Satan.

Satan! If humans knew of the existence of vampires, most mortals would claim that vampires were the creation of the same hand. It's funny how the two species were no different when it came to things they couldn't explain or understand, both driven to rash decision by fear because they lacked the facts.

Grace Marino's human pregnancy advanced at a normal rate. Nine months of gestation and a thriving, healthy fetus. Both she and her husband could ask for nothing more. But when the time arrived for Grace to give birth, it became the defining moment of their immortality and they'd recalled it each day since.

"It's a girl! A healthy, baby girl!" Doctor Donovan Hansen yelled to his good friend and father of the infant, Vincenzo.

"A girl, Grace, do you hear that? She's beautiful, just like her mother." Enzo caressed his wife's face, a creamy complexion, covered with sweat and fine lines of exhaustion.

"What do you wish to call her?" The new mother looked to her husband, eyes filled with love.

He offered his wife a glance of adoration before he made his suggestion. "I've always been fond of the name—Gianna."

She smiled with the same sincerity that stole his heart from the first night they met. "It's perfect...Gianna it is."

He looked to Donovan for an indication that the infant thrived. The doctor's creased brow, struck fear. In an attempt to offer further confirmation, the good doctor requested to see his longtime friend outside. Enzo knew that look, the one that Donovan couldn't hide.

"Donovan, what is it?" Enzo studied his expression.

"There seems to be a problem with...Gianna." The doctor purposely avoided eye contact with his friend.

Enzo arched a brow. "What sort of...problem?"

"She's not like you, Enzo, or Grace for that matter. With your permission, I would like to run some tests but at first glance, judging by her mannerisms she seems to be something...else."

"Something...else?" He held his hands up in the air and begged Donovan to enlighten him.

"Her heart beats yet she possesses a set of retractable fangs. I have never seen anything like it and I do not wish to define it before I know more. The one thing that I can assure, is that she is in no *immediate* danger."

"How do I deliver such news to my wife?" Enzo raked his hand through his hair, then stroked the back of his neck.

"We should not be quick to rush to conclusions. For now, I would allow your wife to enjoy her daughter until we have confirmation. Then we will address the issue should there still be one."

"Can I trust that you'll speak of this to no one and keep my family safe?"

Donovan paused, his eyes cold and serious. "I am offended that you thought to question my loyalty. That child is as much a part of my family as you are. I will protect her as I would my own child."

"I meant no offense, Donovan." Enzo drew a long, tired sigh. "The pregnancy was very much uncomplicated and her birth, equally routine but now the thought of Gianna's very existence is miraculous."

"That it is, my friend. That it is."

*Two years later...*

Enzo and Grace rushed through their picture-perfect cottage in the rolling mountains, far away from the populous. "Hurry, Grace! We have to hurry!"

"I'm afraid, Enzo. What if something happens to her?" Grace said as she frantically shoved clothing into a bag.

"Nothing will happen to her. I swear it on our lives. She will be safe, always. Please, trust me...now we have to leave."

"But where do we go? Who will accept her should we not return?"

"Donovan has a daughter her age. He would never turn Gianna away, and the two girls would be raised together. But it will not come to that, my love."

He looked to his wife, the mother of his precious Gianna. "I have always vowed to protect you both, at any cost. You need to trust me."

"I do trust you, my love. I always have. I should have listened when you wanted to relocate to Italy. But I wanted to be close to my family. I thought it would be safe here."

"There is always a risk no matter the location, Grace. Don't fret over what we cannot change."

Enzo took a moment to cup his wife's face in his hands before he resumed his packing for the family of three, but he mostly packed supplies for the child and hoped Grace didn't notice.

He crushed a letter in his hand that he'd received over a week ago. The formal correspondence instructed Enzo to accompany the child to a secluded location for examination. At first, Enzo dismissed the letter as nonsense until Donovan confirmed the document's authenticity. And since Donovan inconspicuously practiced medicine along side of humans, he was adept in all things vampire.

Enzo and Grace were about to face a vampire. One who had learned of their secret, sent on behalf of another to seek the truth of the matter. If their news displeased him, it could mean their end and Enzo took little chance. He armed himself with the weapons necessary to kill one of his own before leaving with his family in tow.

While Enzo was determined to attend the meeting alone, not willing to risk his wife or daughter, Grace refused. She stood toe-to-toe with her husband on the issue and swore allegiance. "Remember, we are in this together," she said.

"I wish you would reconsider," he pleaded.

She faced her husband, and with her arms crossed, gazed firmly into his eyes, "Never."

"We agree, then. We leave Gianna with the Hansens until our return."

"Yes, we are in agreement."

He took her hand and they fled their once peaceful home to meet with the doctor and his family.

Upon their arrival, they explained their dilemma to Donovan and his wife, Mary. "Of course, we will care for Gianna for as long as it takes. Donovan and I will see that she is treated no different from our own children," Mary promised.

"Grace and I will be forever in you debt."

"There is no debt, my friend. We consider you family. And as family, we take care of each other," Donovan said.

"Thank you."

Donovan rested his hand on his troubled friend's shoulder. "No thanks is necessary. May you be granted a quick return, my brother."

With Donovan's well wishes, Enzo and Grace traveled to the rendezvous, prepared to face judgment.

Their arrival at the meeting place came quicker than anticipated. The full moon cast silver onto the clear field, shielded by a number of trees. The landscape would conceal the pending activity and the potent fragrance of spruce was overshadowed by the uncertainty of things to come. Enzo held his wife's hand tighter than usual. Then a man, richly dressed from head to toe in black, approached on foot.

The man was strikingly handsome. His dark hair brushed his black clothing and if not for a small breeze, Enzo wouldn't have known where the hair ended and coat began. One look at his dark, unfeeling eyes told Enzo that the vampire he faced had one objective and no sense of reasoning. Nothing would steer him off course once set.

"Vincenzo and Grace Marino?" he asked in a tone meant to seduce or lure a victim in for a kill.

"Yes, I am Enzo and this is my wife, Grace. May I ask, sir, who may you be?"

"I am Mattias Vitale. I come seeking evidence of the existence of the half-damned."

"I beg your pardon?" Enzo winced at his tone.

"The child is a product of your human wife and yourself, a vampire, is it not?"

"My wife is a vampire as well."

"Do not toy with me, sir. I know well that your wife was human at the time of conception and at the time of the child's birth. Your wife was turned within the past year. That would make her a newborn, herself."

"Yes, that is an accurate account." Enzo could no longer hide the fact that his daughter was different. Mattias knew too much.

"Where is the child in question?"

Enzo grew uneasy and Grace exploded with rage. "You will not threaten my child, you insufferable bastard!"

She slapped him, open handed across the cheek. "You'll never find her! Never!"

Mattias's eyes widened, his pupils dilated, and his fangs extended, in preparation for an attack when he asked the fateful question. "The child is...female?"

Grace swallowed. Her eyes glowed in the darkness as she looked to her husband, their expressions quickly turned into a look of terror. They'd betrayed what they vowed to protect and judging by his every gesture, Mattias had his answer.

Mattias grew silent for a moment. Then he met Enzo's gaze and addressed the couple, "Please forgive me for what I must do...and for what it may be worth, I am terribly sorry."

# 1

*London, England – Modern Day*

On the wet, dimly lit streets of London, a pounding against puddle and pavement was a cause for concern. Nicholas Sutton ran faster than his once human feet could carry him. The roads were dark, but his ability to see never faltered, and his destination wasn't yet decided. Wherever it was, he needed to get there—fast. Bright headlights gained speed while he heard the voices behind him, belonging to both men and women, filled with sinister laughter, as if their chase were a game instead of an assassination attempt.

Assassination may have been an overdramatically drawn conclusion, but he knew that those who followed in the vehicles behind him were indeed, not human. Only one, high-ranking individual could order such lowly creatures to do his bidding. And from the appearance of things, he'd received the message that Nicholas had arrived, and intended to prevent him from making contact.

The scent of smoldering rubber grew near. He snapped his head in its direction, hoping to remain out of sight. The minions were close, close to being rid of him—the one person who stood between their leader and the desire for vengeance. Or so Nicholas thought.

In an instant, the rain stopped—and started again.

*Goddammit.*

He despised this city. It was far too dreary for his liking. He appreciated a town with spirit and this one dampened his.

With the wind at his back, Nicholas detoured through an alley far narrower than the vehicles that gave chase, and climbed the brick buildings. He leaped from the ground to the side of the brick wall, on to the roof with little effort. As he jumped from one structure to another, he caught a glimpse with his peripheral vision, of something moving fiercely though the darkness, striking at will. He could only see a reflection of light that appeared to move along with him, rather than toward him. Although tempted to investigate the phenomenon, he paid it no further mind. He had bigger problems.

While he understood the fascination with this metropolis and the haven London became for those like him, the constant cover of fog and rain was enough for even a vampire to develop suicidal tendencies. He wanted to impale himself on the nearest stake. Aside from the antiquity blended with modernization, there was nothing he liked about London that convinced him to stay. Nothing.

He thought repeatedly about his quest and practically forced himself to make the journey. If not for the situation at hand, he would've remained in his more familiar habitat. His life, while predictable and monotonous, was what he preferred. No surprises, no expectations. Just comfort, plain and simple.

Looking over his shoulder, however, wasn't how he wanted to spend his future. He spent too much of his past waiting to be discovered, hunted and wondering which moment would be his last. But no longer. One way or another, the high-ranking individual Nicholas was so desperate to meet, would listen to reason. Even if he had to be forced.

Nicholas ceased jumping and remained perched on the edge of a building, listening in on the ground below. When he detected nothing but a few human heartbeats, he figured his stalkers had ended their pursuit. He jumped to safety and hurried along.

He found keeping pace with the humans around him, an annoyance. He didn't wish to draw attention but just this once, couldn't they move a little faster? He feared for them, a faint attachment to a past life. His concern wasn't relative to the danger that could turn a corner at ninety miles per hour, but because he was what they truly feared. And they were completely unaware of the existence of his kind.

The rain began to pummel the asphalt, misting the perfection of his eyesight. Damn. The visual interference was a pestering reminder that while vampires were immortal, there were things that disrupted their lives, simple things such as weather. Although precipitation wouldn't cause them harm, it either shielded them or caused one hell of a delay.

He detected something other than the vehicles on his path. A powerful entity teased his senses, tracking him. He felt it, heard it. The presence wasn't the sports cars full of the approaching carnivores. He was already aware of them. He placed the sound of metal clashing against metal, flesh on flesh and a wielded weapon, a sword—maybe.

*Ugh!*

He despised the few times when he was slow to identify anything in his path, the result of a distraction. His only comfort was he wasn't the target. That he knew. He overheard a struggle, followed by silence and then once again striking, sharp metal. Only this struggle was not among humans.

Humans were betrayed by their fear, their screams. The way their hearts raced with increased adrenaline gave them away, making them such simple prey. To taste them during their rush was enough to drive even the most regimented of his kind over the edge. But the presence he sensed tracking him in the night, possessed a charismatic strength. One he couldn't place, its source a mystery.

Imagine being in London a few hours and attracting such an audience. It was one hell of a welcoming committee. He laughed at the thought when he was spotted. Once again the same lights appeared, gaining speed. Increasing his own pace, he made a sharp right turn. Since the streets were dark and misty, combined with his celerity, he was sure they didn't see his maneuvering. Yes, he was proud of himself and the gift of unnatural speed. He owned it.

Without warning, swift darkness startled him. Nicholas had little time to react. He was cornered by the loud screech of a black Maserati, headlights off. The lightless vehicle spun to face the opposite direction from where it came, missing Nicholas's legs by mere inches. He was caught. Game over. Its revving engine faded to a soft purr as the tinted passenger side window lowered and a woman's voice commanded, "Get in."

Nicholas understood the tone of the woman's voice meant business, but her demand sounded far more compelling than it should. His gut reaction suggested he trust the woman and usually, those instincts were good ones.

He hoped the odds were in his favor when he opened the door and met her tempting scent. His nostrils flared with hunger over the sweet harvest of fruits. But now wasn't the time to lose control. He took a deep breath, composed himself as best he could, and jumped into the passenger seat of the lustrous, vehicle. In an instant, he was aware of the possibility that he'd made a fatal mistake.

At first, the woman behind the wheel didn't speak a word. She gripped the wheel and stared forward, avoiding eye contact. She kept her attention fixed on the road ahead. Her expertise at weaving in and out of traffic, plus her determination to lose his pursuers, reassured him—a little.

He watched carefully, not missing how her gaze darted to the rear view mirror several times, looking to see if anyone dared to follow. She engaged the clutch, shifted gears, and held the pedal to the floor, the RPM needle pushed to maximum velocity. He dug his fingers into the pliable leather of his seat and caught a whiff of the upholstery, the infamous 'new car smell'. She drove like a professional on an off-road course, except London contained millions. Her glances in the mirror became fewer. Once she appeared satisfied that their assailants were lost, she took a deep breath.

Nicholas straightened, and attempted to assess the situation when the woman's hand disappeared behind her. She reached between the small of her back and the cool leather of the seat she occupied. His nerves were unraveling when she returned holding a retracted blade freshly coated with traces of its recent victim. As his eyes widened at the sight of the thick burgundy liquid attached to the blade, the fluid gave off a musty odor. His keen sense of smell alerted him. Her victim, as he suspected, was not human.

She carefully placed the weapon on the floor behind the black leather seat, keeping it within reach to wield at a moment's notice, he presumed.

She shot him a quick glance. "Try doing this with an eight inch blade down the back of *your* pants." She turned her head in his direction but kept her eyes facing forward. "It seems you have some fans. Are you always this popular?"

"Not in this part of the world."

She raised an eyebrow. "You shouldn't be running around drawing attention to yourself at this hour. You never know what sort of creatures are waiting in the dark."

*If you only knew.* "Where are we going?"

"Somewhere safe...at least for now."

"Were you the one tracking me in the darkness?"

"You didn't think you made it this far in one piece, without help did you?"

Of course he did. Then again, the legion of doom pursuing him was unexpected. She had no idea how much gratitude he felt for coming to his rescue but it was way too soon to be giving thanks. For all he knew, she intended to lead him straight into the lion's den. "Why are you helping me?" he asked.

"Because apparently, you're being hunted and I'm feeling generous."

No doubt about it, he needed her help and somewhere to regroup until it was safe to resume his mission. But could she be trusted?

The woman peeled off her hip-length leather jacket. She kept her eyes fixed on the road and the rear view mirror at all times, poised to take action. She fidgeted with her jacket, having difficulty.

"Do you mind?" She gestured her arm toward him for assistance.

He reached over and pulled at her sleeve, freeing her arm from the material.

"Thanks."

"No problem."

His curiosity piqued, he forced himself to look away. But he wanted to see what was hiding underneath the bulky material that shielded her body. A black tank top beneath all that leather revealed more of her immaculate skin.

At first glance, the mysterious female appeared average, yet beautiful. She wasn't the kind of woman to grace the covers of newsstand magazines, a type he'd never really favored. No, she possessed the type of beauty that men used to create works of art. Michelangelo and Leonardo da Vinci would both be awed by the sight of her. To Nicholas, she was absolutely stunning.

She appeared to be in her late twenties with dark hair that dangled well past her shoulders. Her skin glistened in the moonlight as she gripped the steering wheel tight. Although not terribly thin, she obviously took care of herself, taking pride in her physique.

The woman caught him staring. *Damn.* She released her hands from the wheel for a brief moment, and pulled her dark hair back into a ponytail, revealing the length of her luscious neck. Through dark eyes, she cast a sideways glance and a half-lipped smile. He was sure she meant to test his restraint, and fought back his own grin. A move so bold, she earned his admiration. So sexy.

Fighting a smile, Nicholas held her gaze and matched its ferocity. He couldn't deny the attraction. His body reacted despite the warning signs and a pleasant scent filtered through the air.

*Human*, he thought.

***

Nicholas and the mysterious woman pulled up to a twelve-foot high iron gate that eased open then swung closed behind them. His body jerked in response to the sound.

"Relax. You'll live at least one more night in peace," she assured.

She parked her car in a garage attached to a large home, larger than most he'd ever seen. Its gray stucco exterior boasted modern Victorian architecture. Judging by the appearance of the structure, this wasn't merely a home, but a fortress. A fortress designed to keep the unwanted out.

He opened his door and quickly followed the woman through the portion of the cottage-size garage that connected to the main home. For a moment, it seemed as though they were running.

"It's nearly dawn and I'm sure you want to rest. There are spare bedrooms in the basement. Follow me."

"I can't stay here."

She drew a long, tired sigh. "I don't see how you have a choice. Need I remind you that *you* are being hunted? You can stay the day, and live another to kill or be killed. The choice is yours. Or you can leave now. There's the door. Let me know what you decide."

She stood still for a moment, crossing her arms at her chest. He gave her a wry look and she reciprocated.

"I assume you're staying?" she asked.

"It appears I truly *don't* have much of a choice and your walls are far better equipped to provide a bit more safety than the nearest five-star hotel."

"You're right and I'm glad you've decided to see it my way."

She led him down a long hallway where the walls were painted a rich burgundy red. After a few turns, they arrived at what he assumed were his temporary living quarters.

As if she sensed his persistent tension, she faced him. "Don't worry. There are no dungeons or torture chambers. They are merely sleeping quarters in a place where you won't be disturbed. I would hate to have the comfort of my guest interrupted. With that addressed, the room contains most of the things you'll need and I trust your accommodations will be comfortable." She turned, with the intent to leave.

"Do I at least get to know your name?"

She paused and hesitated before she faced him with her answer. "Gianna. Gianna Marino. Oh and Nicholas? Do try your very best not to make a mess of things."

At the moment, too many questions ran through his mind for him to retort.

*How does she know my name?*

*Does she know what I am?*

*Does she know that I have the potential to kill her at any time, without warning?*

While he wanted to demand answers, dawn was near and he was famished. If he didn't feed before he slept, he'd awaken weak and ravenous.

Gianna led him to a beautifully decorated room that would provide both comfort and privacy. Nicholas surveyed the space that rivaled a guest suite at New York City's Plaza Hotel. The wall décor held neutral, earthy tones and the tapestries were of rich antiquity, which led him to believe they were chosen with care.

Curious, he walked into the bathroom. It contained both a shower and a bathtub of generous size, enough to fit at least five or six adults. Nicholas turned and walked out. His eyes drifted to the king-sized bed where he'd soon take his rest and he *was* exhausted. How he wanted to fall onto it and regain his strength with a long day's sleep.

Gianna approached the bed, bending ever so slightly over the top of the mattress to smooth out the sheets. It beckoned him further. As her hand ran over the glossy comforter, the lighting in the room revealed the sheen of the oils in her skin. Soft, warm, healthy skin. His mouth watered at the sight of her.

Still leaning, possibly stretched to her capacity, she closed the distance between her breasts and the bed linens. Her tight black pants cupped curves so fine, he wanted a bite. In fact, a bite wouldn't be enough. He wanted to take his time and nibble on her all day, giving but a sample of his talent, while showing her that a bed so large should never go to waste.

Nicholas's libido took control of his mind as he considered pinning Gianna to the bed to have his way with her until they were both breathless and sweaty, or until she begged him to stop, whichever came first. He didn't doubt her ability to satisfy his appetite for both blood and body.

He gazed at her in naked hunger and imagined how amazing she'd look completely bare to him, how her voice sounded while moaning in his ear and the feel of her scoring his back with her nails, on the brink of a fierce orgasm. Licking his lips, he nearly panted over the momentary fantasy, but those wicked thoughts all but disappeared the second he noticed a small refrigerator and the two goblets that sat upon it.

***

Nicholas stood at six-feet-two inches and didn't appear more than twenty-five years old. His lean, muscular build was enhanced by his tailored Dolce and Gabbana suit.

He was absolutely breathtaking and if Gianna could be swept off her feet by a sight, this would be it. She'd always been a sucker for a man in a suit and judging by his taste in fine fashion, it was apparent he came from wealth, a person of importance, in his own right. His black attire was offset by the green silk shirt beneath the jacket, a perfect match for his eyes.

He left the first two buttons unfastened, revealing a hairless chest. The favorable sight caught her attention and she wondered if the rest of him looked so tasty. His hair, which was longer than she thought at first glance, was so dark it looked like obsidian in a spiked, just-rolled-out-of-bed style. In an instant, heat flooded her body, seared by arousal.

Every inch of him, from his dark hair, flawless clean-shaven skin, down to his confident stride delivered sexual promise. Even his scent drew her in. His vivid green eyes reminded her of the finest of emeralds. And when he looked at her, it was such a feral stare that said he wanted to eat her alive.

For a moment, she feared he sensed her desire, yet she couldn't force herself to look away. The man was sex on two legs. Finally, she pulled her gaze from his and let it travel down the length of his body. Chills teased her spine, tormenting her with need.

Worse, she didn't know him, not at all. He was a stranger, in a strange town and a *guest* in her house. A tall, dark, and very handsome stranger. Honestly, he was downright hot. That fact only increased her desire.

*Just strip him naked and screw him until he begs for mercy, already.*

*It's not like he isn't interested.*

*Stop. Just stop!*

*You know better.*

*It's not only dangerous; it's stupid, very, very stupid.*

Still, the thought of wrapping her legs around his strong, lean waist while he devoured her with his eyes, nearly caused her to cast aside all sense of reason and pull him on top of her for an entire day of play to test her theory. She managed to jerk herself free of her trance and returned her attention to the matter at hand.

Wondering if he was disappointed with the room, she broke through the silence. "Will this do?"

Nicholas cocked an eyebrow at her while directing his attention back to the mini-bar. "I suppose so."

She understood his curiosity and began to excuse herself. "It's time to rest *myself*. It's been a long night and we have another one ahead of us. I'm sure you will have many questions. Until then, take your rest and I'll see you at dusk."

Nicholas stopped her before she exited the room. "Wait, how do I know that you won't try to kill me while I sleep?"

"You don't...but I guess you'll just have to take your chances and trust me. Sweet dreams." She gave him a devilish wink before walking away, convinced she'd have sweet dreams of her own. Dear god, he was gorgeous.

***

Relieved to be alone with his thoughts, Nicholas walked to the small refrigerator and opened the door. Inside sat containers of blood. For a moment, he wondered what type of poison they held, but needed to placate his appetite. Without further delay, he removed the seal, emptied the contents into a goblet, and consumed the liquid within seconds. Much to his surprise, the crimson delight he swallowed wasn't human blood and for that, he was grateful. He placed the glass down and paced around the room.

*Shit!* He raked a hand through tousled hair. His unusual behavior upset him. Normally vigilant, he found himself lowering his guard, which could prove unwise. Unfortunately, the options were limited and he couldn't risk frailty. Should Mattias Vitale–the leader of the most notorious vampire coven in all of Europe– detect so much as a hint of weakness, Nicholas could fall victim to his fury, and his journey would reach an abrupt, wasteful end.

Mattias's dealings were legendary. Covens spoke of him with great fear and respect like some renowned mob kingpin, a god among vampires. With fellow vampire Dante Diakos at his right hand, they were a force to be reckoned with. No one would be foolish enough to attempt what Nicholas dared to, but the danger was worth the potential outcome, and his determination almost always got the better of him.

Nicholas needed a mere moment with Mattias who was always well guarded. The vampire had nearly as much protection as the President of the United States or Great Britain's Prime Minister. As if his coven, which consisted of noteworthy opponents Kyle Turner, Cassius Whyte, Dante Diakos and dearly departed Lucas Ashby weren't enough, he had additional security, people who would die for him when he couldn't die himself. A ludicrous concept. Considering that Nicholas was no stranger, once he reached Mattias, he would certainly be granted access to the notorious coven leader. Since Mattias and Nicholas did have a brief but significant history, he didn't imagine he'd be welcomed like a brother with opened arms, but he would be allowed to speak.

While what he was about to present to Mattias was a bit of a stretch, he'd take his chances, offer a proposal, and wait for Mattias's decision. What if his request was denied? He'd have to come up with a plan B, and soon. Although he'd hoped it would be easy, what happened tonight wasn't exactly an indication of progress.

Now, he had a brand new dilemma—the woman who left him moments ago. Why did she grant him such easy access to her home? Why was she *really* helping him? He could kill her with ease, but first impression led him to believe that she wouldn't let her guard down. She didn't seem the type to be so careless. He wondered about her agenda until he recalled the sight of those tight black pants hugging such lush curves, and *her* agenda no longer concerned him. Why did she make him so hard so soon? The woman and her form presented a distraction, one he didn't appreciate.

After feeding, he gazed into the large mirror placed on the wall of his temporary resting place. His stunning green eyes complimented his raven-colored hair. His lightly bronzed skin appeared flawless against the light, but he did look weak and in dire need of rest.

Before allowing himself to retire for the day, he walked to the bedroom door and locked himself inside. Not that locking the door provided much security, but it made him feel a little less anxious. Nicholas removed his pants and shirt and lay on the bed when a wave of comfort washed over him. The feel of the soft mattress and comforter was divine, and he needed it more than he thought possible.

# 2

Several floors above the first level of Mattias Vitale's famed nightclub—appropriately named Haven, he yelled like a stark-raving lunatic. "Is there anyone in my employ who possesses a single ounce of competence?" Dante and Kyle ran toward the commotion.

The coven resided here. The exterior of the building blended in with those around it, a dark colored warehouse in a district where few traveled without purpose. The height of the building, combined with the questionable neighborhood, would lead no one to guess that they took their rest in the same place where they operated a business, luring their victims. It was a one-stop shop. On a nightly basis, they rose at dusk, dressed to impress, fulfilled both their sexual and blood thirsty appetites, and rested again—all without walking out the door. Mattias was savvy and he knew it. It's what had made him untouchable for centuries.

Many of the ancients in other cities around the world opposed Mattias's concept, believing it reckless and allowed for the possibility of exposure.

No one wanted that to happen, not even Mattias, which is why he chose to be so dauntless with having his covens' next meal delivered instead of hunted. However, he did have his limitations.

Dante and Kyle entered a room designed for private and mealtime entertainment. The sleek leather furniture, seated upon a tan-colored Italian marble floor, was strategically placed throughout. The fountain at the center of the room resembled a shallow infinity pool and contained fragrant exotic blooms. But at present, the tranquil scenery had no effect on the mood of the coven leader. Mattias stood at the bar in the corner, poised to kill someone, and Cassius was his target.

As usual, Dante tried to get a handle on the situation. "What's going on?" he asked.

Mattias narrowed his gaze. "Well Dante, I sent Cassius and his group of minions to drive our little problem out of town and even with horsepower on their side, little Nicky managed to escape on foot! Do you know how that makes us look? He is laughing at us, I have no doubt."

"What? Cassius, you have minions?" Kyle laughed, revealing a hint of fang.

Cassius's anger flared. "Shut up Kyle!" Cassius shoved him in a similar manner children would taunt for reaction. Kyle responded with a sneer.

Mattias paced heatedly around the room. "I suggest that you all make yourselves scarce before I'm forced to do something I could regret."

Kyle and Cassius spoke with caution as they made their exit. "You know, if I didn't know better I would've thought that you were trying to get me killed with your little smart ass comment."

Kyle rolled his eyes. "Please Cassius, he may be pissed, but he wouldn't kill you. He just needs to get laid and that little dick tease of a girlfriend better jump on for the ride of her life, or I might make her pay for the inconvenience of Mattias's piss-poor attitude."

Cassius laughed at Kyle's declaration as they continued down the hall to their respective rooms, intending to retire for the evening.

"Don't pretend to disagree with me, Cassius."

"Oh trust me, I'm not. Although I find it amusing how they play off each other, I often wonder who will win...the cat, or the mouse?"

Kyle shook his head at the nonsensical description. "I'm so over their stupid fucking games. It was amusing for the first thirty seconds. It's why I stay away from her. It's not right, what she does to him. Not to mention, she's so hot, I don't know how he controls himself in the first place. Over a year without sex has to do something to a guy, immortal or not, it's fucked up."

"Hey, it's his choice. He made that decision all on his own and now he has to endure. He feels that the end will be worth the means."

"Fuck, he's a better man than I am."

"Yeah, you could learn a thing or two from him."

Kyle gave Cassius a wide-eyed look. "Oh no, not in *that* department. You don't see *me* walking around with a release-impaired headache that I punish the rest of the world for, do you? I'd rather die than change that. The worst part of the whole situation is that they are perfect for each other. It makes me want to fucking gag."

Cassius laughed at Kyle's disapproval and released a sigh, extending his arm over Kyle's shoulder in a brotherly manner.

"Oh little brother, when you live as long as Mattias has, and share his experiences, you will learn that there are some things that are more important than others. You'll realize that you need to choose your battles wisely and begin to appreciate the simpler things."

"Sounds like fun. Can't wait."

Cassius continued to laugh, his arm still draped around Kyle, lightly punching his side.

Dante lingered behind while Mattias finished his tirade. Finally, Mattias calmed down and stared out the window that overlooked the moonlit city when Dante spoke. "He's right you know...Kyle. You do need to get laid."

Mattias marched straight to Dante, standing only inches from his face. "Fuck you, Dante."

"It's true. How long has it been?"

Mattias backed away and released a long, tired sigh. "Too long."

Dante took a few moments to feel the weight of Mattias's sigh. Although he believed that Mattias brought his torturous feelings on himself, he couldn't let the coven leader lose himself in the process. He took a seat at the bar to engage in casual conversation. "I hate to ask how long it's been since you've fed on fresh blood, all because you want things to be right when she finally offers herself. You never did manage to make the transition from the ways of the old world. It's a new dawn my brother, you need to take what you want, when you want it, or you will perish."

Mattias closed his eyes tight before staring out the window. "While I appreciate your concern, I'm managing. I don't need to make a fresh kill to be satisfied. Trust me, it will be worth the wait."

"Maybe you should forget about her and move on. What she's doing to you is torturous."

"I'm not giving up. I will wait forever if necessary."

Dante laughed at the thought. "Great, can't wait to see how pleasant you are at the end of forever."

"I'm sorry I can't laugh with you right now. I have to figure out how to deal with the Sutton coven representative."

"Why do you have to deal with him at all? He wants a meeting, so let him have one. Let him come to you face to face. If it's counterproductive, then we will take appropriate action. After all, he will be in our house where we know things best. Let him be the fool."

"So what do you suggest? That I invite him into my house? He'll know everything Dante. Where we feed, congregate, and take our rest! Do you think that to be wise?"

"I was thinking more about, trapping the prey."

Mattias took a moment to ponder his statement. "You may have a valid point."

"No...I do have a valid point and it's a damn good one. Why stand here and drive yourself mad with the thought of someone as meaningless as Nicholas Sutton? You have bigger problems."

Mattias raised an eyebrow. "Such as?"

"Your tease of a girlfriend."

"Don't worry about her. Her time is running out."

"So are you going to toss her aside for someone more willing?" Dante's eyes grew wide.

"No, never...I'm going to seduce her. I had sworn against it but I'm at the point of insanity."

"It doesn't show."

"Fuck you."

Dante smirked at his ability to revive Mattias's more rational attitude. "So what's so special about her anyway? Why this incessant need to have her?"

"Have you seen her?"

"Yeah, I think everyone who has ever walked into and out of this building has seen her. Is that all it's about? How she looks?"

"Oddly enough, no. I honestly can't explain it, Dante. There's something about her that beckons me on a level beyond rationale."

Dante placed his hand to his head as though he were suppressing the symptoms of a pounding headache. "Stop...you're depressing me. She'll be here soon enough."

"In about eighteen hours to be exact. Now I have to get her out of my mind long enough to rest."

"Gods, you're pathetic."

Mattias extended the kind gesture of his middle finger to Dante as he continued to gaze out at the city in anticipation of his woman's arrival.

***

Twilight was near. Nicholas felt his strength return. He rose and noticed the clothing he'd removed prior to his rest, was cleaned and pressed. Next to the neatly folded pile sat a gift box with a note.

The note read, *"A gift...London has a tendency to be unpredictably cold."*

Nicholas couldn't imagine who'd left him such a gift or what the box could've possibly contained. Opening with hesitation, the box revealed a long black coat made of a wool and cashmere blend. He read the designer's tag, the same label as his suit. Someone paid a great deal of attention and it cost them, considering a coat like this usually cost about twelve hundred dollars. Moreover, the coat was a perfect fit, his exact size. He arched a brow at the precision.

*Wait. Didn't I lock the door?*

He shook his head, closed the box, and headed to the shower before seeking out the elusive Gianna Marino.

***

Gianna had been awake for what seemed like ages. She anxiously awaited Nicholas's arrival and needed to remain occupied. She was desperate to take her mind off that man's exquisite physique and peeling the clothes away from it. How does one do such a thing? She changed into workout attire similar to what she wore last night. Her wardrobe was vast, but when it came to her current situation, it seemed to consist of tank tops, black microfiber pants that allowed for free movement when attacking a target, the sexiest of dresses, and shoes of all styles. She needed to be prepared for anything, including saving herself—possibly from her most recent houseguest.

Gianna walked to the lower level of the home. Most would call it a basement but hers was far from the standard definition. It looked similar to every other level of her extensive residence. She believed such a dwelling was too large to accommodate herself and her minimal trustworthy staff, but the larger homes offered the most privacy, one thing she needed and valued. Her home was chic and contained everything she needed, leaving little cause for complaint.

The thought that disgusted her, was how she was able to sustain such luxuries. Gianna obviously didn't practice normal means of earning a living. No, she came from money, and in her mind, it was tainted with blood. She would've rather burned the entire fortune that was left to her, but Sofia—her most trusted assistant, refused to allow it. Thank god for Sofia talking sense into the woman. She had been right. In order for Gianna to live comfortably, compensate her staff, and fund necessary extra-curricular activities, the money was imperative. It also came in handy for the vehicle collecting hobby she'd acquired. But it would never replace what was lost and she'd give up every dime to gain back what was taken. The money was a constant reminder of a shattered future and she despised every last cent.

Another feature her home boasted was a security system equipped to protect Fort Knox. She wasn't the overly paranoid type, but it had been Sofia's idea. She had the home fitted with a security and intercom system that Gianna thought to be a bit ridiculous, but if it allowed Sofia to sleep easier at night knowing Gianna was safe, so be it.

Sofia had been with Gianna for years, now. Their families were close since Gianna was a small child. Her father employed Sofia's Mother and various relatives for several generations. They were a trusted unit that understood everything her family had gone through, the depths of their secrets, and were handsomely rewarded for their loyalties.

All of those years of service to Gianna and her family didn't compensate for the void Sofia hopelessly attempted to fill. Never having a husband or a child of her own, she so-to-speak, adopted Gianna as her own.

As loving as Sofia had been to Gianna over the years, she carried sadness with her. At forty-three years old, Sofia was past her prime childbearing years and Gianna couldn't help but feel every bit responsible for her missed opportunity.

Still, Sofia carried on. She continued being the strong and independent woman whom Gianna dearly relied upon. As a result, she indulged Sofia's every wish because she understood the sacrifice Sofia made to remain in her service. Gianna vowed to one day find a way to return the favor and bestow happiness to at least one person in her life. If anyone deserved all of the bliss that the world had to offer, it was Sofia and someone would be lucky to have her.

Traveling down the crimson tinted hallways, she paused at her secure gym. She turned the hand print recognition handle and walked inside while the door armed the security system when it closed and locked behind her.

*** 

Nicholas exited the bathroom wearing a dark blue towel wrapped around his toned, lean waist. He hastily dried off and dressed. Pausing to look in the mirror, he fitted himself with the coat that his hostess had left. It looked good, real good. He removed it to remain casual, draped the coat over his arm, and exited the room to begin his search for the mysterious woman.

He made his way down the hall, retracing his steps from the night before, when a remarkable scent caught his attention. He succumbed to the essence and allowed it to lure him.

The aroma was intoxicating, noting the warmest of strawberries. A human, might describe it as fresh jam spread over a piece of warm toast or a fruit filled pastry cooling from a bakery oven.

The scent desiccated his throat as the thirst continued to pain him. He wasn't used to this kind of treachery where the thirst was concerned. It was something he was normally able to control.

Still in the basement, he turned a corner. The scent grew warmer. He was close to losing control and giving into the one thing that constantly disconnected him from life itself. He heard music playing and recognized the tune. "Bring Me to Life" by Evanescence reverberated through the walls around him. He approached a glass door and through it, he saw Gianna in a personalized gym. One side of the room was paned with mirrors and most of what remained was painted white. The large sound system that transmitted through speakers in the corner of each wall was the source of the music he'd heard from a distance. Considering the room appeared to be soundproof, his hearing was a remarkable ability.

Inside, Gianna trained vigorously. She kicked a weighted bag at full force, beads of sweat dripping from every inch of her voluptuous body. Her hair, pulled away from her face was soaked from her efforts. She wore a tank top with tight black pants made of what had to be the world's most flexible material. Black fingerless gloves clothed her hands. He continued to watch her fight. With every passionate grunt and spin, she unquestionably imagined someone on the receiving end of each strike and thrust. But who was she fighting?

She was *indeed* human and the incredible scent causing him to suffer, was hers

Nicholas could take no more. He wanted her. Raw hunger surfaced as he envisioned her sweet blood saturating his mouth while he thrust his hips against her naked body.

It would either be the closest thing to Heaven that he'd ever know, or the final nail in his proverbial coffin as he inched closer to damnation. He was out of his mind with the need to possess, willing to sacrifice everything to claim her. He reached out for the handle on the door.

*Gasp!*

His breath hitched in reaction to the pain. He smelled the flesh of his hand sizzling. Silver, an allergy he couldn't escape. The agony of the thirst was replaced by the stinging heat of his palm as an alarm sounded and cool air filled the entire room that Gianna occupied, clearing the area of any heat or scent.

When the room cleared, she still stood calmly on the opposite side of the door. She appeared collected, as if expecting the situation. "Are you through or do I have to take drastic measures?" She smirked, daring him to challenge her. He wasn't sure if she intended to laugh or strike him with the closest object that would do the job and take his head. If she knew of his nature, why was she so brazen? She showed no fear, no hint of anxiety. Her pulse didn't even race or jump at the sound of her security system. It made absolutely no sense.

*Who the hell is this girl?*

Nicholas looked at his charred hand. The damage to his flesh was now a memory. He had completely regenerated. "I'm fine. You don't have to fear me," he assured.

She smirked. "Oh Nicholas, fearing you would be easy. However, it is you that should fear *me*," she warned.

The tension between the two broke as the voice of an older woman addressed Gianna from an intercom. "Gianna, are you alright?"

"Yes Sofia, I'm fine. Thank you. I'll be up for dinner shortly. Can you please set a place for my guest?"

"Of course," the woman said.

He looked at Gianna with eyes full of confusion. "Dinner?"

"Yes dinner. You know, an event, usually in the evening, where you eat to satisfy a hunger? In case you're not familiar, it involves chewing and swallowing. Nutrition at its finest, it's quite scary stuff."

Nicholas was beguiled by her level of sarcasm and fought back a laugh. She was witty and quick with her comments. "I'm going to clean up. Meet me in the dining hall on the main level in twenty minutes," she said.

He watched with a tilted head as she left the room, enjoying her pendulum sway, left to right in a rhythmic tempo, and he gave his fangs a sweep of his tongue in response.

He retreated to his room while Gianna prepared. To his surprise, he felt guilty for almost taking the life of his gracious host moments ago.

*This is what we do.*

*This is the nature of our species.*

*We take what we need and then move on.*

*So, why are my emotions becoming an issue?*

*To feel this way is unacceptable. I have more pressing issues to concern myself with.*

Specifically the names and faces behind the bright headlights that chased him last night. He hoped Gianna had the answers he sought.

Nicholas made his way into the dining hall Gianna mentioned, when he heard voices and immediately recognized hers.

"There's something different about him Sofia. I can't pinpoint it but I find him intriguing," she admitted.

Realizing that the other voice must be Sofia's, he listened attentively.

"You must be careful Gianna. If he is what you think, you need to protect yourself. I do not want to see this destroy you."

"I know Sofia. Trust me. I know."

As he approached the dining hall, Nicholas increased the weight of his steps, so as not to catch them by surprise. He heard shuffling, making it appear as if Gianna was alone the entire time, and that the conversation he'd overheard never occurred.

Gianna sat at the head of a dining table that could comfortably seat at least ten. She looked spectacular. She wore a white three-quarter-sleeved dress with a plunging neckline, revealing the deep cleavage of her breasts where Nicholas longed to sink his teeth. Her lightly olive colored tone looked perfect against the material that clung to her like a second skin. She suggested a seat where a full cup and an empty plate were set. He balled his fist deep into the pocket of his pants and walked to his place.

He draped the coat on the back of the ornate chair and sat before speaking. "Thank you for having my clothes cleaned...and for the coat. You didn't have to do that."

"I know I didn't. I wanted to. Did it fit properly?"

"Perfectly." Nicholas folded his hands.

"Good. I'm glad."

He sat in silence for a moment, recalling events from the night before. "I could've sworn that I locked that door."

"You did. I have master keys to every room in this house. I took the liberty of letting myself in while you were sleeping so that you'd have fresh clothing when you woke. It was then that I noted your size and decided to add to your ensemble."

"It's not wise to intrude on a sleeping stranger. You never know how I could've reacted."

She studied him like prey, wondering how to adequately paralyze it. After the few seconds of awkward silence, Nicholas spoke, "I'm Nicholas, Nicholas Sutton."

"I know who you are. What I want to know is what you're doing here in London?"

"I'm here on family business. I attempted to arrange a meeting last night and it did not go as planned." He gave a quick response while disclosing little information. He wasn't sure of Gianna's level of hostility but one thing was for certain, he was still alive which meant she hadn't tried to kill him while he slept, a positive step in the right direction.

Honestly, Gianna couldn't kill him if she wanted to. She was too focused on those spellbinding green eyes that had kept her awake for some time this morning. She swore she stared at her closed bedroom door for hours until just before dawn. Gianna prayed it would open and that he'd be standing on the other side, unable to control himself, and need to have his way with her in order to rest. Sometimes she wished life was like a motion picture where the gorgeous and mysterious stranger falls madly in love with the heroine at first glance and *has* to have her. No, instead, hers has to have an excessively inquisitive don't-throttle- me-in-my-sleep demeanor. Great, this should be a fun time.

His gaze penetrated her very soul and while he intimidated her, she'd never let it be known. Never show weakness, never be controlled, and most importantly...never, *ever* fall for your intended target. Still, she wondered if he really knew how to apply the skills his bedroom eyes possessed. A rather copacetic quality that would easily lure her beneath his bed sheets had they met under different circumstances. Oh yeah, she would've definitely liked to return the favor by keeping *him* up most of the morning.

"What is the nature of your business here, Nicholas?"

"I have information that may prove useful to a few acquaintances."

"You are *obviously* not a local. You've traveled a great distance to deliver such information." She made it a point to indentify his American accent that was similar to her own.

"I could say the same about you."

"Where about in the United States are you from?" she asked.

"Cape May. It's a small beach town at the southern most point of New Jersey."

"I know it well."

Of course Gianna did. That prick Lucas, a member of Mattias's coven met his maker while trying to claim a victim in Cape May last year. The poor girl happened to be a young vampire that was coming into her own. Unfortunately for Lucas, the headstrong bastard wound up assaulting the wrong vampire. The girl had a clan close by and they made an example out of him by sending a message to Mattias and the rest of his coven...never fuck with family. Good for them for defending their own. Gianna only wished she had the same defense.

She thought the very reminder of losing Lucas as violently as they did, would've surely set Mattias on the path of straight and narrow. It did just the opposite. He was hell bent on making the girl's coven pay and wasted no time issuing warnings of his own. Although the girl's clan was indeed justified in their actions, Mattias wanted vengeance for Lucas's death. It's an ironic situation, considering that vengeance itself was close to knocking on Mattias's own door.

Gianna hunted Mattias Vitale for what seemed like an eternity. Up until a little over a year ago, she'd been unsuccessful. Frustrated, she came to London to clear her thoughts. When she stumbled across a vampire coven, she had no idea Mattias was the leader until a formal introduction and an overheard conversation. Jackpot.

Law enforcement wasn't her expertise but she didn't appreciate those who took the law into their own hands, enforcing their own rules without the benefit of a council. Any creature deserved judgment from more than one vampire with a serious god-complex. Individuals such as Mattias, needed to be punished for the belief that *his* word was abiding. She would make that bastard pay for everything that he'd done and everyone that he'd made suffer, who were undeserving of such treatment. Oh yes. He would pay dearly if Gianna had anything to do with it and she'd make certain that she did, even if it killed her. She'd do whatever it took to see it though. Whatever. It. Took.

\*\*\*

Concerned about the wealth of information Gianna seemed to know about him, Nicholas was eager to learn the details. "What do you know about me?" he asked.

"I assume that you're referring to the small vampire detail? It so happens that I can easily recognize your kind. I can tell by the way that you move. It's unlike anything I've ever seen. There is such grace in your movement, almost liquid-like that is undetected by most humans. Actually, most humans are in too much of a hurry to notice such things.

"Then there is the appearance of your skin and your unearthly beauty is a matter of fact. A smooth, porcelain characteristic with a reflection that is almost surreal. Most would believe that it was a result of a heavy rainy season in London so you're safe."

"So *you're* not in too much of a hurry to notice the characteristics of a vampire?"

"I wouldn't necessarily say that. I would say that I am a little more educated in the subject than most."

Nicholas paused before asking his next question. He didn't want to seem too antagonistic.

"How did you manage to track me last night?"

"Your presence has managed to upset some major players in this city. When something causes a disturbance, I'm always looking for it," she said.

A petite woman in her early forties approached Gianna. Nicholas assumed this was Sofia. She was dressed plainly with pale blonde hair and she spoke tenderly, like a parent to a child as she cleared the table. "Not hungry Gianna?"

"Not tonight, Sofia. Perhaps I'll grab something later. Sofia, could you please see that our guest's room is tidy before the evening ends? Otherwise, I have no other requests and your time is your own."

"I'll be sure to take care of it."

She reached out to touch Gianna's shoulder as a means of comfort to the girl.

Sofia left the room and Gianna attempted to explain the foundation of her relationship with the woman. "Sofia's a good lady. A little overprotective at times, but she loves me."

"Is she your family?"

"Not biologically. She's my most trusted assistant. Sofia is like a mother, doting over me like the child she always wanted and I try to appease her wish, as she deserves far more than that."

She cleared her throat. Nicholas noted her discomfort and he casually steered their conversation back on course.

"Where were we? Oh, I was about to ask where you're from and why you reside here in London."

"My Mother was from America and my Father was an Italian. I was born and raised in the United States. On the western coast of the United States, I call Astoria, Oregon home. Should I choose the eastern coast, Philadelphia, Pennsylvania is where I reside. However, when the need for time away is necessary or any unforeseen situations that may require my attention arise, I come to London."

"Are you alone here?"

"I have my help but my Mother and Father have long passed on."

After briefly assessing the situation and appreciating her honesty, Nicholas reached for the cup in front of him and drank the warm crimson that occupied it.

"Surely you are not in London alone. What about your family?"

Without hesitation, Nicholas answered. "I belong to a small coven in Cape May. My father, sister, and I remained together despite difficulties."

Their conversation took a serious turn. "Was there a way that you could assist me?"

"That depends. Do you feel that you may need some? I've been following you. I know where you have been and who you have come to see. There are individuals in this city that you want no part of. Vampire or not, you should heed my warning, Nicholas."

"How did you know my name and what I've been doing? I think I would remember if we had met before."

"Look, I know that you're trying to locate Mattias Vitale and you were chased away before you came close. He's a ruthless creature that will stop at nothing to get what he wants. He is power hungry and ultimate power for his coven is his goal. Mattias will not stop until he is the final council of your species. I'm sure he had you followed to see where you'd lead him and that you were in London acting alone. I don't want blood spilled for sport, Nicholas. That is my *only* concern."

Nicholas became angry, raising his voice.

"Your *only* concern?" You know nothing about me! Does my utter presence not cause you to shudder?" Nicholas hissed through his teeth as the thirst returned. Her aroma was tantalizing. Nicholas's anger only sharpened his senses. He'd reached his limit. Thoughtlessly, he lunged for her with the speed of a wild cat. He reached her instantly and stood behind her, his breath grazed her neck. "Never, underestimate what I am *or* doubt the extent of my ability."

She stood slowly, turned to face him and without an ounce of fear in her eyes, she held up one hand, freezing him where he stood, leaving him powerless against her.

"It's rude to attack your hostess without provocation. I suggest you hone your people skills and take the seat that I so graciously had prepared for you."

*Did I mistake her for a human?* "What is happening? How is this possible?"

"So...about those people skills?" Nicholas quickly calmed down when she shifted her hand and guided him back to his seat, while holding his attention with piercing eyes.

"Please accept my apology. I didn't mean to lash out. My anger was misdirected and I'm sorry."

Oh yeah, he could turn on the charm and even make it sound sincere. She wanted to trust him, wanted to believe that of all the awful things in the world, that he was genuine. It was unlikely.

"Leave it to a vampire to believe that *they* are all powerful. I have what you would call a telekinetic ability."

"So you can move things with your mind?"

"Yes, with a single thought. I've had this ability since I was very young. It's been confusing, frightening and has taken a great deal of time to control. Now, if you would please excuse me, I have a prior engagement that I need to attend. I wouldn't want to keep anyone waiting."

"Of course. Will I see you later?"

She gave him a bewitching smile. "Sure, if you're lucky...You can feel free to stay as long as you wish. Something tells me that I can trust you, Nicholas. If I felt otherwise, you wouldn't have survived the ride. Don't make me regret my assumption."

She walked out of the room and Nicholas felt the emptiness of her absence. That feeling could only mean trouble. Serious, fucking trouble.

# 3

GIANNA LEFT NICHOLAS WITH AN ABUNDANCE OF UNANSWERED QUESTIONS. While he hadn't anticipated her ability, there was something appealing about the woman. The essence of her blood and the physical attraction aside, she was exotically charming. Meanwhile, what could he do until he could see her again? He decided to become more familiar with his new setting and make a second attempt at reaching Mattias. The sooner he met him, the sooner he could leave and not risk growing closer to Gianna.

As Nicholas wandered through the lower levels of Gianna's home, he found himself in the extra-large garage. Two motorcycles were parked in the corner, a black Hayabusa with lime green accents, obviously custom-made, and a black and red Ninja ZX-14. He had to give the woman credit. She had impeccable taste for speed. The keys and helmets for the cycles hung on the opposite wall and he thought to help himself. He walked the Ninja out to the iron gate and leaped over with the motorcycle in hand as if he was carrying a child's toy.

He had unfinished business and with Gianna gone, he'd be undistracted. Yet, he couldn't erase the girl from his mind. Smooth, satiny skin and an aroma beyond intoxicating, all he could think about was possession. She was the one thing in this world he wanted for himself and while she angered him to his very core, it only made him crave her. His body tightened at the thought of her naked beneath him while he fed, begging for more. He'd hold her against him tightly as he lapped at her wound and the only thing she would feel was sexual satisfaction. Yeah, she'd like it. He'd make sure of that.

Driving at a dangerous speed, he weaved in and out of traffic with ease. Nicholas neared his destination. He noticed several dark warehouses that appeared abandoned, but he knew better. He parked the cycle in an inconspicuous place and knocked on a steel door. A rugged looking man answered without speaking.

"I'm Nicholas Sutton. Mattias is expecting me."

The man smirked and allowed him to pass by while he followed a short distance behind.

No doubt, Mattias was expecting him. The bastard tried to have him chased out of town before he had the opportunity to make contact. Mattias seriously underestimated Nicholas's persistence. At least here, in the open, Mattias wouldn't attack without being provoked. If Nicholas remained calm, Mattias would return the favor and, at the very least, allow Nicholas to plead his case.

Nicholas needed to take advantage of his few moments with Mattias. How do you convince a vicious vampire leader that the death of his coven member was completely justified, without him lashing out in a demand for retribution? Nicholas was about to find out.

The dark warehouse was merely a mask, covering something much larger. He passed over into another warehouse before realizing that the space where Mattias and company resided was the size of an entire city block.

Music played throughout the building, shaking the walls, and floor beneath his feet. Soon, he took notice that this was no ordinary meeting place. It was a nightclub that contained many people and vampires, alike. He had to give Mattias credit, the nightclub front was a clever idea. The appearance of the rundown warehouse buildings was intimidating to the general public. As a result, no one would vandalize or search them for suspicious activity. Mattias and his cronies could feed, sleep, and congregate with the public in one place while having their meals come to *them*. It was novel, really. Clearly, Mattias got off on hiding in plain sight. Camouflage—nature's craftiest trick.

Once inside, the view was a different story. Judging by the exterior of the buildings, one wouldn't have expected too much but it blew Nicholas away. The interior was dimly lit, denying any suspecting being, human or otherwise, to see something they shouldn't. The walls were painted a tasteful red and sconces hung throughout that were filled with flickering candles. The light of the dancing flames reflected off the dark floors, creating a calm ambiance. The room itself was huge, far beyond the normal square footage for an average nightclub. Mattias obviously spared no expense for his own comfort.

There was no wait at the door tonight, although it was still early. Nicholas must have entered from a private location instead of the front door used by the general public.

From the main entry, Nicholas saw Mattias from where he stood. The security guard led him to the left side of the room where he ascended two stairs and met another guard that stood outside of a roped-off area. Nicholas's escort gave the guard a quick nod and lifted the rope, granting him access to their boss.

Mattias stood in the far left corner of the room as if anyone who entered should approach him with care. Standing at six-foot-three-inches tall, his head was shaved nearly bald. He looked more like a well-built celebrity than a vampire, making him difficult to miss. His eyes were as dark as night and his arms were crossed at his chest as he slowly scanned the room as if looking for someone or something in particular. He was extremely muscular, threatening and looked just shy of thirty human years old. His stance indicated that he clearly led this coven.

As Nicholas caught Mattias's attention, he tensed and straightened from his more relaxed position. Mattias couldn't have appeared less inviting if he'd punched Nicholas across the jaw.

Approaching slowly, Nicholas was the first to speak. "Mattias."

Mattias uncrossed his arms and nodded at Dante. "Ah, Nicholas, we've been expecting you after last night's incident."

"I'm terribly sorry about that. Your less than warm welcome had me questioning my safety."

"Now, I'm offended that you felt my coven was hostile. I do apologize if we've given you the wrong impression, as I meant nothing more than to extend a friendly welcome. Perhaps someone was mistaken when instructions were delivered." Mattias let out an evil snicker.

Mattias took Nicholas for a complete fool, as the visitor blatantly tested his authority. As if Mattias would allow such an act. There were countless times in the past when Mattias ordered elimination to anyone who disrespected or questioned his position of power. He found Nicholas amusing, humoring himself until he could kill him and be done with the nuisance. "Dante! Please make our guest comfortable."

Dante approached and handed a drink to Mattias. He stood an inch taller than his leader. His slight widow's peak gave way to a dark head of hair that rested below his chin with eyes a hazel-gray-like color and equally well dressed. His temperament, calm and observant, gave the impression that he wasn't far from Mattias in the coven's ranks. He seated Nicholas next to Mattias. "Would you care for a drink, Nicholas?"

"No thanks, I don't plan on staying long."

"Sorry to hear that. I was beginning to enjoy your company."

Yeah, he bet he was. He could see Mattias enjoying the thought of mocking his pleas while inching his way to slaughter. He wanted to rip his heart out and show him how black it was.

Nicholas was careful with his words and actions in the presence of the coven. One wrong move could mean his instant demise. On the other hand, maybe they should put him out of his misery. He smiled at the thought of death over the present company. He wondered how, even with immortality on their side, anyone could be so shallow and callous. Both vanity and lechery seeped though the pores of everyone that stood around him and it was aggravating at best.

Nicholas and Mattias were surrounded by two other males. Nicholas knew them well. Cassius Whyte frequented his hometown as the tourist season grew near.

His sandy blonde hair and olive skin were all too familiar. He blended well in Nicholas's shore town like a local surfer, looking the part. Kyle Turner was to his right. His bronze locks waving on his head in a James Dean-like style, in combination with his nothing-can-touch-me attitude, made him the epitome of a careless vampire. Kyle's cold, vengeful eyes studied Nicholas's every move, remembering how he had been with Cassius and his now departed friend Lucas Ashby while he met his demise at Nicholas's father's hand. It was obvious that Nicholas and his family did not rank high on their most welcomed guest list.

Like a breath of fresh air, a familiar voice carried from across the room.

"Mattias...are you playing nice?"

Nicholas recognized the fragrance that accompanied the divinity of the voice. Gianna walked across the room like a goddess. Every eye watched her make her way to her destination and many of the present company stopped, mid sentence and stared as if she walked on air. She was still wearing her white dress that fell to her calves with silver shoes that made her stand at least three inches taller than normal. Gianna moved with the grace of royalty and not one male was ignorant. Her long brown hair was straight and blew lightly in the breeze of her strides. She was the sexiest woman he had ever seen, a feast for the eyes and there was not a single male present who didn't share his opinion.

If Dante *could* be breathless, he looked it, as he gaped with subtlety. Nicholas could read his body language. He looked uncomfortable, as if he had spoken those thoughts aloud.

Kyle licked his lips before wiping his lower one with his thumb while he looked Gianna up and down as she passed by. Cassius shook his head and rolled his eyes at Kyle while he raised a respectful brow to her beauty. She approached Mattias who flashed a pleased grin.

"Gianna...I've missed you. It's been far too long."

"Baby, it's only been about sixteen hours."

"Yes, and that would be sixteen hours too long."

She then kissed him passionately and he happily returned her affection.

*What. The. Fuck.* Nicholas's rage ignited when he watched Mattias embrace Gianna. His frigid body boiled with jealousy and he wanted to tear Mattias apart. But the sting of Gianna's betrayal seared him like a newly forged lance.

*Bitch!*

*How could she do this to me?*

*Was her mission to get information for Mattias's coven?*

*How could I be so fucking stupid?*

*I should've killed her when I had the chance.*

Gianna caressed Mattias's arm. "Mattias, aren't you going to introduce me to your new friend?"

"This is Nicholas Sutton. He's here to pay a debt by giving me some valuable information, information that could give my coven more power that we've ever dreamed...What is it that you have to say Nicholas?" Mattias smirked, feeling all the more powerful with Gianna at his side. "Whatever you need to say, it's perfectly alright to do so in her presence." Mattias pulled Gianna into his lap and nuzzled her neck.

Nicholas hesitated. "Very well...in exchange for my Father's life, I am willing to divulge privileged and rather classified information." He paused, glanced around, and then continued. "I can prove the existence of Dhampires."

Gianna's jaw dropped.

Mattias released a low, humorless laugh. "This is how you expected to pay for your father's debt? By revealing the existence of Dhampires? Half breeds? They are fictitious creatures invented by an author somewhere with the purpose of selling a few books. Dhampires do not exist." He stopped nuzzling Gianna for a moment to take a swig of his drink, downing the entire glass.

"They do exist! Their power is possibly limitless! With one of them placed within your coven, you could use that to your advantage. In fact, I know—"

"Oh Nicholas, you have indeed amused me this evening. What am I going to do with you?"

Mattias looked at Gianna with lust lingering heavily in his eyes. "Gianna my love, what do you think we should do with Mister Sutton?"

Gianna looked at Nicholas with care and wanted him thrown out of the club before things escalated. Although misplaced, she could see the disdain Nicholas held for her. Never would she intentionally hurt anyone undeserving, but he didn't know her from Mattias and she didn't blame him for the way he felt toward her. The longer he remained in Mattias's presence with his irrational claims, the sooner he'd seal his fate and damn himself to Mattias's revenge. She owed Nicholas nothing and barely knew him, but she couldn't have that happen. "Clearly he is delusional. Don't we have better things to do? Let him go. He is of no use to you...Mattias, please baby let's go. Who cares what you can do with him? Think of what you could do...with me." She gently tugged at his hand.

Mattias gave Gianna a searing stare and then returned his attention to Nicholas. "You should thank Gianna, for she has chosen your fate tonight.

"Never let me hear of such nonsensical claims again, for the next time we meet, I may not be as generous...Dhampires."

Gianna led Mattias away. Nicholas watched as Mattias wrapped his arm around her waist, allowing his hand to travel down her side. Nicholas wanted to kill them both and it took every ounce of his being to control the urge. But he had a mission to complete. His family's well being was of utmost importance but that did not stop him from plotting Gianna's swift death.

Before leaving, he was sick from the sight of Mattias pinning Gianna to the wall for a hot make-out session, which they both seemed to enjoy. Mattias couldn't keep his hands to himself as he explored every bare inch of her body while savoring her lips.

*Disgusting.*

Nicholas wanted nothing more than to walk over to Mattias and cut the lips off his face. He smiled at the thought.

Shaking his head at the foulness of the situation, Nicholas exited the way he came, walking so quickly, that he flashed himself to where he parked the cycle and drove back to his temporary accommodations. He was livid. Gianna had deceived him. He was torn between the decision to kill her quickly or make her suffer as his victim, the pawn in his, and Mattias's little game. She knew too much; the location of his coven family, the possibility of the existence of Dhampires, and who knows what Mattias had already shared with his human pet.

*Why do I feel the need to stay under her roof? I have to leave before I hurt her...or worse.*

Just as soon as the thought popped into his mind, he realized if he hurt Gianna, there would be no hope for his father, no decision to be made about his fate. He'd be tormented by Mattias through the rest of eternity and Nicholas wouldn't jeopardize that, no matter the price. He couldn't show his face to his house with that kind of news after causing them so much worry.

He also knew a bit about her. He discovered her gift—her power. She felt comfortable sharing her own information as if they'd reached a mutual understanding. In addition, she didn't admit to Mattias that the two of them were acquainted. She could've done so instead of asking for an introduction.

*That's it!*

That was his clue that she was hiding something bigger. Why else would she walk into the pit of hell wearing a sexy dress and a smile? There must be something more to this woman. He hoped.

# 4

Forty minutes passed between the time Nicholas left Mattias's club and his arrival at Gianna's home. He hoped she'd be there to confront. Not likely. She'd still be with King-fucking-black-heart. His blood seethed at the thought of Mattias's hands traveling all over her body, violating her in various ways. The more he thought about it, the more rage consumed him. He was spiraling out of control. His vow of emotional detachment was about to betray him.

*Get a hold of yourself.*

*You don't feel anything but the adrenaline rush from the ride and the meeting. Nothing more.*

He walked through the garage, as he came to know the particular area of the house well, and searched for Gianna. The main dining hall was empty, as was every other room on the main level. He headed to the next floor, which he had not yet explored. Nicholas roamed feverishly; opening door after door until noticing a pair of french doors at the end of the hall. He pushed them open and met the sound of running water. As he inched his way deeper into the room, he noticed Gianna was showering.

Nicholas could see the shape of her naked body though the frosted glass, private enough not to give away too much detail. He was fascinated. As he continued to watch, the water stopped suddenly. She was quick to reach for a towel before she stepped out of her watery escape. Nicholas fled the room before she realized his intrusion. If he decided to kill her, he wanted to give her the respect of allowing her to face him when it happened.

Continuing down the hall, with every intention of returning to his quarters, Nicholas stumbled upon a room that was more or less a memorial. Old photos and paintings, some worn over time, were displayed throughout. One that caught his attention was a small painting of woman in her twenties, a man slightly older, and a child no more than two years of age. They looked like a typical family that believed in the delusion that their lives where just beginning and looked forward to the years ahead, not having a care in the world except each other. Sadness befell him, a feeling that he hadn't experienced in over two centuries. This room was history, *her* history and the fact that she was alone could only mean that the story ended on an unpleasant note.

*Who were these people?*

"My family."

Nicholas turned to face her. Her hair was soaking wet. She seemed at ease as she casually leaned against the frame of the door with her arms crossed.

"I envy you Nicholas and the fact that you have one. I have paper photos of people far from recollection. This room is a reminder that this is as close as I will ever be to mine. I only hope that yours is grateful for the risk that you are taking. They are equally as fortunate to have you," she said.

Truth be told, he was interested in the details of her pain and felt a strange need to comfort her. She drew a deep breath. "What happened to them?" he asked.

"My mother and father were killed. Both were victims of a vampire sent out to serve justice for something that he didn't understand, and it's my fault, my fault for existing. If it hadn't been for me, they would still be—"

She hesitated to finish the sentence.

"I don't understand. Does this have anything to do with your involvement with Mattias?"

"Mattias and I aren't involved in the literal sense...at least for my part. He has something I need and I'll do whatever it takes to get it. My attraction to him is merely animal magnetism. He's strong, sexy, and ambitious. But ultimately, he's evil and I'm aware of the fact. I hold no emotional bond with him whatsoever, and he'd more than likely return that feeling by ending my life with little hesitation."

He looked at Gianna and wondered how she managed to make the drive from the club and shower so quickly. She was with Mattias as Nicholas exited the building. The timing didn't make sense. "How did you get here so quickly? I was leaving when I saw you making yourself comfortable, and you managed to get here...fast."

"Did you not get into my car and drive with me last night?" She laughed as he remembered how well she operated a vehicle. Her smile was mesmerizing, pure illumination.

"I guess you're right. How did you manage to leave in that short time frame?"

"Faked an illness."

"For me? I'm touched."

"Don't mention it. I thought you'd want either an explanation or blood. Either way, I figured I'd be here waiting...and clean. "

He returned to the photo he held. "Your family...is there anyone else left...siblings, distant relatives?" he asked.

"I have extended family across the United States, friends, and cousins from Washington State to Florida. We're not related by blood but are united for a common purpose, which I guess by default, it makes us family, but at the end of all things, I am alone. My kind don't exist in great numbers, like vampires and humans."

Nicholas's growing frustration mounted. He needed to know where he stood in what was beginning to look like a tangled web. "Enough polite conversation and riddles Gianna! Why did you betray me and run to Mattias the first chance that you had?"

"Mattias doesn't know you're here! If he did, don't you think that you would've been dragged out by now? He's fueled by jealousy, and believes that because I'm human, I belong to him. It's a game, a vicious circle, Nicholas. Mattias    doesn't know this place exists," she assured.

"Tell me something. Whose side are you on Gianna?"

"Mine."

She turned to exit the room. Nicholas stopped her. He grabbed hold of her arm when the metal frame he still held, sliced through her skin like a knife through warm butter. Blood spilled from the wound and Nicholas was taken aback. The pain of his thirst was overwhelming. He held her arm, and before he encountered the only blood he truly desired, Gianna, with panic-stricken eyes, covered the wound with her hand.

"Gianna, are you alright?" Sofia came running toward her holding a white cloth.

"Yes. Thank you." Gianna wrapped her arm and the cloth fell to the floor. The evidence of her wound was visible but the injury nearly healed. A small pink mark remained. It took a week, maybe several, for a human to heal from such a wound.

Nicholas began to question Gianna. "How is it, that you healed so quickly...Gianna, w-what are you?"

Her eyes swelled with tears, no longer able to bear the burden of her secret. "I am an abomination, a monster. I brought death to the only two people I needed more than anyone and you were so eager to rest my secret in Mattias's hands. I am the half-damned...a Dhampire."

He took a brief moment to absorb her announcement. He blinked his eyes several times, in obvious denial. But when he met her gaze, the truth was there and it shook him. "You...a Dhampire? Are you fucking kidding me?"

He studied the length of her. "Your appearance and your scent are so innately human that I wouldn't have believed you were anything else. Are you immortal?"

"It would appear so. I also have a pulse. On occasion, I've been referred to as a hybrid. It's ironic that I am everything and yet, I am nothing. I belong nowhere."

He shook his head, straightened, and looked at her with a lover's tenderness. "You are not a monster, Gianna. You are Mythic."

Nicholas never understood the existence of her kind. Although he knew the truth, most were blind to the fact of their existence.

Most believed the Dhampires were legend, a scary bedtime story designed to keep the vampire species in line. But the real reason vampires feared the very thought of them was because the Dhampire would be the greater predator.

Gianna wasn't comforted by his term. She lost her family to a vampire's injustice and standing before her was someone who knew what she was, and redefined her. Even so, she couldn't accept the compliment and would continue to punish herself for something in which her only role was—living.

"Mythic? I'm a nightmare and I constantly live one. I'm so torn over what I am that I find it difficult to belong to either side. It would be easy to be with Mattias and casually disregard all things, living or dead. He'd provide for me and fulfill every need and desire."

"Please don't elaborate on that last part."

"I don't intend to, but I'm sure you get the idea. Our relationship would be mutually beneficial but it would never be enough for me. The one thing I truly want was ripped away from me so many years ago and no matter how much I try, I'll never get it back. It's my sentence for being and I have to endure. I am alone in this world, Nicholas, and the only thing that will give me any sense of peace is to avenge the death of my family. I want my vengeance. I deserve it."

She stared at him in silence as her eyes filled with tears, fighting like hell to prevent the overflow, but Nicholas wasn't about to argue with her. In fact, he agreed, but felt that in the end, dealing out death wouldn't bring her satisfaction. He feared that her hunger for vengeance could turn her into the very thing she was fighting against. "Why should you be feared? It seems to me that you are a unique treasure...an anomaly, even."

"Everyone should fear me, Nicholas, because the possibilities are endless. As you stated, I am a unique creature. I know few like myself. I remain in the shadows and live among the humans, but clearly, I'm different. I keep Mattias close, but at enough of a distance so that he can't bite without warning. Draining the blood of a Dhampire could have severe consequences. I could be impervious to a lethal bite and nothing could happen, or my power could be intensified as I become a different kind of immortal or...I could be consumed by my predator."

He looked at her as if what she said was ludicrous. "Gianna, it's the same set of scenarios with vampires."

"Yes, but the difference is you know what you're dealing with. It's difficult to say which of those scenarios would come to pass if I were ever to receive a lethal bite. To an average human, being bitten by a vampire is poisonous to their system. An enzyme releases into their bloodstream, binding with their DNA and transforming into something else. Depending on the human infected, anything could happen. A human might not simply change. It affects each one differently. The change could cause some to go insane while others go on living while trying to adapt to their new lifestyle. The means of survival are the same for both you and I...drinking human blood. However, the result of a lethal bite combining with *my* genetic coding, when it is already different from humans and vampires, is unknown. It disturbs me to even think about it."

He nodded his head. "I guess that is a disturbing thought. What about your weaknesses? Are they similar to ours?"

"I have several. If I told you what they were, it would leave me vulnerable and I'd have to kill you."

*Interesting*, he thought. So for now, killing him wasn't on her agenda. "Fair enough...but why does Mattias believe so strongly that Dhampires don't exist?"

"I can only guess it's for the same reason *any* vampire wouldn't believe we exist. Imagine humans knowing about the existence of vampires. Think about the fear and uncertainty they would have, the mass hysteria. They would constantly look over their shoulder for life threatening danger. It's the same for vampires when it comes to Dhampires. We are the product of evolution, of vampires living among and breeding with the humans. My human mother fell in love with my father at first sight, as is the case with most human-vampire attraction. When he informed her of his immortality, she accepted it and their relationship continued. During her mid-twenties, she became pregnant. She survived the birth, which was a miracle in itself. The odds of her survival were not favorable."

His eyes widened. "Wait, do you mean to tell me that if the pregnancy didn't kill her, the birth should have? If that is what you're saying then...she lived, Gianna. That proves that it was meant to be...*you* were meant to be."

"Some things are not that simple, Nicholas. My story obviously doesn't end well. With careful consideration, my father decided he didn't want to watch his family grow old and die while he continued to exist in misery.

" After my birth, while my mother was still human, my father disclosed my nature and offered her immortality to protect me. She gladly accepted his offer to forever remain with the loves of her life. A few years later, a vampire discovered what I was.

He dismissed it as fabrication but still thought my family should be eliminated to eradicate the possibility. My parents realized what could come to pass and took me to a familiar vampire coven until it was safe to return. I never saw either of them again. The vampire took justice into his own hands, murdering my mother and father because they created life."

Something didn't add up and he wasn't sure he liked where this was going. "I understand everything you've said but what I'm still confused about is how Mattias fits into the mix of things."

"Mattias is the vampire in question. His hands are stained with innocent blood."

Suddenly, everything made sense. Mattias believed Gianna's kind didn't exist because he thought he'd eliminated the likelihood.

Nicholas was almost speechless. "That's the reason you didn't reveal the fact that we'd already met. You're infiltrating." He felt a strange sense of relief at the discovery.

"Yes. I'm biding my time, like the predator I am, waiting for the right moment. *I* will end *his* reign...I have already thought of several ways to arrange for Mattias's downfall, but none would leave him suffering in a way that I see fit. However, it would be amusing to influence Dante. Once he got closer than Mattias would allow, it would pit them against each other and the entire coven could crumble beneath the weight of their jealousy. All of you alpha males are victims of your own doing."

Gianna, emotionally spent, felt a dire need to change the subject. "Enough about me and my problems, tell me about *your* family Nicholas. They must mean a great deal for you to come all this way."

"We all have our share of tragedy but I grew up in a loving home. My mother died during childbirth. My father is related biologically. He was turned in the early eighteen hundreds. It happened during his late thirties working, as a college professor in New York. He walked home one night, later than usual, he came across a student who appeared gravely ill. When he tried to carry the boy to a doctor, he bit my father. After coming to terms with what he was, he looked to his only family and didn't want to watch them die when he couldn't follow. He thought of leaving us for our protection, but with our mother dead, who would care for us better than our own father?"

"That's commendable."

"Indeed. He faced a terrible decision and made the best one he could at the time. I remember my own transformation in great detail. I was twenty-two and working to help support our family when I noticed my father looked more like an older brother. I asked questions. He succumbed to the thirst that night and now, I stand before you."

A terrible sadness overcame Gianna as she imagined his memories. "So, you weren't given a choice?"

"He made the right one and I understood. Don't get me wrong, I don't resent him. I accepted what I am a long time ago. Years later, we came across several covens and learned techniques that kept us alive. And when my biological sister, Elizabeth turned eighteen, my father turned her at her request. Then Josephine came along, and we've adopted her as one of our own."

"No mother figure?"

"My father never found someone he thought could handle our delicate situation. He thought it was a much better idea to play the role of a single father."

She nodded her head, concentrating on all of his details. "Now for the question of the hour, how does Mattias fit into *your* situation?"

"My father eliminated a member of Mattias's coven. A coward of a vampire named Lucas who deserved a fate far worse than death. Lucas, Kyle, and Cassius frequent Cape May Point in the summer months. Lucas pursued my sister close to our home and nearly killed her. I heard her piercing screams and came to her aid. I fought as long as I could but he proved to be a stronger opponent than I thought. My father followed the sounds of my sister's cries and after a struggle, destroyed and disposed of the vampire."

She covered her mouth in horror, reliving the event with him while he continued to replay the memories. "My father knew there would be consequences for his actions, but a family friend, who happened to be a Dhampire, suggested that my father hint at the possibility of his existence, believing that the information alone was worth more than vengeance for Lucas's death. When I learned of this information, I assumed it was some sort of myth but I needed to use something that would peak Mattias's interest."

No longer angered by his desperation, she understood the need to use whatever tactic he could to grant his father a pardon. "I would've done the same thing if our roles were reversed."

"You see, Gianna, I came to London to plead with Mattias. I was providing information so he and his coven would withdraw their conflict with my family. I thought that if he believed my claim, then he'd research the information himself and come up empty. I had no idea that I'd stumble upon one in my travels. Please understand that it wasn't my intention to place you or anyone else in danger in exchange for my father's life. I know now that I'll have to handle it another way."

For more than two hundred years, Nicholas believed he knew everything there was to know about his vampire brethren. Gianna was different, she was one of them, yet she was something else. She had everything a vampire could desire, to be able to walk among the living without fear that someone may notice that she was different. Gianna's news took Nicholas by surprise and he needed to collect himself.

"I think I've heard enough for one night and I know we've both been through a great deal this evening. I'm going to regain my strength and we'll talk again later. I'm so sorry for your loss."

Gianna nodded as he left the room, in too much pain to vocalize any feeling. Her constant survivor's guilt choked her. She wanted someone to hold her, soothe her, assure that the blame was never hers, and tell her that everything was going to be all right. However, she wasn't a fool and she'd will herself endurance. She watched Nicholas's retreat, her heart heavy.

***

Nicholas returned to the lower level of the house. Breathless, he entered his room. Vampires never lost breath but now, he was suffocating. He opened the first few buttons of his shirt—a lingering human impulse. The thirst was agonizing. He needed to feed and found a warm glass of blood next to his bedside, prepared by Gianna or one of her assistants. Once again, it wasn't human blood. He imagined Gianna understood that if the blood *were* human, the amount in the glass wouldn't be enough to sate his appetite, and he'd continue hunting until he achieved satisfaction. His actions would attract the kind of awareness that neither of them wanted—a body count.

Damn, he was frustrated. Frustrated over wanting to comfort her, the feelings brewing inside him, and the images he couldn't shake.

# 5

For the next several nights, Nicholas woke and sought Gianna. Tonight, he'd found her in the same place, at this time, every night since his first—at the dining room table. A plate was set for both of them and although his remained empty, it was set just the same.

"I know you don't typically eat human food so I've taken the liberty to have a nightly beverage prepared."

He looked over to the usual crimson filled glass placed at his familiar seat. "What is this exactly?"

"In your glass? Tonight I believe it is Kobe beef imported from Japan. Sofia will only have the finest in the kitchen and I try not to argue. Personally, I think it's too much."

He laughed in agreement, as she smiled at the light-hearted moment. "That's different."

"What is?"

"I've been here a week and I think this is the first time I've seen you smile. It suits you. You should make that a habit." Nicholas reached for his glass and sipped slowly.

She poked at her steak, a few bites missing, while what remained sat in a pool of pale pink.

She grew disinterested in her meal, distracted by what he might possibly be thinking. "Do you want to get out of here?" she asked.

"As long as it doesn't involve handing me over to your boyfriend."

"I assure you, Mattias is not my boyfriend."

"In that case...definitely."

She led Nicholas to the garage and her Maserati.

"Do you mind if I drive?"

She laughed. "Only *I* drive this baby."

"Is there any *baby* that you'd be willing to let me navigate?"

She had an extensive collection. Nicholas was familiar with some of the models as his family had their own noteworthy stock. A dark silver Aston Martin was parked in the far corner of the garage, the Maserati that was obviously her favorite, a Mercedes, a Bugatti Veyron, which made Nicholas's eyes widen in surprise, and a few cycles. Yet, she chose none of those to show off his driving skills. She approached a pale blue Alfa Romeo Spider.

"How about this one?"

Nicholas shrugged. "I guess it will have to do."

"Be careful Nicholas. These aren't even off the assembly line."

He drove to the riverbank where they could both walk and have an excellent view of the Tower Bridge. St. Katharine's Docks was safe enough for them to be in the open among the human tourists. They'd blend with ease. Nicholas parked the Spider and opened Gianna's door. He extended his hand to help her out. She sharply denied. "Thanks, I've got it."

*Damn, she's headstrong.*

Gianna prided herself on her independence, needing no man to save her. She viewed such a dependency as a weakness, a distraction she couldn't afford. Moreover, she didn't want to give Nicholas the wrong idea. But what was the wrong idea? As much as she hated to admit it, Gianna found herself falling for him and thought *that* idea to be a terrible one.

A thick overcast loomed in the sky and the air held a crisp chill, one for which she wasn't prepared. He could feel her tenseness in his presence, like that of a living statue, and wondered why she was on high alert. They continued walking along the edge of the Thames and down St. Katharine's Way. The whiff of sea air reminded him of home, oddly calming. Ornate lampposts lined the damp cobblestoned street and a glow of warm orange light emanated from the fixtures, enhancing her beauty. He noticed that she grew more beautiful the longer he stayed in her company. *Keep it professional.*

Gianna feared that her growing attachment to him could get them both killed.

*What the hell are you doing?*

*You are playing with fire, Gianna!*

Her thoughts began to run rampant until Nicholas broke the silence. "The moonlight agrees with you."

"I hope so. I'm a little sensitive to sunlight. I mean, I won't spontaneously combust but there is occasional discomfort that keeps me indoors. So as a result, I've adopted the vampire sleeping schedule."

Gianna shivered as Nicholas draped his coat around her shoulders. But it wouldn't give her comfort as it recently clung to his frigid body.

"Thanks." She closed the coat around her.

"It's my pleasure. I'm so curious, Gianna. The night we met, you defended me, leading me down a safe path. Are you a...slayer?"

"A Slayer? No. Slayers hunt with the intent to destroy vampires. I don't seek them out, Nicholas. I understand your nature. However, should I notice a vampire taking an unwilling participant...that is a different situation altogether. I *will* defend the innocent. And that night, *you* were innocent. You had done nothing to warrant your death. Mattias rushed to judgment even when he knew all the facts. It was easier for him to run you out of town or to kill you rather than listen, as though he felt the need to save face."

With a blank stare, he looked ahead, considering her points. Of course, Mattias had to save face because he had yet to take action for Lucas. His retaliation was expected to be swift, but that's not how Mattias handled things. "Forgive me for pestering but I still have so many questions about what you are."

Gianna stopped and turned to look at him. "What do you want, a complete bio?" She extended her arm and shook his hand as if meeting for the first time. "Hi. I'm Gianna Marino; I'm two hundred fifty three years old. I'm five feet nine inches tall and I'm roughly one hundred thirty five pounds. I enjoy long walks on a moonlit beach, adding music to my playlist, my extensive DVD collection, fast cars, anything Italian, books by Sherrilyn Kenyon, and occasionally type O-negative. My favorite movies include The Godfather, Interview with a Vampire, The Lord of the Rings Trilogy, and Troy. My favorite music includes Seether, The Foo Fighters, Sinatra, Dean Martin and anything by Evanescence. Does that about cover it?"

She turned away from him and continued walking while Nicholas looked at her in disgust. "Interview with a Vampire?"

"Hey, have you seen Brad Pitt?"

"So you're serious, then?"

"Like a human heart attack."

"I assume Sherrilyn Kenyon is an author?"

"Yeah, she's a romance novelist. If you haven't read anything, you should. Her Dark-Hunter series is addictive. She has this one character, and trust me, if the guy actually existed I'd—"

He interrupted. "Please, I don't think I want to know what you'd do."

"Hey, you were curious, pal."

He shook his head and met a harsh reality. She used sarcasm to lighten an uncomfortable situation, burying anything that could cause her pain, a defense mechanism. "Am I ever going to win with you?" He nudged her arm with his.

"I guess it depends on what you're trying to win."

"Okay, now that I know *who* you are, I'd like to know more about *what* you are."

"Actually, this is the part where you would say Hi. My Name is Nicholas Sutton. I'm insert-appropriate-age-here."

She sighed in spite of herself. "What do you want to know?"

He paused before speaking, trying not to seem anxious. "How do you sustain yourself? What do you eat?"

"You've already seen that I eat human food but occasionally, blood is a necessity. Blood consumption leaves me stronger, but there comes a point when I need blood to sustain my strength and human food is no longer an option. Usually that happens after a long period without feeding. That's why I make it a point to eat at the same time every evening."

"Do you prefer human food to blood?"

"It's less complicated and there's no guilty conscience after I've eaten a cooked meal that I can chew and swallow."

"I know that sun doesn't affect you but what about other things, like your bite, for instance?"

"My bite isn't lethal if that's what you're asking. I've bitten before. It's easy to cut through flesh, which is another characteristic that you and I share but with one exception, I cannot alter humans. I am most thankful for that. I would hate to turn my victim without either one of us being prepared and I wouldn't want the responsibility."

Nicholas nodded in agreement. "Where do you hunt for blood when it becomes necessary?"

"Actually, I don't kill for it. I don't need to. I have the benefit of having it provided without my involvement and most of my staff is kept in the dark. Sofia is the only one who knows what I am. She acknowledges, accepts it, and has been with me for years, assisting me personally while the rest of the staff believes I have a rare condition, making it necessary to keep it on hand. A fresh supply is ordered every so often."

She made it sound so simple but Nicholas wasn't finished. "You knew of my vampire nature but didn't offer me the nourishment of human blood. Why?"

"I know I can control my thirst. You pose a greater threat and I wasn't aware of *your* restraint. It turns out that I made the right decision when you tried to attack me in the gym."

"A wise move."

"Thanks. Vampires have been known to be unpredictable. I needed to proceed with caution."

"How did you become involved with Mattias's coven?" "Being a Dhampire comes with several benefits. One of which allows me to sense the presence of vampires and other creatures with abilities."

"Other creatures?"

Gianna laughed. "Do you think we're the only special creatures walking the earth? There are others who possess different abilities. I've run into them from time to time, undetected of course, and since my quarrel is not with them, I simply move on."

*Interesting.*

She continued. "I sensed some activity at the warehouse that doubles as a night club and it turns out I was right. My senses led me to Dante. However, when a conversation occurred between the two of them about an eliminated abomination in the states years ago, I realized that Mattias murdered my parents and headed the coven. I set my sights on him but I didn't have to. Once Mattias and I met, he staked his claim and no one else dared to pursue me. It took the game to an entirely new level."

Nicholas continued to ask questions that were fueled by jealousy. "So, where is he tonight?"

"Mattias is attending to business matters. He'll call if I'm needed."

"So are you posing as a sort of business partner?"

"I'm an advisor of sorts. Mattias values my opinions and sees them as genuine. He believes I'm a fragile human and plans to turn me at some point. He also believes that by doing so, I will become his for eternity...etcetera, etcetera. It must be my irresistible berry-like scent." She laughed.

Nicholas's eyes widened at the remark. "You're aware of that?"

"He tells me all the time." She rolled her eyes as she spoke.

He laughed under his breath.

"Are you jealous Nicholas?"

"Absolutely not." He lied and she was surprisingly disappointed.

"Good, I wouldn't want to complicate things."

"Gianna," he reached for her hand, "I think we've crossed the threshold of complication a long time ago."

"Uh oh, be careful Nicholas, someone could possibly consider this a date."

"Who said that it wasn't?"

Nicholas set an intimidating gaze upon her, leaving her weak and speechless. His wicked smile followed, revealing a flash of fang when she felt her cheeks warm with blush. Was *she* embarrassed? That never happened. Not to her. If anyone made such a comment, she'd simply roll her eyes or shake her head and walk away laughing on the inside at their poor attempt of a pick-up line. But not this time. And the foreign feeling inside of her unlocked the woman that wanted to be ravished. She'd had her fair share of bedmates, but her need was physical and it ended almost as quickly as it started, which is how she liked things. Lovers would beg her to stay and she politely declined with one believable excuse after another, and made her way out the door. Sure, she enjoyed the uncomplicated once in awhile but this, this was quite the opposite. This was absolutely, positively complicated and for the first time, she wasn't repulsed.

Suddenly, as if on cue, the sky opened up and it began to rain. The thunder and lightning sent many running for cover, but Gianna and Nicholas stood still, allowing the rain to penetrate their clothing while they stared at each other. Both had nothing to say, only gazes to exchange. She hoped that the cool precipitation would be enough of a distraction to keep her emotions under control and extinguish the fire he'd started.

There would be no repercussion for their actions. Neither of them would fall ill because of the toll inclement weather took on the human body.

Instead of joining the masses in running to a dry place, Nicholas took her hand in his, and reveled at the feel. It was both softer and warmer than he thought. He wondered what it would feel like if she reached that warmth down his pants to touch him where he throbbed for her. One intimate touch was worth his death sentence. He looked to her face for a reaction, but stared past her expression and noted how the curls of her hair held the beads of rain, shining like diamonds. Before she could react, he caressed her face and slowly kissed her. At first, his kiss was gentle. Then it grew passionate and hungry.

Gianna wanted to pull him closer so she could feel his hard body against hers. His lips were full, palatable and begged to be sucked on. As she gently nibbled his lower lip, sucking it seductively between her teeth, he moaned in approval of her method. God help her, he tasted like sin and she loved it. She pulled back rather surprised when her sarcasm took control. "No...That doesn't complicate things *at all*."

Nicholas could kiss her all night and into the daylight hours. Only he wouldn't stop there, he'd continue kissing every inch of her flesh until his lips were raw and that would only be the beginning. Her breath combined with his own, ignited him to an unimaginable level. He too, had experienced his fair share of lovers but nothing ever came close, physically or emotionally, to how he felt with Gianna. It figured he'd come to London with news that would backfire because fate pushed him into Gianna's car. He no longer had the will to convince Mattias of the existence of Dhampires and expose Gianna's secret. He'd find another way to vindicate his father.

Gianna once again, took the opportunity to lighten the mood. "Ok. Now it's my turn to ask the questions."

Nicholas sighed. "So be it."

"How old are you?"

"Two hundred and twenty seven years old."

"Ooh...I'm robbing the cradle!"

He laughed at her wit. "No one would ever guess."

"Sweetie, any human in their mid twenties could only dream of keeping my pace. They have nothing on me."

"I know. I've seen your handy work."

"Do you listen to music?"

"Sure, I listen to everything...Metallica, Linkin Park, and even The Beatles. No matter how long ago the music was popular or how the styles have changed over the centuries, good music is good music."

"Agreed. So, what do you do to amuse yourself?"

"Amuse myself?"

"Please tell me you are familiar with the phrase."

"Do you really want to know?"

"Did I not ask the question?"

He pressed himself against her so that she could feel his breath on her skin. "I invade the homes of gorgeous, single women and have my way with them until they scream my name. It's a night they don't soon forget."

Without a hint of intimidation, she laughed hysterically. "Wow, I'm trembling. It's like a bad horror movie...a night they don't soon forget. Don't answer the phone...the killer is already in the house."

Although he'd intended for his words to be flirtatious, they had the opposite effect. Nicholas laughed aloud.

"Oh my God! Did he just laugh?"

"No, I was choking on the dense fog that seems to constantly shroud this city which made stretching my lips a necessity."

"Well...*choking* is definitely different from your normal static expression."

Nicholas looked at Gianna with a hint of regret. He could use her as leverage with Mattias and thought about it momentarily but he could not and would not do that to an innocent person, especially one that he'd unintentionally grown so close to over the past week. It was all he could do to refrain from admitting his true feelings. "I want you to know that my intentions with Mattias won't involve using you. At first, I thought that you'd prove useful but I've become fond of your company and don't want to place you in any sort of danger."

"I'm glad to hear that you want to return the favor."

Nicholas suddenly felt as though they were being followed. "We'd better head back. It doesn't look like the rain is going to let up anytime soon."

She agreed. While trying to not have it appear obvious, Nicholas hurried back to the car and drove back to Gianna's home.

For the duration of the drive, Nicholas didn't see anything out of the ordinary. He parked the Spider in its original position and headed into the house.

Gianna stopped outside door that led to the basement. "I had a nice time Nicholas. It was a much needed change of pace."

"I enjoyed myself too."

After a few moments of awkward silence, Gianna spoke. "We only have a few hours of night left. I'm going to head to bed. I'll see you tomorrow?"

He nodded. Damn, he wanted to do things to her that would prohibit any kind of rest.

"Goodnight."

After Nicholas retreated to his room, he recalled his father's warning. He'd always disregarded his father's advice about how he'd find love when he wasn't searching.

He often wondered if his father possessed the gift of foresight and always knew Nicholas would come to London and reason with Mattias.

*Did he see Gianna coming or was he simply referring to the love that came about with my mother?*

*A love so vast that when he lost her, she could never be replaced by another? I don't know that I would ever want to experience that kind of loss first hand.*

*Wait! What am I thinking?*

*Feeling this way for someone I barely know!*

He was angry with himself for the betrayal of allowing himself to open up to her. But the truth was obvious. He enjoyed being with her. It allowed him to remember how it felt to be human. Damn. Nicholas felt that his emotions were a rather large drawback, one to which he clearly wasn't accustomed. The notion of her blood drove him mad. A recollection of sweet, sun-kissed berries from summer days of his human youth came to mind. He fought to suppress the scalding feeling that made its way into his chest when he drank from the glass left for his consumption.

The relief was immediate. Thoughts of her flooded his mind, her warmth, her deep dark eyes that could penetrate his very soul, if he still had one, and those lips. The notion of those luscious lips, how they tasted, and the fact that he'd sacrifice his next meal to suck on them all day, made him hard and frustrated. He needed to preoccupy himself with plotting his next move against Mattias and his coven, but thoughts always led back to Gianna.

To avoid further complexities, Nicholas was left with only one conclusion. He needed to leave. Packing what little he had, he left it on the bed while he sought her.

He imagined she was still preparing for her nightly slumber and did not want to leave without saying goodbye and thanking her for the hospitality. It was the least he could do considering she was risking her life by being near him. Nicholas wondered if his reason for searching for her was to say a bittersweet goodbye or to end his aching.

# 6

No. This couldn't be happening. After their stroll by the Tower Bridge, Gianna walked upstairs and immediately prepared to sleep; the only thing she could do to suppress the urge to be with Nicholas. She enjoyed him terribly and it scared her.

Her secrets were many and she lacked faith in others, but there was something about Nicholas that differed from the rest. She knew far too well that a week wasn't nearly long enough to get to know him but when living an eternal life, the measurement of time blurred. He was beautiful and she'd find herself lost in his eyes, swearing to conceal what could only be described as a school-girl-crush. It wasn't love, definitely *not* love.

She convinced herself otherwise, but knew something more existed between them than she'd intended. But what were his intentions? He made the first move. If Nicholas planned to use her against Mattias, he would've already made his trade and gone back home bearing good news while she'd be silenced in one way or another for drawing breath.

Gianna couldn't help recalling the kiss she shared with Nicholas, his sweet breath mingling with hers, the feel of his tongue searching for a taste. But she knew he couldn't stay forever. And when it came time for him to leave London, his departure would be unsettling but she'd be busy enough to forget him. She would remember their time as two individuals who simply crossed paths and leave it at that. She'd rather accept his loss through his departure than accept that he would stay to see where their relationship could possibly lead. It was a childish fantasy. Things never worked out in her favor and hanging on to what could've been would be wasted time when Mattias needed to pay for his actions.

Speaking of Mattias—what could she say? He all but defined sexy. She found her attraction to him difficult to explain, as if she was lured and lost the will to struggle. It always took an extensive amount of energy to fight her urges. She knew he could fulfill each and every desire. She ached for him and often found it hard to force the breaks when she took things to the brink. God only knows she embarked upon moments when she secretly begged for Mattias to take her, teetering over the line that dared to be crossed.

*Maybe that's what I want. For him to take control.*

She repeatedly thought about Mattias in ways she shouldn't, and surely, he was aware. It was difficult not to have indecent thoughts and dark desires. His body was rock solid, displaying a tribal tattoo that stretched from his shoulder to his hip on the right side of his frame and the thought of it pressed against hers drove her mad. It almost seemed like a waste to kill him.

A relationship with Mattias would be mutually beneficial. She'd have the power to do what she wished because people shuddered at the very mention of his name. And once she became his companion, her accomplishments could be many. She could double cross him easily, but would find it most difficult when he'd keep her positively blissful in the bedroom. Worse, she knew he wanted her in his bed with a fierce desire that bordered on delirium and she used the constant presence of his lust to her advantage more often than not.

The question was, could Mattias actually live up to the expectation? Or would he be unable to deliver? The latter would be disappointing, but not likely the case. Her chief concern was that being with him would be earth shattering, leaving her ruined. She'd no longer be able to think with a clear mind and more importantly, unable to achieve her goal, retribution.

*Am I really weighing my options?*
*Do I want them both?*
*Damn my human impulses!*

God help her, she did want them both, and for very different reasons. Her highly regarded independence began to wear thin.

At times she wished she could simply ignore humanity and join the ranks of her other half. It would be so much easier to be selfish but she didn't have it in her.

Gianna rushed to bed—alone, hoping to banish her wicked thoughts. At least her dreams were safe.

*** 

Nicholas inhaled long, savoring breaths. Her bouquet caught his attention and led him to the familiar set of double doors at the end of the hall. He didn't bother knocking.

He didn't want to disturb her slumber. Instead, he opened the door to a dark room. Heavy drapes danced in the cool, damp breeze as Gianna slept on a bed of black satin. The black marble floor reflected every inch of light, which made it look more like a celestial observatory than a bedroom.

Relieved by her state of unconsciousness, Nicholas ran his hand across the soft material of the duvet. It didn't seem possible but Gianna was even more beautiful when she slept. She looked like a goddess—the personification of perfection, one that he'd stop at nothing to protect. He shuddered, fighting the connection. But he'd never felt more alive and he'd forfeit his life for her, a stranger. Yet if he lost *her* to death, he'd be destroyed.

*Leave. Leave now!* If Mattias knew of Nicholas's presence here, he'd want blood and he couldn't risk hers. He would never allow Mattias the opportunity to consume her. He couldn't imagine her under the influence of someone so evil, losing her forever. Nicholas fought against emotions he hadn't felt in ages. Watching the pattern of her relaxed breathing while she slept, he reached out and gently touched Gianna's face. She exhaled what sounded like a sigh of relief. She woke suddenly. "You're leaving."

"I have to...but before I do, I wanted to thank you for... everything."

"It's was my pleasure...really. I'm not surprised though, I knew you'd leave eventually."

"Please don't misunderstand, Gianna. I don't *want* to leave but I have a responsibility to my family and it's best for your protection. I will not be the cause of your extinction."

"I don't need protection, Nicholas. I'm not one of those knight-in-shining-armor types that need saving. I'm more than capable of taking care of myself."

"I know." It was one of her most endearing qualities.

"Look, I know we've only known each other for a short time but I can't help but feel this unexplainable sense of security with you, safer than I've felt in a long time."

Nicholas trembled, betraying the feelings he hoped to conceal. But when she confirmed that hers were mutual, it weakened his will. She looked to him for a reaction. Part of him wanted to devour every inch of her delectable body, slowly, until sunset. The other part couldn't fight the desire to be with her and see the world through her eyes. He closed his eyes tight. In his mind, the voice of reason screamed, telling him to leave her without threat. But the man that fought to remain a part of him wanted more, so much more. He drifted off into thought and after a moment of silence, she touched his hand, bringing him back to her, exactly where he wanted to be.

"Hey, it's all right."

"No it's not all right. I never planned to—"

Gianna reached forward, cupped her hand around the nape of his neck and pulled him to her lips. She kissed him so deeply that he could taste her blood through her lips. She couldn't contain her feelings any longer.

God, she loved how he tasted, forbidden. A spicy mix of masculinity wafted through the air. He smelled of sandalwood with a hint of evergreen. The heady concoction unlocked the moisture coating the all too sensitive area between her legs that begged for his touch. She felt his will weakening, he didn't have the desire or strength to end this, and she no longer wanted to be alone.

Nicholas pulled Gianna close, her arms locked around his neck. Little did she know, he wanted this moment more than Mattias's pardon. His cock hardened as her lips moved across his, carefully avoiding his fangs. Each time she came close to his teeth he moaned in anticipation, balling his hands into fists. *Dear, God.*

He silently begged for a flick of her tongue across his elongated fang, the sensation pleasantly agonizing. He unbuttoned her satin chemise that matched her linens, revealing a near perfect silhouette. He ran his hand up the entire side of her body as though trying to study the contour to brand her shape into memory.

Nicholas claimed her mouth, listening attentively to her racing pulse. He slowly reached his hand beneath her hair, under her ear, to the nape of her neck and felt her temperature rising. Her body, incredibly warm against his, shivered at his frigid touch. He wanted to consume every part of her and bathe in the scent of humanity that flowed through her veins as she enveloped his body, his mind, his...heart.

Danger presented itself by simply walking into this room. He intended to make love to her. They both wanted it and he was through denying his part. This was the kind of intimacy she deserved as though it was the last time they'd ever see each other. He wanted her to know how he felt and would continue to feel for all eternity.

Gianna understood that their contact could end with grave consequences. He could drain every last drop of her blood and leave her to whatever fate was waiting, or tear her to shreds without warning.

*Do it and put me out of my misery. But let the ecstasy from your touch be the last thing I feel.*

She pulled away from his lips, panting, as he stared longingly at hers, aching to taste them.

"Make love to me Nicholas...please."

"God, I want nothing more."

Permission granted. With a seductive glare, he kissed her hard like a cursed man who, for but a moment, tasted salvation. He moved slowly with his hand, creating a torturous path leading beneath the waistband of her black panties. His eyes never left hers as he separated the warm flesh that conveyed only a hint of hair. Then, his fingers traveled the length of her heat when he smiled devilishly in surprise of how wet and ready she was for him.

She moaned at his touch that brought her to life and encouraged him to explore, grinding against him. Having long forgotten how it felt to be impatient with a lover brought the reminder of need, of wanting someone so badly that the ache grew into hunger, starvation. She was about to burst at the seams.

Now he wanted her. He needed to be inside of her with a madness so profound he was sure he'd die. Gianna bent her leg at the knee as he removed her panties, dragging the garment from her hips to her ankles until she was bare to him. He paused for a moment, looked at her from head to toe and back again before his eyes met hers. "You have to be the most beautiful woman that I have ever seen."

Evidently touched by his words, she sat up to meet him and delivered a kiss so sweet, he swore his heart fluttered with life. Still wearing his pants that were only unbuttoned due to their impatience, she reached for them. Breathless from the anticipation, Nicholas was at the brink of insanity. "Gianna, touch me baby. I want to feel your hands all over me."

Gianna pulled the belt from the loops of his pants, and tossed it to the floor. Losing herself in the moment, she tugged at the button on his pants, unable to peel the clothes from him fast enough.

His eagerness proved he shared her enthusiasm. Each piece of clothing shed, gifted an arousing surprise. Every inch of him displayed perfection. Before she stripped him completely naked, she paused and rose to her knees while he stood at the foot of the bed. She ran her hand down from his collarbone, over the detail of his pectoral muscles, down his washboard abdomen and gently slid her hand inside his pants.

Reaching down through the soft, short hairs, she closed her fingers around him where he ached, throbbing at her touch. As she stroked him, he closed his eyes and whimpered in satisfaction. He loved the way she touched him as though she'd been waiting for him for centuries. Her hands felt like heaven on his skin, which only made him harder and seeping—famished. She shed what remained of his clothing, allowing it to fall to the floor.

Finally, when Gianna had him bare, in all of his glory, she sat back on the bed, admiring the complete picture before her. She exhaled a sharp, wicked breath and bit her lower lip with the tease of a vixen as her eyes met the length of him. Oh yes, he was impressive. His chiseled upper body was that of a god with immaculate pectorals and six-pack abs. A light trail of dark hair rested just below his naval that led the way to his jaw-dropping erection. She knew that he'd be gorgeous beneath that suit, but she wasn't expecting—*that*.

Nicholas stood at the foot of the bed and gently pushed Gianna down onto mattress. He met her lips and kissed her with a fierce desire while his hand delved into the warm, moist skin that begged to be touched. He did the most wicked things with his fingers and his eyes never left her face, watching her expressions closely as his touch sent waves of pleasure tearing through her.

Gianna threw her head back and cried out in sweet bliss as he lowered himself to replace his fingers with his mouth. He growled, low in his throat at the taste of her, the sweetness of her femininity even better than he'd imagined. With a firm grasp, he held her hips as a means of control. He paused. "Do you have any idea how good you taste? I could be here all day, licking every inch of your body until I can taste you in my dreams."

God, she was so turned on by his words. Chills ran the length of her at the sensation of his cool touch between her legs, replaced by sinful pleasure, his for the taking. She sensed herself growing wetter still, combing her fingers through his hair while he tortured her. She was losing herself in the feel of his skillful mouth. So hot. So close. She bit into the heel of her palm. "Oh...Nicholas!" she cried out.

Nicholas delivered a long slow lick before she tensed, shuddering from orgasm. He kissed a trail up her stomach and continued to dominate. God, he enjoyed watching her come for him. He took pride in her obvious gratification. But he wanted more. He needed more.

Her body begged for his entry and he was eager to comply. "I need to be inside you Gianna. I want to feel your legs wrapped around me the next time I make you come."

Nicholas suckled her taut nipple and paid equal attention to the other, while reaching his hand between her legs to spread them wide. With a single thrust he dove inside her and snapped his head back, moaning in ecstasy at a meaningful connection.

She was more than a warm body. Gianna arched her body to guide him deeper while she wrapped her legs around his waist.

His control diminished with each thrust against her hips. He'd never felt anything so good, so right and he wanted blood, her blood.

Gianna panted and pulled him close.

"It's okay Nicholas. You don't have to be gentle. I promise you, I won't break."

He quickened his thrusts, couldn't help being shameless. But he felt the human in her and the sight of her body, naked beneath his, was almost more than he could take. His fangs made an untimely appearance and he didn't bother to conceal them.

She met his gaze and witnessed the extent of his lust but she didn't stop at the sight of his fangs. No, she met him thrust for thrust.

Nicholas was lost in the feel. His mind spun. Hazy.

*Yours. Take her!*

He ran his hands over her breasts, kneading in time with his hips and she climaxed, screaming his name.

When he heard the sheer bliss of his name on her lips resulting from the wave of pleasure, he met his own almighty release, an expulsion of lust and conflicting emotion. Tremors. His body shuddered, but not because of the act. Unlike past encounters, this one wasn't meaningless.

Their sexual appetites satisfied, Nicholas held Gianna tight, naked in his arms. He was embarrassed. His bloodlust was tested and he'd almost failed. "Gianna, I'm sorry, my control, I almost—"

She interrupted by placing her finger against his lips. "Shh...it was perfect."

Perfect, yes. He pulled her close and showered her with soft kisses until she fell limp as she succumbed to the inevitable sleep that she'd been so desperate to fight.

He'd treasure this perfect moment for as long as he lived, for it would be etched into his memory.

The feeling of her soft, berry-scented skin was nothing short of pure rapture.

Once he was certain she'd fallen asleep, he took the opportunity to freshen up. Nicholas entered the large bathroom inside her bedroom and showered. He dressed himself in the same clothes that were crumbled on her floor when he took a moment to admire her beauty. Her naked body glistened in the moonlight, a combination of both her own moisture and his, and her dark hair fell perfectly over her lush breasts. She was an absolute masterpiece.

If she'd awaken at any moment, asking him to stay, he'd fall victim to those warm brown eyes and give in to her every wish. Nevertheless, he feared that the longer he remained in her company, the greater the risk. Hell, he'd almost taken her blood tonight and could've killed her, a consequence he couldn't live with. He sighed at the next cowardly thought. And even though he knew the ramifications and that it was an awful, clichéd way to do it, he decided to leave her a simple note—one he feared he'd regret leaving more than anything.

*My Dearest Gianna,*

*Words cannot begin to express how painful it is for me to leave you this way. If I stayed the night, I would've never been able to leave you. I feel that this is the only way to keep him from finding the truth and to keep your secret safe. I wish I could've taken you with me. I can only hope that fate will be kind and that one day, we will meet again.*

*Yours always,*
*Nicholas*

# 7

The dark, cover of night arrived as it had countless times before. For the first time, Nicholas felt emptiness where his heart once thrived. He could love Gianna Marino. Correction, he *was* in love with her. And even though the feeling was alien, it didn't excuse how he left things. Leaving her home wasn't easy but he needed to time things correctly, sneaking out just before sunset, before she woke.

He stayed in bed next to her all day, basking in her scent, in the satin feel of her skin. Forcing himself to remain fully clothed, he draped a sheet over her body but couldn't resist touching her, running his hand up the curves of her body, around the perfectly rounded bounty of her breasts. All were now memories.

She deserved better. She deserved a face-to-face explanation—one he'd never have the chance to give. He worried that his departure ruined any possibility of reciprocation, and the longer he endured without her, the more emptiness would grow. It served him right. *Coward.*

He wanted out of London but needed to contact his house before his departure. The coven would want to know his status. He waited until sunset arrived back home. Pulling his phone from his pocket, he sighed heavily in preparation for a verbal lashing. Luckily, his sister answered the call.

"Elizabeth. It's Nicholas."

"Well, it's about time you called."

"I'm sorry, but I've run into a bit of a dilemma."

"A woman."

Nicholas froze momentarily. "What?"

"Your voice gave you away. I had a feeling something was going to delay you." She giggled as his discomfort.

"She's...something else, Elizabeth. A Dhampire."

Elizabeth grew silent. I'm sorry?"

"You heard correctly. She found me causing somewhat of a disturbance during an altercation with Mattias's coven. Not to worry, though. It's over and I'm coming home."

"Will you be bringing company?" She pried.

"No." He answered sharply.

"I'll see you tomorrow, then."

He ended the call and tried to swallow past the lump in his throat over the agony of his cowardice and the thought of the look on her face when she saw what he'd done. He started for the airport with a one-way ticket home, vowing never to return.

***

Gianna opened her eyes and expected to find Nicholas in her bed. Instead, she found his gut-wrenching note. After everything that happened, he decided to leave believing it was for *her* good.

*As if he had any idea what was good for me.*

She crumbled the letter in her hands.

*How could I be so reckless?*

She wanted to die from humiliation over what she'd done and wanted to punish herself with the world's largest I-told-you-so. She had betrayed herself by thinking Nicholas was different, that it was permissible to feel for him. This is exactly why she preferred solitude.

*Let this be a lesson.*

She found her nightly nourishment that Sofia prepared, ate quickly, and walked to the garage. She knew Mattias would be waiting and needed to make her way to him to play her usual role. However, tonight, she was on a different kind of mission, one to mend at nearly any cost. If she wanted to reclaim her iced-over feeling, Mattias could give it to her.

Upon her arrival at the warehouse, she realized it was more crowded than usual. The doors were lined with velvet ropes. The crowd was large and they were eager to gain entry. She noticed Mattias's usual security placed at the front door when she effortlessly walked past the patrons waiting their turn. No one protested. She walked passed Michael Larsen, Mattias's head of security and he nodded in consent.

A vampire in Mattias's employ, Michael didn't appear terribly intimidating. He stood less than six feet in height, lean and muscular. His dark hair and eyes, black as night, stood out against his tan complexion. The gleam of his smile extended invitation but his exterior deceived. A native of Polynesia, he studied every fighting style known to man. Given his age, he had the time. The man possessed the most dangerous of all weapons, a *once* human body and his was one of mass destruction.

On a few occasions, she'd witnessed Michael's capability. She never wanted to experience punishment dealt by his hand or suffer his wrath. In fact, she took advantage of his knowledge when he offered his instruction, teaching what he mastered. He told her she possessed a great deal of skill for a human, an apt pupil. If he only knew what she was truly capable of, it would blow his mind.

She dressed her very best for the evening while setting her plan into motion. Temptation was chosen carefully, a red Diane Von Furstenberg dress. The collar stood erect, drawing attention to her lush neck. The top half of her hair was pulled back, while the lower half fell past her shoulders in long chocolate curls. Not only did she always look exquisite in red, complimenting her dark features and skin tone, but it also happened to be Mattias's favorite color.

As Michael greeted Gianna at the door, she heard the voices of jealous, catty women gathered at the velvet ropes outside the front entrance.

"Excuse me. What makes her so special?"

She looked to the woman in a metallic silver dress, carrying on, waiting to gain entry with three of her equally vain girlfriends. The woman's appearance screamed prom queen. The type of woman Gianna loathed, perpetually waiting for a man to save the day when it took less time and effort to finish the job herself.

The woman was a walking stereotype—an emaciated blonde of average appearance, a mouth that rattled off random thoughts, overcompensating for lack of intelligence and wore entirely too much makeup. Cassius would love to get his hands on her.

She was his type, the shallow dimwitted woman who'd give herself to him the second his sandy locks fell into his eyes displaying that come-hither look. She should introduce them.

"Are you kidding Leyla? She's gorgeous!"

"Well, she's not us." They both giggled. One girl smoothed her hair while the woman in the silver dress adjusted her breasts.

No, she wasn't like them. Gianna appreciated that she was nothing like those women. Realistically curvaceous, she never tired easily in the bedroom and wouldn't break during childbirth if, given her complex genetics, she could actually perform the task. She fought and held her own without the worry of a broken fingernail. She wondered why people like Leyla existed. What was the point, really? She'd run home and lock her doors if she knew what awaited her in the darkness. No prince charming, no happily ever after.

The Goth group stood a few people behind the prom queen. While she respected the type of woman that exuded an individual creative style, not one vampire she knew wore such heavy paint on their faces. Most she knew appeared human and blended the same.

The Goths looked pained or possibly craved some, but they had no idea the magnitude of anguish an individual bore as a result of becoming a vampire. Goths were Kyle's type of women, those who wanted vampires to approach. But they only saw the beauty and power. Or maybe it was the lust, the loss of control with the thought of being bitten. She could see that, but why did they think vampires looked similar? It was something she never understood but thanks to their fashion sense, some vamps found it easy to fold into modern culture. *Idiots.*

Strangely enough, not one woman who stood in line fit Dante's criteria. She couldn't pinpoint his type. She thought he'd like a strong, independent woman who could both submit and dominate when the need or desire struck. She'd witnessed Kyle and Cassius showing off women around the club, but never noticed that type of behavior with Dante, as though he patiently waited for someone, the right woman perhaps. At the same time, she wasn't oblivious and was in tune to Dante's attraction. He never tried to hide the fact and made it very clear on more than one occasion. But she knew Mattias would never allow for such a union. He'd sooner see Dante dead.

Always gorgeous and difficult to resist, Dante was no exception to the vampire trait. In a timeless fashion, his black hair rested midway between his neck and shoulders. His hazel eyes were mesmerizing and seemed to change color according to his mood. She imagined him in old world London dressed to the nines in a classic tuxedo with tails and a long cape. She often allowed her mind to wander into fantasies starring Dante Diakos.

All the vamps in Mattias's coven were attractive but she remained detached, careful not to lust. But it was impossible not to notice desire emitting from all who'd approach. Women went crazy for Cassius Whyte. Although blonde was not her type he was unquestionably handsome.

He resembled a stereotypical surfer. He donned straight, sandy blonde hair that he'd constantly brush away from his perfectly chiseled face, was lean bodied and of average height. His sun kissed skin in contrast to that light hair, combined with a smile to die for, made him stand out from the rest of the coven.

Evidence of his approachability was apparent several nights a week. He'd often have two at a time, one on each arm. Dinner and dessert she called them. But she wasn't fooled by his radiating smile. She knew the kind side of Cassius, but she'd also met the cunning hunter.

Finally, Kyle Turner came to mind. The youngest of the clan, appeared no less than nineteen human years old. His youthful allure and chiseled jaw line appealed to many. The way his bronze locks rested on top of his head, in a model-like style, mirrored a billboard in Times Square. He spent quite a bit of time concentrating on his appearance and it suited him. However, his vampiric infancy always led to his carelessness.

He jeopardized the coven in several instances by taking victims people would notice once they'd vanish, people of high social status, celebrities, and political figures. It gave him a greater rush. Mattias warned him about such behavior but always sent Cassius to clean up any and all evidence. No one, including Gianna, ever understood why Mattias allowed such insubordination.

Kyle's actions toward her were colder than the rest. He'd comment here and there about how she and Mattias were so appropriately matched and how she'd prove useful to their coven, but they didn't interact. He wasn't important and was completely expendable if the situation ever arose.

Gianna wondered how Sofia would react if she knew her intention. Sofia worried, and for good reason. She often placed herself in danger and although Sofia would understand the motives, she'd be upset.

The fact that Sofia thought of her as a daughter was ridiculous. Gianna was older than Sofia's Great-great grandmother. She knew that she appeared as a woman in her twenties, equally conflicted and stubborn.

If Gianna had the ability to turn Sofia, she wouldn't give it a second thought. She'd be a trustworthy and important ally, both of which were rare in her world.

Still, she couldn't change what she was about to do. Part of her wanted it and the other was terrified. Mostly, she wanted to be—numb. She was willing to take it as far as she could, aware of the recklessness of her actions.

As she continued her way into the warehouse, she overheard comments from the men, as well. Whistles and banter not meant for a female of her nature, although many would feel complimented.

"Hey baby! A hottie like you shouldn't be going inside or leaving alone," one man yelled.

The males obviously lacked in other departments where it actually counted. Men that Mattias and Dante would kill with ease for lack of toleration and what they would consider disrespect. She laughed at them, shook her head, and walked through the doors.

The rock music was loud and the lights were dim. Gianna stepped up slightly onto the floor where Mattias was visible, and walked to his usual seating area in the very back of the room. Several seats were blocked by more ropes and security. He was the walking definition of temptation. Any woman would ache by simply looking in his direction and almost all wanted to jump on top of him with the promise of a night of extreme gratification, the kind that would serve as a reminder with each tender movement the next day, like a good workout. In fact, she knew they did. She was the object of immeasurable envy.

The women didn't appreciate the way she captured Mattias's interest, but neither cared much for the opinions of others, and when he kissed her, he let the world know she was his. Anyone out of their mind enough to pursue her quickly learned she was off limits, and never made the same mistake a second time.

Mattias's shirt was slightly unbuttoned revealing a hint of a smooth muscular chest and neck. He offered sinister smiles while speaking casually with Cassius as he held a drink he'd sip to appear more human and blend in with his crowd. His body language hinted at his comfort. He'd tense during more serious situations. It was sad that she knew so much about him while she plotted his end, almost as if she cared how he felt. She quickly shook off the unsettling feeling of empathy, talking herself down. *Keep your eye on the prize.*

He stopped mid conversation and gaped at the sight of her. The rest of his company stared as she glided across the room to greet him. He stood and welcomed her with a powerful embrace, delivering a playful nibble to her earlobe, his approval obvious.

Her position in this coven was crucial. She acted as his advisor while he planned for something more. Her relaxed demeanor allowed Mattias to instruct her in the ways of his dealings and believed her capable of making an informed decision, one he relied heavily upon. He valued her opinions and she was able to coax him into making any decision in her favor, for he believed it was for the good of his organization.

Gianna gained the knowledge of Mattias's secrets, potential weaknesses and investigated him much further. But she grew closer to him. A victim of his own desire, he deemed himself unable to look at another woman. She alone was his conquest.

Confident, he felt he'd eventually succeed in wearing her down but evolved into something else. In Gianna, he found his eternal companion. She laughed at the idea. *Mattias and I, one infinitely dysfunctional couple. I wonder if they have counseling for our situation.*

They'd spend half of their time together trying to kill each other. The rest they'd spend ripping each other's clothes off to throw down 'bedroom-style'.

She intended to give herself to him tonight. He'd waited long enough and she'd run out of excuses. Why not? She could use the disruption. In fact, she'd welcome one.

Still gaping, Mattias managed to snap his jaw closed and found the words to speak. "Wow, Gianna. You look...amazing."

*No kidding.*

He kissed her harder than usual. Betrayed by his actions, she knew his thoughts. He was no different from every other man she'd come across. Both alive and dead, they were all so easy to operate. One small act of persuasion and they were for the taking. Upon kissing Mattias, she quickly identified the Irish whiskey on his breath. "Mmm...Jameson?"

"Of course. Did you expect anything less than the best?"

No, she didn't. She licked her lips, enjoying the spice of the alcohol. Noticing him watching her every move, she pulled her bottom lip in between her teeth and let it slide out ever so slowly, seductively as she gave him a searing once over.

***

Mattias wasn't exactly sure what had gotten into Gianna, but he'd be damned sure he took advantage of it.

She made him painfully hard every time she was in his presence, as if his body was instantly aware of her essence. If it weren't for his promise not to press the issue until she was ready, he would've had her begging every night since he first laid eyes on the beauty. When she stood by his side, he felt even more empowered by the paradise of her presence. He knew his weakness when it came to her, in too deep, but he wanted no cure for his addiction.

He envisioned bending her to his will, of charming her to give into his every whim. Damn him for wanting her to come to him freely. He wanted nothing more than for her to drag him away from business for a naughty romp that would last for days. And he would most definitely deliver, make her suffer for every night she'd denied him, every night she could've satisfied his lascivious appetite. He knew she'd be a vixen in the bedroom. No one had a body like hers and lacked deliverance. It would be an absolute sin against man to be able to tease with the sight of her, and not be so talented. Centuries later, he knew that even though the world was indeed a cruel place, it seldom worked that way. Would tonight be the night? Damn, he sure hoped so.

He leaned into her and whispered, "Seriously baby, that dress looks incredible."

She gently pressed herself against his side, allowing her breasts to touch him, and spoke softly enough so only he'd be able to hear. "How do you think it would look off of me?"

He smiled. "Mmm...I think I have an idea." His eyes darkened with the potency of lust.

"Let's go and test your theory." She gave a coy smile.

"Really?" He couldn't believe his ears.

"If you feel differently then—"

"It's not nice to tease, Gianna," he interrupted.

"Then we're wasting time that could be used elsewhere."

Mattias looked at Dante and gave him instructions along with a heeded warning if they weren't followed. "No one disturbs us Dante. Do you hear me? No one. I don't care if the building catches fire."

Through long hair, Dante glared in jealousy. "Got it."

Mattias stood behind Gianna wrapping his large arms around her waist as she took his hand, leading him away, burning for her with every step they took toward his bedroom.

# 8

Gianna and Mattias entered his penthouse on the highest level of the building. He led her to his bedchamber, and allowed her to enter first. Gianna stared at his bed, having second thoughts. When she turned to face him, he'd already removed his shirt. He didn't waste any time. She cast a slow, hot gaze and knew she was a goner, but continued to play the game.

God, she'd dreamed of gripping those broad shoulders. Every single detail of his body bulged with perfection exactly where necessary. And the art, hugging his entire right side, from his neck to his hip was simply delicious.

Her heart raced. She nearly salivated. Damn, the man was ripped and she wanted to trace the detail of his tattoo with her tongue. She was hot all over, dripping with arousal. Shit. She wanted him. Actually, it wasn't him she wanted. No, it could be anyone with that body, charm, and hint of diabolic aura. Yeah right. She was done for.

She thought of this moment too often. His muscular build pressed against hers, her resistance dwindling as she grew weak, unable to hold back when she reached the breaking point, begging him to take her and do what he wished. But he's a coward, a murderer. Isn't he? Why? Why did he have to live up to her fantastical expectation?

*Relax. You're just using him and that delectable body.*

There he stood, in a position meant to seduce, to overpower. He looked deep into her eyes with a ravishing glare that made her knees weak and smirked in spite of himself, curling one corner of his lip into an evil grin. "We'll eventually end up in the bed."

She cocked an eyebrow. "Eventually?"

Just then, he kissed her so fiercely that her head spun in a passionate haze. Moaning at the taste of him, she tried to put forth the effort of a struggle but felt herself being pulled in, beginning to lose control. Secretly, she loved the taste of the alcohol on his breath. It drove her mad as her tongue longed for the flavor.

He lifted her against the wall and bound her hands with his own, pinning her with his body. Locked. Trapped. Foreplay. Who had the upper hand in their game of seduction? The roles began to blur. He released her hands. But before he lowered her to her feet, she'd removed his belt and unfastened the button on his black pants.

She pulled him close, placing her hands on his back. Not a single inch of him was soft. Duly noted when he pressed his lips to hers as he unzipped her dress. The garment floated to the floor, revealing the sexy black lace underneath. They were both breathing heavily. "I've been waiting for this for a long time," he panted.

She smiled, hoping to keep her wits about her. "And you've been patient."

He leaned his forehead against hers, towering over her with a six inch advantage. "I want you so badly Gianna, you do realize I could hurt you."

She tugged at his unbuttoned pants, an aggressive move on her part. "I'm hoping that you do."

"It will be difficult to use restraint. You have no idea what you do to me."

"Show me."

He leaned in for another heated lip lock before she interrupted.

"First, I have one condition."

He sighed. "Of course you do...what is it?"

"No biting. Not tonight."

His eyes widened and he backed away to meet her gaze. "You have *got* to be kidding!"

Didn't she? To expect this sort of control when all he wanted to do was lose it? If she hadn't made him wait so long he could almost guarantee his resistance, but he hoped she'd reconsider. He imagined her blood tasted as good as her body, but if he couldn't have both, right now, he'd settle for one. He'd have her blood later. She would eventually beg him to taste her. He was that sure of himself.

Gianna knew this was his greatest challenge but she needed something over him, something that could keep him under control, *her* control, until the time came to play her ace. She knew that asking was nothing short of cruelty, but took her chances and made the request. Hell, if he was as good a lover as he was a cunning, lying, killer, she might offer herself to him on a platter. "Not kidding. Can you control yourself for me? I promise I'll make it worth your while."

He leaned into her, pressing his rock-hard erection into her hip. "You don't make things easy Gianna."

"Baby, nothing worthwhile is easy, but if you don't agree I'll understand. We can always wait for another—"

"No. No more waiting. Too long have I watched you, wanted you while not being able to touch you. It has been nothing short of excruciating and I'm through with it.

"I guess we have a deal, then?"

He never answered. He took hold of her with a fervent kiss.

She almost felt guilty for making him feel this way.

*Do I want to be with him?*

It was debatable. He exuded undeniable sex appeal. But she knew her reasons for engaging in this situation. She wanted to forget Nicholas, trying to heal her broken, beating heart, and all because she desired to be closer to him. She wanted to erase him from memory as if she wasn't partly responsible for giving him the green light. Now she'd seduce Mattias to fill the void in a moment of desperate contact.

After savoring every inch of her lips, Mattias reached her neck and collarbone. He tilted her neck and slowly licked the area where he'd typically sink his sharp teeth. There was something to be said for anticipation as he felt a shiver through her body by simply touching the forbidden area, teasing it by testing the boundaries. Then he kissed the same area and grazed ever so lightly with his fangs. He earned a sound of approval.

Deliberately disobedient, he turned her on. She was primed and ready. "Are you going to violate the terms of our deal, Mattias?"

His body pressed against hers, his breathing ragged. "I should. Really, I should. I want to taste you and drain you of *every last drop* but I think I'll give it a few more minutes.

That's how long it should take until I have you begging." His confidence made her ache in every place that was distinctly female, making her so damn hot.

He felt the blood rushing through her veins as he ran his tongue over her warm flesh. Only a thin layer of skin separated his life force from hers, and the thought nearly caused him to lose his sense of reasoning. He could taste the sweetness through her skin and smell the blood on her breath. The distinct sound of her tripled heartbeat confirmed her fading inhibitions. Once he was inside her, she'd want it. It was only a matter of time before he would bind himself to her and her to him. *Just one bite and I'll have everything. Power, a kingdom and a queen.*

His cool touch ignited her lust as he raised Gianna's toned legs, wrapping them around his waist. He lifted her to the bed and managed to shed the remaining lace garments from her body. He appraised her with a stare that burned. Then he grinned and proceeded with a penetrating kiss.

He held her so tightly that she thought she'd choke on elation. His naked body was exactly how she imagined all the way down to his substantial erection. She swore her eyes bugged at the size of him, but he didn't seem to notice. Listening to his low growls of victory, she traced the planes of his back with the tips of her fingers, earning an ecstatic groan. She'd passed the point of no return. It was impossible to end things now.

Drunk. She was drunk on the aroma. His scent, a provocative hint of amber and woods, compared to rolling around naked amidst crisp autumn foliage. His hands migrated all over her body and she lost track of his movement.

He caressed her hip, teased the deep valley of her breasts, and tangled himself in her honeysuckle-infused locks. Ten fingers pulling, demanding. Fuck. He was right. And no, she didn't care who he was or what he'd done.

Hard kisses crawled higher and she made an offering, a pulsating temptation. She tilted her neck further...further, felt the warmth of his proximity and braced herself with bated breath. Ringing. The chimes of victory, warning bells? No.

His cell phone rang. Saved by the glorious sound of modern technology, their intimacy interrupted. In a flash, the phone was in his hand.

"What the hell did I tell him?" he sneered.

"What is it Dante? Someone had better be dying." He paused.

"He's on the move? So, bring him in. ...Why do you need me?" Another pause.

"Fine, I'll be right there."

Mattias ended his call with a slam of his phone, less than thrilled. But as luck would have it, either by coincidence or in a fit of jealousy, Dante saved her.

Mattias sighed in dismay. "I have to handle something. I won't be long. Promise me you'll be right here when I return because I am *not* finished with you. In fact, I hope you don't have anything planned for this evening because you'll be busy warming my bed."

She pouted, firing his libido. "I'll do my best. In the meantime, let me give you something to come back to."

She pulled him on top of her, kissing him passionately. Nothing compared to the way his tongue worked hers. Grasping his shoulders, she spread her thighs, allowing his painful erection to caress the warmth between them, and he growled at the contact.

As much as she tried to convince herself that she was teasing him, she wanted it, silently begging him to penetrate and ease the aching. "Stay with me Mattias. I need to feel your strength inside me."

He trailed his way down her fit body until he stood at the foot of the bed and aggressively pulled her hips to the edge to meet his. He stepped back for a moment to admire the one woman he wanted with every part of his being. He was in awe of her beauty. Every inch of her was bare to him now and she was a goddess, *his* goddess. She alone could be his eternal bliss or his ultimate ruin. Tonight he intended to show her just how much she was missing. Upon his return, there would be no interruptions, no abrupt reason for either one of them to part ways.

Mattias leaned over Gianna and, with his hands, eased his way into the flesh where she yearned for him. Amazed by how primed she was, he wanted her more than anything, even power. He inserted two fingers deep inside of her and she screamed in ecstasy. His erection grew more painful as he thrust his hand deeper, watching her face, throwing her head back as he pleased her. She looked down at him with starvation in her eyes when he withdrew and licked his wet fingers with a murmur of approval.

"Mmm." His eyes pierced hers. "Even better than I thought."

His phone rang again.

"Damn it! Please tell me this is someone's idea of a sick fucking joke. Someone will pay...dearly."

"Mattias please don't go. I can't wait. I need you." She wanted this now before she lost her nerve.

"Baby you know that I wouldn't leave *this*," his eyes swept over her, "unless it was important."

"Oh this is so cruel, Mattias." She balled her hands into fists and took her anger out on the mattress.

"Now you know how I feel on a daily basis. I've been walking around for over a year with a constant hard on that you caused, but trust me baby, this is hurting me far worse than it's hurting you."

She looked down at his huge erection with wide hungry eyes. "You know, I can take care of that for you."

She lowered her gaze and smiled at both the impressive specimen and the meticulous grooming habit. She pulled him close, pushed him onto the bed, and lowered her mouth to his shaft. Suction increased as she covered him, sliding from root to tip. Although unexpected, she enjoyed the salty taste of him, the velvet feel of his cock on her tongue, and it felt too good to play with fire. He cupped her head as she worked him and moaned with such guttural agony, unlike any sound she'd ever heard.

\*\*\*

God, she was talented as she continued to take more of him. The way her tongue teased, left him balling the sheets in his fists to fight back the urge to release over a year of frustration. So close. Oh yes, Dante would pay for this!

Mattias reluctantly withdrew from her. Confused, she looked at him. "What's wrong Mattias?"

"I'll tell you what's wrong, I'm hard, you're wet, and we're still teasing each other. It's torture, Gianna."

"Well, what do you suggest?"

He wanted her and didn't want to wait any longer. But he knew his time was limited due to Dante's urgency, and he wanted no intrusions. Mattias wanted to take his time, for the moment to be perfect and he would in fact, turn her tonight, with or without her permission. Consequences be damned.

"We'll resume this when I return. In the meantime, I want you to conserve your energy...because baby, I promise you're going to need it."

He stood and dressed himself quickly while taking the time to admire what he was leaving. He shook his head in disbelief that he finally had her in his bed and was being called away. Dante could handle the urgent situation on his own while Mattias indulging himself with Gianna. But if he wanted things dealt with correctly and didn't want to appear weak, he needed to be the one to see it through.

Fully dressed, he crawled on top of her and claimed her mouth. Gianna pulled back, slightly. "Isn't there anything I can do to convince you to stay with me?" She reached her hand inside his pants and cupped him.

He growled at her expert touch. "You're relentless."

"Yes and don't you just love it?"

"More than you'll ever know."

He kissed her deeply as she played with him. "I have to...go. I promise...won't be long." He delivered one more scalding kiss and had a sinking feeling he was going to regret leaving her as he exited the room.

***

Once she was certain that Mattias had gone, she stood and began dressing. Clothed in a pair of panties, she'd managed to hook her bra back into place, when she heard the appreciative groan of a male. Dante entered the room. She gasped and quickly covered herself with one of the bed sheets. "Do you know how to knock?"

Dante laughed. "Please don't stop on my account."

"Could I have some privacy?"

"Sure, sure. I was however, hoping I could take his place."

Uncomfortable, Gianna laughed as he pressed himself against her.

Although she found Dante incredibly sexy, something about him made her skin crawl. This was one of those moments. She tried her best to hide the repulsiveness when he became so bold.

"I don't think Mattias would approve," she said with an unsteady tone.

Dante gave a quick laugh. "We've shared many things, Mattias and I. What's one more? I could do things to you that would make you melt."

She didn't doubt it for a second.

"You need better pick up lines, Dante. That one does not suit you. In fact, you may want to consider subtlety."

Her harsh words delivered a lashing for his audacity.

"I know there's something between us Gianna. You know it too. Just give me a chance to show you." He leaned in and sniffed the surrounding air, invading her personal space.

"You smell...ready. All I'm asking for is ten minutes. I promise it will be the best ten minutes of your life."

"Stop...really," she said with a sideways glance.

He fell silent and she shook her head. She tossed the sheet onto the bed, finished dressing, and left the room with Dante still inside.

Gianna should've thanked him for the save but fury overrode her gratitude and she needed to move on. Waiting for Mattias would be a mistake. Now, he'd want her even more. Allowing him to think it was a greater possibility would give her more power over him than she thought. The power to destroy him from the inside out.

Trouble emerged. She was far too convincing during their little incident. If she'd been with him, she would've loved every minute. Fear struck her. Would she be able to resist him next time?

*Oh, come on Gianna, get a hold of yourself and stick to the damn plan!*

*Get your head in the game...this is nothing.*

*You've taken down better men.*

*Yeah, but none were nearly as tempting.*

In her need to forget what happened moments ago, to forget Nicholas, to forget everything, she decided to intermingle with the humans. Yeah, that would definitely take her mind off things. After all, this was a nightclub and the point was to get lost in a horde of people. If she could do that, maybe it was possible to alleviate her frustrations, at least for one evening.

Gianna approached the bar. The bartender walked to greet her, a handsome man with dark hair and equally dark eyes who appeared in his mid-thirties.

"Vodka, please."

Drinking wasn't something she practiced on a regular basis. She never had much alcohol. It didn't have the same effect on her as it did on a pure human, but since she played the role of a human instead of her true self, she embraced it. The bartender poured the drink.

"Mattias says to get you whatever you request without any question."

Mid-swallow, she looked at him and nodded, rolling her eyes before she turned away. The temporary burn of the alcohol eased her mind for a moment. The bartender tapped her shoulder wearing a look of concern. She could've sworn she caught him scowling. The man must've had a death wish. "Here is another for you, miss. From the, ahem, gentleman across the way."

*Dante...that smug bastard.*

Dante winked, nodded and held up both hands, in reminder of his ten-minute request. Gianna made no attempt to thank him when she tossed back the pathetic gesture and disappeared into the crowd.

# 9

Mattias was on a warpath. Tense, frustrated and with a hard-on that could etch glass, he threw open the door of his limousine, nearly tearing the door from its hinges.

Startled, Cassius jumped from his seat. With the exception of their chauffeur, they were alone on what Mattias hoped would be a short journey. Silent, Mattias lingered in thought and fantasy, but Cassius wouldn't allow for a moment of peace.

"What's up, Mattias?"

"Isn't it obvious?" He answered with a scowl.

Cassius laughed uncontrollably as Mattias referenced his erection. "Wow I'm sorry. That umm, that really, really sucks man."

"I should consider gutting Dante for having the audacity to interrupt. There she was, Cassius. I finally had her where I wanted her. She was begging for me and then...Dante rang. So, I stopped to answer him. Then, she pulls me back and tries to persuade me to stay while literally going below the belt, and, as if he could see everything, Dante rings again. Remind me to rip his fucking throat out." He adjusted to a more comfortable position, a useless effort.

Cassius chuckled then sighed. "Maybe you shouldn't have waited so long. You do have the pick of any woman you choose and it could've prepared you for Gianna but you refused all of them and made yourself suffer for her. You put her on a pedestal that no one else can measure up to. I hope she's worth it, man." He clapped his friend and leader on the back.

"You have no idea. I can still feel her, taste her even." He sighed.

"Why didn't you just have Dante come with me?"

"I wanted to handle this delicate situation myself."

***

Nicholas neared the airport. He heard the sound of a vehicle slowing. A trendy black limousine, windows completely tinted, stopped beside him. The back door opened. Cassius stepped out and invited him inside.

Momentary hesitation and Nicholas saw no alternative. If he declined the invitation, they'd kill him where he stood. He walked to Cassius and ducked inside the vehicle, only to be met with Mattias.

"I thought you may be leaving town soon. Before you do, I want to discuss some things. Won't you please come along where we can have a more comfortable conversation?"

"Absolutely."

Mattias handed him a drink. "I have one small order of business to handle. Then you will have my undivided attention."

The three vampires took their seats and the door closed behind them.

The limousine pulled up alongside a building, another nightclub. How many of these could one person have? They stepped out of their transportation and entered the building.

Inside, they traveled for a few moments until they reached the same building where Nicholas had taken his prior meeting with Mattias. The establishment was even larger than he thought, appearing to be four or five levels high. And the crowd was so large, he thought that all of London's youth were in attendance.

The loud music provided a veil of distraction while Mattias conducted business of every sort. They walked up to a second level that closely overlooked the first. This was where Mattias and company took their places, keeping a watchful eye on their surroundings while being close enough to the door to make a quick escape.

Upon reaching the second level, Nicholas noticed Kyle walking by with a girl on each arm. They were laughing, flirting, and touching in ways that were indecent. Cassius wasted little time finding a victim and a dark corner then fed in such a way that it looked more like an intimate moment rather than a predatory slaying. The woman still had her hands clenched on his ass, obviously reacting to the pleasure of his feeding. Nicholas smelled fresh blood everywhere. Not good.

Dante's presence was unaccounted for. Nicholas figured that he intentionally watched from places unknown while protecting Mattias's best interests. The coven leader displayed his hospitality and offered his apologies. "Please excuse me for a few moments while I handle a small matter. I'll be right with you," Mattias said. Cassius, who finished his meal, handed Mattias something to sign.

"No problem," Nicholas answered.

"In the meantime, feel free to unwind and enjoy yourself for awhile. I'll send for you when I'm through." Mattias walked toward his office, Cassius followed close behind.

Nicholas wandered about Mattias's establishment, making his way through what seemed like hundreds of dancing humans with a desire for entertainment. Many of them were intoxicated, frantically trying to numb themselves with the promise of escape from the everyday chores and stress of life. They moved slowly compared to his stealth, though they would never know how much they paled in comparison.

He counted them quickly. Six hundred fifty seven potential prey on this level of the building alone. A few of them would experience their end of days here. They appeared to dance innocently but in reality, they were entertaining Mattias, the type to play with his victims before taking their lives. He feared that Mattias would no doubt do the same to Gianna if he uncovered her little mystery.

Many of the unsuspecting humans took notice of Nicholas's perfection. He always considered it more of a curse than anything else, the face of an angel without a soul. Most were awed by his beauty and tended to shy away. However, there was the occasional individual who considered themselves outgoing and pursued him, thinking they had nothing to lose. He'd politely express his disinterest toward the advances and continue on his way.

The bar lined the entire perimeter of the room. He imagined the remaining floors he hadn't yet visited were of similar design. The dance floor was larger than most he'd seen and welcomed people from all walks of life. The lights were dim and an occasional color or two flashed across the room, while people danced to the rock music that resonated through the floor.

Something in the center of the crowd caught his attention, glowing in the darkness as if highlighted by a spotlight.

It was her. She flaunted her human impulses for the entire world to see as she moved in cadence with the mortals. He and Mattias were not her only admirers. With her alluring personality, she was a beacon for both men and women alike who approached and danced beside her. She was so convincing in her human portrayal that she almost had him fooled.

***

There were times when Gianna thought it was nice to be among the living. To blend in as one of them and to have them accept her as such periodically reminded her that she was not as disconnected from that half as she believed and was surprisingly enjoying herself.

She wished her alcohol consumption had the same effect on her as it did the humans. To be able to drink her problems away seemed like a good idea. She was falling in too deep and couldn't shake thoughts of Nicholas, his cool touch, his passion. But she wouldn't grant him power over her emotions. She would not let him win.

Despite her distress, she masked her sorrow, flashing gleaming smiles as if she were having the time of her life. Looking up through her long brown tresses, Cassius stood before her. "Hey you." He smiled.

She smelled fresh blood on his breath. "Hey yourself."

"Dance with me."

They danced, an oddly comfortable moment between them, until she backed into a solid piece of ice...Dante. He danced behind her and she was caught between the two vampires. Humans watched, and a girl approached Cassius. It was Leyla, little miss prom-queen, and she fought like hell for his attention. He turned toward her, mildly attentive while Dante took advantage of both Cassius's and Mattias's distractions and ran his hand up Gianna's inner thigh.

Oh yeah, this could work to her advantage. Initiating plan B, she leaned her back into him, teasing him. His rigid erection pressed at her from behind when she curled her fingers and dragged them up the sides of his legs. Dante hissed in pleasure but she stopped suddenly when something caught her eye. Nicholas.

***

Nicholas enjoyed observing Gianna from afar. She appeared relaxed in the belief that no one noticed her, unaware of the attention she drew. But Dante's nearness to her, set off his fury. Nicholas, all of a sudden, felt the uncontrollable need to make his presence known. As he approached, she tried to make her way out of the crowd. A moment of desperation, she wanted to avoid contact. He didn't blame her.

What she didn't know about, was his gift of speed. Using his advantage, he didn't allow her to get far. He dashed and stood before her, blocking her exit. Wrapping a possessive arm around her waist, he pulled her close. She gasped in surprise. It was vital that she knew exactly how much she meant to him even through the most restrained touch.

Careful to be appropriate in the presence of their common enemy, few words were exchanged but with every expression, he knew how she felt. He relaxed his grip. They had little time to communicate when Kyle appeared out of nowhere and advised him that Mattias was ready.

Kyle guided Nicholas to an area of cushioned couches and chairs behind velvet ropes, clearly reserved for 'important' people, and showed him to one of the oversized chairs.

"Have a seat," he said in a thick British accent.

Nicholas took his place and looked to Gianna, seated beside Mattias like a prize, *his* prize. Mattias caressed her arm several times as if she rendered him powerless. Nicholas watched the two, and begrudged the vampire leader every second.

Lust lingered heavily in Mattias's eyes as he smiled and exchanged playful conversation. He placed an arm around Gianna and leaned close.

"You didn't wait for me," he said in a husky tone.

"I needed to amuse myself in your absence. But I'm trying to decide whether to feel insulted that you left the bed for *this*. I might punish you for it later."

"As long as it involves your naked body beneath mine, I'll gladly pay any price."

Mattias stroked Gianna's bottom lip with his thumb and she gave it a quick playful lick.

Her crimson dress and knee-high black boots looked spectacular. Nicholas recalled the feel of the curves of her body, now a memory. He studied her for a reaction but she looked away, and in Dante's direction. Nicholas knew her game but had a difficult time sitting quietly on the sidelines.

Dante winked and Nicholas saw the plotting in Gianna's eyes, the knowledge that she could easily lure Dante away and set her downward spiral into motion. She removed Mattias's hand from her leg and whispered something into his ear. He nodded. Too aggravated to focus his attention elsewhere, Nicholas watched her walk away. Dante followed seconds later.

Oh hell no, Nicholas wasn't going to sit by and allow this to continue. Cassius and another man approached Mattias with a clipboard and Nicholas made his move. He turned to Mattias "Would you excuse me Mattias? I'll just be a minute."

Preoccupied with business, he waved him away. "Sure...sure."

*** 

Gianna started down the long dark hallway toward Mattias's office. Dante followed her just as she expected. When she reached the door, she turned to find him paused behind her. "Are you stalking me now, Dante?" She placed a hand to her hip.

"Don't pretend that you didn't lead me here, Gianna. Mattias flaunts you like some sort of trophy and I can't take it any longer."

"I do *not* understand you." Before she could ask another question, he threw her up against the wall, cupped her face firmly with both hands and kissed her. His kiss was rough, primal and he wanted more than she was willing to give. He wanted the impossible.

She shoved him away, giving a light push, as though she didn't possess the strength to throw him through the opposite wall. He smiled at the opportunistic moment, proud of his actions.

Her expression bore disgust. "Mattias would kill you if he knew your intentions. You're a little late, Dante. He already staked his claim."

He closed the distance between them, taking the bait. "I'm willing to take the risk if you are."

His breathing was ragged and his voice ached, sealing his own fate. She knew exactly how far Dante would go. She smirked, and resumed their kiss, running her fingers through his hair, pulling him closer to entrapment.

She opened her eyes and met the unexpected. Nicholas stood behind Dante. Surprised, she immediately backed away and once she sobered, saw the truth. Nicholas wasn't there by obligation. He wanted to stop this from advancing any further simply because he cared.

Head down, Cassius appeared just short of missing what occurred. "What's going on?"

Dante quickly recovered. "Nothing, Cassius. I thought that Gianna needed some assistance and Nicholas must have agreed with me. It turns out that I assumed incorrectly."

Cassius arched a brow. "Is there a problem Gianna?"

"No. Not at all. I wanted a quiet place to return a phone call. I must have made it look more urgent than it was. A simple misunderstanding, that's all. No harm done." She scrambled, but it was the best she could do under pressure.

"Good. Mattias is waiting."

\*\*\*

Mattias stood to welcome Gianna back. "Is everything all right, baby?"

"Everything's fine."

He leaned in close and whispered, "I can't wait to be finished with this irritation so that I can take you back to bed. It's all I can think about."

She looked down and flashed a rather pleased grin in response to his words as he ran his hand from her knee to her inner thigh.

Mattias turned to address a wide-eyed Nicholas. "I was thinking about the news you delivered the other night and came to a decision. If you can lead me to a Dhampire to prove your claim, I'll consider your debt satisfied and spare your father's life."

*Oh God...no.* Her stomach lurched. In an attempt to avoid the conversation, she looked away and out at the crowd, but feared for her life.

Distracted, she bit into her bottom lip, creating a deep puncture. Blood seeped from the wound. Mattias and his inner circle focused their attention on her, inebriated with her essence. She was centered in a circle of death.

She watched the effects of temptation. Erratic breathing, reflective eyes, the bloodlust was in full effect. Dante's quick breaths echoed while he dug his nails deep into the arm of his chair, tearing the material, no doubt recalling their illicit encounter. Kyle licked his lips, his eyes changing color. Cassius closed his eyes tight. He managed to talk himself down and directed his attention elsewhere. Dante reached the breaking point and began to lose control. He stood and approached her with cat-like reflexes. She braced herself for what might follow, when Cassius stopped him. "Easy Dante, relax man."

Taken aback, Gianna sat guarded. She took comfort in the fact that humans were present and no one would dare risk exposure by acting on their thirst. They'd have a crowd control issue. She anticipated each of their next moves, waiting to defend herself.

Mattias breathed heavily. He gripped her leg and bared his fangs, looked at her lips and licked his own. He composed himself quickly and gave a sinister laugh as he retracted his teeth. "Wait. I want to change the terms of our deal. Let's make this a little more interesting, shall we?"

Mattias looked at Gianna and back at Nicholas. "A simple test of restraint...if *you* can taste her blood and remain in control, I'll let you leave with your obligation fulfilled." He laughed, "And since the Dhampire is a dead end and I know that you won't be able to handle Gianna, I'd much rather save myself a trip across the ocean to settle this."

Nicholas rubbed the back of his neck and brought his hand over his hair. He sighed.

Mattias laughed. "Seriously Nicholas, kiss her. Don't let it go to waste."

The remainder of the coven, and Gianna all looked to Mattias, four mouths dropped wide open, eight eyes bulged over the challenge.

"This is ridiculous Mattias. Just end it now and be done with it," Dante protested.

Surely, he had to be joking. "Mattias, you can't be serious!" Gianna panicked.

He caressed her face with the back of his hand in long, gentle strokes. "Trust me Gianna. It will be over shortly. Just do this for me and end this quickly so we can resume more productive behavior." He sat back against the seat, hands locked behind his head as he watched.

She deliberated for a moment and stood. Colorful curses muttered under her breath, she sighed heavily and conceded to Mattias as an act of good faith, prepared to do his bidding. She'd come too far and sacrificed too much to throw it all away over refusal of a simple kiss.

Nicholas looked at Gianna's blood stained lip. Restraint was dwindling, becoming less optional. He wanted to ravish her completely, with or without an audience. No, he had to focus. He wouldn't give Mattias the satisfaction. It took everything he had, to refuse the demands of thirst and lust. He placed his hand behind her head and carefully kissed her. His tongue touched her blood, a coppery blend of exotic fruits. He'd never tasted anything so sweet and helped himself to another serving. The beast inside roared to life and his cock grew rigid, painful. "More," he whispered against her lips.

He pulled her closer and kissed her deeply, while pressing hard against her lip to open the wound. God, he wanted to tear into her soft skin while he slid himself deep inside her. Blood saturated his mouth, igniting a fire that inched through his body.

Awkward. The vampires were delighted with Mattias's choice of entertainment. But it was no longer an innocent suggestion. "Okay, I'm convinced. You can stop, now," he ordered.

However, they continued. Mattias couldn't believe his eyes and rage consumed him.

"Nicholas! That's enough!"

Dante walked to where Nicholas sat and intended to shake him free of his distraction before he further crossed a line. Nicholas stopped suddenly and bared his bloodstained fangs.

The air around them clouded. Nicholas couldn't form a rational thought. Eyes cold and full of hatred, he walked up to Mattias and stood as an equal. "You think you deserve her?"

"Careful Nicholas, my patience wears thin." He set a narrow gaze upon him.

"Fuck your patience." He closed his fist and delivered a devastating right hook across Mattias's jaw.

Gianna's hair fluttered in the breeze of the impact, the force of fist meeting face, and she gasped in horror. Mattias staggered backward. The coven moved in for the kill when someone noticed their quarrel.

"Fight!" Someone yelled.

Cassius snapped his head toward the voice. The crowd grew unruly and huddled around the vampires. A diversion, exactly what he needed. The vampires lost focus, preoccupied with the growing attraction of their patrons. Nicholas crept into the crowd and before she had the opportunity to protest, he put one arm around Gianna and, with his gift of speed, fled the building with his love in his arms.

# 10

Rapid footsteps crashed heavily against the drenched street. Uncertain breaths mingled with the surrounding mist. Gianna and Nicholas raced to safety. Her panic turned into anger.

She stopped to shove him. "What have you done? You've ruined everything!"

"I'm keeping you safe, away from that masochistic asshole. It's only fair that I return the favor."

"The favor? I was safe Nicholas, safer than you'll ever know. But thanks to your quick thinking, we'll be hunted. I hope you're satisfied." She looked away and walked ahead of him, disgusted.

"I have a plan Gianna." He caught up in a flash.

"Great. I can't wait to hear it since your other plans have worked so well."

She rehashed his latest attempts, adding insult to injury. "Sure let's try to convince the leader of the most powerful coven in Europe that Dhampires exist. Actually, I have a better idea! Accept his backhanded offer as a test of will. Wait, don't stop there...stand toe-to-toe with him and cut a right hook across his jaw. Disrespect him in front of all of his power players.

A brilliant performance, Nicholas. Next time, don't do me any favors."

Nicholas fired back. "Oh and I suppose that throwing yourself at Mattias, Dante and maybe even Cassius were better options?"

"Well at least I would've had them turning on each other. That was the idea. Remember? Instead, you've managed to make *us* moving targets. Hey, while we're at it do you want to save them the trouble and paint big bulls-eyes on our backs?" He gave her a less than amused glare.

They continued down the road. He looked to her and attempted to calm her fears.

"Mattias won't be looking for you... he'll be looking for me." He searched around them, quickly turning his head from side to side as though looking for something specific.

"What is it?" she snapped.

"I was thinking a car would be a better means of transportation."

She sighed. "I parked a Mercedes two blocks from the warehouse, intending to remain incognito and not raise suspicion. Considering that I'm *typically* in no danger, I usually walk the rest of the way."

"Nothing about what you do is typical...let's go."

He tugged at her arm and helped her keep his pace.

Before long, they arrived at her vehicle without any sign of jeopardy. Nicholas hopped into the passenger seat while Gianna took the wheel and sped off into the night.

Silence and tension drifted between them. She wanted to throttle him for his idiocy. Worse, she knew what was coming. The thought of being without her would drive Mattias mad and he'd use every available resource to extract her. He wouldn't care about the number of casualties left in the wake of his path. She feared for Nicholas's life, for the lives of his coven members. They had no idea what was coming.

She stared out at the lines of the road, appearing deep in thought, but the crease in her drawn brow hinted at distress. Déjà vu. The quiet killed him. He needed to speak, to open the lines of communication. Swallowing, he turned to her. "Gianna, look, I—"

She held her hand up and cut him off before he finished. "Don't. Don't even say it." She shook her head. "I just hope you know what the hell you're doing."

So did he. And with that thought, they continued in silence for the remainder of the ride.

Gianna pulled into the garage at a faster speed than normal. She brought the car to a screeching halt. They both jumped out, ran into the house and up the stairs to her bedroom. She paced for a moment. "What are we going to do?"

"Pack some things and make it quick. I don't want to spend more than twenty minutes here. You're going to need your passport."

"I have to advise the staff of a possible breach." She started for the door. Nicholas took hold of her arm and stopped her.

"You can do that after you gather some belongings. Don't leave anything that could lead them across the Atlantic."

"I have nothing here regarding my home in the States. They wouldn't know anything about it...Where are we going?"

"I told you, I have a plan or at least I will. I know it's difficult and I haven't given you much of a reason to, but you need to trust me. We can't pull this off alone. I have to consult with my father. He'll know what to do."

Bags in hand, they quickly descended to the lower level where they came across Sofia. "What's your hurry, Gianna?" Gianna's eyes filled with tears of concern.

"Oh Sofia, we may have been followed. Please warn the others to leave immediately. I armed the security system behind me as I came into the house. If at any point, the alarm is triggered and people are still here, take the hidden elevator on the southern most point that leads to the safe house. No one will find you there. Be sure to take the keys with you. The safe house is equipped with a monitoring system that will allow you to see into every corner of the house and the surrounding grounds. There are enough supplies to last six months, although I don't think you'll be there for that long. I'm going to leave with Nicholas and will return when it's safe. Anyone who doesn't wish to stay should leave now and that includes you."

"I'll go with you," she offered.

"No. I couldn't bear it if anything happened to you because of your involvement with me. I appreciate all that you've done throughout the years and I'll completely understand if you decide not to return."

"Now you know that I'd never do that. You're the daughter that I never had. I could never leave you." She smiled.

Gianna flashed her own smile of comfort and embraced Sofia.

"We have to go. Take care of yourself, Sofia and give my best to the others."

Before they parted ways, Sofia pulled at Nicholas's coat. "Take care of her Mister Sutton or you'll have *me* to answer to."

He nodded. "I will protect her with my life."

The couple turned and ran back to the garage where they stepped into a vehicle and sped off.

Nicholas drove as if the wind were behind him, assisting his velocity. Monstrous engines roared overhead and the rumbling grew closer. The airport was near. Twenty minutes later, landing strips and lights were visible. They arrived at London's Heathrow-Airport where a private jet awaited them. With passports in hand, they boarded the aircraft.

In approximately eight hours, they'd land at Atlantic City Airport where they'd drive another hour to Cape May Point where Nicholas would have much explaining to do. Fortunately, due to the privacy of their travel, the wait was non-existent. They boarded the jet where a familiar pilot greeted Nicholas. "Evening Mister Sutton." The man nodded his head.

"Good evening," he replied, while showing Gianna to her seat.

"We were under the impression that you were flying alone."

"Change of plans."

"I see. Welcome aboard Miss."

"Thank you," she said while taking her seat.

The pilot quickly took their bags and stored them away. Gianna noticed that her seat was equivalent to a luxury sofa, a sign of traveling in style.

Nicholas sat beside her while she stared out the window, fussing with her hair. She sat back against the seat then leaned forward and back again. She reached down and fidgeted with her shoes, all the while not saying a word. God, he wanted to reach out and touch her, do something to break the silence. He covered her hand, with his. "You're awful quiet."

"What's there to say?" She retracted her hand and clasped them both together.

"I'm sure there are several things going through your mind. Don't worry...I have a feeling that Mattias's bark is far worse than his bite." He laughed.

She shot him a less than amused glance. "You underestimate him. You have no idea what you've set into motion."

"And you underestimate me." Again, he reached for her hand and gave it a gentle squeeze.

"You doubt so easily, Gianna. You have no grounds on which to base your fear. Sure, Mattias is ruthless but you don't know what I'm capable of...have a little faith."

She scowled. "The fact, Nicholas, is that I don't know what to say, think or feel. You're absolutely right. I hardly know you and I know even less about your family. But from what I've learned, you act with emotion, with fear for your father's life. You present yourself as cool and reserved but your conflict with Mattias has escalated and you have much to lose."

He didn't argue. She was right. She knew him better than he thought. He sighed and caressed her cheek. "Now, I have even more to lose."

Gianna grew silent and closed her eyes as Nicholas tried to speak to her. She didn't want to have *that* conversation. God knows she wasn't ready to confront him or her feelings.

*I'm confused. Yes, that's it.*

He leaned over her. "If I didn't know better, I'd think you were asleep."

Her eyes shot open in annoyance. "Well I am half human and need rest as one. What is the plan when we arrive?"

"Well, when we land in Atlantic City, we should pass through customs with little delay. After that, we'll have an hour drive to Cape May Point. Upon our arrival, it will be approximately forty-five minutes until dawn at which point, my energy will be at its lowest.

We'll be greeted by my family and will only be able to give them a very brief explanation before I'll need to rest. You can feel free to join me. At dusk, we'll have the opportunity to explain in greater detail, before I feed."

Fear mounted. "I'm sure they'll be thrilled with my involvement and for inflicting Mattias on their coven."

"You did no such thing. My quarrel with him set this whole thing into motion. You were unexpected, but I appreciated the distraction as frustrating as it was at times."

"Was it always frustrating?"

"No. Not always. I let my guard down. In fact, I think that I might l—"

She didn't want to hear the end of his sentence, not wanting to open old wounds though she knew it was inevitable "Yes, I got the note Nicholas." She looked away, unable to face him.

He was silent. For a moment, it seemed he tried to find the right words. "I'm so sorry it was sudden. I wish I could've stayed to tell you everything." He sat, hunched over with his elbows on his knees, his hands folded and looking at the floor.

"You don't have to explain yourself. I told you, I understand. Our friendship is mutually beneficial, at least where Mattias is concerned. Now, if you don't mind, I need to recover the strength that I've lost."

Gianna had felt the worst kind of rejection when she read his letter, and she'd be damned if she'd make the same mistake twice. She shielded herself from the pain as best she could, but now was one of the few moments when she couldn't hide. The downfall of being near Nicholas, was that she knew he studied her every expression, every movement. She wanted to say more but restrained herself for fear of an argument. Instead, she fell silent, praying that the woman in her remained quiet.

Nicholas wanted to continue their conversation and explain the reason for his actions. Eight hours aboard a private jet seemed like the perfect opportunity. But Gianna wasn't interested. She may have needed her rest, but at the moment, sleep was security. Having to lay all of their feelings out to dissect obviously made her uncomfortable, and he didn't want to force the issue.

Inches away, sleeping beautifully, she mesmerized him and he spent most of the time fantasizing. He recalled how it felt to sleep next to her, holding her close, with only a thin sheet draped between them, teased with the enticing scent of her hair, the feel of her breath, all with the promise of waking up next to her. He wanted to die from cowardice. How could he have left her?

The gentleman in him reached for a blanket to keep her comfortable while she slept. But the animal, the feral beast within wanted to strip her naked and have his way with her until she begged him for mercy. He could still taste the lasting remnants of her blood. The aftertaste combined with the recollection of the way she screamed his name on the brink of orgasm, was almost enough for him to wake her with the intention of a repeat, or in his case, a do-over.

*** 

She woke just as the pilot announced their descent into landing. Their flight arrived much sooner than anticipated, seven hours instead of eight.

*Great.*

More time with the family that she wasn't looking forward to meeting considering the circumstances. The quick trip through customs led them outside to the parking lot within minutes. Nicholas unlocked the doors of a pristine silver Jaguar XE.

*Nice.*

He took her luggage and placed it carefully in the trunk. She couldn't shake her feelings of uncertainty.

He opened the passenger side door when her cell phone rang. She looked to Nicholas before stepping into the car. "It's Sofia. I need to answer this."

"By all means," he said.

"Hello? Yes, Sophia, we've made it safely. We're in the car and should be there in about a half hour...The alarm hasn't sounded?....That's good to hear, no I'm not sure how long I'll be here...I may head back to Astoria for awhile. It will be nice to be home. Why don't you head there as well? ....Great, call me when you get there. See you soon."

Gianna ended her call.

"How are things in London?" he asked, staring intently.

"It doesn't sound like there were any intruders so I want Sofia to leave while she has a chance. I'll meet her at home when things die down and then return to London to handle things with Mattias."

He pressed his lips together tightly and bowed his head toward the ground, evidently disappointed by her eagerness to return.

She felt a sinking feeling about the warmth of his covens' welcome. "What should I expect of your family, Nicholas? It just occurred to me that I don't even know what they look like. I should probably be prepared for the onslaught."

Nicholas hadn't given it much thought. He knew his clan would adore her. He imagined Elizabeth, Josephine, and his father would be thrilled to learn he'd found a possible companion. Unfortunately, at this point, she more than likely hated him.

The direction in which their relationship was headed wasn't an appropriate topic of discussion.

The timing was terrible and to make matters worse, he wasn't sure how she felt. Sure they'd had an amazing time playing naked together, but did she feel anything more? His family would also be in awe of her nature and how she lived her life in the open. He sighed and tried to think of the best characteristics that would both justify the members of his house and calm her fears. "Well, my father is proper and very likable. He'll adore you."

She looked away trying to take it all in. What she really wanted to do was haul ass and high tail it out of there on the next flight back to London. She'd much rather take her chances with Mattias. Hunting and killing she could deal with. The idea of vampire family bonding didn't exactly leave her feeling warm and fuzzy.

Nicholas continued. "Then there is the matter of my sister. Elizabeth, my biological sister is free spirited. I see a great deal of human youth in her, and I admire her for that. Josephine is also part of our clan. She's completely non-judgmental. Did I mention that she is a fertility doctor?"

Gianna arched a brow. "A vampire fertility doctor? That's certainly interesting."

"Indeed it is. She'd suffered like no one should and still insists upon helping others," Nicholas explained.

She took a much-needed deep breath. "Actually, it doesn't sound too torturous. I'm still expecting an execution for endangering their son and brother."

"I keep hearing you blame yourself for all of this but I'm the one who pushed Mattias when I could have left well enough alone. You were a bystander who became much more."

"We'll see if they share your opinion Nicholas."

He smiled. "We're here."

He pulled up to a large, lightly colored house, the only one on the street. The Suttons valued their privacy for obvious reasons. She nudged him. "You were intimidated by *my* home?"

He took another glance at his home and had to admit, the house his father built on the ocean front lot, was a bit excessive. However, they required a gated home in a quiet community. The house boasted a cream stucco exterior with white accents. His family strived to adapt to their surroundings and their house did just that. Most of the ocean front homes on *The Point*, as the locals called it, tended to look different, more posh from the rest that occupied the surrounding streets.

She delivered an honest compliment. "It's beautiful Nicholas. But I have a question. Why a beachfront location in New Jersey? It seems like a strange choice for a vampire's residence. You're without the benefit of a constant overcast and run the risk of sun most days."

"That's the very reason my father chose this location. It's not like there is an influx of vampires wishing to set up residence. Besides, houses here are typically winterized for seven months of the year. We're the only coven for miles and we like it that way."

She drew her brow. "I didn't mean any offense."

"None taken."

"You must always have to plan around the weather and that has to be difficult. You wouldn't want to step outside thinking it's going to be down pouring all day and suddenly the sun blazes through the clouds."

"Wouldn't that be a nice surprise? Well, relocation is always an idea. One that I'll be sure to pass along to my father once the time is right."

He shifted the gear into park and gave her a sideways glance. "Are you ready?"

She was surprised he couldn't hear the pounding of her heart or the gulping she just forced down her throat. She nodded. No, she wasn't ready. Not at all.

# 11

Gianna opened the door and stepped out of the car. The briny fragrance of the sea invaded her senses. She closed her eyes and concentrated on the sound of the crashing surf—a brief moment of relaxation, and took a deep breath.

Nicholas took her hand in his as they approached the front door. He gave it a gentle squeeze. "Don't worry. Everything will be fine," he promised.

He gave her that sexy smile with a hint of fang. Confidence seeped through Nicholas's pores and made her heart race. Damn he was sexy. He walked to a security system placed on a neutral colored brick wall, and began to enter a code on the keypad. Before he could finish, the door swung open and an adorably petite teenager emerged from the darkness, excitement in her light eyes. "Nicholas! I've missed you."

"Elizabeth, it's four o'clock in the morning. You may want to keep it down."

"Oh right. Sorry," she giggled.

Petite and slender, Elizabeth's peridot green eyes were complimentary to her ebony hair. Her youthful appearance made Gianna forget she wasn't among the living. She resembled a human in the beginning of adulthood. To the naked eye, she was an average teenager.

Her gaze focused on Gianna. "Wow, Nicholas. Who is this?"

He held her hand tighter. "This is Gianna Marino. Gianna, this is Elizabeth, my sister."

"It's so nice to meet you Gianna." She looked at her brother with hopeful eyes. "Nicholas, she is gorgeous!"

Gianna laughed. "Thank you. It's nice to meet you too. I've already heard so much about you."

Elizabeth shot a look of concern to Nicholas. "I hope you've been kind with your words, Nicholas. Well don't just stand there, come in. Father is looking forward to seeing you."

He entered first and Gianna took a deep breath before she followed, crossing the threshold. *Well, so far so good.*

Through the entry, they stood upon a sandstone floor in a large foyer. Gianna's eyes spanned the area. Long winding stairs made of a royal mahogany, led to the second floor and beyond, while ivory colored walls were decorated with classic artworks, adding to the timeless appeal.

Out of nowhere, a man who closely resembled Nicholas appeared before the couple. Gianna was awestruck by his appearance. She could've sworn she blushed. The man was handsome, an A-list-Hollywood-leading-actor sort of handsome. His eyes were glittering pools of blue that sparkled even in the moonlight. They were set against skin that held onto a slight bronze hue, most likely from his youth. "Nicholas," he smiled.

The man's voice was hypnotic and she'd only heard a single word. He could seduce a woman through conversation alone, but she couldn't see a killer in his eyes. Could it be possible that they were a different kind of vampire? Domesticated even?

"Father," Nicholas said.

"You've been doing well for yourself." The man quickly looked to Gianna. "Who is this exquisite young lady?" He sniffed the air as he spoke.

"This is Gianna Marino. Gianna, this is my father Bennett Sutton."

"Well, Miss Marino, I am pleased to make your acquaintance." Bennett reached for her hand and gave it a gentle shake.

"Likewise. Your home is beautiful."

Bennett offered her a warm smile. "Thank you. We enjoy it. Please, make yourself at home for as long as you'll be gracing us with your presence." He made a sweeping motion with his hands. "Our home is yours," he said.

Gianna nodded. "Thank you."

"It's my pleasure," he said with a heart-stopping smile.

Nicholas spoke up. "Actually, since it's nearly dawn we were thinking of turning in. We'll talk tomorrow. Will that be all right?"

"Absolutely. Take some time to recover. We'll chat later." Bennett left them alone.

Gianna smiled and turned to Nicholas. "He seems wonderful."

"He is. Now, follow me."

Nicholas took her hand and led her to a bedroom at the end of the hallway on the second floor. He opened the white door to an enormous room.

The square footage of this room alone took up half of the second floor and was complete with an oversized bed, bathroom, and gorgeous fireplace, the hearth made of stone. "I hope this is private enough for you."

She laughed, recalling the first night she'd met him. Of course, it was more than enough but she couldn't resist a witty comment. "I guess it will have to do."

He smiled as though he'd heard her thoughts. "I'll have your things brought up. Try to get some rest. I'll be back in a little while." He left her with privacy and headed back downstairs to gather their belongings.

*** 

A lengthy interrogation was something he was trying to avoid and hoped to retrieve their luggage without being noticed. He imagined his family gathered, half on one side of the room and half on the other, while his father played referee. Shaking his head, he prayed silently that he'd be able to have a moment's peace before the tirade began.

Voices in conflict echoed as Nicholas walked downstairs to the stone-covered foyer. He intended to collect the baggage but saw a gathering in the living room.

*Don't go in there.*

*Go and be with Gianna while you can.*

Unfortunately, the voice in his head usually went unheard.

He turned a corner into the living room and saw his father and sisters gathered. The group paused as he entered. Nicholas shook his head. "I expected for this to wait until nightfall."

Nicholas stood in silence, waiting for a reaction. He wanted a reason to unleash his rage.

"Nicholas, we're just concerned with a human being in the house. The temptation will be far too great," Josephine said.

"I don't think you need to worry yourself," Nicholas smirked.

Elizabeth, the only one who knew Gianna's secret, chuckled at their banter.

Nicholas and Elizabeth were always close. They were the only two Sutton children who shared the connection of being biological siblings. When times were tough, they had each other. She was his rock. If anyone accepted Gianna, Elizabeth would. He smiled at the thought and a weight lifted from his shoulders.

Josephine stood furthest from the rest and quietly observed. She assembled facts before adding her opinion. Nicholas waited for something profound.

He gave them a sheepish look. "Tonight. I promise. I don't want to keep Gianna waiting."

Nicholas walked out of the room and up to his bedroom where he found Gianna with her eyes closed. She listened to music on her MP3 player and he wasn't sure if she was sleeping again, or concentrating intensely on the melody. Either way, he left her at peace. Her presence kept his tired eyes wide open, fascinated. He'd watched her sleep before, but this time he paid attention. Her tranquil breathing reminded him of a spring breeze on the ocean.

Concern engulfed him. He desperately wanted her to find a place in his house, to be comfortable and maybe even consider staying. He worried she'd be eager to return to London and he wouldn't even be an afterthought. For the first time, he appreciated his immortality and the thought of forever waking up next to her gave him a reason to look to the future.

Too often had his thoughts been consumed with defending her against the likes of Mattias, that he didn't address the issue of their relationship.

It was times like these when he wished his immortal gift was the ability to read thoughts. Then again, if he could, it might not be such a wise idea.

He couldn't linger in thought. Gianna would need to find nourishment come dusk, he'd have to consult with his family and like it or not, preparation was necessary. Mattias was coming.

# 12

The burning sun finally set in London. After dealing with the rowdiness of last night's crowd, Mattias and company thought it best to keep a low profile. But Mattias couldn't relax.

Anger pumped heavily through his veins while he sat in his usual seat. In a methodic rhythm, he rapped his nails on the edge of the chair and cast a gaze so feral, it should've incinerated the entire building. Since Gianna's disappearance, he was in a constant state of unrest. He looked to Dante. "What is taking so long?"

Seated, Dante leaned forward. "Look Mattias, I know you're anxious. We all are. We just have to calm down and take this one step at a time. You know that jumping into a situation with both feet, without planning, is careless. We'll never have the upper hand if we rush into retaliation."

He knew Dante was right, but it didn't stop him from cutting a scowl. He relied upon Dante's levelheaded rationale like a crutch to the wounded. It had saved the coven numerous times when Mattias's temper could've led them to their demise.

Kyle quickly entered the room and spoke quickly. "Mattias, Allyn has some information." Allyn smiled as she approached Mattias. A slender blonde-haired woman with light eyes and one of Kyle's numerous companions who envied the relationship between Mattias and Gianna. She stood beside Kyle and Cassius, while Dante and Mattias remained seated.

Mattias grew impatient. "What is it Allyn?"

"I followed Gianna and Nicholas. It appears that she went willingly," she purred.

"Impossible." His eyes widened with rage. Beside him, Dante balled his fists.

"There's more. They were spotted entering a large house just outside the city. The way that it's placed on the road, you'd never know it's there."

Mattias crossed his arms at the chest. "Can you lead us there?"

She gave a wicked smile. "I can take you anywhere you want to go, baby." She reached out to caress his thigh.

Mattias caught her wrist in his hand before she made contact and gave a look of pure evil.

"I'm not interested in your advances. I want only *one* woman and you can't hold a candle to her," he said between clenched teeth and threw her arm away in disgust.

Everyone sensed Mattias's fury. No one would dare antagonize him in this state, or it could mean the end of their lives. Right now, he was unpredictable, and with Gianna being the center of his world, he wouldn't bat an eyelash over killing Allyn for practice. Kyle took Allyn by the arm and led her out of the room, glancing at Mattias one last time.

"Be sure to get that address." Mattias ordered.

Mattias looked to Dante. "Make sure the car is ready. I don't want to waste anymore time."

Dante nodded in agreement. Moments later, Kyle entered the room. "The car is waiting. Let's go."

Mattias and Dante followed Kyle.

Dante took the driver's seat and Mattias sat comfortably as his passenger. While Dante drove he looked at Mattias. "I have a bad feeling about all of this."

"I want him dead Dante."

Dante sat in silence and allowed Mattias to vent. There were several times when he would've loved to watch Mattias dwindle in the wind like a flying kite. The coven leader's end would benefit him, but if he allowed Mattias to perish at any moment, he'd have plenty to answer for, and would be hunted like an animal. There wouldn't be a power on earth that could save him from wrath. Now, he shared Mattias's anxiety, in addition to his feelings for Gianna, and even though she didn't reciprocate Dante's advances, there was something more between them than what appeared. He was just as eager to learn of her whereabouts and bring her back.

Dante's secret longing for Gianna left an emptiness inside him that no other could fill. He knew that his days left with Mattias were numbered, the longer Gianna remained in his presence. He longed to touch her in such a way that would be punishable by death. Still, he dreamt of ways he could have her come to him, to make Mattias respect him as an equal and as his competition. *One day...*

Mattias balled his hands into fists and struck the dashboard. "I was so close, so close to making her one of us. You have no idea, Dante. Now that I've seen every last remarkable inch of her, I won't stop until she's mine. And I'm prepared to do whatever it takes."

"I thought that is what we are doing."

"Then you'll understand when I tell you that her safe return is my highest priority. I don't care who dies in the process. Furthermore, should anyone place a hand on her other than myself, I will personally end their existence. I just want to be clear should the body count rise."

They continued the remaining thirty-minute ride outside of London in silence. After what seemed like an eternity, they reached their destination. Dante pulled the car up to the wrought iron gate of the secluded property. Noticing that the security system was armed, Mattias, Dante, Kyle and Cassius exited their vehicles and jumped over the gate in a single bound.

A blue laser was breached by Kyle's pant leg, most likely tripping a silent alarm. "Fuck!" he whispered.

"Shh!" Cassius yelled.

They stormed the doors of the home. Once inside, they investigated openly, peering into every room on each floor of the house looking for clues to the beauty's whereabouts. The vampires began on the lowest floor of the house, and worked their way up. They stood in hallways with red-colored walls when Mattias placed Gianna's scent. He closed his eyes and leaned his head back, reveling in the essence. "She's been here. I can smell her."

Behind him, Cassius's phone rang. He quickly answered while Mattias looked on. "It's Dante. You need to see what he found upstairs."

Their voices echoed through the dining hall as they advanced into a large parlor near the front door, and up the stairs. Mattias entered the room where Gianna's family history was prominently displayed. He reached for an ornate glass frame.

Dante's eyes searched the area. "What is all of this?" he asked.

Silence fell over all in the room. Without warning, Mattias threw the frame against the wall, shattering it into pieces. "Find them!"

A brisk walk down the hall led Mattias to a set of doors. He threw the doors open and froze in place at the sight—Gianna's bedroom. He slowly approached the king sized bed, neatly dressed in black and silver satin. He ran his hands over the soft material as he walked to where he imagined she slept. "So, this is where you go when you leave me aching, wanting...where you dream about me." He leaned down to inhale her scent from the sheets when he recognized another, and hissed in anger.

"Sutton has been here. In this very room! He should know better than to take from me like some common thief. His head will be my prize."

Suddenly, Cassius entered the bedroom holding a woman by the arm. The woman appeared in her mid-forties, petite with short blonde hair. She bore a look of terror. Cassius tightened his grip on the woman while she struggled. "I found her hiding in the kitchen. When we approached, she tried to run. What do you want me to do with her?"

Mattias advanced cautiously. "What's your name, love?" He cupped her face.

"Sofia. Sofia Smythe." She trembled.

"Hello Sofia. Where is Gianna?"

"I'll never tell you anything."

Mattias grabbed her by the arm with such force it hindered her circulation. "Now, listen to me very carefully. If you don't tell me where she is, when I do find her, I will kill Nicholas first. Then I'll kill Gianna ever so slowly and make you watch. Now, where did Nicholas Sutton take Gianna?"

She stood silent as Mattias lost patience. "Kill her."

Sofia panicked. "Wait! Cape May Point, New Jersey, United States."

Mattias smiled at Sofia's cooperation. "Very good. We're going to the States, tonight."

He shoved Sofia toward Cassius. "Bring her along. We could use her."

Cassius pulled Sofia out of the room as Mattias looked to Dante. "Make the arrangements, including a private jet. The clock continues to tick."

Dante nodded and left the room as Mattias sat on Gianna's bed.

*Soon baby, I'll be there soon and we'll be together again. Only, this time, it will be forever.*

\*\*\*

Gianna woke before Nicholas in time to see the sun set. She'd seen them numerous times, but this one was different—amazing. It could've been because it felt like it might be one of her last, or perhaps because she was in Nicholas's home watching from his bedroom window. A pure salt breeze flowed from the calm ocean and she took in as much of it as possible.

"You're awake." Nicholas startled her.

She recovered quickly. "Only long enough to watch the sunset. I now see why you live here. The view is breathtaking."

"I thought the same thing." She felt the weight of his stare and knew he wasn't referring to the scenic views from the ocean front bedroom.

For a moment, he imagined waking to find her staring out of his window every night, a perfect immortal existence. Just when he believed himself damned, she'd become his haven, his breath of fresh air through the desert heat of eternity. But now, he wanted to make her comfortable instead of burdening her with his dreams. "I guess it beats staring out the window onto the streets of London."

"Without question." She laughed.

She walked to the bed and sat beside him. His smile faded as he paused to listen to the pacing from below. His coven grew restless. Their concerns were great and the questions would be numerous.

Gianna composed herself for the inevitable confrontation. "I guess it's time. They've been patient enough," she admitted.

"It won't be brutal. They just want to know what to expect."

"You don't have to reassure me Nicholas. I'm alright."

"Oh that's right for a second I forgot who I was talking to."

Gianna smiled at Nicholas's sarcasm. "You've been around me too long. I think I'm starting to rub off on you."

*I'm hoping you'll rub off on me.* He smiled. "I suppose it's possible...okay, I'd better get dressed before they plow through the door." He stood and dressed quickly. "Let's go."

She took his hand and followed to where his family waited.

Nicholas and Gianna descended the stairs and heard the family whispering. The couple's audible ranges were so advanced they could distinguish the murmuring from where they stood. Before long, they were in the presence of his family. Bennett stood. "Nicholas. Gianna. We're so glad that we finally have the chance to speak."

Nicholas remained calm but held a tone of remorse in his voice.

"I have some news. Most of it I regret to inform isn't good. As you all know, after the situation that occurred last summer with Elizabeth and Lucas, I decided to go to London.

I didn't want anyone to follow and didn't want to make our father a mark while in the presence of Mattias's coven. I eventually met with Mattias but he wouldn't see me my first night. In fact, he had me running through the streets while being pursued by a convoy of vehicles. Gianna happened to be in the right place at the right time and came to my rescue. That's when *our* journey began. I spent several days as a guest in her home and discovered she was working with Mattias."

"Wonderful," Josephine said with a hint of hopelessness. Her short, light brown hair and eyes gave way to a soft and innocent appearance.

Nicholas continued. "Initially, I jumped to conclusions. I immediately thought Gianna was a messenger sent to obtain information then betray me. However, that wasn't the case. Gianna is infiltrating Mattias's organization, posing as an advisor and Mattias is enamored with her. He is smitten to the point of weakness. Gianna uses that weakness to her advantage by any means necessary."

Gianna stood beside Nicholas while carefully examining Bennett, Elizabeth, and Josephine. She never revealed a hint of discomfort, which was a relief. The last thing he wanted was for her to be intimidated. And he buried the urge to clear the room and savagely make love to her. She turned him on with a force so powerful, that he had to hide his agonizing erection.

"Nicholas, why is she so important to Mattias? What is she...human...vampire?" Josephine asked.

Already in the know, Elizabeth smiled. "This should be good."

Bennett attempted to calm them. "No. She's something else. She's Mythic, the subject of legends. Half human. Half vampire. A hybrid. "

Gianna closed her eyes waiting for the snide remarks, a criticism. Nothing but quiet followed the revelation. Bennett rested his hand on Gianna's shoulder, a feeling of assurance. "Don't worry, you'll be safe here."

Nicholas knew Bennett was astounded. He too, thought her mere existence was nothing short of miraculous, an endangered species on the verge of extinction, while others would be terrified of what she could be capable of, and what it could mean to the future of their species.

Hunger struck. Gianna doubled over in pain and looked to Nicholas for support. He rushed to her side and met both her gaze and a surprising sight. "Gianna, your eyes..."

"What color?"

"Burgundy, like a glowing wine."

"Damn it." Her breathing increased.

"What does that mean?"

"I've gone too long without feeding. I need...blood."

The Suttons huddled around the couple like spectators.

"I'll get some," Elizabeth offered eagerly.

"No. Thanks, Elizabeth but I need to feed, as well. I'll take her with me."

"Nicholas—"

"Josephine, I understand your concern. But I brought her here. I thought it would be the safest place to form a united front. A place to be prepared not if, but when they decide to attack."

Bennett stepped up. "You've made the right decision Nicholas. We need to be prepared. They are a powerful coven and would love nothing more than to catch us off guard, at each other's throats.

It makes their job much easier. We'll have to devise a plan as soon as possible. We'll start tonight. In the meantime, take her to the vault."

Nicholas nodded.

He looked to Gianna who now spoke a language he understood too well...blood.

# 13

Away from the intrusion of prying eyes, Nicholas held Gianna close as he led her away from the living room. Moments later, he reached for a handle, and opened a large oak door. The descending stairs indicated they were headed to the basement.

"What's the vault?" Gianna asked, growing weaker by the minute.

"It's where we keep our emergency stock." He pulled her tighter against him.

"Your emergency stock?" she asked, panting from the painful hunger.

"Just wait. We'll be there shortly."

They moved down the stairs slower than he liked, but he knew what hunger felt like, the agonizing torture equivalent to internal fire. A quick left turn at a corner stone wall, and she almost lost balance. He reacted quickly and caught her by the arm before she hit the cold floor.

"Almost there, Gianna. Hang on."

"I've got it. I'll be fine," she said.

Before long, they faced an eight-foot steel door equipped with its own electronic security pad. Nicholas entered a combination and the system disarmed. When the door came open, they entered the freezing space inside. Even in the dark, the heat of her breath was visible. He found the light switch and brightened the room. Gianna's eyes widened at the sight. Every wall, from floor to ceiling, was shelved with collection bags of blood. It made sense the room was freezing to preserve the blood and prevent spoiling.

"Oh my god! You have your own blood bank."

"Well, we have our suppliers. All are reputable, I assure you. We need to keep a supply. It's the only way to sate the thirst without harming humans." He didn't make eye contact, but moved quickly as he reached for a bag labeled O-Negative.

"No human blood," she muttered. Her eyes clenched shut as the sharp pains attacked.

"Gianna, I need you completely focused. You'll have to trust what I'm about to do," he implored.

"Please—"

He cut off her plea. "Trust me. I'll be right back. This will only take a minute."

Nicholas dashed out the door with three bags in hand, leaving her to the frigid space, and headed for the living area of the basement. In the kitchen, he reached for two glasses, emptied one bag in each, and added a few drops of the third bag, before placing the glasses in water at the bottom of a large pot atop the open flame on the stove. Ninety-eight-point-six degrees, and five minutes later, the cocktails were ready for consumption. He ran back to the vault with the third bag, and glasses in hand.

When he entered the room, she was on her knees, falling victim to the agony.

"I'm here. I have what you need," he said with urgency, handing her the glass.

She winced at the sound of his voice and reached for the container. Once her lips touched the crimson, she didn't waste time. He joined her in rejuvenation.

***

In unison, they lowered the glasses. He smirked with a flash of fang that made Gianna's body react.

"What are you smiling about?" she asked.

"I was imagining the blood was yours," he confessed.

His admittance should've been the most repulsive statement she'd ever heard, but it only made her hot.

"I thought I said no human blood. What have you done?" she asked, wiping the few lingering drops from the corner of her mouth.

"It was animal blood with a few drops of O-Negative. Clearly you needed the charge," he said, proud of his concoction.

Nicholas placed the human blood on the shelf, and took the glass from her hands. "Shall we go?"

"Yes."

He reached for her hand and kissed her fingers. His touch gave her unnatural chills, even through the sub zero temperature of the blood bank, but she feared he had false hope concerning a relationship. It was damned near impossible to pursue one with Mattias being very much in the picture. Regardless of her choice, Mattias would always be around...always.

She frowned at the hopelessness of the situation, and sighed in frustration.

"What is it?" Nicholas asked.

"Do you think we can head back upstairs? I'd like to shower. I just don't feel right after feeding."

"Whatever makes you comfortable," he said, securing the vault door behind them. He reached for her hand and led her upstairs to his bedroom.

"I won't be long," she said.

"Take your time. I'll be back soon." He turned and left her with privacy.

Gianna needed time alone after everything that happened. She walked into the large bathroom, took her time undressing, and stared into the mirror. Her tough exterior masked her true feelings. She was genuinely terrified. The kind of power that Mattias and his clan possessed only validated her fear. And they'd be ruthless in their pursuit. She placed a hand on each side of the sink and supported herself from the weight of her worry. Concern grew for the lives of the Sutton coven. To lose Bennett and Elizabeth would destroy Nicholas. Regardless of how they felt for each other, he'd be lost.

Her thoughts took another turn.

*Would I actually be able to kill Mattias?*

She had every right to take her vengeance. He deserved death but could she deliver? She was rattled to the core over the possibility of this one decision. Here she had it. Two vampires. Both cared for her and both nearly irresistible. One tender and one callous. Both believed they knew her best interests. She'd be with one for the thrills of sex and the luxury of supremacy. Power wasn't her forte, but she could accomplish many things with Mattias by her side.

*The asshole killed your family!* A fact which she knew, but did she actually care for him? To a point she did—her capricious human nature again. But she played a dangerous game with Mattias, starring in a role that could quite possibly distort reality if she continued. Yes, he needed to die but how could she complete the task when she constantly wanted him in ways that should be considered illegal?

However, she knew she'd be with Nicholas for different reasons. Not out of obligation but because she cared, really and truly cared. She felt differently about Nicholas than she did Mattias. He didn't deserve pain or suffering. His passion for all things made him so appealing. Not to mention, he was one of the most beautiful vampires she'd ever feasted eyes on, and didn't lack talent in the bedroom. Attractiveness aside, she couldn't live with herself if any harm came to him. Suddenly, a realization! *Do I love him?*

***

Nicholas walked to the end of the hallway and out to a balcony overlooking the beach. He looked to the stars set high in the night sky and inhaled the warm salt breeze propelled from the sea. The familiar squawk of a seagull flying overhead on a search for unsuspecting sea life, brought a short-lived smile to his face. He placed his elbows on the balcony rail, pressed the heels of his palms against his brow, and used his fingertips to cradle his head. Damn, he wanted to run to Gianna and tell her how he felt, that he'd protect her regardless, no matter the price, and it scared the shit out of him.

"Women tend to have that effect, Son." Bennett startled him. Nicholas sighed as they both looked at the calm sea.

"And you weren't even looking for her," Bennett said.

"What do you mean?" Nicholas flashed defensive eyes at his father.

"I can see it in your eyes, Nicholas. They're warmer, tender. Love has found you."

Nicholas diverted his gaze back out to the open waters, avoiding eye contact. "You don't know what you're talking about."

Bennett laughed. "Nicholas, I've been around for a long time and I think I'd recognize love in my son's eyes. The question is, are you going to do nothing and lose it, or will you claim it for yourself?"

Nicholas sighed. "Look, I don't know what I feel. I certainly don't know how she feels. Maybe it's for the best if things are left unspoken. It would make it easier than rejection or regret."

"Rejection or regret? Son, like life, love is a game of chance. You take a risk and hope that your heart is cared for when you place it in someone else's hands. Sometimes it works out and sometimes it doesn't. That's why many would choose death over the loss of a loved one."

"That's reassuring." He rolled his eyes.

"I won't lie to you, Nicholas. It won't be easy. You're very different creatures, you and Gianna. I can see she cares for you, and like you, she holds a great fear in her eyes."

Nicholas looked down at the sand and imagined rubbing it into his eyes, a better fate than subjected to his father's philosophical views of love. While Bennett had wisdom of the ages, Nicholas tried to enjoy his moment of tranquility.

Bennett didn't give up easily. "Nicholas—"

"Father, I don't want to have this conversation."

"Forgive me, but you're being foolish."

"Foolish? I know I'm going to lose her. It's an absolute matter of fact. When Mattias arrives, he'll find a way to lure her back. One way or another, she'll leave with him."

"Maybe she will and maybe she won't."

"No...she will." Nicholas hung his head dejectedly.

"Then you're wasting time."

"I'm not wasting time. I'm simply saving her the pain of having to choose. Excuse me for being a realist."

"She's a grown woman, capable of making her own decisions. If she knew you felt this way, how do you think she'd react?" Nicholas looked up and glanced sideways.

"She'd probably kick my ass."

"Exactly. What advantage do you have over Mattias? The answer is simple. Gianna is here with you and he is across the ocean on another continent. If the roles were reversed and she was with Mattias, do you think he'd be standing here giving Gianna the same courtesy? Or do you think he'd seize his moment while there were no interruptions? You see, you wouldn't be a fool for giving love a chance. You'd be a fool for doing nothing at all. And when she goes back to London without knowing the depth of your feelings, only then will you truly know what it's like to live with regret."

Bennett turned to leave the balcony but not before he gave his son one last piece of advice. "Go to her Nicholas...or risk losing her forever."

Nicholas closed his eyes tight and dropped his head in defeat. He knew Bennett was right and couldn't insult his father with denial. And he'd be a damn fool to throw it all away. After several paces across the balcony, he weighed the options.

*What do I have to lose? Possibly everything.*
*What do I have to gain? Possibly everything.*
*Damn it.*

\*\*\*

Gianna exhaled a tired sigh, turned the knob, and unleashed a stream of relaxation. She made sure it was one of the hottest showers she'd ever taken. The scalding water proved a welcomed relief, a momentary freedom from her conflicted emotions.

The constant flow of water rushed over and massaged every inch of her body. If only it would do the same for her mind.

Now wasn't the time to evaluate loving Nicholas or wanting Mattias. Would there *be* any other time?

Nicholas walked back into his bedroom and heard the sound of running water. He paced around the room for a few seconds in heated contemplation.

*Fuck. Do I or don't I?*

*What the hell.*

He undressed and walked into the bathroom. There he met the sight of her hourglass figure through the beveled glass of the shower door. God, he hoped she wasn't watching. Opportunity knocked. He wanted to make up for the stupidity of days past, wanted to catch her off guard. She wasn't going to run away. He'd have his moment and he'd have *her*.

Gianna faced the showerhead and allowed the water to pummel her eyes. The heat felt too good. With her hands, she brushed through the soaked strands of hair and smoothed them away from her face. The steam intensified the scent of her shampoo. She closed her eyes and basked in the aroma. When she turned away from the stream, to rinse the remaining suds from her locks, she sensed a presence and opened her eyes, only to face a pleasant sight. Nicholas invaded her shower. Nice trick.

*How in hell did I miss that?*

Goodness, he looked even better soaking wet. His raven-colored hair held droplets of water that begged for a finger comb-through. A day's worth of facial hair added a sexy, rugged look to his appearance and she enjoyed the rough texture of his new growth during their lip locking. Rock-hard, hairless pectorals and washboard abs gave way to the small dark patch of hair that pointed the way to his best asset.

"Nicholas...," she trailed off as he took a step forward, closing the space between them.

"Gianna, I don't want any regrets or missed opportunities. Especially when I don't know how much time we have left together."

"Nicholas, I don't know what you want from me! We met under interesting circumstances, I invited you to stay and remain in my home for as long as you wished, you tried to kill me...twice, we became friends, had amazing sex and then you left...period. There's really nothing left to say about it." She averted her gaze, only to have him reach out, and force her to look at him.

He fired back, "Look, I'm sorry I left the way that I did! I'm sorry I suck at this but in over two hundred years, I've never met anyone like you. You drive me crazy and it turns me on, which might mean that I'm a glutton for punishment. You can call it whatever you want, but I want you. I want to be with you, even if it's for a fleeting moment. And I don't want you to leave without knowing how I feel."

They stared in silence for seconds, swallowing past the lumps of fear. He reacted, dipped his head, and kissed her with all of the passion that consumed him. Nicholas savored the moment, every second of it. She let out a soft moan as his lips skated over hers and his tongue begged her mouth for invasion.

He ran his hands over the exquisite curves of her slick, naked body and pulled her close. Her breath hitched at his touch, at the contact of their skin. With a low growl, Nicholas lifted her to the tiled wall. She wrapped her legs around his waist while he cupped her delicate ass.

*Gasp!*

The slam of her back against the ceramic wall surprised her for a moment, until their gazes met. His hypnotic eyes pinned her with hunger while his palms lay fiat against the tile, on either side of her head.

The position made his arms bulge with definition and she gaped at the luscious expanse of his chest. She'd underestimated his strength as he supported all of her weight with his body pressed against hers. He licked his lips with a primal sweep of his tongue. Her throat went dry.

Power emanated from his body, the persistent growls from deep within proclaimed dominance and she was willingly at his mercy. It was as though every nerve in her body was in tune to his touch. She ground herself against him with a need to ease the aching and with a single, powerful thrust, he drove himself into her slick heat and didn't dare hold back. That single move, cleared her head of all previous thoughts, and she could think of nothing but how amazing he felt inside her, filling her.

Pain transformed into cries of erotic bliss as Gianna's body stretched to accommodate him. He hissed between clenched teeth, thrusting repeatedly from tip to base. The heavy bounce of her breasts against his chest drove him crazy and couldn't get enough. In the euphoric moment, he brought his lips down on hers and pulled away, breathless. Emotion tore through him, weakening his defenses. He closed his eyes tight before he held her gaze. "Gianna, I'm in love with you."

Speechless, she stared and blinked several times. She couldn't have been more surprised had he slapped her. But, she knew he awaited her response and words couldn't express her feelings. Suddenly, she realized that with or without Mattias, she'd always want Nicholas, just like this, in a genuinely perfect moment. The moment when he broke through her walls and made her—feel.

Uncomfortable silence followed. Their lovemaking halted.

"I'm so sorry. Fuck!" He screamed at the ceiling, "I really know how to kill the mood," he said in disappointment.

"I...um...hmm...," she choked out.

*Think, Gianna, think! Say something!*

She winced and feared his lust for both her body and blood were equal but God help her, she wanted to show him how much he'd come to mean to her. Could she trust him? She took the gamble and made a quick decision that crossed a line and tested their restraint. A teasing grin flashed across her lips but instead of speaking, she kissed him savagely, nibbling on his lips between kisses. And with a sharp fingernail, she sliced through the skin at the top of her shoulder, allowing blood to flow.

Fangs elongated, he panted, staring at both the incision and the willing participant.

"I trust you," she said with hooded eyes

Shocked by everything she offered, he placed his hands on her waist and released her. Gianna's slick body slid down his, as he placed her on her feet, standing before him. He studied the wound, and watched, for a second, as the blood combined with water and cascaded in a single trail down the outer contour of her breast. Hunger built and he bent to one knee. He placed his tongue against the hot flesh at her waist and caught the long track of crimson. In a slow and torturous pattern, he dragged his tongue the length of the blood trail, over her breast, and back to the origin.

He closed his mouth over the gaping wound, and lapped so sensually, her breath hitched. The suction he applied as he drew more blood caused her to grow molten. And the contact only enhanced the thrill of their intimacy.

She lifted her leg and wrapped it around his waist when he raised her back against the tiled wall. Still working her incision, he released a low growl, and buried his cock deep inside her. She rolled her head in the opposite direction and bit the inside of her cheek to keep from screaming in pleasure. Dear God, he felt amazing and she wanted to lose herself in this very moment. Who was she kidding? She was already lost.

Holy, fuck. He couldn't believe this was happening—again. He was sampling her very essence, and this time, she'd offered. She tasted incredible and was wrapped so tightly around him that his mind spun. He penetrated in time with the sweep of his tongue as she met his thrusts and fuck, he wanted to bite down.

Drunk from lust and love, Nicholas took his fill of her blood before he lost control. She moaned at the feel of his lips and tongue as he drank. She cupped his head against her and ran her free hand down the rippled muscles of his back.

"Oh Nicholas, is the taste as good as you'd imagined?" she whispered.

He paused briefly and gazed into her eyes, lips coated with her blood, and fangs present. "Baby, you taste just as good as you feel."

The sight of him enjoying the taste of her caused her blood to boil with pleasure. She stared at his lips and kissed him fiercely, moaning at her own flavor combined with him.

Suddenly, he needed more. Oh, shit, he needed so much more. He pulled away from her lips. "I can't get enough of you," he said.

He lowered her to the floor and faced her toward the sleek ceramic tile. She pressed her hands against it, and without warning, he entered her from behind.

"Oh God, Nicholas!" she groaned.

"Is this want you wanted Gianna? Is this how you dreamed I'd take you?" His breath was hot in her ear.

"Yes," she answered, breathless.

As he filled her, he crushed her back to his chest and continued feeding. The act aroused them both to blinding levels, when Nicholas brushed his fangs against her incision. Gianna moaned in anticipation.

Now it started to become interesting. His fangs heightened her ecstasy and he continued to tease her. She tilted her neck, exposing herself further. He ran his hands over her full, swollen breasts and pressed sharp teeth against her, delivering a long, light scrape. She reached back and grabbed a fistful of his hair. He growled deep in his throat at her forwardness.

With clouded judgment, Gianna silently begged for the change. She imagined the sting of his bite, the burning excruciating pain that the transformation could bring. She welcomed it. Was this her humanity again? Is this moment the sole reason why most humans desire to become a vampire, or at least be with one? The sexual encounters were legendary and far exceeded the expectation. Torn over her feelings, right now, she didn't care to sort them out. She longed to be claimed, to be his, to belong.

The steam filled the space with the aroma of mixed fruit and raw sex. More than anything, he wanted to pierce her skin with his hypersensitive fangs. He thought about it, as he tasted her life force, her passion, and her lust. Finally, he gained insight to her feelings and it was enough to drive him mad. So blissful, a high unlike nothing he'd ever experienced and he was so hard for her, like velvet stretched over marble.

Nicholas could sense her climax mounting and he wanted to give her an orgasm so fierce, she'd never forget. He reached between her legs and let his hands work magic on her sensitive nerves, as he continued to thrust his hips against her.

She hissed between clenched teeth at how good his hands felt on her body. "Ah..."

"That's it Gianna, come for me. I want to hear how good I make you feel."

Within seconds, she came, screaming his name in such a blinding wave of ecstasy, her body shook with every spasm.

Once again, he turned her to face him and he lifted her to support her weight. She locked her legs around him. He thrust himself all the way to his base when he came so furiously, he almost lost his balance. The release he found with her was unparalleled, while Gianna fell limp in his arms, grasping his shoulders to steady herself. He held her tight and spoke softly. "God, I love you."

She laughed airily in his ear. Her wound healed quickly and he continued to hold her in his arms, still kissing her with everything that he had. He lowered her to the floor where she leaned against the wall for support. A woman could absolutely get used to that kind of stamina. He stepped out of the shower and tossed a towel in her direction, then grabbed one for himself. He walked back into the bedroom, and she made a mental note that he had the nicest bare ass she'd ever seen.

Gianna took a moment to recover, when the reality of what he said, set in.

Nicholas tried to break the ice, "Gianna—"

"Nicholas, I need a moment."

He dressed himself quickly and turned to speak to her. "I'll be downstairs for a little while. Take your time and come down when you're ready."

He pulled her in for a gentle embrace, his finger caressing the place from where he'd just fed.

"Thanks. I will," she said.

He kissed her softly on the lips and was instantly hard. Wrapped in a towel, she gave him a wicked grin. "Want another go round?"

His eyes widened in anticipation of her answer. "Really? Hey, just drop that towel."

"It was more of a half loaded question. I'm surprised I can still stand."

"I'll take you up on the offer later, then. See you shortly."

He left the room elated, while Gianna was left to catch her breath.

***

Nicholas walked downstairs. Nothing could defeat him now. But he needed to get a feel for the current emotional state of his house. He didn't want Gianna thrown to the wolves. Elizabeth cascaded behind him, embraced him in a big bear hug, and spoke with enthusiasm.

"Hey Nicholas!" Did I tell you how happy I am that you're home?"

Nicholas laughed. "I think maybe once or twice."

"I really am though...So about your friend, Gianna."

"What about her?"

"I like her, Nicholas. I think she's good for you and I know that you probably don't want to talk about it but I really think—"

He interrupted with a truthful admittance. "Yes, I'm in love with her, Elizabeth."

"I thought as much...Yay! I haven't heard or seen you this pleasant in a long time and I'd like to see her stick around for awhile."

"Well, I've made my intentions clear. The rest is up to her."

"Well she seems intelligent. Let's see how it goes after she's had some time to weigh her options."

"I've missed you too little sister."

# 14

Emotions rattled and fully clothed, Gianna left no trace of the romantic interlude. Unable to hide forever, she stepped out of his bedroom and into the hallway. Nicholas's room occupied half of the entire second level of the house. To her left, the staircase led to floors above and below. To her right, was a door to another room. Curious, she walked to the entryway and opened a large oak door to a study, designed for both solitude and entertainment. Books, too numerous to count, graced the shelves that accounted for most of the wall space. And the comforting scent of wood burning in the fireplace across the way, mingled with the surrounding air.

Expensive artwork that was time-period specific, adorned the space. The study contained a great detail of history, both public and personal. She now understood how Nicholas felt when he came across the room that told her own story. Amidst the surrounding memories, sadness and loss loomed. She could sense it.

She reached out and grasped a photo frame seated on a marble mantle above the large fireplace.

Suddenly, Bennett cleared his throat and she nearly dropped the frame. He had a knack for appearing out of thin air.

"That was my family. Well, before the change. The woman was my wife Kathryn, Nicholas's and Elizabeth's mother. Nicholas has few memories of her while Elizabeth has no recollection. Kathryn died while giving birth to her," he said.

She placed the photo in its original position and looked to the floor. "I'm so sorry for my intrusion and for your loss. I have no right to be here."

"Please don't apologize for caring, and being curious. I've had many years to come to terms with her death. When I look at my children, I see Kathryn. Especially Elizabeth, she looks just like her mother."

She winced at his hardship. "It must be difficult sometimes. I imagine when you notice the resemblance, it opens up the wound all over again."

He smiled and raised his brow. "No, not at all. Kathryn's love is a constant presence in my life. It's what gave me the strength to accept others into our coven. Even without her, the family continues to grow and she would be proud. She loved children and we'd always wanted more."

"I apologize in advance for anything that sounds obtrusive, but how do you endure without your greatest love? It can't be much of an existence without a companion," she said.

He sighed and extended his arm, his palm met the mantle, and he gazed into the fire. "It's been centuries since I've searched for one. The humans wouldn't be very receptive and the vampires have just as many complications. I'm happy with my arrangement," he admitted.

Gianna nodded. Bennett sacrificed his own happiness to care for his family. If that didn't signify a decent person, she didn't know if anything would.

He shocked her with his own set of questions. "Please forgive me for asking, but I was interested in knowing how you came about, your family, and the reason for the impending conflict. Please stop me if I am being ignorant, Gianna."

She offered her best cordial smile. "Bennett, I don't think you *could* be ignorant. Nevertheless, I warn you, it's a story without a happy ending."

She dug deep into the pain within her soul and rehashed how she came into being. The same story she'd told Nicholas; her father and mother, their forbidden relationship, the miraculous delivery, the betrayal and assassination. All of it leading to Mattias as the culprit and her infiltration of his coven.

He listened intently and spoke only when it seemed necessary. "Leave it to my son to fall for such a fiercely passionate woman."

She smiled. *You mean emotionally challenged.*

She ignored the fact that he alluded to Nicholas's feelings, and prayed he didn't hope to learn her own. In response, she did what she'd always done, and flashed a smile at his comment.

"I'm terribly sorry for the difficulty that you've had to endure. However, with that said, you play a dangerous game Gianna. The outcome could be unfortunate and I'd hate to see any losses."

She straightened. "I don't plan on losing, Bennett."

"Those that do lose, seldom plan to. You seem confident now, but can you really end Mattias's life? I feel that your attachment to him has more depth than you're willing to admit. When you have the opportunity to deliver justice, you may not be as quick to kill as you'd think," he said.

She folded her arms across her chest. "I've killed when necessary. And I find it only gets easier with practice."

"Please don't misinterpret my words as lack of faith. I only want to be sure that you are aware of the difficulty of your intentions."

"I appreciate your concern, but now that I've played my part, and inadvertently brought this conflict to your family, I must follow through."

"Fair enough, but know that if you are faced with the decision and find it difficult to choose, I won't fault you."

"Thank you, but I don't think it will be a problem."

Bennett narrowed his gaze upon her. "What of your gift Gianna, the telekinesis? Have you had it your entire life?"

She sighed. "For as long as I can remember. I could move things as a child, but the power seemed to intensify a few years later. My ability took a great deal of time to understand and control."

"Do you know your limitations with regard to the size of the things you can move?" His eyes widened with a thirst for knowledge.

"I haven't tried much more than a person or a vehicle. Those, I can shift rather easily," she said.

"Interesting...Have you ever tried to move elements?" He eyed her curiously.

"Elements?" she asked.

"Yes, as in the basic elements of nature? You've already mentioned moving vehicles, so you're capable of moving metal. How about water or fire?" he asked.

"I've never actually tried," she admitted.

He looked to the fireplace in the study. "Do you mind if I test your ability?"

"I guess not," she hesitated.

"Look into the fire and imagine the flames in your hands. Can you hold the flames?" he asked.

"I'm afraid of what would happen if I could," she admitted.

"Just give it a try Gianna. Trust me. You can always stop if it becomes overwhelming."

She hesitated before agreeing. "Okay."

She concentrated on the flames raging within the mantle walls. She cupped her hands and held them palm side up. Suddenly, she was cradling a ball of flame in her left hand. To her surprise, there was no heat to bear.

"It's not burning," she said.

"Amazing."

"Did you know I was capable of this?" she asked.

"I've known a few with your ability and thought it could very well be possible. None of my acquaintances could move elements quite as well, but I knew one who could move wood, and as a result, was able to move entire structures. Your ability has endless possibilities, Gianna."

"Why did the fire not burn?" she asked.

He looked as though confused. "I believe it's because you did not create the flame, you mirrored it. You are moving it from one place to another and I assume you can direct it elsewhere. Try to throw the fire into the wastebasket."

"Are you kidding?" she asked with raised brows.

"I trust you, Gianna. You can do this," he encouraged.

Still holding the ball of flames, she turned her hand with an outward force and threw the ball into the trashcan with ease.

"That's unbelievable," he beamed.

Gianna surprised herself, and Bennett shook his head in wonder.

"I would like very much to continue to analyze your ability, but I don't want to keep my son waiting. It's no surprise that he eagerly awaits your arrival," he said.

"Thank you for...everything," she said.

"No, the pleasure was all mine. Speaking of my son, I wanted to give you a few words of advice."

She sighed. Here comes the awkwardness.

"Don't be afraid to open your heart. If it's loss, pain, or sorrow that feeds your fear, it's worthwhile to take that kind of risk sometimes. Eternity can be a lonely existence. Trust me. I speak from experience," he said.

"I'll take it under advisement."

*** 

After Nicholas left Elizabeth, he surveyed the rest of the house, when he heard the creaks of Gianna treading lightly down the stairs, her steps no doubt, matching her angst. And when she arrived in sight, she stole his breath. He offered his hand. "Are you ready?" he asked with a gentle squeeze.

She sighed. "As ready as I'll ever be."

When the couple entered the room, Bennett, Elizabeth, and Josephine were seated on the couch. "So, shall we discuss how we are going to handle what's coming?" Bennett asked.

Nicholas urged Gianna to sit while he remained standing. "Let's begin by saying that we're all on the same side. We all want the same thing, to protect each other without any casualties. However, if we find ourselves in a predicament where that is not an option, we will need to defend ourselves, and each other. Now, clearly most of us know how to do that, but we should consider alternate means of defense."

Elizabeth leaned forward and braced her hands on her knees.

"We can't all be destroyed the same way. It's the beauty of individuality. We should consider different possibilities when it comes to eliminating our kind, if need be," she added.

Bennett nodded in agreement. "Okay...well, there's the old stake through the heart which may or may not be effective, decapitation, fire, silver, and a few others. Since a vast majority of our kind can walk in the light, sunlight may not be a wise option. Whatever we decide to do to defeat them will affect them all differently and we will have to act quickly. Wasting time could prove to be fatal."

"Wait. You can walk in the light?" Gianna asked.

Bennett smiled. "Most of us can. It's not something we necessarily like to do as it causes us to grow weak quickly. For that reason, we sleep during the daylight hours."

"Our species has evolved just as the humans have. Some of our kind have become impervious to old methods of elimination," Josephine added.

Bennett looked at each of his children individually. "Choose your methods and weapons wisely, as there isn't much time. A few weeks at best, but an attack could occur in an instant. Watch yourselves, and each other."

After his words of wisdom, Bennett led them to the basement entertainment area. He removed a large painting from the wall, and pressed a button behind it. "I was hoping that I would never have to show this to anyone because I prayed there wouldn't be a need," he said.

A wall opened to reveal an arsenal. Weapons of all kinds, futuristic, UV lamps, spring-loaded syringes, explosives, bullets, stakes, blades, and pistols were displayed throughout.

"I want to point out that I do not condone this kind of behavior. This is only for a means of self defense." Everyone gawked at the vast collection of ammunition.

"Father, I never knew this existed. Why didn't you confide in me?" Nicholas asked accusingly.

"It wasn't necessary at anytime, Nicholas."

Gianna approached a weapon. "May I?"

Bennett nodded. "Be my guest."

Gianna reached for a pair of close range pistols. "This will do."

Bennett offered an explanation of her weapons. "Gianna, those pistols require two different kinds of ammunition and are for close range combat."

While Bennett's wisdom was wealthy, his statement was one of the many misconceptions that men had regarding women. Even though not human, the same rules and ways of thinking applied. He knew nothing of Gianna's background nor considered the possibility of the extensive training that she'd undergone with such weapons. Quite honestly, she could've given instruction. Instead, she remained humble. "I'm aware. One is for ultraviolet ammo and the other is for silver, correct?" she asked, closely examining the pistols in her hands.

"How did you know that?" Nicholas asked

"I've done a lot of training. I want to look them in the eyes so I'm the last thing they'll see while staring down the barrel of a loaded gun," she said, aiming the weapons at the wall.

While Bennett's collection was admirable, and she was glad to have the pistols, she still preferred her own. She came equipped with a shiny weapon and a special gift. Combined, both were deadlier than anything Bennett stored in his treasure chest.

The ammunition was an efficacious insurance policy. If Mattias or one of the others attacked with similar weapons from a distance, Bennett believed they should have the same advantage.

Gianna corrected herself. "Actually, I'd prefer no weapons at all. I have my own that I'm used to wielding, and I'd choose the pistols if I'm left with no other option. I'd rather defend myself with my mind and bare hands. After all, what is the use of being a powerful creature if you don't use what you've been given?"

The Suttons chose their means of defense. Each one different than the next, making their individuality evident. Nicholas and Gianna had killed other vampires before but not like this. This was different; they could very well have a massacre on their hands. One thing was definite, Mattias was coming, and preparation was necessary. For each life they took, another would take their place in Mattias's coven and each one could be worse than the last. Gianna was distraught over the thought of using the ammunition in her hands but she, Bennett, and Nicholas knew exactly the kind of tactlessness they were dealing with. If given the opportunity, Mattias would insist upon an attack from a distance, so as not to get his hands dirty. Gianna armed herself in case that possibility became a reality.

*** 

Nicholas was overcome with a horrible feeling of trepidation. What would happen should he and Mattias come face to face? He would fight to his own death for her and Mattias would no doubt do the same. Gianna had spoken of how easily Mattias would take her life as if to discard her like an unwanted animal but Nicholas knew differently.

He saw something else in the way that Mattias looked at her. He longed for her in such a way that sent a jealous rage through Nicholas's entire being.

He understood the need, the desire for her, and because he'd dared to taste it, he had become insatiable. And he'd fight for her with everything he possessed.

Still, Nicholas had left her once because he believed it best for her. He thought that if she continued to be with him, it would be revealed that she wasn't exactly what she claimed, and it would place her in harm's way. Nicholas was fortunate that most of his family accepted her willingly, eagerly even, but not everyone would be that receptive. Some would see her as the abomination that she considered herself, and death would be her sentence when judged. It was a sentence that he could never allow. He wondered if he could be her protector. She didn't need one, and that was obvious, but he would always consider her safety his responsibility. Call it an old-fashioned way of thinking, but he wanted to be that for her or at the very least, he would surely die trying.

# 15

After a grueling flight, Mattias's plane landed at the airport. "It's about time. I could've swam faster."

He knew the rest of his company was beginning to grow impatient with his obsession but at the same time, they understood the frustration. They glided through customs with no issues, and walked to the vehicles they requested—two exquisite limousines. Mattias liked to travel in style and while he loved the feeling of being behind the wheel of a fast car—which was ironic considering that he was a dead ringer for Vin Diesel from *The Fast and the Furious* having the same look, build, and equally deep, hypnotic voice, he was far too distracted to concentrate on the road. All he could think about was her, what she was doing, who she was with, the earlier situation he so foolishly left. He wanted to kick his own ass for that one. It would be his single greatest mistake to date.

Kyle couldn't help but look at Mattias, his mentor, in sorrow. Who knew that it would lead to this? Sofia struggled against Cassius. "Don't worry. It won't be too much longer until we'll see just how loyal you and Gianna are to each other."

"You had better pray that you're up to the task." Sofia spat.

"Look lady, it will take more than your attempt at intimidation to cause me to shake."

Mattias opened the door to the first limousine. Dante rode with him while Cassius, Sofia, and Kyle rode in the limousine that followed. Mattias slid down into the seat and noticed two women, dressed very provocatively, waiting for them. The girls smiled as the men took their places in the car. Mattias glared at Dante. "Is this someone's idea of a sick fucking joke?"

"No doubt, it was Kyle. Relax Mattias, he meant well."

Dante addressed the girls. "Do you ladies have names?"

"I'm Madeleine."

"I'm Seleyna."

"I'm Dante, this is Mattias. It's nice to meet you, ladies."

Mattias didn't miss how Kyle had done his very best to see that Seleyna looked very similar to Gianna. He glanced at her every so often, but his expression turned to yearning, and the woman seated before him, couldn't measure up. No one could.

Dante spoke softly to Mattias. "Look boss, I get that you're aching for a taste of your precious girlfriend, but please, you need to eat. You'll never be able to fight for her if you allow yourself to grow too weak. I'm not asking you to fuck Seleyna, but hell, you could at least feed from her."

Mattias draped his arm across the top length of the seat. Lost in thought, he gazed out the window. Then he felt an unwelcomed touch.

Seleyna reached for his thigh and gave him one long caress from knee to groin when he jerked out of his seat and sat across from her. Seleyna jumped back, apparently startled by his reaction. She looked to Dante. "Is he gay?"

Dante roared with laughter, which was rare for the methodically cool vampire, but her statement caught him by surprise. "No love, he's definitely *not* gay, a little stubborn yes, but definitely *not* gay."

Mattias rolled his eyes and sat frozen in his place with his arms crossed, wishing he would've walked.

Soon thereafter, they pulled up to a lavish beachfront property close to the Sutton's home. It was close enough to keep an eye out for any action, or sight of Gianna, but at a distance that was safe to remain undetected until the time was right for them to make their move.

Mattias was so anxious to see Gianna that the thought of her already made him hard. When he finally found her, he'd waste no time making love to her, ravishing her body and taking his fill of her blood. How he needed her. He used the palm of his hand to adjust his swelling cock.

Seleyna made the mistake of her life. She knelt before Mattias, on the floor of the vehicle, and reached for his fly. He drew his fangs and snarled at her, with a firm grip in her hair. How dare she touch him! She let out a piercing scream when Dante interceded. Mattias grew tired of their games, and released the girl while jostling her toward Dante. "Deal with her and be sure to clean up the mess. Oh, and Kyle should be warned about his gifts to others. My patience wears thin."

"No problem."

As they climbed out of the car, Dante leaned into Mattias. "Aren't you going to feed?"

"I'm fasting until my meal of choice manifests."

"You're unbelievable. Regardless, I'm not watching you waste away only to fall victim to insanity."

Dante turned to Seleyna and sunk his fangs deep into her carotid. She screamed and then hissed in pleasure before they vanished, leaving Mattias with deafening silence, exactly what he wanted.

***

Gianna walked out to the beach with Nicholas in tow a short distance behind, desperately trying to catch up to her elongated strides. She was fast-paced and troubled.

"Are you alright?" Nicholas asked.

Sitting on the warm sand and staring out at the ocean, she closed her eyes and spoke softly. "I'm fine. I just wish you would've let me handle things my own way instead of escalating such unnecessary dramatics. All of this could've easily been avoided," she said.

He grew tired of her dwelling on his actions and fired back. "Well, I didn't. I reacted the best way I could at the time and there's no turning back now, so if you want to condemn me for acting with emotion, then condemn me. But, I'd do it again and wouldn't change a thing. To be honest, I don't think that our time here has been all that bad." He caressed her neck.

She looked at him with a smile so warm, it touched his very soul.

He dreaded asking the question that was torturing him, but thought he may never have a better opportunity. "Have you ever thought about what it would be like to become a full-blooded vampire?"

She cocked an eyebrow. "Of course," she admitted.

"Have you considered being changed?" he asked sheepishly.

"Several times. Take the shower for example. The passion was so intense that I was pleading for the change and, it only gets worse the more I'm with you."

"Damn it! Why didn't you tell me? I would've changed you in a second. I nearly did. Being with you has an effect on me." He pulled her close, wrapping he arms around her.

"I don't want to get caught up in the heat of the moment, Nicholas. First off, I don't even know if I *can* change. Secondly, what would happen if I regretted it when the transformation ended? How would *that* make you feel?"

Gianna paused briefly, taking in the purity of the salty air. "I've weighed the pros and cons. Should I be faced with certain death, I'd want to attempt the transformation, without question."

Nicholas smirked an evil one before teasing her, "So if I were to say, slit your wrist deep enough that healing would simply take too long, I could help myself?"

She answered with equally sarcastic banter that he found endearing. "In self defense, I would throw you miles from shore in the middle of the ocean where your only friends would be sharks." She twisted out of his arms and placed her hands on her hips.

"Then I would swim to shore, find you, have my way with you, and then take your life in revenge. I would be completely justified. Even *you* can't argue that."

"I really think my sarcasm is rubbing off on you."

"I think it may be more than your sarcasm."

Laughing at his argument, Nicholas leaned into her, rubbing her bare shoulder in comfort. "I noticed that you didn't reply to my earlier statement."

She tried to pretend she didn't know *exactly* what he was referring to, but the silence would give her away. Instead, she took his hands into hers and looked meaningfully into his jewel-toned eyes.

"Nicholas. I want to be fair to both of us. I have feelings for you that run deep. So deep in fact, that it scares me to no end. With that said, I allowed you to sample my blood. It was just the two of us, no one to take action if you, for lack of a better phrase, slipped up. Yet I trusted you could stay controlled, which should tell you something. But love is a very serious emotion, and I want to be sure that I'm comfortable calling it love. I want to mean it when I say it."

Her words created a lump in his throat that he hadn't felt in centuries. It delivered a mild sting, but one that he could live with. As long as she entertained the possibility, he would not pressure her. He was relieved that they were finally being honest. Now, it was his turn, and taking his father's advice, Nicholas spoke freely, not withholding anything for the sake of feelings. "I want you to know that I meant every word. You make me feel more alive than I've felt since my first moment as a vampire. Being near you sends electricity though my entire being, bringing me to life and I swear to you Gianna, I'll give my life to keep you safe."

"I distinctively recall that I don't need your protection or sacrifice. I can handle Mattias and the others on my own."

"It's not Mattias and his coven that you need protection from. The only person that you need to be protected from is...yourself."

"Wow, that's quite an epiphany you've had. What makes you think that I need protection from myself?"

"Come on Gianna, you are constantly accusing me of acting with emotions, yet you act before thinking things through. You put your life on the line carelessly, and you run from the one thing you know would do your life any good."

"You've managed to describe a lot of people I know."

"I mean every word that I just spoke. Baby, I'm here for you. I will always be here for you, wanting to be the one to pick you up whenever you fall."

His words were chilling, and she was sure that one day they would haunt them both. Still, she attempted to swallow while holding back the tears that welled in the back of her eyes at the beauty of his words. They were poetic and forthright and no one had ever spoken such things to her. She knew exactly what stood in front of her. Salvation. *He* was her salvation. She wanted to hold him tight and never let him go, but she didn't dare. She knew she didn't deserve him; somehow, she would end up having to leave him, she just knew it was coming, and didn't want to hurt either one of them.

Gianna remained silent while her thoughts unleashed unspeakable agony in her mind.

*You don't deserve him.*

*You destroy everything you touch.*

*Your mere existence has caused suffering to so many.*

*Even if you claimed to love Nicholas and stayed with him, how long before you destroyed him and those he holds dear?*

She couldn't cause any of them to endure an ounce of pain. The Suttons were good and decent people who only had the best of intentions. She would leave them that way, the same way that she'd found them.

Why couldn't she find a soul equally as lost and tortured as hers, so that they could heal each other's pain? No one on earth could have suffered as much loss as she did and still be walking, could they? The thought of an immortal soul mate was something out of a random paranormal romance novel. It could never *really* exist. Could it? No, she could never be that lucky. She and luck weren't on good terms. Hell, they weren't even acquainted.

She glanced at Nicholas, her poor, poor Nicholas. She shook her head at how he thought luck knocked on his front door. *Newsflash! It was doom and you should never have answered. Why the hell did he ever get into my car?* Fuck fate for throwing them together. It was a cruel, sadistic universe.

She felt Nicholas's palm brush high over the arch of her cheek and downward to her jaw line. As though he couldn't contain his feelings any longer, he kissed her. Her senses upheaved, he tasted of warm salt air, desire, and love. God, it scared the hell out of her. Pulling back, she smiled. It was what she did when she didn't know what to say or do, in an attempt to avoid an awkward situation. She sighed before changing the subject. "Is there any place for me to train? A gym, or something?"

"We have one on the lower level. It's not as extensive as what you're used to, but it's something. Come with me. I'll show you." He led her away from the beach and back to the house.

# 16

Mattias sat in an oversized black leather chair in the living room of his temporary oceanfront rental. Elbows placed on his knees, and his hands folded, he was deep in thought. He remembered Gianna from the past evening. He remembered the intimate feel of her, the scent of her skin and hair, the taste of her. In a fit of anger, he knocked glasses off the long coffee table before him, sending them shattering to the floor. Dante walked into the room ever so cautiously and handed him a goblet.

"What's this?" Mattias asked.

"Your sustenance."

"I beg your pardon?"

"Even though Cassius, Kyle, and I indulged ourselves, we couldn't let you starve, Mattias."

He inhaled the contents of the cup and licked his lips like an addict offered his drug of choice.

"Drink it Mattias."

"No."

"Look, do you want to be prepared when Gianna comes home, or would you rather mistakenly and carelessly end her life, because you were too cantankerous to curb your appetite until you could take your fill of her and turn her properly?"

Dante had a point. He was indeed the one who could talk sense into Mattias at a time like this. Cassius was too vain to care, although he would appease Mattias by putting forth a formidable effort. Kyle was too impatient to give any kind of solid advice. He'd rather kill now, and ask questions later.

Feeling deflated, Mattias reached for the cup and quickly ingested its contents. He pulled the goblet from his lips and gave a satisfied growl.

"Is there anything left?"

"I managed to salvage some for you."

Dante handed him another goblet. Mattias gave an appreciative nod. Dante waited until he was mid sip before he asked about a strategy. "So what's the plan?"

"I have a few things in mind but I was thinking of simply observing from afar for now. I need to know what we're up against."

"Good, have Cassius survey the area and kindly report to me upon his return."

"Ok. Where are you headed in the meantime?"

"It's nearly dawn, I'm retiring. You may want to consider the same. I wouldn't want to be in this room in a little over an hour. Oh, and one more thing, did you dispose of the mess that was made with your entertainment this evening?"

"It's being handled as we speak."

"Good."

Mattias headed to a bedroom in the back of the house as Dante sipped the contents of a similar goblet while scowling at his leader's back.

Mattias entered his room, undressed, and laid on the bed. He closed his eyes and took a deep breath. He well remembered the night when he had first laid eyes on his lady love. It had been a night like any other, although it didn't feel like an ordinary one. Mattias felt uneasy as if something was about to happen, it made him unusually nervous and he couldn't focus. Instead, his eyes were drawn to the front doors of his nightclub for most of the evening.

Mattias could do nothing else. He sat in his usual gathering place and stared at that door, frozen with curiosity. Why couldn't he pull himself away from the entrance? With one last glance, he saw a familiar sight...Dante crossing through the threshold. He was smiling from ear to ear. Following closely behind him was a sight so divine, that it took him by surprise. He sucked his breath in sharply, and recalled being speechless when Dante introduced them. "Gianna, this is Mattias."

She was breathtaking...literally. She wore a black strapless dress that hung just above her knees, trimmed in red, and was tight enough that it hugged her every luscious curve. Her black stilettos wrapped up each leg below her calves. His eyes traveled up her body, examining every inch.

Her hips were that of a woman, full and curvaceous. They gave way to her smaller waist and full breasts. Although she wasn't thin, she was fit with a body made for stamina. She had strong, yet delicate hands that would know exactly how to touch what was beneath them. His eyes traveled to her collarbone, to the point of her neck where he could see her pulsating with life. In an instant, he wanted to whisk her away and drain every last drop of precious crimson from that soft, delectable body.

The goddess's hair and eyes were a perfect shade of chocolate against light olive skin, possibly Italian or Greek in descent. Her lips held a light layer of gloss that shimmered with a frosty cream hue, lips that begged for his and it was her name that was immortalized into memory—Gianna.

After their introduction, Mattias reached for the softest, warmest skin he'd ever known and placed a gentle kiss to her hand. It was then he caught her scent, one that would intoxicate him forever. "Dante, you've brought a goddess with you. To say that meeting you is a pleasure wouldn't do this moment justice."

She parted her lips to give him a smile of glowing white teeth that melted his soul. His eyes raked her body and this time, it didn't go unnoticed. "It's a pleasure to meet you too, Mattias." Her gaze bore into his.

Dante gaped at what unfolded, and shook his head as if he were in a fog of a nightmare. Mattias could charm the panties off almost anyone, and that was his exact intent with Gianna. Little did he know, he'd met his match. She silently excused herself. He winked at her as she made her way to the dance floor. Dante started after her when Mattias, who was in front of him, held his hand up to Dante's chest to stop him, an obvious act of claim that rendered Dante powerless. He would not deny his leader's demand of Gianna.

Yes, in the beginning, Gianna was Dante's conquest. That original plan came to a screeching halt when Mattias wanted her for himself. Mattias was ignorant to the lust that seeped from Dante's pores. Though he was aware that Dante would most likely always harbor feelings for the one that got away, Mattias relentlessly pursued her none the less.

He followed Gianna to the dance floor where she could seduce the room with the sway of her hips. Due to their nature, Mattias kept the room dimly lit which made their encounter more intimate. He circled her as if he were partaking in a predatory ritual. Her come-hither look was all too tempting as he approached. Standing only a few inches apart, he could feel her heat, her desire. He found himself needing to touch her. She crooked her finger at him and he eagerly obliged. When he did, she wrapped her arms around his neck as he glided his hands from her waist to her hips where his palms rested.

They moved together among the living in time to the music, when his lust took control, and her eyes, rich with life and passion, met his. He reached both hands beneath her long, soft hair that smelled of honeysuckle and strawberries, cupped her head just behind her ears and kissed her so deeply that he could taste her. He remembered how she moaned in response.

She was intoxicating. So much in fact, he was overcome with such uncontrollable desire and he had to have her. Now. He grabbed hold of her hand, and led her to his bedroom where he continued to kiss her fiercely. He couldn't get enough of her as he pinned her to the wall, reaching his hand underneath her dress to become better acquainted with her. She stopped his hand mid grope.

"What's wrong?" he asked, his lips against her throat.

"I think we're moving a bit too fast don't you? I mean "nice to meet you" was what? Five minutes ago?" she said breathlessly.

"Ten but who's counting?" He continued with gentle nips to her neck, her ears.

"Mattias."

"I'm sorry, but there's something about you that I can't get enough of. I assure you, I'm truly out of character...Look, I don't want you to be frightened by my actions, or repulsed by me. I don't want to pressure you. I'll understand if you leave and never want to return, but if you decide to continue seeing me, I'll gladly wait until you are ready to take things further and I won't ever touch another woman, none could compare."

"I appreciate taking things slowly and I am *far* from repulsed by you. I don't see how *that* could be possible...and as far as touching other women is concerned," she looked him dead in the eyes, "baby you'll never want to."

It was from that moment on that he knew he couldn't live without her and that he would both love and desire her incessantly.

Jerking himself from his memories, he whispered into the air, "Where are you, baby? I need you."

He reached his hand down to his swollen cock and cupped himself. He imagined the feel of Gianna as he rocked himself against his own hands, dreaming that he was making love to her. No, he wouldn't be careless with her life or her body. He wanted to savor every morsel, and he would indeed be ready.

***

Nicholas and Gianna entered the house and walked to the lowest floor where he showed her to the training area. She admired the machines that equipped the room. "It will most certainly do."

She didn't necessarily need to enhance her performance, the act of training sharpened her skill. She was perfectly capable of her own defense. "Do I have to worry about hungry vampires?"

"Well, I'll make sure that everyone is out for awhile. Just in case, I'll remain close."

"I would appreciate not having to use one of your friends as target practice."

Nicholas lightly laughed and left her to her solitude.

A half hour passed. It was maddening to not be near Gianna. Nicholas wanted to check on her, and walked down to the gym. He peered through the window in the door. There she was, training. She wore a black tank top with spaghetti straps, and the tightest of black pants that flattered her curves better than anything he'd ever seen. He remembered watching her like this once before. Beads of sweat glistened like diamonds on her body. He needed her so badly right now, and could barely stifle his erection.

Watching her bounce with vigor wasn't helping the situation. As he fought back the thirst inching up his throat, he heard the blood coursing through her veins, combined with her accelerated heart rate. One bite could satisfy so much. She could satiate his thirst for her blood, and fulfill his sexual appetite, while becoming his for as long as they both existed. He wanted all of that, and would gladly take it, but she made herself clear. Gianna wanted nothing of his life unless faced with the grim possibility of the loss of her own mortality.

He knew it was daring, but entered the room, interrupting her session. She watched him as if prepared for an attack and he was the intruder. He practiced tremendous restraint as she danced around him like a predator circling its prey.

The mirrors that lined the walls made her moves appear all the more methodic as she spoke in warning, "Are you calm? Or shall we dance?"

"That depends, is this a mating dance?"

"Vampires don't mate."

"If they all looked like you, they would certainly try."

Teasing, Nicholas aggressively bared his fangs and crouched low to the ground. She drew a stunning weapon from behind, which she must've kept on her person at all times. At first her piece resembled a small spear, but was so much more. Once the weapon was in her hands, she pressed a switch on the side, and extended it to the length of a javelin. Nicholas gaped at her means of defense. The detail was immaculate. It combined both ancient Roman and Grecian weaponry, with a futuristic touch that allowed for convenient transport.

"Stunning."

She continued to circle Nicholas with warning. "One wrong move and I could take out your heart and remove your head with very little effort."

"I believe it. I was just wondering what was stopping you."

Gianna retracted her weapon to its original, compact size. In a flash, he spun and crouched low with one leg extended, and swept her off her feet, knocking her to the ground. When she hit the floor, he laughed.

"Never let your guard down, Gianna." Breathing ragged, she lay still as he knelt over her. He ran his hand up her leg, over the curves of her waist, and kissed her. The sweat that clung to her body intensified her scent, almost enough to make him conveniently forget her choice and take what he wanted most from her.

Nicholas couldn't get enough of her. The urge was the only sympathy he had for Mattias. He now shared the need for Gianna, and would stop at nothing to keep her. He imagined how wet she must be in this position, and wondered if she wanted him as much as he wanted her. "Should we take this upstairs?"

Gianna cocked an eyebrow. "Yes, for a shower. I could really use one right now."

They entered Nicholas's bedroom where she peeled off her clothing in front of him and headed for the bathroom. An avid fan of her hip movement, he swore she moved with a hypnotic rhythm. It was then that he heard the sound of running water, and without invitation, took the liberty of removing his own shirt to join her. He walked through the door to see her shadow behind the fogged glass as she lathered her body in soap. He found himself envious of scented glycerin and froze in place at the sight of her. All he could do was observe the unbelievable view.

He couldn't imagine anything more beautiful than the woman who stood before him. Sure she was flawed, and had her own demons, but that only made her like every other creature that had ever existed. As he wasted time, she turned off the water. Nicholas closed the door to allow her some much needed privacy.

She stepped out of the room with only a towel wrapped around her. Her hair was combed, but soaked. Could it be possible that she looked even better wet?

"I needed that. I feel so much better."

"I bet I could make you feel even better, Gianna."

Smirking, she agreed. "I'm sure you could."

Nicholas approached, and kissed her once again. As she reached up to tangle her hands in his hair, her towel fell to the floor and he wanted to devour her. He laid her carefully on the white, plush throw rug and suckled her breasts slowly moving from one to the other. Soon after he had kissed a trail leading from her breasts to her navel, he spread her thighs apart. He lowered his head to her warmth and took her with his lips. She tasted like pure, unrefined sugar.

As she moaned in response to his timely actions, he knew she was primed. "Are you ready for me Gianna?" he whispered against her moist heat.

"Yes, I need you inside of me, Nicholas."

He crawled up the length of her, and in one fluid motion, he drove himself deep inside of her. She was tight around him, and he imagined her slippery skin stretching with welcome. As ecstasy began to crest, it was he that begged her, "Let me change you Gianna. Please let me bind you to me."

When she urgently pushed him away, he realized his mistake. "Gianna, I'm sorry if—"

She placed a finger to his lips, gesturing silence. Like a true temptress, she grinned, then lowered her head to his shaft and took him into her mouth. He growled at the sensation of her tongue swirling around him, making him convulse with pleasure. He placed his hand on the back of her head as she continued to work him senseless. He ran his fingers through her long wet curls that draped over his hips and she made a sound of appreciation at the taste of him. In an instant, he came for her in a way so profound, that she continued until every last drop was spilled, making him shudder for another full minute.

Curious, he looked at her as she spoke with a bewitching smile. "There you go, I've tasted you."

Breathless, he answered, "Yes, you have."

Still reeling from pleasure, he pulled her toward him to claim her lips. To his surprise, he was instantly stiff. She laughed lightheartedly. "Are you never satisfied?"

"Trust me. This only happens when you touch me. I think I'm addicted to you." He sat up and held her on his lap.

Gianna kissed him hard, curling her tongue around his sharp teeth, scraping her flesh against them. He nearly lost all control as she urged him back to the wall and he remained seated upright.

She faced him, and placed herself expertly atop his shaft, arching her back to pull him in deeper as he caressed her breasts while she rode him.

He leaned his head slightly to the side and her eyes met his neck. He noticed her eye color changing to the glowing wine hue, which he knew meant that she needed to feed. Looking at his bare skin, she licked her lips, heightening his pleasure. He taunted her, testing her convictions by giving her permission. "Have at it baby."

She continued to thrust hard against him. The feel of him inside, and his verbal consent to taste, caused her fangs to elongate and appear to him for the first time. She quickly honed her thirst as unimaginable pleasure set them ablaze.

He couldn't believe the control it took to suppress the anguish of the thirst, the need for blood. It was amazing to watch, and he never thought her more beautiful. When they could no longer contain themselves, they came in unison with orgasms so fierce, they were both left shivering.

Gianna shifted off him and ran a hand through wet hair. Unashamed of his nakedness, Nicholas stepped into the light from the fireplace. The glow of the flames that reflected off Gianna's skin reminded him of autumn foliage. He reached for a blanket, and covered them. Neither had the desire to dress or move. They were content with remaining in each other's arms.

"Stay with me Gianna."

"Where would I go? I'm completely naked and satisfied. I'm not going anywhere."

"I meant to say that I want you to stay...here and not return to London."

*Oh.*

She sighed. "Can we make this decision slowly and just enjoy each other right now? I can't think of anywhere else I'd rather be at the moment."

He held her close and kissed her softly.

Suddenly, she sensed trouble. His breathing was labored, and he appeared ill.

"Nicholas, are you alright?"

"I'm fine," he threw his head back against the wall, "I just forgot to—"

"Feed."

He looked at her with a guilty conscience. "I know it's rather forgetful, but I was far too hungry for other things, and I let time escape me."

"What am I going to do with you?"

He raised his brow in mischievous thought.

She extended her arm, and sliced it with a finger nail. His expression startled her for a moment.

"Is something wrong?"

"I'm just thinking how wonderful it would feel to sink my teeth into your skin."

"Stop...you're turning me on." She steadied her arm.

"Is that all it takes? I'll keep going if you give me the green light."

"Nicholas..."

"I know, I know...only with the possibility of certain death, got it the first time. I just wanted to see if I could be convincing."

He smiled before lowering himself to taste her.

She steadied her arm as he fed, and her body reacted to his actions. Her breasts hardened and her nipples puckered as the moisture between her legs returned.

Hissing with pleasure at the connection with her blood, he crawled on top of her and continued to sustain himself, nudging his erection at her hip.

He made a guttural sound against her, and without so much as moving his lips from her wound, he reached between them and spread her thighs wide, with his free hand. He was so hard for her. He couldn't remember the last time he felt this way with anyone, the last time he acted so recklessly and didn't care about the consequences. What he didn't know, was that she wanted him so badly she would've given anything to feel him inside her again, even her humanity.

She ran her hand down the length of his naked body, caressing his smooth muscular back, his tight buttocks, and finally reached between them to feel the length of his cock. Nicholas reached for her breasts before planting himself deep within her slick warmth. He thrust against her so quickly and mercilessly, that it made her dizzy. This time, it was primal and rough. It was even a little uncomfortable and she loved every second of it. This was the side of Nicholas she wanted to experience, the unleashed animal. She was so regimented in her day-to-day life that she secretly desired to be overpowered and she wanted to see if Nicholas was capable. Oh yes, he was far more than capable. He was masterful.

His animalistic growl set fire to her being and she knew he could feel it too. He penetrated her harder still, as he released her arm, taking his fill of her blood. "Have you had enough?" she asked.

"Of your blood, yes but I'm not quite finished with your body."

He leaned into her lips, and growled with a burning need for his own release, when he kissed his way to her neck and placed his lips where her heartbeat was most rapid. He pressed his mouth on the pulse, and gently created suction. The anticipation nearly killed her, as she came in his arms, and he joined her a moment later.

"Like that did you?"

"What gave it away?" She laughed at his boldness.

He smiled before steering the conversation in a more serious direction. "We need to make it to the bed and actually sleep. It will take quite a bit to recover from our little marathon."

In agreement, they stood. Nicholas lowered the electronic shades, blackening the room until nightfall, and walked the few feet to the bed where they'd lay naked, intertwined, and sated.

# 17

Mattias slept later than he'd planned. He did not rise peacefully, rather he came awake to bickering between Dante, Cassius and Kyle. Cassius was mediating the disagreement when he heard Kyle raise his voice.

"Well what the fuck do you want me to do, Dante?"

"I want you to tell him."

"He can't give him all of the details, Dante. There is no telling how Mattias will react. You and I both know that he hasn't been right since the other night, when all of this shit started."

"Yes Cassius, I know, but if you aren't honest with him, he will most definitely have you pay, and I wouldn't want to be on the receiving end of his wrath. He's done a great deal for you, for both of you. You need to disclose everything you know."

"I couldn't agree more." Mattias stood in the doorway, aggravated.

Unnerved, Kyle spoke, "Mattias I didn't—"

"You didn't what? Expect me to be listening to your conversation? I'll make this easy Kyle. You tell me what you know, and I'll forget that you even considered withholding the details."

Mattias waited as Kyle looked to Dante and Cassius for support but Cassius stood in silence while Dante raised an eyebrow instead of voicing his *I told you so.*

"I saw them."

"Saw whom, exactly?

"Gianna, Nicholas and a few others that I can only assume are a part of their coven."

"And...?"

"Gianna and Nicholas were sitting on the beach. She didn't seem to be receptive to him. And then...well I can't be too sure." He couldn't continue, for fear it would mean his certain death.

Kyle was skating on thin ice already where Mattias was concerned. He'd taken his carelessness a step too far by hand selecting their latest meal, and though he meant no harm, Mattias was offended.

"What do you *think* you saw Kyle?" Mattias asked through clenched teeth.

"I—"

Cassius intervened. "He saw Sutton caress her cheek and kiss her."

"What!" Mattias's lips were white with rage.

"I couldn't be sure of the situation, Mattias. It was more like a peck and she seemed uncomfortable as if she was waiting it out but I just can't be sure. I can't read thoughts or emotions but it could've gone either way."

"I see."

Mattias's rage mounted, and Dante tried to talk him down as best he could. "Look Mattias, why don't you go and relax for a little while, and we'll all feed?"

"How do you suppose I do that?"

"However you need to."

"Fine, I'll be back to discuss this."

Cassius nodded as Mattias turned to walk away.

Cassius looked at Dante and Kyle. "Look, we can't afford to have him burst at the seams. Let's try and tone it down a bit."

Mattias quickly turned around and addressed Kyle.

"Kyle! Why don't you go and meet some people? I'm thinking a small gathering would do us good."

"Are you serious?"

"Deadly."

Mattias walked into his bedroom as Cassius and Dante gaped at his cavalier behavior.

Kyle was baffled. "What the fuck got into him?"

"Ever hear the expression never look a gift horse in the mouth? I'd get moving if you want a party," Cassius said.

Kyle smiled before he bolted from the room while Cassius and Dante looked on.

Mattias stepped into the shower and turned the water to its hottest setting. The water pounded away at the tension of his rippled back, and as thoughts seeped through his mind, he leaned a hand against the tiled wall as if supporting his weight, then he struck the wall with such a force that he should've shattered the tile. He was pissed, pissed at what had led to their situation, but mostly because as much as he wanted to berate Kyle, he knew that everything the boy told him was the truth, and it was of his own doing.

He feared that because of his actions, every second he was without Gianna, was one more that Nicholas was getting to know her in a way that Mattias would end his life for. How long could Gianna resist? He ground his teeth at the thought. He turned off the water and stepped out, toweling himself dry, all the while plotting Nicholas Sutton's destruction.

***

Gianna woke to a strange scent of garlic and wine. Still naked, she rolled over to see Nicholas sitting upright in bed, completely dressed and staring in captivation. He brushed the hair away from her face and tucked it gently behind her ear before he spoke.

"I was wondering when you would wake. I was afraid you'd sleep the night away and leave all of my hard work to waste."

"What do you mean?"

"I'll show you shortly. Why don't you take a few minutes for yourself? I need to make a quick phone call."

"Okay, but you're making me nervous."

He winked before he stepped outside the room. How could his wicked smile tempt her so much?

Gianna took Nicholas's advice and stepped into a quick shower. She was hasty to towel dry, dress, and prepare herself. When she stepped out of the bathroom, she met a sight that caught her completely off guard. Nicholas had taken a small window of opportunity to have a meal prepared. For a second, she was dumbfounded. On the opposite side of the room was a small table dressed with cream-colored linens, white candles aglow, a pair of wine glasses, and a place setting for two. Gianna knew for a fact that Nicholas didn't plan on joining her in consuming the meal, but wanted to be polite. The centerpiece displayed a single red rose. It was simple, elegant and, so thoughtful that she fought back the tears in her eyes. God she was a fool and she was well aware of the fact. What was she to do? *You should turn around and run.*

Gianna collected herself. "What is all of this?"

"Well, you did say that you liked anything Italian, so I snuck out before you woke and had a dish of chicken marsala prepared."

"Nicholas this is too much."

"Please don't be polite. I wanted to do this for you."

"No, I mean, this dish could feed your entire family."

"Oh. Well, it is the most sought after Italian restaurant in the area."

"I'm impressed."

"It's only food and wine."

"I'm not impressed with the meal. I'm impressed that you have to be the first in the history of men to have paid such close attention."

"Gianna, I always pay attention to the important things."

"Thank you." She kissed him on the cheek, in appreciation.

The flames housed by the fireplace set a magnificent backdrop and a romantic mood. Nicholas poured a glass of wine as she took her seat, but couldn't help being mesmerized by the sight of her dark, wet hair against an emerald green dress that hugged her tightly and flattered her features. He watched while she cut through the meat and placed it carefully in her mouth.

Gianna's eyes widened at the taste, savoring each bite. "This is amazing."

"I'm glad."

"Would you like some?" she asked.

"I haven't had human food in centuries."

"You don't even want a taste?"

Gianna held her fork out to him, and as he leaned in for a taste, he sampled her lips instead.

"Mmm...you're right. I forgot how divine the simple things are."

"You're incorrigible."

"Not really. Anything is possible with the right persuasive tool."

Gianna reached for her glass and took a slow sip of wine.

"So, I was wondering if you would dance with me," he said.

Gianna laughed. "What?"

"Will you dance with me?"

"Is there music playing in your head? I don't hear any out here in the world of the relatively sane."

Nicholas walked to a docking station to turn on his MP3 player.

A familiar tune played through the speakers, *Frank Sinatra's, If I had Three Wishes*.

"I have to be honest, I never figured you for a Sinatra fan," he said.

"Nicholas, my name is Gianna Marino. It kind of goes hand in hand."

He laughed at the blatant nod to her Italian heritage as he held his hand out to her. She placed her hand gently in his, and he pulled her close, inhaling the essence he hoped would cling to him forever.

They continued to dance and he didn't want to let her go. He couldn't believe how she could be such a perfect fit for him. And as tenacious as she was, he handled her as though she were a rare gem, so precious that it shouldn't just be held, but cradled gently in his hands. He was in love with her. He wasn't sure when it happened, but he was positively in love with her.

\*\*\*

As Mattias prepared for the evening, he instructed Dante to bring Sofia into the living room, unrestrained. Dante and Sofia entered the room where Mattias offered her a seat on the couch. "Trust me when I tell you that it's not my intention to cause you harm. I only want what I came for, and you can return to London just as you left."

Sofia laughed. "You really think it's that simple? You have no idea what awaits you here. Sure you have physical strength on your side, but you've grossly underestimated the strength in numbers."

"Sofia, you underestimate my knowledge of things. No one, human, vampire, or otherwise will come between me and Gianna."

"Listen to yourself! You consider her a prize. Do you know how pathetic that sounds? I would rather die than allow you to claim her as a victory."

"She's not a mere victory. She is the only woman I have ever dared to love."

"You're saying that you love her?"

"With everything that I am."

Once again, Sofia laughed, and this time, Mattias was vicious.

"Your outburst of humor won't be tolerated much longer. I will not be ridiculed by the likes of you," he warned.

"You speak of love as if you've experienced it. Yet, when you describe it, you clearly have no concept of the definition. We're not talking about intimate details of your bedroom, Mattias. That girl is like a daughter to me and I will not allow for such a union to be had."

"But you're not her mother are you Sofia? What scares you the most is that I know the truth of what became of her parents. It shakes you to the core doesn't it? It's why you've protected her for so long. Your entire family has protected her since the day of their disappearance. As one passes, another fills the shoes of the caregiver. But you, you became more invested than you should have. As a result, you have forgotten your place."

Mattias smiled as Sofia tensed.

"You know I have no intention of hurting you or Gianna. If Nicholas or any member of his pathetic family stands in my way, they will die by my hand. I've killed more worthy opponents...I will seal our fates before this battle is over and once that happens, everyone will be powerless to stop it."

"You have no idea what you are saying Mattias."

"Believe me, I do. I promise you."

Cassius brought a meal for Sofia as Mattias continued speaking. "You'll want to eat, Sofia. You wouldn't want Gianna to be upset to see you malnourished, and I certainly couldn't have that. I need her to come to me as calm and rational as possible."

"You are a ruthless bastard. You can't bend her to your will."

"I've been called far worse and I don't have to bend her. She is already more than willing to submit. You'll see."

"She will hate you for this."

"Will she? Or will she hate *you*?"

"She will forever hold nothing but contempt for you. Not desire, not love, but pure hatred. That is a feeling worse than the emptiness of death."

"Forgive me for disagreeing. Now if you'll excuse me, I have an event that requires final preparations." He exited the room, leaving her alone with her meal.

***

Nicholas stared at Gianna as they finished dinner. They enjoyed every bite, each gentle touch, and every bit of conversation. The longer she stayed with him, the more she felt...normal, which was lunacy, considering the facts. She was not *completely* human.

He was *definitely* not human. In the world around them, they shouldn't exist. But they did. How do you explain the unexplainable?

While some things just didn't make sense, others were pronounced, and if the mythical existed, then why couldn't the idea of them being together be a reality, as well?

As she battled with her mind, Nicholas grew anxious. "I'm going to clean this up."

She sprang from her seat. "Wait, I'll help you."

"You'll do no such thing. We're not finished. I'll be back shortly."

He leaned in and gently kissed her lips, tasting the hint of wine. "Mmm...now don't run away while I'm gone. I'll have to hunt you down."

"I'm not going anywhere."

He stepped out of the room as she smiled. She was falling in love with him and if she valued him as much as she thought, she could never tell him what he wanted to hear.

Minutes after Nicholas left the room, there was a knock at the door. Gianna thought it was Nicholas, trying to charm her as usual. "Back so soon? You really don't waste time."

But, instead of seeing her handsome vampire consort, it was young Elizabeth. "Hi Gianna. I'm so sorry to bother you."

"You're not bothering me at all. Nicholas will be back shortly if you'd like to wait."

"I'm actually here to speak with you," Elizabeth admitted.

"Come in," she said.

Elizabeth took a seat on the bed where Gianna joined her, the two sitting like long time girlfriends.

"Is there something wrong?" Gianna asked.

"No. Well, I hope not. I know it's none of my business, but there's something I need to know. How do you feel about my brother?"

Gianna blinked several times, while Elizabeth studied her wordless response.

"I'm not sure how to answer that, Elizabeth."

"Oh, I see."

"Please don't misunderstand. I'm not confirming nor denying...but now I feel I owe you an explanation. I don't blame you for trying to protect your brother, for holding his best interests close to your heart. I admire that. The truth is, I'm not sure what I feel. It could be love, but I don't know."

Elizabeth looked away. "Please don't hurt him, Gianna. I beg you. I haven't seen him this happy in centuries and he deserves happiness more than anyone I know. Please don't take that away, it would kill him."

Gianna desperately wanted to humor Elizabeth. She wanted to tell her what she felt, what she wanted to hear. *What the hell.*

"I can tell you this...what I feel for your brother, I've never felt for anyone else...ever. If that's what love feels like, then I guess it's love."

Elizabeth beamed from ear to ear similar to a toddler who'd been given a new toy. "You have no idea how glad I am to hear that. He loves you too, Gianna. He loves you so much that he'd give his life for you. Do you know what that means?"

Gianna sighed at the realization. "Unfortunately, I do. Now with that said, you need to understand something. It's imperative that nothing is lost in translation. You, above all people, know the danger that lies ahead of us. If at any point I have to make a decision that grants Nicholas a reprieve, I will not hesitate. There will be no thought involved, no deliberation. I will not allow him to suffer, no matter the price that I have to pay. Do you understand what I'm saying?"

She looked at Gianna with tears in her eyes. "I love you already and I'm so glad that my brother found you."

"Be careful with your kind words Elizabeth. The night is not over and you may find yourself retracting your statement."

"Trust me Gianna. Anyone who would put my brother before themselves deserves my respect. You not only have my acceptance, you have my allegiance. I will forever be indebted to you for saving my brother from a lonely, miserable eternity."

"I haven't saved anyone, Elizabeth. In fact, if he manages to continue chipping away at the ice that coats my heart, it will be Nicholas who saved me."

Elizabeth embraced Gianna, and for the first time she felt as though she was part of a real family. Someone who was welcomed.

\*\*\*

Nicholas pushed the door open and met the sight of Gianna and Elizabeth in a warm embrace, both of them in tears. "What happened?" he asked.

Gianna answered. "Nothing. Everything is fine. Your sister needed to speak to me for a moment. I think that we understand each other."

"Elizabeth, are you alright?" he asked.

"I am now. I'll let you get back to...whatever you were doing."

Nicholas shoved her out the door. "I would appreciate it if you did."

Elizabeth wedged her knee between the door and the frame. "Oh, before I forget, a few of us are going to a party a few blocks down the road. It's should be a fun time. Would the two of you like to join us?"

"Who is going?" Nicholas asked.

"So far, just Dad and I."

He glanced at Gianna with a half-lipped smile. "Thanks but we'll be busy."

"Eeew...Gross!"

"Elizabeth!"

"All right, all right I'm going...thanks again Gianna."

"Anytime."

Nicholas closed the door and turned to face Gianna with an inquisitive look. "So what was your conversation with my sister really about?"

"It was girl talk...you know, you hurt my brother, and I'll rip your heart out with my bare hands, sort of stuff. It was really brutal. I had to bare fang and all. It was almost bloody"

"Really?"

"Oh yeah...she was pulling my hair and I had to paralyze her. It was quite funny, actually. Too bad you missed it."

"Yeah, I'm devastated," he said.

He walked closer. Beneath his arm, he held a white box.

"Should I even bother asking what that is?" Gianna asked.

He removed the lid and revealed a variety of small pastries. "I thought you may be in the mood for something sweet."

"Actually, I'm quite full at the moment, but I appreciate the offer."

"I'll leave them here in case you change your mind."

"Thank you."

He took her hand and led her out of the room, toward the balcony that overlooked the beach. The moon was full and cast a gorgeous light over the calm ocean. It was almost too calm, as if the peaceful breeze should be enjoyed while it lasted. The couple sat down on chairs facing the sea. He pulled her from her seat with a forceful jerk. "What are you doing?" she asked.

"You're entirely too far away," he said.

He seated her on his lap and wrapped his hands around her waist, pulling her close to rest against him. He leaned forward, inhaled the aroma of her hair, and imagined having her locks draped over his hips once more, as she made him feel like the man he once was.

***

The emotions were too much for Gianna to deny, and she was finally able to admit...something. Nicholas, I can't stand the anticipation, the waiting for what is coming. I'm...afraid."

His expression serious, he gathered her in his arms and held her tight. "Baby, I can honestly say that you are the last person who should be frightened. One thing that Mattias and I agree on is that no one will dare lay a finger on you. I won't allow it."

Gianna wasn't afraid for herself. She knew the truth of his statement. But was terrified for him, and couldn't let the man she loved, fall to Mattias. Nor could she grant Mattias such a victory. They were coming, and she felt the tribulation within her soul.

*This is not going to end well.*

She shivered at her thoughts, when Nicholas felt her trembling. "Are you cold?"

"I guess I am."

"Okay, I'll be right back." He left her seated and stepped inside the house for something to keep her warm.

# 18

Nicholas's intention of finding Gianna something to warm her chill was sidetracked. He needed to find his father. Bennett was likely the only person who had the answer to the question stinging his mind. Thankfully, he didn't have to search long.

He found Bennett standing in the study as he often did, staring at the pictures of his deceased mother. Nicholas now knew what the possibility of that kind of loss could feel like, the utter emptiness that could be left in its wake, and finally understood every action that his father had taken to keep what remained of his family intact.

Without turning to acknowledge him, Bennett was aware of Nicholas's presence. "You've come looking for answers."

"I need to know something. Can I trust that you'll be honest with me and not rush judgment?"

Bennett nodded. "What is it that you want to know?"

"I want to know about blood bonds."

The shock in Bennett's expression told Nicholas, it was not something he'd share willingly. "I can't tell you Nicholas."

"Father , I am begging you. Please tell me how it is done."

"Nicholas, before I tell you anything about the ritual, I need you to know a few things. First, you must never enter into a bond lightly. It is a powerful and emotional connection on a level that you cannot possibly fathom. Second, you need to be sure that the bond is mutually desired. You cannot take from her without consent. To do so will lead to devastating consequences. Lastly, you will need to use utmost restraint when taking your partner's blood. One drop too much and they will die. Do you understand?"

"Yes. I know you know how it's done. You turned me and Elizabeth."

"I almost lost Elizabeth during her transformation. She was weaker than you. She was still so young."

"Father, is turning Gianna possible?"

Bennett sighed deeply. From the moment Bennett learned of Gianna's unique genetic makeup, he feared this very question would be asked, and that he would have to be the one to answer it. As a result, he saw the longing in Nicholas's eyes, the panic that he may not be able to do anything at all. He could only advise him as honestly as possible. "I feared this very moment. The truth is...could you alter a human? Yes. Could you alter someone who is half of what you are? That, I cannot answer."

"Great," Nicholas said dejectedly.

"It doesn't mean that you can't try."

"She already knows that her bite cannot alter a human," Nicholas said.

"Well, that small detail may work in your favor. The worst that could happen is that it doesn't work."

"That *is* the worst thing that could happen."

"Is it her desire to become like us?"

"Not exactly, but I'm working on it."

"Nicholas. I cannot stress enough that she has to be a willing participant. Should she change and resist, you will suffer her malevolence for the rest of your existence."

"I understand."

"In the event that you are prepared to partake in the ritual, you must first make sure that she is aware of what is going to occur. You will then take of her blood until her heart slows. You will know when this happens. She will grow weak and will have to feed from you for sustenance. If she doesn't, she will perish. Understand that due to the nature of your relationship thus far, the exchange will become extremely sexual and you will want more than anything to lose control. You must keep all of your senses about you," Bennett warned.

Nicholas made note of the details. "Let me see that I've followed your instructions correctly. First, be sure that she is a willing participant, I bite and feed until she's weak from blood loss, it becomes sexual, I need to stay focused, she feeds and that's it?"

"She must bite. It won't work at all if she doesn't bite. That's usually how it works for humans. Let's put it this way, you at least have a fifty percent chance that it will work. I'm sorry that I couldn't be more helpful and that I couldn't give you the answer that you sought but it just may be worth the effort of an attempt."

"Thank you Father."

"You're welcome son. Now go and be with her. We'll be down at the Alighieri home for the festivities. Enjoy yourself."

Nicholas left his father feeling hopeful. Now all that was left to do was convince Gianna that it was what she needed. That may be the hardest task of all. He quickly entered his room, chose a heavy blanket for Gianna, and made his way back to where he'd left her.

\*\*\*

Gianna sat alone on the balcony. She was at peace listening to the waves crashing into shore until she swore she heard her name called on the wind.

*What the hell? They're close. I know it.*

She tried desperately to sort through her melting pot of feelings, those of lust for both Nicholas and Mattias, fear for those around her, and...love for Nicholas. She winced at the thought that she couldn't fight. It was the perfect time to tell him. They were alone, and things were peaceful. She may not have the chance again.

*Don't you dare!*

*Once those words leave your mouth, the sting of your absence will constantly be a fresh wound. Just keep your mouth shut and spare him the agony.*

Nicholas stopped a few feet short of walking onto the balcony. Her beauty stole his breath. He watched her from a distance for a few moments and remembered how they'd arrived at this point. While it seemed fate was against them, they were somehow thrown together to deal with one another's quirks until they could part ways, but couldn't. He wouldn't change anything about what happened, only the way that it did.

If Mattias weren't the obstacle standing in the way, he was sure he'd have her naked, bloody, and altered. The thought of her wine red eyes and drawn fangs, thirsty for his blood, made him hard for her. She looked equally as beautiful in her vampire state. He just had to be able to bind them. He had to.

Gianna turned to see Nicholas staring. He appeared to be lost in thought. "Nicholas, How long have you been standing there?"

"A few minutes."

"What were you doing?"

"I was thinking about how you leave me breathless."

How could she not love him? He said all of the right things and he treated her exactly how she'd dreamed a man would. Only he wasn't a man—minor detail. She didn't care that he was a vampire. It seemed to be what she attracted, or perhaps, vampires were what she sought. She'd be a fool to not let him try to alter her. They'd always be together and there would be no needless concern for the frailty of her human half. She considered the possibility of changing her mind, but it would have to wait until their conflict with Mattias ended. If what she thought she heard on the wind was real, the end was near.

***

Dante paced nervously around the great room. Cassius entered quickly, and took notice of Dante's uncharacteristic behavior. "What's wrong with you?" he asked.

"I'm just nervous about this little soiree."

"Why? It'll be like anything else. Like the club. They come to us and we discreetly dispose of any evidence left behind," Cassius said nonchalantly.

"It's a little different, Cassius. We're familiar with our surroundings at home. We have no idea what could be walking through that door."

"Yeah...I love American women."

Dante rolled his eyes as Mattias entered dressed to impress. "Are things arranged as I've instructed?"

Dante nodded. "Everything is taken care of."

"Good."

Cassius looked at the two who seemed to be speaking in code. "What's going on? Is there something I should know?"

Dante indulged him. "No. It's nothing important...just Mattias being Mattias. How are things progressing for tonight's entertainment?"

Cassius relaxed. "Things are far better than expected. Surprisingly, there are many tourists left in town. But come tomorrow, this place will be desolate."

Mattias smiled. "Perfect. Where is Kyle?"

"He should be back shortly. He was mingling with the locals, attempting to turn on the charm and lure them here tonight."

Dante cringed. "How many are we expecting?"

"Oh I don't know. A few hundred, give or take."

"What! A few hundred people?"

Mattias intervened. "Calm down. We can handle it. Compared to what we're used to, it's a small crowd." He walked back to his room to add the final touches to his wardrobe.

***

Dante knew what Mattias was really thinking. He'd arranged his entire presentation. All it needed was Gianna and she wouldn't be making her appearance just yet. He walked into Mattias's room, which was larger than most he'd ever seen. The walls were tan and the furniture was modern, right down to the wrought iron bed with white silk sheets. The owner of this house spared little expense on luxury. Thankfully, the owners were vacationing in Europe and their home was available to accommodate their last minute needs.

Mattias adjusted the belt of his pants while Dante spoke. "What are we to do with Sofia?" Dante asked.

"Well, she'll be in attendance of course."

"Is that    a wise decision?"

"Well, it would be rude of us to have a party in the home where she's a guest, and not invite her to join us."

"I'm not so sure about it."

"You worry too much Dante. I've selected something suitable for her to wear.

She'll cooperate. Don't worry. Can you see that she's ready? Our guests will be arriving soon, make sure she knows how to keep her mouth shut."

"Whatever you say." Dante was growing tired of being a puppy at everyone's beck and call. Dante's jaw tightened, insulted by truths. The tension between Mattias and Dante was about to thicken.

\*\*\*

Guests began to arrive. Kyle and Cassius stood at the door, greeting the unsuspecting residents. The house looked spectacular. The dark marble floors beneath the black furniture in the great entertaining room, added an elegant touch while reflecting the moonlight. The beach area just outside their doors was lined with torches for the outdoor adventurers. Rock music played from every area. Neighbors wouldn't mind, most were already in attendance. The guests helped themselves to the extravagant food display, and the beverages continued to flow.

Cassius nudged Kyle as guests continued to pour into the house and congregate outside on the sand that still held its daylight warmth. "I'm going to head outside. I see a few delicacies that I'd like to add to my menu," Cassius said.

"You are insatiable! I can't believe we don't come here more often. Look at them all!"

"Like I said, you will learn to appreciate the simple things."

"Do you mind if I join you?"

"Come along my brother."

Dante stood behind as Cassius and Kyle walked from the doors to the beach. Oh yes, he'd have someone tonight as well. All the while wishing she were someone else.

\*\*\*

Mattias was anxious. He'd secretly hoped that Gianna would be attending his function. He knew it was unlikely. The Sutton coven wasn't foolish. If they expected Mattias's arrival, they'd be protecting her and wouldn't allow her to walk freely until the threat passed. What if they dared to turn her? What if Nicholas took her for himself? Rage tore through him. It had been far too long since she'd left his side and he couldn't stand another minute. Tomorrow night, he would end things once and for all.

He left his room and almost instantly, women attached themselves to his side. Who could blame them? He was as sexy as any mortal man. Hot. Alluring. Deadly. All of the exact ingredients for a glorious bedmate. He politely refused their advances.

*One more night.*

It would be well worth the wait.

# 19

Moments following the conclusion of the party, Mattias overheard Kyle arguing with Sofia over Bennett Sutton. From the sound of things, she'd engaged in an intimate conversation with Nicholas's father, unaware of his identity. In the middle of his tantrum, Mattias appeared outside the door to the room. "Leave us Kyle."

"But—" Mattias cut him off.

"Leave us." he hissed.

Kyle turned to leave at Mattias's request. "So it appears you have a new roommate, Sofia. Meet Elizabeth Sutton," he said with a smug grin.

"What have you done?" Sofia ran to the bed, scooped up Elizabeth, and cradled the young vampire in her arms.

Mattias stood with his back firmly against the wall and his arms crossed over his broad chest as he watched Sofia with Elizabeth. "Is that how you've held Gianna?"

Sofia looked at Mattias in disgust. "How dare you take this girl against her will! Do you think Gianna will look favorably upon you after she learns of your treachery?"

"I assure you, I had nothing to do with the abduction of young Elizabeth. She was in the wrong place at the wrong time when Kyle and Cassius happened to bump into her. However, after I learned her identity, my plans changed. She now has a larger role to play."

"What is that?"

"She will make a far better pawn than you have, Sofia. Soon, I will grant you freedom. When you leave, you will find the Sutton home and tell them that we have Elizabeth."

"What else?"

"There is nothing else. That is the only message that you need to deliver. After that, everything else will fall into place, beautifully."

He smirked as he unfastened the buttons on the cuffs of his white shirt.

"You are revolting."

"I've been called worse. However, if you continue to feel sympathy for Elizabeth, feel free to provide her nourishment. I'm sure she'll wake quite famished."

Mattias strode out of the room and down the hall when he heard a gasp from Sofia's room. He returned to the doorway and witnessed Sofia feeding Elizabeth. "Well, isn't this touching?" His wide shoulders filled the doorframe.

Both women gazed at Mattias with contempt. "I would consider myself incredibly fortunate that we've already satisfied our appetites this evening, Sofia."

"What do you want, Mattias?"

"I wanted to inform you that you will be released at dawn. You will be given strict instructions."

Elizabeth spoke, not concealing her hatred. "My brother will kill you for your intentions. He will not allow you to take Gianna."

Mattias laughed. "Oh my sweet girl, I won't have to take Gianna. She'll come to me, and by the night's end, Nicholas will be bowing at my feet, pleading for a swift death."

Mattias scowled at the women. "Of course, I have no intention of harming anyone. I just want what I came for and I will be on my way. However, let this be a warning for you not to mistake kindness for ignorance. Should anyone so much as attempt to cross me, I will kill you without a hint of remorse."

"Understood."

"I will need to see you in the hall, Sofia."

Sofia stepped into the hall behind Mattias, away from Elizabeth's sensitive hearing before he spoke. "Here is your cell phone. Once you're away from the house, I want you to call Gianna and let her know you're there."

"She sleeps during daylight," Sofia said.

"Then I guess you'll have to wake her."

"Have you ever woken a sleeping vampire household? It's not wise."

"Like I said, make contact, and kindly disclose the details of my proposal....Elizabeth for Gianna."

"And then what?" she asked.

"Then I will expect to see her at dusk. One way or another, this ends tonight, either by bonding or a bloodbath. It doesn't have to be difficult, and fate rests in your hands. Do a good job, Sofia and we'll all be sleeping peacefully in London in no time."

It was much easier said, than done. One wrong suggestion and it could end badly. Would Gianna go to Mattias without a fight? Would Nicholas allow it?

"What of the girl?" Sofia asked.

"You have my word that Elizabeth Sutton will remain unharmed, but you have until sundown tomorrow to set everything in motion. If you are unsuccessful, we'll move in and take matters into our own hands, as we see fit. Trust me when I tell you that you don't want that to happen."

It took everything for Mattias to remain as calm as possible. The truth was, he was angry and dangerous. He knew he could only last another day in a rational state before he pillaged the entire town in search of Gianna. God, he needed her; needed to hear her voice, sense her essence, touch her...something to know she was close.

Sofia agreed to do as Mattias asked, and took the cell phone from his hands.

"The sun will soon rise. Remember, you have limited time to work with."

"Elizabeth—" Sofia's eyes searched his for some sign of compassion.

"She'll be fine. She is one of us and will sleep until dusk. I will of course, have to seal her room for our own protection."

Sofia nodded and made her way toward the door when Mattias called to her. "Oh and Sofia, no trickery or I will make sure Elizabeth suffers."

"You wouldn't."

"No, of course not, but I do know two vampires that would love to deliver a bout of justice."

Mattias recalled how Kyle and Cassius would not show Elizabeth a bit of mercy and would act with all the brutality that they could muster.

Sofia walked to the patio doors that faced the beach and opened them wide. Mattias was correct. Dawn was near. He grinned at Sofia's back as she stepped outside onto the cool sand that would warm upon the kiss of sunlight.

Tonight would be the last night that they would be in this house and in this town, biding time in dealing with a delicate situation. Tonight he would make Gianna his and heaven help anyone who dared to interrupt. He'd stake them himself and deal with the consequences. He was hard at the thought of touching his treasure in a matter of hours. It will all begin with a single phone call.

*** 

Nicholas and Gianna lay in bed, comfortable, naked, and settling into a day's rest. He reached around to the warm flesh just beneath her breasts, and held her close, inhaling her sweet scent.

Gianna placed her hand on top of his. She pictured herself night after night in this very position, loved, wanted, and belonging. For a moment, it was tranquil and she concentrated on the feel of his large arms wrapped around her while wishing with everything she had, that she wouldn't have to let it go. She tried so hard not to love him, and he was breaking down walls she spent her entire life building. She wasn't sure if he was a blessing or a curse, but she loved him regardless.

She checked to see that Nicholas lowered his electronic shades so they'd be in total darkness, with the exception of the last of the burning embers in the fireplace. Eyes were heavy. She was fading into a state of unconsciousness while relishing the pleasure of Nicholas's embrace. She concentrated on his rhythmic breathing and closed her eyes.

Seconds passed and she came awake, startled by her phone, moving with violent vibration. *Who could that be at this hour?*

She glanced at the caller ID—Sofia. Surely, Sofia was aware it was almost dawn and that she would need to sleep to recover her energy. The reason for her call couldn't be a good one. Gianna was quick to answer. "Hello?"

"Gianna?"

"Sofia, is that you?"

"Yes. Please come outside to the beach."

"You're here, in New Jersey?" Gianna said incredulously, sitting upright.

"I'm just outside the back door watching the sunrise on the horizon," Sofia said.

"Is it safe?"

"Gianna, you know I wouldn't put you in a dangerous situation. It's safe. The sky is a mixture of pink and peach. It is as safe as it gets, for now. We need to talk and the topic is severe."

"I'll be right there."

She knew Sofia would never betray her. In fact, she'd wager her very life to prove the fact. But it didn't mean that Sofia's hand wasn't forced. Gianna couldn't exactly step outside naked and the need to change was necessary, but she also wanted to buy time for sunrise, negating the possibility of an ambush. Twenty good minutes was all she needed to ensure safety for all of those around her.

She took her time dressing, then walked to Nicholas and gently kissed him as she left the room and closed the door behind her. Along the long hallway, light streamed through windows in geometric patterns.

She saw the sunrise through a large window above the patio doors that faced the beach. It was stunning and it had been at least a century since she'd last witnessed one.

She was also amazed to learn that vampires could walk in the light. Well, most could, according to Bennett. What did that mean for others and their fate where stepping into the light was concerned?

She walked down the stairs and out the back door. When she stepped off the wooden deck, there was Sofia, sitting on a mound of sand, looking upon the sea. Sofia turned to Gianna, stood, and embraced her tightly. "Oh Gianna, are you safe?" She reached for Gianna's hand, examining her from head to toe.

"Yes, Sofia, I've been welcomed into such a wonderful home with equally wonderful people."

"I'm so glad," Sofia said.

Sofia's expression turned from relived and happy to acute concern.

"Sofia, why are you here? How did you know where—"

Her words trailed off when she realized exactly how Sofia came to be here. "Mattias."

Sofia's eyes filled with tears and she began to apologize profusely. "Gianna, I'm so sorry. I didn't know what else to do. I would've much rather offered myself as a sacrifice to keep them at bay, but they threatened your life and once they abducted Elizabeth and decided to use her as leverage or they'll kill her, I had to come, if only to warn you. They will kill her if you don't comply," she announced.

A raging heat consumed the hybrid. "Wait, did you just say that they abducted Elizabeth? Are you sure?"

"Positive. I just left her side not minutes ago," Sofia said while wrenching her hands.

"How is it that Bennett, Nicholas or the rest of the family aren't aware?"

"I'm assuming they were preoccupied with other things."

Gianna almost blushed at Sofia's insinuation. "Did they hurt you?" Gianna asked.

"No. In fact, they were quite hospitable. They even entertained most of the tourists with an exquisite party."

"Bringing their food to *them* instead of hunting, no doubt."

Gianna began to piece things together, "Oh my god, do you mean the party that Elizabeth was speaking of earlier tonight?"

"That would be the one."

"But Bennett and Josephine made it back safely?"

"I was speaking with Bennett during most of his time at the house. I had no idea who he was. You cannot give them what they want, Gianna."

"Oh yes I can."

"I will not allow you to do such a thing, it's suicide."

Gianna's rage built so furiously that her eyes changed to a bright violet color and sand started to swirl as if in the midst of a violent storm. She was losing control of her power. This is what Gianna feared most, when emotion controlled her. It commanded her. She was its passenger.

Sofia placed a gentle touch to Gianna's skin. If she wasn't successful, the hybrid would reveal herself to the public, and things would become dangerous for the entire world. "Gianna, you need to calm down."

Still, the sand swirled, stinging her eyes. "Gianna, please, you need to relax. We will figure something out. We don't have much time."

Gianna's fury subsided and her eye color returned to the warm chocolate, reflective of her subdued demeanor. She breathed rapidly for a moment. Then she spoke rationally. "What do you suggest we do, Sofia?"

"They've given me until sundown to bring you to Mattias and no further threats will be dealt. If not, they *will* kill Elizabeth. Then they'll come after the family."

"I won't wake the Suttons. They will need all the strength they can get. I will need to rest as well, but before I do, please understand that I will do whatever it takes to see that things are left as they were before our arrival. Whatever it takes."

"I don't like the sound of that."

"No one ever does."

Gianna walked Sofia into the Sutton home and showed her to a large sofa in the study located on the same floor as Nicholas's bedroom. "I know it isn't a bed, but trust me when I tell you that it's comfortable. I don't want to take the liberty of showing you to a room in a vampire's home, nor do I want the wrong person to stumble upon you when you're most vulnerable. You'll be safe here and I will meet you here when I wake."

"This will be just fine. We will get through this together," Sofia said.

"You're right about that," she said as she closed the door behind her. She felt something brewing, something she wasn't sure she'd be able to stop.

# 20

Gianna stepped out of the study and walked lightly back to the bed where Nicholas slept, stripped off her clothes, and crawled beneath the sheets, draping his arm around her. Now, thoughts flooded her mind...their means of defense, the safety of those around her, and Elizabeth's welfare. She only arrived to one conclusion, and no one would agree with what she wanted to do, no matter how convincing her argument.

Nearly ten hours later, while the sun was still high, Gianna rose while Nicholas still slept. She showered, dressed, and walked past Nicholas to the bedroom door.

"In a hurry to get somewhere?" he asked.

Startled, she turned to see Nicholas seated upright, with a sheet draped over his lower half. He propped himself up on his arms, bent at the elbows and his upper body was exposed to his navel. Goodness he looked like a god, which brought about instant arousal. She lost focus and forgot what she was about to do. "I...umm...I was going to—"

"Did I finally leave you speechless?" he smirked.

Gianna shifted her weight in an attempt to alleviate the discomfort between her legs where the need for him was unbearable, and she was sure that he felt it, too. "You caught me off guard."

"It seems like I've been doing that rather frequently...but surely you weren't leaving without a kiss," he said.

*No! Don't do it. You won't be able to leave.*

She approached him and the closer she moved toward him, the more she swore she'd melt into a puddle of molten lust. She ached. Her body was seething and her breath was ragged. But his look of pure rapture, was almost enough to trigger an orgasm, even without his touch.

Nicholas sat erect, waiting, watching her every move. It felt like eternity for her to stride across his room. When she finally reached the edge of the bed, he grasped her wrist and jerked her toward him.

She stood at the side where he was resting when he reached out and caressed her hip, slid his hand beneath a sleeveless red shirt and pulled her closer for a mouth-watering kiss. He tasted wild and dangerously sexy. Sliding his hands inside her pants, beneath the waistband of her cotton panties, she saw the desire in his eyes. He was starving for her. "God, I hate when you wear these things. It makes it so hard to play," he said.

"You know how I love to present a challenge."

"Mmm...and I do appreciate a good victory."

His fingers played, stroked her while she threw her head back with a breathless moan.

"You're rather devious today," she said.

"Is that a complaint I hear?"

She cried out softly and forced everything from her mind. The only thing that remained was Nicholas and the sensations he created. Gianna spread her legs wider, growing weak in the knees.

"You are so wet." He plunged a finger inside of her and she had to brace herself against his chest from the force of pleasure she hadn't expected so soon.

Yes, oh yes...no, wait," she said.

She remembered leaving Sofia in the study.

"What's wrong?"

"Something has come up and I wanted to have a better handle on it before anyone else had a chance to wake."

"Yes, something has come up, and it's beneath this sheet. Now, how about we do something about it?"

She withdrew his hand from her and caressed his arm.

"I really do hate being a mood killer, but the situation is grave. Sofia is here, she's in the study."

"What? How?" Nicholas was at full attention.

"Get dressed and come with me. I'll explain everything."

"This can't be good," he said.

Nicholas dressed and joined Gianna as they walked to the study. "I'm a little nervous."

"Like, I said, it's not a good situation. Just promise me that you'll try your best to contain yourself. I'll come up with something. Don't worry."

***

Not worrying was easier said, than done. Nicholas was constantly worrying on the inside. He feared for his family. But most of all, he feared losing Gianna.

She was the most unexpected addition to his life, and he wasn't about to give her up without a fight. He'd even take on Gianna herself, if necessary.

Nicholas opened the study door to find Sofia reading. "Mr. Sutton, it's so nice to see you again. I see you've been keeping Gianna safe." she said with a warm smile.

"Yes, I gave you my word."

"And a man is only as good as his word, even an immortal one."

"So, what brings you here, Sofia?"

Gianna nodded for Sofia to proceed with her explanation. "Nicholas, before Sofia begins, you may want to sit down and whatever you do, please keep your voice down."

"Alright, but I don't like the feel of this."

Nicholas took a seat on a brown leather sofa.

This was the moment of truth. Nicholas's reaction would determine how things would be handled. Sofia began her story. She started with the invasion of Gianna's home, the threats made against her, the idea of using Sofia as bait and finally, she couldn't say the worst part of all. Gianna stopped her. Sofia was trembling.

***

Gianna sat next to Nicholas, held his hands, and sighed before she delivered the bad news. "Last night, while we were having dinner, do you remember Elizabeth mentioning a party she was attending with your father?"

"Yes, what of it?"

"It was no ordinary party, Nicholas. It was Mattias and the coven, luring prey," Gianna said.

"They're here and they're that close?" Nicholas stood, hands at his side.

"Yes. It gets worse, I'm afraid."

He shifted and crossed his arms at his chest. "Continue."

"Sofia spent the evening speaking with your father. She didn't know who or what he was. After all the guests left for the evening to return to their homes, Sofia retired to her room. When she opened the door, a girl, or what seemed like a girl, lay on the bed, unconscious but unharmed. It was then Sofia realized what happened."

"The girl...where is Elizabeth?" Nicholas asked.

"Nicholas, stay calm," She said.

"Where the fuck is my sister, Gianna?"

"They have her, Nicholas. I am so sorry." Her eyes searched his.

"No, please tell me you're joking."

"I think you know me well enough to realize I would never joke about something like this...I'm so sorry."

Gianna watched Nicholas slowly, waiting for a reaction. Then, it finally came. "How long have you known, Gianna? How long did it take for you to tell me the truth?"

"I only learned this morning as the sun was rising. Mattias was kind enough to release Sofia with a cell phone and told her that she had until sundown tonight to deliver me to him."

"What? That has to be the most ridiculous thing I've ever heard."

"It's a fair trade Nicholas. Me for Elizabeth. He wants you to make the most difficult decision of your existence and I won't let you do that," Gianna said.

"I need to wake everyone."

"Nicholas—"

"Don't you dare try and tell me to stay calm. This is my sister we're talking about. She's been through enough and I won't sit here another second and allow her to suffer a moment longer than she should."

Nicholas started for the door and Gianna held him in place with her mind. He tried to fend off her ability but was powerless against it. "What are you doing? Why won't you let me help her? Is it because you're helping Mattias?"

His voice grew as loud as the sting of his accusations.

Sofia and Nicholas watched as Gianna's eyes glowed with a violet color just as they had that very morning, showing that she was no longer in control of her ability. Her emotions were besting her. Books swirled in the air by the hundreds, forming a vortex in the center of the room. The priceless Persians that dressed the floor curled at the edges and the furniture levitated. Sofia panicked. "Nicholas, you need to try and calm her down."

"What's happening?"

"It's the telekinesis. She's developed a level of control over the years but when her emotions become disorderly, the ability controls her."

He was out of line with his accusations and he knew it was the reason for her conniption. She was hurt by his words. To be affected so deeply, she must care for him a great deal more than she'd admit. He took a deep breath. "Gianna, baby I'm sorry for speaking out of line. Please forgive me, I was wrong."

Unresponsive, her eyes glowed beautifully violet as the vortex spun faster as though it would swallow the room, and the house would implode with everything and everyone still inside.

"Please try again. You have to break through. I'm begging you. It could kill her," she implored

"Gianna, I love you," he said.

Suddenly, the tornado of literature stopped. The books fell to the floor with a thunderous crash along with everything else that was levitating. Gianna's eyes darkened from violet to deep purple, and finally, to brown. She looked around the room and guessed at what happened.

Gianna crouched to the floor and looked at Nicholas who was staring in amazement. He ran to her, examining for injuries. "Are you hurt?"

"I'm fine, I always am."

"Gianna, I'm so sorry. I should've never thought those things about you. You know I was speaking out of fear and anger. I was out of line and I apologize."

"You don't have to apologize. You were acting as anyone would in this situation. Please, go wake your family, they deserve to know."

Nicholas nodded. "I'll be right back, please just sit and relax."

Crouching to the floor, Gianna began to feel twinges of pain. Sofia ran to her aid, but before she could reach her, Gianna held out her hand, re-categorized the books, and organized the room as if it were never touched.

"Gianna, when was the last time you fed?"

"I consumed human food last night. I'll be all right."

"You can't go another night without feeding. If you don't eat daily, you'll look for blood. That is never pleasant for you."

She had no idea how wrong she was. The fact was, the rush of new blood was strangely erotic, and she did not want Sofia to know.

It would've made the situation all the more uncomfortable so she masked her pleasure with sounds of agonizing pain. If a man had been there such as Nicholas, she would've begged for him to be inside her as she fed, to intensify the sensation. Just the thought alone made her quiver.

Bennett stormed into the study with Nicholas. His terrified expression needed no explanation. "Nicholas told me what happened."

"I'm so sorry. I will make this right, Bennett. I swear it."

"Gianna, this has been coming for a long time. We've been dealing with the aftermath of last summer's incident for an entire year. You have nothing to do with this."

"I have everything to do with this. It's better to be threatened from a distance than to have the enemy standing on your doorstep."

Bennett sat on the couch with his elbows on his knees and his hands on his cheeks. "I don't know what to do without Elizabeth. She is the closest thing I have to their mother. What if they hurt her, or worse?"

Gianna crouched down to meet Bennett's eyes. "I will not let that happen. I promised to not allow any harm befall your family, regardless of the price."

"Why would you do that for us, Gianna?"

"Because of what you've given to your children; some of which aren't biologically your own, and yet you think nothing of it. Most of your kind knows no such emotion and I think it's a most admirable quality. Your children are very lucky to have you, Bennett."

Sofia sat next to Bennett. "Bennett, I'm so sorry that I couldn't stop them, but I didn't know. I didn't know who you were and what they might do."

"I know, Sofia."

Gianna looked down to Sofia's injured arm. "Sofia, I thought you said that you weren't hurt."

"This isn't from them, Gianna. Elizabeth needed to feed and since they captured her with silver, I knew she'd be weak. I know the signs. I couldn't stand by and watch her go mad."

"Despite our difference in age, I've always thought of you as a mother figure which is frightening considering that I knew your great, great grandmother. You remind me so much of her. She was a mother figure to me as well. You have done so much for me, Sofia. You've protected my secret from the world, and thanks to you, I continue to flourish. I couldn't thank you more."

Sofia looked at Gianna and then to Bennett who was stunned to learn the level of loyalty between the human and the hybrid. "Gianna, why does it sound like you are saying goodbye?"

"I fully intend to march straight down that beach and into Mattias's house. If it's me he wants, then I'll give him what he's asking for."

Nicholas was first to argue. "Like hell you will. There is no fucking way that you'll do such a thing."

"Nicholas, you are in no position to give me orders."

"Father, tell her. Tell her that she can't do such a thing."

Bennett touched Gianna's shoulder. "Sweetheart, I appreciate the sacrifice but regardless of the outcome, someone will lose and I can't hurt Nicholas by losing you."

"Mattias won't hurt me. You know that."

Sofia spoke. "Gianna, I can't let you do it either. It's insanity."

"I'm sorry, it was the best idea I could come up with. It solves our problem quickly and efficiently."

"And it gives some of us a brand new one," Nicholas scowled.

Josephine entered the room and braced herself. "It is time. They are staying at the beach house where the festivities were held last night. They've captured Elizabeth hoping to lure us out of our home and into the open. Let us be swift and accurate. This ends tonight. We will recover Elizabeth and settle this issue once and for all," Bennett said.

Josephine nodded. "Got it. Let's go."

As she left the room Gianna knelt to Sofia and made sure that Bennett could overhear. "I love you like family, Sofia. The only thing that I regret is that you were so dutiful that you neglected your own needs. I'm sorry you sacrificed your opportunity for a husband and a family. I know how badly you wanted children. I could see it in your eyes, the pain that you've tried to mask. You would've made a wonderful mother, Sofia, and any man would be crazy to let you get away."

Tears flowed down Sofia's face. "Thank you." Gianna turned to leave the room and Nicholas followed. But she didn't miss how her information piqued Bennett's interest.

# 21

Nicholas chased Gianna through the hallway, and into his room. Frustrated with both his sister's abduction and Gianna's willingness to offer herself to Mattias, he grabbed her arm, forcing her to stop. She turned to him, pressed him against the wall and drew the spear-like weapon from the back of her pants, concealed at the base of her spine. She viciously held it to his chest. "I don't know who you think you are trying to handle me the way you just did, but don't ever make the mistake of grabbing me that way again."

"I know you're scared, Gianna. I can protect you."

"No you can't, no one can."

"Oh, I know this game...you mean for me to despise you. You're trying to deliberately push me away so you can go to Mattias with a clear conscience. Well, I have some unsettling news for you. You won't change how I feel...ever."

Gianna withdrew her weapon and placed it back securely where it was originally hidden. She walked to her luggage and began packing her things. Nicholas baited her, begged, pleaded, and she didn't respond. Now, she was trying the silent treatment.

"Why are you packing and why won't you talk to me?"

"Because, this is all *your* fault! You have this habit of playing with fire, Nicholas and because of your obsession, look at what happened!"

"I am so tired of running around in the same circle, Gianna. How many times do I have to say it? I don't regret a single thing that I've done. Why? Because it led me to you and for that, I wouldn't change a thing."

"Really? I seem to remember, not ten minutes ago, you accusing me of working with Mattias. How can you claim to feel the way you do, when you were so quick to jump to conclusions?"

"I'm sorry. I was out of line with my comment. It was misdirected hostility and I am truly sorry. I never meant to hurt you."

"You could've fooled me."

Even with her back toward him, Nicholas felt her pain. If she was testing his loyalty, he had no doubt failed her. For a fraction of a second, he thought that she may be assisting Mattias, but as soon as the thought formed words, he realized how ludicrous it sounded. In the short time he'd come to know Gianna, he knew that much to be factual. The woman had remarkable integrity and fortitude, two qualities that were endearing to him. But he was worried that as much as he tried to convince her to stay with him, he may have just done the one thing that would push her away.

He then remembered the purple glow of her stare. She lost control of her ability when her emotions overrode her logic. Nicholas witnessed just how powerful Gianna was, capable of complete destruction. Both halves of her were constantly at war. The human emotion and compassion made her vulnerable, but the predator in her possessed all of his strengths and none of his weaknesses. That heady combination made her the most dangerous creature he'd ever come across, and the sexiest.

***

Nicholas was right. Gianna was trying to find a way to push him to a point where he'd hate her and force him to make a clean break. She'd devised a flawless plan in her head. He wasn't making things easy, seeming as though he anticipated her next move and deflected each one. This is what Gianna did best. She pushed everything and everyone away that ventured a little too close, because feeling numb was safe, it never had the opportunity to betray, and never hurt. Yet, despite all of her efforts, there were two men, both built like Adonis, that were pining for her attention. Yeah it was some pity party she was throwing herself. But this wasn't about her. This was about saving those who didn't hesitate to help her when they had every reason to send her away.

Nicholas walked to Gianna and placed his hand on her shoulder. "Gianna, I'm so sorry. You know that I wouldn't want to cause you an ounce of pain."

Gianna melted under his touch. The very feel of him sent chills down her spine and caused every nerve to tingle.

In a perfect world, she'd stay here and spend all day allowing him to use his hands to work over the rest of her body, but time was of the essence.

The sun would set soon, and then all bets were off. She armed herself and turned to Nicholas. "I know that hurting me wasn't your intention. Now, if I were you, I'd prepare for battle."

A piercing scream came from the study, distracting Gianna. She ran down the hall with a weapon in hand, and opened the door. She stopped, frozen in her stance, witnessing something impossible. "What. The. Hell."

On the other side of the room, on the brown leather sofa, Sofia lay limp in Bennett's arms, his fangs embedded in her neck. "No! What the hell are you doing?" she cried.

Bennett looked to Gianna with fangs bared, hissing at her intrusion. She started after him with her weapon when Nicholas pulled her back, restraining her from attacking. "Let go, Nicholas."

"I can't do that, Gianna. Just wait and watch. Trust me."

Tears fell from Gianna's eyes, fearful of Sofia's demise, of losing the only true ally that she'd ever known. She held onto Nicholas's forearm, tightly gripped at Gianna's chest. She watched in horror as Sofia's chest heaved. Bennett turned to her as if nothing happened and offered his wrist. Sofia placed her mouth over the incision. "Oh my god, he's turning her," Gianna said.

"Yes, he is."

"Was she—"

"Yes, she was definitely willing. My father would never risk turning another person without their consent, but this is more than merely turning Sofia. This...is the bonding ritual."

"Bonding...why?"

"Because this is what they both want. My father has lived for hundreds of years without a mate because no one fit the mold. Sofia comes along and they both get what they want. My father has a companion. Sofia has a husband and a family in a world that she both understands and accepts. My father will adore her, love her and will see that she never wants for anything for the rest of eternity, while her children will be devoted and loyal. What more could she ask for?"

She wanted to say something, anything to stop what was happening but he was right, this is what Sofia wanted, and if Gianna didn't have the power to give it to her, at least she could lead her to Bennett. "Well, I guess it beats the stress of planning a wedding, giving birth, and changing diapers."

"I don't think that sounds as terrible as you make it seem."

Gianna watched carefully as Sofia continued to take from Bennett. At one point, he threw his head back and cried out with a long moan. He reached for Sofia's face and caressed her cheek. When he released her hold on his wrist, she sat up and began to undress him frantically as his lips skated over hers with sincere passion. How strange that they didn't even realize that Gianna and Nicholas were standing across the room. Gianna whispered to Nicholas. "Umm, does *that* fit into the ritual?"

Nicholas's breathing grew ragged and in the most seductive voice she'd ever heard, he answered. "This is how the blood exchange affects us all. It is the world's most potent aphrodisiac and we vampires...deliver *everything* it promises."

Gianna's body reacted to his husky voice, to his declaration. God, *she* wanted it too.

\*\*\*

Nicholas felt the pressure of her chest rising and falling. It wasn't as steady as it had been only moments ago, the result of a positive reaction. Could she finally be convinced to be turned? He didn't want to wait another second to find out. "We should see ourselves out, and leave them with privacy or it could become extremely inappropriate."

"Uh-huh."

Nicholas led her out of the room, closing the door behind them. They managed to walk a few feet away from the room when he pressed her against the wall, his eyes glowing like emeralds and his fangs revealed. As a result of witnessing the bonding ritual, his decision was made. He wanted it with Gianna. He didn't care about the possible complications due to her breeding, didn't care that his lethal competition was only blocks away, holding his sister captive. He was far too hungry...hungry for her.

He kissed her hard, fierce. With a single motion, he reached for her leg and wrapped it around his waist while the other responded willingly. He pressed his erection against her core, moaning at the contact. At that moment, the only thing that mattered was being inside her. *Take her!* "I want you, Gianna."

Gianna answered with a moan while deepening their lip lock, curling her tongue around his fangs and the power that they possessed. Something about him seemed so much different than the Nicholas she'd come to know. She listened as he growled low in his throat, rubbing himself against her. He was possessive and demanding, starving to be with her and she loved every second. God, she wanted to lose control with him, wanted him to make the decision to claim her. She didn't need the pressure of having to weigh the odds. Her life was complicated enough.

Nicholas moved away from her lips, to her ear and to her neck where he froze. The heat of his breath gave her an amplified state of arousal. And when he pressed his fangs lightly against her skin, she cried out, digging her nails into his back in anticipation.

"Bond with me. Taste me," he said.

Her head spinning, she tried to speak but couldn't form words. Thought of how good he felt, and how badly she wanted him, remained.

"Say the word, Gianna. Tell me what you want."

"I—"

"Just. Say. Yes."

She looked at him with a drunken gaze and opened her mouth to give him the answer he so desperately wanted to hear.

Like an omen, the study door flew open, interrupting their interaction. Nicholas gently lowered Gianna to the floor. They watched carefully as both Bennett and Sofia exited the room and walked toward them. Sofia looked the same, but different, as though she was happy and ironically full of life. Gianna was all too familiar with how the change from human to vampire altered DNA and the effect could prove disastrous for some. She prayed that it didn't have the latter effect for Sofia.

Bennett paused when they closed in on Nicholas and Gianna. He'd obviously looked for a reaction, but Gianna was still panting from the tryst in the hallway. Sofia peered from behind Bennett and Gianna gaped at the sight of her. "Sofia, are you all right?"

Sofia folded her arms across her chest. "Never better.

Now do the two of you plan to continue making out like teenagers just caught in the act, or are you going to prepare for what's coming? There's not much light left outside and I would say that we have about an hour left to make a decision."

Gianna smiled at Sofia's normalcy. "Well, I guess we had better decide quickly," Gianna said.

Nicholas patted his father on the back as a congratulatory offer while Bennett squeezed his son's hand for luck. Gianna watched Bennett and Sofia continue down the hallway, his arm draped around Sofia like a loving couple who'd been together for quite some time. Nicholas wrapped his arm around Gianna's waist. "Why do you look so worried?"

"Doesn't it concern you that they just met and now they're...together forever in a blood bond?"

"Sometimes when you know, you know, and time doesn't matter. Do you want to know what I find amusing?"

"What is that?"

"You and Sofia seem to have switched roles. You are now the mother figure and she's the rebellious teenager."

She nudged her elbow into his side. "You're not funny. Let's go. Sofia was right, there isn't much time left."

Gianna and Nicholas followed behind Sofia and Bennett, and     gathered in the downstairs living room. "We believe the beach is where they will attack since it provides the least risk for exposure," Bennett said.

"So why are we here?" Nicholas asked.

"I wanted to inform you of the strategy. The plan is to work our way toward their house where they are keeping Elizabeth. Once the way is paved for anyone to make a move, they will take it. Then we'll distract the coven long enough to allow that person safe passage...Now, gather your weapons and follow me," Bennett said.

Sofia held Gianna back as Nicholas and Bennett walked off. "I know what you're thinking, Gianna and I whole heartedly disagree."

"I'm sorry to hear that, although it was expected."

"You love Nicholas. I see that...but you don't have to make such a large sacrifice. He wouldn't want that from you."

"No one ever does. Unfortunately, it's not Nicholas's decision."

***

Mattias paced back and forth through the house, rattling off items repeatedly as if reading off a checklist, making everyone around him nervous. "Is the room prepared?"

Kyle rolled his eyes. "Yes, for the fifteenth time. White linens with threads too numerous to count...was that really necessary? I mean, I think the last thing she'll notice is the thread count of the sheets."

"I want it to be perfect."

Cassius chimed in, "Do you think you could be wasting your time? I mean, do you think she'll show up?"

"Absolutely. I have no doubt."

Kyle continued. "You're acting like you're a virgin preparing for your first time. Mattias, she obviously isn't lily white, and probably has a pretty vast bag of tricks. For fuck sake, anyone with decent vision could attest to that."

Mattias turned and snarled at Kyle who was laughing, obviously baiting him. He was two steps away from snapping his neck with his bare hands. Dante entered the room and addressed his brothers. "It's nearly sundown. Are we ready?"

Cassius looked at both Dante and Mattias to confirm their arrangements. "So we're approaching offensively and then we'll hold off on an attack once we know Gianna is with Mattias. We'll wait for word. You'll instruct how to proceed?

Mattias answered. "Yes. If they attack, you have the right to protect yourselves, as well."

Kyle smiled. "Got it."

Kyle and Cassius made their way out to the beach, leaving Mattias and Dante alone in the room. "You seem nervous, Mattias."

"I am."

"Is this not what you wanted?"

"I want her...by any means necessary. This could be quite a mess."

"I don't think so."

"Did you call in reinforcements?"

"Oh yes. I had no idea the number of covens that live in this area. There must be hundreds of our kind and they're all on standby."

"Excellent."

Mattias stood at the rear doors looking out at the moonlit sea, collecting his thoughts. He was nervous about tonight. He wanted it to be a night that Gianna would never forget and he arranged all of it, down to the last detail.

He envisioned her walking though the door, hair tossing about with the wind as she begged him to take her.

He grew hard at the thought and he could have her soon enough. He shook himself from his wandering thoughts. "Dante, keep an eye on things for me. I am going to check on our guest upstairs."

"Very well."

Mattias unsealed Elizabeth's room and opened the door. "Miss Sutton, how are you feeling this evening? Is there anything I can get for you?"

Elizabeth looked up at Mattias. "Fuck you."

"Oh, you are terribly sweet, but you know that I only have eyes for one woman."

She instigated. "She's been with my brother you know. I made the mistake of passing his bedroom on more than one occasion and heard indecent sounds coming from behind closed doors. I actually heard her scream out his name." She smiled triumphantly in spite of herself. Mattias lunged for her, pinning her to the wall by her throat.

"This does not help your cause. Never, ever speak of such things again."

Elizabeth gasped at the power behind Mattias's threat. She backed down and remained silent while he lowered her to the floor. "If you remain docile, this will be over shortly. Try my patience again, and you will regret it."

***

Nicholas walked outside to the beach behind Gianna. She faced him and noticed his weapon of choice, a long sword. Gianna immediately studied the design, a renaissance period weapon in nearly pristine condition.

The weight alone required the wielder to be skilled in their handling of such a fine blade.

The way he mastered the sword made him appear knightly, and her thoughts, indecent. "Nice choice in weaponry. You have excellent taste."

"Tell me something I don't already know." He arched a brow.

The Sutton coven and their new addition of Sofia were positioned and ready for battle. The large silver moon lit up the clear night sky. The air was crisp and warm with only a hint of humidity as it danced amidst the sand. This is the moment they prepared for, the inevitable. Gianna felt uneasy. Something was going to happen that threatened to ruin lives. Her decision was made. She knew what she had to do. The only thing she needed was the opportunity to make it all happen.

Bennett stood on the front line, representing the family. Sofia stood behind him for support next to Nicholas who reached out for Gianna's hand and held it tight, joining the three of them side by side. The rest of the family held positions close by and would file in when necessary. Gianna's heart pounded, she swore that Nicholas could hear it and if he could, he showed no sign.

Bennett saw movement ahead. "They are approaching. They'll be here in roughly ten minutes. Stay calm and focused. Do not allow them to provoke you."

They nodded in unison. Nicholas turned to Gianna. "Don't worry, I have your back."

"You should worry less, sweetheart. I have never seen you handle a weapon."

"Prepare to be impressed my love," he taunted.

"Promises, promises."

Suddenly, Dante, Cassius, Kyle and a few unnamed faces approached. They carried no weapons, but Gianna knew better. Whatever they had as a means of defense, they'd keep hidden until the precise moment. They were all about the shock factor. Dante spoke for the coven. "Bennett Sutton. We finally meet in person. I am Dante Diakos. Mattias wishes only for you to release Gianna. Upon her safe return, you will receive Elizabeth, unharmed."

"We will not surrender Gianna. If you want her, you will have to take her."

Gianna, Nicholas, and Sofia gaped at Bennett's obvious dare. So much for not provoking the enemy.

# 22

Dante's small army stood behind him as he walked a straight line back and forth, meant to intimidate Bennett. "Just to be clear, I want to reiterate your declaration. You're refusing to let Gianna walk away? You're resisting a peaceful negotiation and allowing your daughter to suffer the consequence of your actions?" Dante said.

"I will not allow my daughter to suffer. I intend to walk into your house and free her myself, over your corpse if need be," Bennett promised.

Kyle and Cassius laughed at Bennett's threat. Kyle noticed Nicholas standing behind Bennett. "We should've killed that bitch when we had the opportunity...after I fucked her of course," Kyle taunted.

Nicholas walked forward. Anger lingered heavily in his gaze. Gianna pulled him back and Bennett raised a hand to Nicholas. "This is provocation, Nicholas. They are empty words made for you to act with clouded judgment. Do not play into their hands," he warned.

Nicholas growled, his breathing frantic.

Dante saw Gianna standing beside Nicholas. "Gianna baby, come home with us. Come home with me where you belong and I'll personally see that no one in present company is harmed in any way. Take your rightful place that is being offered to you."

"You give me your word that no one will be harmed? Including Elizabeth?"

"Yes. I give you both mine and Mattias's word. Come along so that we can be through with this situation. Mattias anxiously awaits your arrival," Dante said.

Gianna stepped away from Nicholas to fulfill the bargain. He grabbed her hand and pulled her close. "Don't. You. Dare. Don't do it," Nicholas said.

She met his gaze. "Nicholas, please."

"Are you begging me to let you go?"

"No, I'm begging you to save your family...and yourself."

"I would rather die than lose you."

Death could very well be his fate. Why did he have to be so fucking stubborn? More importantly, why did she allow him to have enough influence over her, that she worried about how her decisions affected him? She needed to conceal her true feelings. It wasn't the time to contemplate mundane details. Dante analyzed her reactions, her mood, and every move she made. She knew the slightest shift in her weight would reveal her comfort level, and the alliance with Nicholas and the rest of his family. She'd be damned if she gave herself away that easily. Dante would have to work much harder to cause her to feel uneasy.

\*\*\*

Cassius sniffed the air. "Something is off. The only human I sense is Gianna. Sofia, have you been playing naughty with the local vamps?

If you wanted to be one of us so desperately, all you had to do was ask. I would've been happy to help."

Sofia simply shook her head. Bennett smiled at his new companion with pride.

Dante looked at Nicholas who held Gianna tightly. He snarled at the sight of his hands on her. "Nicholas, are you prepared to face Mattias once he learns of your defiance?"

"I would sooner face God, Lucifer, and the three Fates all at once. I think I can handle one vampire playboy."

"I can arrange for all of the above," Dante said.

Dante drew a pair of matching short swords from his side and dashed toward Nicholas. Gianna broke from Nicholas's embrace and quickly fell backward, away from the path of the knives. Dante twirled the blades expertly between his hands. He slashed at Nicholas's right. Nicholas blocked the attempt and retaliated with the swing of his sword. He aimed for Dante's head. Dante dodged the blow and stabbed at Nicholas's side. He continued to meet Dante parry for parry as though it were masterful choreography, rather than a battle to the death. It was a beautiful sight.

Dante laughed at Nicholas's skill, attempting to distract him but he had nothing to mock. Nicholas fought like a champion. He possessed such skill with his weapon that no one would've guessed otherwise. The two vampires were evenly matched.

Cassius and Bennett both fought with their hands. Cassius gripped Bennett by the throat and threw him to the ground. Bennett stood and delivered a blow to his chest, knocking him back at least ten feet.

Josephine came out of the shadows, behind the four on the front line and attacked Kyle with a crossbow. Kyle had been prepared. He retaliated with Chinese stars, embedding one in Josephine's arm. The metal dug deep into her flesh. Blood poured from the wound. She removed the weapon with ease and a curse.

Sofia ran to Gianna as the men continued to battle. "Sofia, stay behind me." "What are you going to do?"

"Nothing yet, but I'm ready. Something isn't right. This is too easy. They would never be so headstrong as to attack in such small numbers."

Suddenly, Gianna's fears became a reality. Twenty additional unnamed faces appeared in the darkness. They smiled wickedly, baring fangs and ready for bloodshed. "Fuck this," she said.

The newcomers moved to attack. Gianna leaped in between the two sides of the battle, dividing the groups. "Stand down or you will suffer," she warned.

Kyle laughed. "Move out of the way so the big boys can fight. This isn't the place for you."

Gianna smiled. "It's your head."

She drew her favorite toy from the back of her pants, at the base of her spine.

Cassius's eyes widened at the short spear. Kyle continued to laugh. "What is that going to do, Gianna? I mean really...it's like coming to a gun fight with a knife."

"Oh, little Kyle, Mattias's favorite flunky, you're always underestimating with your overinflated ego. It's sad when you don't realize that you're about to be bested."

She activated the small release with a flick of her thumb that was barely noticeable, extending her weapon to its full, five foot length. She stood out from the rest of the crowd, all in awe of her deadly presence. For the first time, Nicholas saw the fighter that saved him in London, the one that moved like wind in the darkness. She was powerful, sexy, and treacherous. He was glad not to be the poor bastard on the receiving end of her weapon.

Two men charged. She didn't move. Once they came within her reach, she twirled her weapon in the air and came down on one, splitting him in half. The other swung in her direction, and she ducked away from the blow. He then swept her off her feet. She fell to her back. Looking up at him, she smiled before she pierced his heart. In a single movement, she stood to her feet. In a swift Z-like motion, while her weapon was still lodged in his heart, she sliced to the left, through bone, up through the chest, and finally severed his head. She wiped the blood from the tip of the blade on the clothes of her victim.

The enemy continued to approach in impressive numbers, and any who made the mistake of attacking Gianna, met their end on the edge of her blade. She pivoted the weapon with little effort as though she'd undergone extensive training with that single piece of equipment. However, despite her role in this battle, she realized that even though their side seemed to be closer to victory, and the body count of their enemies continued to grow, they still kept coming. This would not end as long as Gianna stood with the Suttons. Mattias was forcing her hand.

The coward wasn't present. He didn't have the balls to face her. What was he planning? She had to know, but she couldn't get to him without someone noticing. How could she get there quickly?

Nicholas possessed tremendous speed, but his assistance was out of the question. Then she remembered Kyle. If what Dante said was the truth, then all she had to do was get close enough for Kyle to grab her, and dash to Mattias in seconds.

She parried her way through the swarm of enemies, deflecting strikes, and continued in Kyle's direction. Once he noticed that she was close, he reacted exactly as she'd hoped. He grabbed her by the throat, pulled her snug against him, and smiled. "Now, we end this. I've been given strict instructions to bring you back unharmed. See, the problem with that is, no one took the time to define the word unharmed. What I really want to know is why you're worth so much trouble."

He held her tight and within less than a minute, they were just outside of Mattias's house. Kyle became rough and rigid. He pulled her hair back to look into her eyes. "If I had the time, I'd fuck you senseless. You need to be taught a lesson, to learn your place." His eyes raked her body.

"In your dreams." It took everything she had not to kill him.

Kyle laughed and kissed her, shoving his tongue into her mouth, while working hands up her shirt. He pulled back, dizzy from the kiss when she closed her fist and punched him across the face. "I should kill you."

"Now that would take the fun out of everything, wouldn't it? Unfortunately, I don't have the time to bed you adequately, so you're going to have to settle for a roll in the sand but I promise you'll enjoy it," Kyle said.

Gianna struggled against him, pushing aside the urges to use her ability and risk exposing the truth of her nature.

"It really is pointless to struggle, and as much as it would please me to kill you, I just don't feel like dealing with Mattias's whining. It's so tiresome...the endless lamenting over his precious Gianna. I want to impale myself onto something every time he gets into one of those moods. I would love to see the look on his face when he's learned that you've felt *my* cock first."

*Two can play this game.* She kissed Kyle, just like he wanted.

"Mmm, that's it baby, show me what you want." He reached up her shirt and cupped her breast. He lost control at her touch. "I want you to rock those hips on top of me."

"I can't wait to please you," she said.

She reached her hand inside her pants as he watched.

"Touch yourself, rub yourself for me."

"Oh yes, Kyle...anything for you."

She stepped closer and reached her hand inside his pants, feeling for him. When she found his priceless manhood, she was disappointed in her discovery. The words he spoke should've accompanied the evidence to back them up. He came up rather short. He shuddered as her hand brushed against his crisp hairs and swollen shaft. In an instant, his expression turned horrified. "What the fuck are you doing?"

He looked down and met her gaze. He was terrified and at her mercy, for she held a dagger against what he treasured most. "Now, lets you and I get something abundantly clear. Never, ever touch a woman unless invited. I don't care if she has a pulse or not.

"Secondly, you talk an awful good game for what you've got going on down here and finally, you'll take your repulsive hands off me and will keep them to yourself. You will now take me to Mattias."

If you ever threaten me again, I will remove what you treasure using most and you'll need to fill your closet with dresses. Do you understand?"

"Yeah, I get it," he squeaked.

Gianna and Kyle approached a monstrous, unlit beach house. Once they were close enough to the back doors, Kyle pushed her inside with one last snide remark. "I hope he shows you the real meaning of pain, bitch."

"Watch out Kyle. When Mattias finds out how I've been treated, I can personally guarantee that you've officially seen your last night. By the time the sun rises, by either my hand or his, you will be nothing but the memory of poor judgment."

Kyle gave Gianna a sullen look before releasing her through the open doors of the house.

Gianna pressed her hands against the sleek black marble floor of the great room, bringing herself to her feet. Black furniture decorated the room along with window treatments of sheer windswept curtains. The only light now was the moon illuminating off the hot sandy beach. The sand still held the memory of the sun's kiss, which she felt on the breeze of the night. The view was magical, causing her to forget she was in a strange house, in potential danger. Yet, Gianna's breathing calmed and she relaxed, as she couldn't imagine why the doors were ajar, open for invitation.

She reached out with other senses, catching several scents in the air. Freshly cut flowers, roses perhaps, were close by. The floral scent was combined with melting wax, arousal, and a familiar cologne. She knew that last fragrance anywhere...Mattias.

\*\*\*

Kyle appeared next to Dante and whispered into his ear. Dante smiled and called out to his comrades. "Fall back!"

Bennett and Nicholas looked at each other as the enemies began to withdraw from battle. They gathered in formation behind Dante. Nicholas was baffled by their actions. "What's happening, father?"

"Something has changed. What could possibly have them standing down after engaging?"

Nicholas searched the area for sight of Gianna but she was nowhere in sight. "Gianna!"

Sofia came to Nicholas's side, her eyes filled with sorrow. "I'm sorry Nicholas."

"Where is she?" he asked through clenched teeth.

"I'm so sorry. She had do what she felt was necessary."

"No. No, she wouldn't. She couldn't. I begged her."

A hurt Nicholas met Dante's gaze. "Where is she?"

He smirked before antagonizing. "She is where she should be. She doesn't belong here. That woman is royalty to us and her place is with Mattias. You knew this when you took her, Nicholas. Why act so surprised? You knew better than anyone that this was coming."

"Don't stand there and claim that she belongs with Mattias. You mean she belongs with your coven. You have an ulterior motive and you forget I witnessed your inexplicable actions."

"I don't deny an attraction. Who would? But I have no right to her. She is wanted by a superior and I can take no claim. But you...you walked into his house as a guest and stole from him."

"I finally understand what bothers you. Tell me something Dante, how does it feel to always be the runner up, to know that you will always be second best?"

Dante answered with a hiss through clenched teeth.

# 23

Gianna walked into the house just far enough so her voice could be heard by anyone left inside. Her anger flared as she yelled for Mattias. "Mattias, where are you?"

"I'm right here."

He spoke so softly it was almost melodic. He walked out of the darkness wearing a half buttoned, white shirt and black pants. The moonlight reflected off his muscular chest. He was devastating. He spoke as though relieved, and in such a tone that set her desire ablaze, "Gianna baby, you are a sight. I thought I had lost you."

"I'm here Mattias. I want you to release Elizabeth."

"You will stay in her stead?"

"You know I will. I want you to call Dante and have Kyle bring Sofia. Elizabeth will be released to her, and she'll return to her family. All will remain unharmed."

He sighed with a smile, and paused for a moment in deliberation before he reached for his phone to dial Dante. "Dante, the package has arrived. Kindly have Kyle bring Sofia here quickly. I'm making the trade, and everyone is to be left as they were."

Gianna heard yelling in the background and identified the erratic behavior as Nicholas. He was worried and angry.

"It appears that your little friend is concerned about your well being. I guess we'll have to let Sofia reassure him when she returns."

"So, we have a deal?" she asked.

"I suppose so, but I feel that it is a small price to pay for your safety. Wait right here."

Mattias walked up the stairs, out of sight. Not a second later, Sofia was standing behind Gianna.

"You have to be the most stubborn woman on the planet."

Gianna didn't turn to face her but continued the conversation. "You know I needed to do this, and you understand the reasons better than anyone. Please don't lecture me. This is my decision, and I have to live with the repercussions."

"He's worried sick over you."

"Well, you can assure him that I'm breathing, when you return home with his sister."

"What are you going to do, Gianna?"

"Whatever it takes...please don't try to talk me down. Mattias won't react kindly to betrayal and I'd hate to see you killed when you just found happiness."

"You'd be stupid to throw your own chance away."

"This is about preservation, Sofia and damn it, I will protect everyone and everything I hold dear, no matter the price. You'd better wait outside for Elizabeth. I don't want Mattias worked up. I need him calm."

"I wish you'd reconsider."

Gianna remained silent as Sofia walked out the back door, waiting Elizabeth's arrival. A few moments later, Mattias returned with Elizabeth following shortly behind him. "Gianna!"

Elizabeth ran to embrace Gianna.

"Are you hurt?" Gianna asked. Her eyes searched Nicholas's beloved sister.

"No. I'm fine."

"You are free to go. Sofia is waiting outside to escort you back to your home."

"What about you?"

"I made you a promise, Elizabeth. Do you remember when we spoke last night?"

Elizabeth's eyes widened. "Gianna, what are you doing?"

"What I have to. Trust me when I tell you that this is an extremely small window of opportunity. You need to leave now, while Mattias is being so cooperative."

"No. Not without—"

"You must go. Do not allow my sacrifice to be wasteful. I only ask that you do one thing for me. Don't let your brother be foolish and attempt a rescue. He'll be killed for the effort."

Elizabeth nodded and exited through the same rear doors, meeting Sofia. She looked back at Gianna one last time before they began the walk back to the Sutton home. Gianna turned to face Mattias. She stood silent, staring. Overcome by his presence, to her surprise she continued to breathe calmly.

"It's time, my love."

"Time for what, exactly?"

He smiled seductively. "Follow me."

He led Gianna down a long hallway and allowed her to enter a bedroom dressed with lit candles. The king-sized bed was fully clad in expensive white linens, adorned with fresh red rose petals. The pleasant scent filled the air, tingling the senses. Gianna attempted to brush off the presentation before her as though nonchalant when she turned to exit the room, but he stood at the doorway, blocking it with his hands on each side of the frame while acting casual. "We've been staying in this house for a few weeks observing from afar. Waiting, watching...and considering all that we've seen, one fact remains clear."

"What is that?"

"I want you Gianna. You can call it selfish, but it's the honest of truths. Join me and I will give you immortality."

She wanted to laugh at his back handed offer. Sure, he presented her with the gift of immortality, but he gave nothing freely. What he desired in return was to have her tied to him permanently. Since there was really no need for his soured kindness, she remained playful, but politely refused.

He smiled that knowing smile, as though he understood her resistance was walking a tightrope. Gianna was struck with a sudden shockwave of lust that she tried desperately to fight, but she wasn't prepared to be in his presence...like this. Resisting him was easy from a distance, but being so close, feeling his steely body near hers was making her ache with want.

He inched closer. "Tell me how you've longed for me. Tell me how thoughts of us being together have consumed you."

His assumptions were not that far-fetched. Heat flooded her body, pulling at her, luring her. It was so sexy and everything he said was beginning to sound like the truth.

With the last of her fading resistance, she drew her weapon from the back of her pants and held the blade to Mattias's chest. He loved her this way, the thrill of the chase that gave her the impression that she was in control. Clearly, she was misinformed. He wasn't surprised by her actions and seemed evoked by her latest endeavor . "Do it, Gianna... end it," he dared.

Her breathing erratic, she lost focus. Mattias backed her into the doorway and deliberately slammed her arm into the frame, breaking the weapon free from her grasp. The blade fell to the floor with a loud clatter as he pressed his body against hers. God he was gorgeous and had a body built for sexual fulfillment. How could she resist? Before her stood the man responsible for her misery, for everything that left her orphaned, and devoid of emotion. So, why was it, that instead of wanting to dig his heart out with her bare hands, she was more interested in crawling in his bed and wrinkling those crisp, new sheets? Yeah, she needed her head examined.

Panting and pinning her to the wall, he leaned his face into the side of her cheek and spoke softly. "How I love your ferocity. I've crossed an ocean to claim you, to touch you, to be so near to you that I may feel the warmth of your breath. You would punish me for wanting that?"

*Fight damn you!*

*Fight! For everyone he made suffer, for all that he's taken from you, from others...fight him! Have your vengeance!*

He reached down between them, running his hand between her thighs causing her to melt beneath the power of his touch. All hope faded when moisture began flowing thick at her core. She wanted this, wanted him, his touch, to feel him inside of her before she ended his pathetic existence.

"Do you feel it Gianna, the aching? I know it well. It's the pain that I feel when I sense your presence, inhale your essence, and when thoughts of you race through my mind driving me further into madness."

She met his gaze through hooded eyes. "I'm so tired Mattias...so tired of...fighting you."

He sighed in relief. "Then don't."

"I—"

"Don't say another word. Just be with me. It's what you want. I can feel your desire. For once in your life, stop fighting and let it happen. Let me worship you."

Mattias grazed her bottom lip with his thumb and stared at her for only a few seconds when he attacked her lips as if he were starving. God, he could kiss. It was penetrating, igniting. As her tongue gently touched his sharp teeth, he moaned in anticipation and it was unclear how long he could contain himself.

In one moment, Gianna found herself weak, and out of control with desire. Every arcane thought that she ever had regarding Mattias was surfacing. He knew how to reveal them, to pull them from hiding. She realized that he too had an ability, but couldn't identify it as manipulation or seduction. Were they one in the same?

*How did I not realize it sooner?*

Not that she cared too terribly at the moment. She lost the will to struggle and wanted to give in. In fact, she intended to. Regardless of Mattias's ability, it was the truth. She wanted him, *really* wanted him and the smoldering heat she felt was about to cause her to combust, turning want into need.

Mattias pulled back from her lips. "God I can't breathe around you, Gianna." He looked deeply into her eyes. "I should've never left you the night Nicholas fled, nor offered you as a test. I should've never answered Dante's call." He shook his head in frustration.

Gianna actually felt sympathetic for him and how regretful he was for leaving her the night she offered herself to him.

"Let me make up for leaving you alone in my bed. Let me savor you, ravish you, and show you passion unlike anything you have ever known."

Gianna's breathing intensified as she completely surrendered herself. He knew exactly what to say, exactly what she needed to hear. He caressed her cheek and kissed her deeply. Every touch of his cool tongue sent a raging fire through her body, as contact with Mattias always did. She removed his shirt as he smiled cautiously.

Mattias's body was the most remarkable thing she'd ever seen. Every inch of him displayed perfect detail, from his luscious, muscular neck, the art that hugged his body, down to his naval and finally to his massive erection, would be branded into memory. Gianna was painfully aware that every time she'd recall him from this moment forward would cause an insatiable yearning that only he could relieve.

Mattias continued to kiss trails down her body while slowly peeling off her clothing. He removed what remained of his own while never taking his eyes off her, leaving her paralyzed with desire.

Every touch was ravenous, every kiss erotic and when he paused to speak, he was breathless, drunk with lust. "I can't take being so close to you. I want to devour every succulent inch of your body."

Gianna took his hand, and he led her to the bed covered in red rose petals. He seated her upon the mattress and ran his hands down her thighs, spreading them apart, feeling the warmth that beckoned him. He could still sense a small part of her that was fighting, trying to deny him but her will was weak and he was perceptive to that fact.

Mattias lowered himself between her thighs and took her with his mouth, growling low in his throat at the sweet taste of her. She threw her head back and screamed in ecstasy while his tongue did the most nefarious things. He enjoyed every second, pleasing her, arousing her to the point when she'd beg his entry. "That's it Gianna, give yourself to me."

It would have improved Gianna's situation had Mattias been a dreadful lover. Despite the malice she felt toward him, she couldn't dismiss the fact that everything he was doing, felt incredibly good. She was at his mercy, easily enslaved by him.

Before she could reach orgasm, she sat up and pushed him on top of the bed while she crawled down his body, allowing her breasts to touch him in such a way that it drove him to the brink of hysteria. She reached his hard cock and playfully licked the tip, enjoying his saline taste when he hissed at the unbelievable feeling of her mouth, teasing him so intimately. He held her head while she pleased him, lifting it gently. Then he pulled her up to meet him. "Easy love, I don't want to ruin this moment by ending it so quickly. I've been waiting far too long to touch you, and I intend to feast."

She gaped at his intentions. "I want you Mattias. I need you inside of me." She spread her thighs wide as he placed her on her back and wrapped her legs around his waist. He was so turned on by the feel of her moisture on the tip of his cock.

When neither one could take anymore torment, he unleashed all of his frustration and drove himself deep inside, moaning from a single thrust, as if he'd waited for eternity for this moment.

Gianna slid her hands up and down the ripples of Mattias's smooth, muscular back, then gripped his broad shoulders with her finger nails in response to his intense performance. He smelled of designer cologne mixed with pure sexuality. The combination was so provocative, that it made her want to submit to his every fantasy.

Mattias knew every maneuver that would keep her begging, and spoke breathlessly. "Do you see what you've been missing? We were made for each other."

He was hard and thick, filling her completely as he leaned in closer to take her left breast into his mouth, teasing the taut peak with his scalding tongue. Gianna rolled Mattias to his back and found herself on top of him. Her nipples swelled painfully hard her body yearned for his touch. Licking his lips, he ran his hands over her breasts, creating a sensation like no other, as she vigorously rocked her hips against his. He was heavily endowed, continuing to swell inside her, and she couldn't get enough of him as she cried out his name.

God, he needed to feel more of her, to be deeper inside her. He turned her on her knees and bent her ever so slightly as he entered her from behind. Pulling her back toward his chest, he took her hand and led it to where they were connected. "I want you to feel this, Gianna. I want you to feel your body welcoming me. I want you to remember how good it feels when we're together."

Thrusting against her, he made contact with her hands and growled at her touch.

She felt as if she were about to burst as he held her closer, tighter, driving himself to his base and running his hands across her breasts while she reached behind herself to embrace him as he took her.

"Tell me how much you've wanted this, Gianna. I want to hear how you've dreamed of my touch."

"You're...incredible...ah."

Truthfully, she did dream of him...often. He constantly played the starring role in her depraved fantasies. "I tried for so long and I should've never denied you."

"It could always be like this, eternity just like this...night after night...forever. Is that what you want?"

She conceded to his will. "Yes."

"Are you sure?"

"Mattias, make me yours." She was consumed with desire. All the fight in her was gone.

"Mmm...come for me, Gianna."

He slowly ran his hands up her body kneading her breasts while thrusting against her. She was so wet that he could barely think of anything other the feeling of sliding in and out of her heat.

Gianna tilted her head to the side when he leaned his head back, growled and bit down as hard as he could at the side of her neck. She screamed out in pain, feeling the sensation of her eyes changing color due to the sudden loss of blood and her need to feed.

The instant pain lasted only a second, until a different feeling washed over her. It was the single most erotic sensation of her entire existence. Never had she imagined that being bitten would increase sexual pleasure to an unrivaled high.

She became more sensitive to sensation and the feeling of him thrusting was enough to make her scream. His incessant moaning at the taste of her blood made him swell even more, and escalated her arousal. He continued to take her furiously.

Holding her neck to his lips while he took his fill, she felt the tickle of a single trail of blood spilling down her chest, between her breasts and down to her naval as she came in a blinding orgasm of epic proportions.

Still hungry, following her fierce wave of pleasure, she turned to face Mattias, seated him upright and placed his back against the head board when she mounted herself on his shaft. Her fangs surfaced, and she didn't care to fight. She bit into his shoulder. He tasted as incredible as he felt inside of her.

He enjoyed the penetration of her bite. "That's it Gianna. Bind yourself to me."

He gave her a pleased laugh as he cupped her head to his shoulder encouraging her to drink while she continued to ride him. She retreated from him and when he saw his blood on her lips, he claimed them fiercely. Their animalistic nature clawed its way to the forefront, and they couldn't keep their hands off each other.

He laid her on her back as he drove himself inside of her. "Baby, I love the way you feel...but do you want to know what I love even more, Gianna?"

"What's that?"

"That you're mine...forever."

He lowered himself to feed from her once again. As his fangs pierced her flesh and his tongue savored her essence, she came with an orgasm so fierce that she screamed his name and writhed in his arms. He loved the sound of his name on her lips, loved when she screamed from the pleasure he gave her, how she tasted, and how she felt beneath him. He was madly in love with her and wanted to share her with no one.

Moments later, he arched his back as he released himself inside of her, driving himself to his hilt. He balled his hands into fists from the force of it.

Gianna's greatest fear had become a harsh reality—an earth shattering orgasm, one that would ruin her for every other man.

# 24

Mattias released Gianna after taking just enough blood that would turn her into one of *his* kind. He laid her back on the bed and leaned against her while he whispered. "That was worth every second that you tortured me, and it was *everything* I thought it would be. Your taste, your touch and how you feel inside have far surpassed my expectations." He continued to kiss her as he ran his hands up and down her naked body.

She awaited the flames, the burning that would seem like it would never end, as he poisoned her life force.

To her surprise, the change never came. The wound healed slowly and she sat to face him. She was still weak, but managed to speak. "You're not...lethal."

"Hmm...Then I guess we should talk about that." He sat back and draped a sheet across them both.

"What are you?"

"For someone who is usually quite perceptive, I'm surprised that you haven't discovered it sooner. I'm...like you, Gianna."

"You're not a vampire?"

"I'm half vampire. I'm also half human. A Dhampire."

She was speechless as tears pricked her eyes, but she knew better than to let him see her so vulnerable. "Your touch, it's cool. I don't hear your heart beating. How can you be what you claim?"

"We are all affected differently and inherit different traits. Vampires are the same."

"I don't understand."

He reached for her cheek to brush away a strand of hair. "Well, as a result of a simple observation, you appear human. Your scent, your warm touch, the sound of the blood rushing through your veins and your loud beating heart are *your* traits. I appear vampire. My touch is cool and my heartbeat is nearly silent, making it appear non-existent. My appearance is that of the predator you are familiar with."

He traced the length of her arm with two fingers, unable to keep from touching her. "Look at the vampire company I keep. Dante is calm and relaxed. He embraces his immortality as a gift. He handles eternity differently from let's say Kyle. Kyle is careless and unruly. He believes that immortality gives him the right to take what he wishes without consequence. He believes that he can play god and he could easily expose us all with his significant appetite that I constantly have to conceal. That is all a result of the change. It affects them all differently."

It made perfect sense but she wasn't not convinced. What were his motives, his reasons for keeping himself hidden?

"Wait, how long have you known what I am?"

"I've always known."

"But my parents, my family, you were responsible for their loss!"

---

"Loss? Gianna, love, they are very much alive. Over two hundred fifty years ago when I heard of the possibility of the existence of one of my kind I sought out your parents. Fearful that someone would search for you and discover the secret, I took your parents into my custody realizing that someone else would not extend them the same courtesy and would surely kill them. If discovered, we would all be killed. They've been under my protection since."

Gianna snapped a fired temper. She was suddenly full of fury and wanted blood, his blood. The walls began to shake and she had to remember to control herself. She reached out and slapped him across the face. "You fucking bastard! You could've had the decency to let them come home and explain before they left! Did you feel justified in allowing a child to feel abandoned and alienated her entire life?"

He ignored the sting of her slap and continued to explain himself. "Doing it the way that I did was the only option. Having everyone feel as if your parents had simply disappeared would cause a fear that would force anyone who was involved to protect the secret. They would be more inclined to do so for fear of someone else's disappearance."

Gianna nodded her head in disbelief. "No, I don't believe you."

"I figured you wouldn't. It's what I love most about you, always guarded...always skeptical. If it's confirmation you need, just ask Sofia."

She narrowed her gaze. "Excuse me?"

"Sofia knows everything." It's part of what she'd sworn to protect. She took an oath to protect your well-being, to guard your secrets, and those of your kind. And she's done a fine job, I might add."

Could he be telling the truth? His words weren't that unbelievable. She had a sick feeling in her stomach.

"I know this isn't easy for you, Gianna."

Gianna shook her head. "What I don't understand is your benefit from all of this. What is your payment for services rendered?"

"I think you know."

Suddenly it all came into focus with a shocking clarity, "Me."

She felt as if she were in the center of a violent nightmare and wanted to vomit. She walked to the window, staring out at the beach. Mattias saw Gianna's horrified look. "Baby I realize that this is a lot to process."

"Don't you fucking dare pretend to know how this feels. It's insulting."

"I needed you to think that I was the one responsible for the death of your parents. As long as you were fixated on your vendetta against me as the enemy, I could keep you close and protect you. I vowed to always keep you safe. I promised your family that when I took control of the London coven and posed as one of their kind. I needed to be convincing and part of the act was to begin a courtship with you and eventually turn you into one of us."

Gianna sat down and tried to comprehend everything going on around her.

"Do you remember the bartender from the nightclub?" Mattias asked.

"Yes."

"He is your father, Gianna."

For a moment, she thought it impossible. She thought she would've recognized him, but it had been centuries and she was not paying attention to detail that night.

Gianna met his gaze. "So you're my protector? Wow...and to think that you were merely acting with the intention to preserve the species. I mean, I shouldn't have expected anything less, but it surely redefines the word offensive."

"It's become much more than that, Gianna. I can't deny that I've watched you from afar for so long and in the beginning, it was a simple duty. Everything changed the night Dante escorted you into my domain. You took me by complete surprise and instantly, duty turned into desire and became something else...I am so in love with you. Thoughts of you consume every part of me and everything I told you moments ago is the absolute truth. I want you to be my companion. Eternity would be twice as long without you."

"Is this the manipulation of your ability speaking?"

"So, you've sensed that? It's not my ability at all. I use my gift to calm you so that you can be free and honest. Your feelings are your own. I just brought them to surface. I can easily manipulate the others, obtaining what I want to hear. That's why I can keep up the rouse."

She yelled in heartbreak. "All this time, all this time you allowed me to believe that my family was dead! All of this time I was alone!"

"Gianna, you have never, ever been alone. You've never wanted for anything."

"Oh no? I may have been raised by a vampire doctor and his wife, in a loving family, but I wanted the one thing I couldn't have...*My* family. So, try walking one fucking day in my shoes! Experience the emptiness that has been my life. Shame on me for being weak, and secretly wanting you, when I should've killed you while you slept."

"You couldn't kill me Gianna. In the beginning, perhaps, you wouldn't have given it a second thought, but now your heart won't allow it. Despite what you say and how much you try to deny it, you have feelings for me. I had to confess the truth to you because a true vampire family has become involved. You must come back to London. We must keep the secret as quiet as we have for the past two and a half centuries, and I have to continue to rule the coven. If the vampires discover what we are, we will be eliminated, and it could mean the extinction of our kind."

She rolled her eyes. "No one has the authority to order our extinction. There is no vampire body of government."

"And because of that lack of organization, no one can protect our existence either. It is a double-edged sword, my love. For such a governing body to exist, would mean that they would have to have cooperation from most, if not all, of the covens through a designated representative. Have you any idea how difficult that is? It's why I need to take matters into my own hands."

Gianna stared blankly at Mattias, deep in thought. She wondered. "How is it that you are able to lead a coven and are recognized as their leader, if there is no system?"

"I lead this coven because power and ruthlessness is feared. Think about it. Instill the fear of a god into someone, and they won't think about challenging authority." She shook her head, trying to make sense of it all. Nicholas invaded her thought. Oh this was not good.

"Nicholas knows everything, Mattias. He knows what I am."

"Well that certainly does complicate matters," he said through clenched teeth.

"He would never betray me...*that* I know."

"What makes you so sure?"

"I just know." They exchanged a glance and Mattias realized she cared for Nicholas on some level.

"So, Nicholas Sutton *is* my competition."

She gave him no response. Mattias kept a close distance behind Gianna as she stared out the doors facing the moonlit sand. "What of the quarrel with the Suttons? They must be left unharmed."

"I have no quarrel with them. I needed to keep an eye on Nicholas to make sure he didn't share his wild story with anyone else. Unfortunately, I have to deliver some sort of retribution for the death of Lucas."

"Or you could just order them to walk away," she said.

Just then she thought of Nicholas and whispered his name in the air. She loved her Nicholas. Yes, she finally admitted the truth to herself, but how could she admit it to Nicholas after making a deal with the devil? Maybe he'd realize the extent of her bargain and walk away.

Mattias sensed her inner turmoil. "I won't hurt him, unless you force me to."

Gianna's eyes widened as she hissed at Mattias through clenched teeth. "If you ever lay a hand on him, or give an order for someone to lay a hand on him, so help me Mattias, you will regret the day you struck a bargain with me. Don't force my hand as I know just how to kill you."

"Already issuing the threats, I see. I have to admit that you're turning me on."

She turned to look out at the picturesque ocean scene when he pressed his arousal at her back, wrapped his hands around her waist, and leaned in to kiss her. "Let's go back to bed."

"Tempting, but we need to end this Mattias. We need to end it now before someone is hurt, and the damage cannot be undone."

"Tell me you'll come with me back to London," he demanded.

Gianna turned to face him. "I will, under a few conditions."

"Why do I have a feeling I'm not going to like this?"

"Personally, I don't care if you like it or not. If you need me to come back with you as badly as you claim, then it won't be a problem."

He arched a brow. "Let me hear your demands."

"First, I want *you* to demand that the Sutton's be left alone. I don't want Elizabeth or any of them left to wonder when someone will try to attack next. Second, you take me to my family the minute we land in London, and third, I want to be included in every decision that you make."

Gianna stood with her hands on her hips as she waited for his decision. "Well?"

"I'm thinking."

"By all means, take your time," she said with abundant sarcasm.

"All right, I'll agree to your terms."

"I thought as much."

"I need your word that you will continue the charade as if nothing happened. I rule and you sit at my side as an equal."

"An equal? How will your peers feel about a human equal?"

"They'd never question my authority for fear of the consequences."

"You have my word but I want to make sure that you understand that if I ever hear that an ounce of harm has befallen any one of the Suttons, I will deal out justice, and leave London so fast, that my trail will be non-existent."

"You forget my love, we have tasted each other. I would be able to sense you as if we were linked."

*Nicholas has tasted me too. So, you won't be the only link in my chain. Until you prove otherwise, you will only be the shackles.*

"We're not bound, Mattias. I've seen the ritual and feel no different."

"No we're not bound. That fact hasn't escaped me. I'm not sure why that is, but if we continue to sample each other, we can sense one another."

Gianna felt relieved that she wasn't forever tied to Mattias, and felt bitter about being deceived the way she was but she'd finally reached somewhat of an understanding with Mattias. He'd carried out the most nefarious deeds, albeit secretly, in the name of the Dhampires. He was vicious and calculating, but she'd misinterpreted his actions. To his coven and anyone who happened to cross his path, he was pure unadulterated evil. To himself, he was the protector of a vital secret, acting solely to guard himself and others. To her, he was something else, something yet to be defined. Mostly, he was so true to his word that even she couldn't fault him.

She wondered if she could love Mattias. He would protect her with his life. She owed him...everything, including herself, and she would give herself to him willingly, sparing all others. It was a small sacrifice she'd make, considering all he'd sacrificed in return. The promises that he made only to be awarded with her in the end, could prove to be worth it in the grand scheme of things.

Gianna hated feeling fickle, but she would be the one to save Nicholas, Bennett and the entire Sutton coven. As much as it would rip her heart out to leave Nicholas who loved her completely, she knew she could protect them all with one act. It was the best way she could love him, even if it was thousands of miles away with an ocean in between. In that instant she realized why Mattias had done what he did on that fateful day, centuries ago.

Trepidation flowed thick through her veins as she thought about what she had to do next. She had to look Nicholas in the eyes and deliver the words that would break his heart. Even though she knew she was saving him from an eternity of torment, it would be Gianna that would kill him—slowly.

Lost in thought, still entranced by the beauty of the coast, Gianna failed to realize that Mattias had left her side to dress. She was tuned into him now, and placed his scent as he entered the room. His aroma bore a hint of sweet chocolate that made her mouth water for a taste. A taste that she knew would be sinfully delicious...another time. She suppressed her temptation, turned to face him, and watched as he buttoned a white shirt over his sculpted, bronze chest. Dear gods, she just wanted one little taste.

"Shall we end this, my love?"

"Yes. By the way, we need to talk about Kyle."

"What about him?"

"He's a threat. I'll explain in detail on the way."

# 25

Nicholas paced, waiting for word on Gianna. Elizabeth tried to calm him, but it was no use. He felt uneasy and knew that no good would come of Gianna's interaction with Mattias. He snapped his head in the direction of a ringing cell phone, and scowled at the enemy line. Dante walked behind his army of immortals while he accepted a call, most likely from his leader.

"Nicholas, please relax."

"Relax! How can you say such a thing, Elizabeth? I could kill her for doing this."

"Yes, Nicholas, I'm feeling fine. Thanks so much for your concern."

"I'm sorry, Elizabeth. You know I was worried. Forgive me for being so selfish."

Elizabeth smiled at her selfless brother. "I know you love her and it's comforting to watch you become so wound up over a woman, but she knows what she's doing. Have faith in her strength and independence. She'll have the upper hand. Just wait."

"Waiting is part of the problem."

Dante ended his call and looked at Bennett. "They're coming."

"They?"

"Gianna and Mattias."

Nicholas stood next to his father. "What has he done to her?"

Dante laughed. "Nothing she didn't want, I'm sure. She breathes, if that's your concern."

Bennett placed a hand on his son's shoulder. "Calm down, son. Anger will do you no good."

The moments waiting for Gianna to arrive seemed like hours. Nicholas looked out to the horizon and spotted the first hints of peach tones. "The sun is rising."

Bennett looked to his new companion and spoke with concern. "Elizabeth, please get Sofia into the house. We do not know how she will react to sunlight just yet."

"Yes, father. Come, Sofia. Let's get inside quickly."

Sofia followed Elizabeth and Josephine into their home.

The first rays of light shot across the sky, heating the sand. Some of Dante's company turned to ash, unaware of their sensitivity to the sun. Suddenly, Gianna was seen approaching with Mattias by her side. Nicholas had never been more relieved to see her in the distance, but as she advanced, he noticed something out of place. She didn't seem like the woman who left him hours ago. Never the less, he dropped his weapon to the ground, and ran to meet her. He wrapped his arms around her and squeezed tightly in a meaningful embrace. Then he planted a heartfelt kiss to her lips that was obviously more than Mattias could take, as he released a low growl.

Gianna glared at Mattias quickly, and pinned him with a look of warning. Nicholas fired back at Mattias with a shit-eating grin before he returned his attention back to her. "Are you alright?"

"Yes," she said frigidly.

Mattias focused. "Excuse me for a moment. There's a matter I need to address," he said.

He stalked toward Kyle, who smiled at their opponents and waited for the go ahead to resume battle. Mattias smirked. In one fluid motion, he punched a hole through Kyle's chest, splattering blood on Nicholas's clothing.

Mattias retrieved Kyle's heart with his hand, the fatally wounded vampire's eyes widened in horror. "You've made your last mistake," he said as he crushed Kyle's heart in his bare hand,  reducing it to ash. Kyle's lifeless body shattered into a thousand pieces and fell into a pile of rubble. Mattias turned and addressed his clan. "Let this be a warning," he pinned Nicholas with a feral gaze, "never touch what I've claimed as my own."

Cassius's jaw dropped in shock. Mattias delivered the final blow. "It's done. She has agreed to return with us. She'll remain with me, and in the service of our coven. This fight is over."

Gianna walked away from Nicholas to the pile of rubble still smoking on the sand—all that remained of Kyle. She approached the pieces of stone, dropped to one bended knee, and spoke in a soft but stern tone. "Goodbye Kyle. May you meet whichever god takes the greatest pleasure in your torture, and I hope they show you as much mercy as you have shown to others." She stood to her feet and with a swift and subtle move, kicked the sand, covering the remains in a form of blatant disrespect before returning to Nicholas's side.

Cassius questioned Mattias, his attitude fueled by rage. "What about Kyle? Lucas?"

"Kyle crossed me. He had it coming. As far as Lucas is concerned, I will consider the debt settled with the agreement of Gianna's return."

"You have got to be kidding me!"

"Is it your intention to be insubordinate, Cassius? You do realize the consequences for such defiance."

"No. It's just—"

"Acquiring Gianna was priority number one. She will serve our coven well. Not to mention, keep me pleasant. We will replace those we've lost. Kyle's days were numbered. Let it also be known that we will cease all conflict with the Sutton clan. There are to be no quarrels with them from this moment forward. My word is final."

With the intent to gloat, Mattias faced Nicholas. "You should thank her, Nicholas. She paid the price for your amnesty. Had I known how much you were worth, I would've bargained much more. But that too, will come with the time she will spend by my side."

He walked to stand beside Dante, his right hand, as he faced the enemy, waiting for Gianna to inform them of her pending departure. Satisfied with how this was going to end, Mattias barked an order. "Back to the house! We'll rest and leave tonight. Will you be joining us to take your rest, Gianna?"

"Not yet."

"I'll send a car for you tonight."

Gianna nodded in silent agreement. She'd already agreed to leave with him. The least he could do was give her one more day to say goodbye. Mattias and company turned their backs and were gone in an instant, disappearing from plain sight.

Nicholas's jaw dropped. He turned and pleaded with Gianna. "No, don't end this fight by striking a deal with *him*. You can't let him win."

Gianna easily saw the hurt in his eyes. If his heart were capable of beating, it would have broken. She felt the burden of his pain and she wished like hell that she wasn't about to be the cause.

She held his hand in hers. "It's over Nicholas. The battle is over. Take comfort in the fact that your family is safe and whole."

Everyone started back to the house. Nicholas and Gianna walked into their familiar sleeping quarters. "We need to rest, Gianna. We'll talk about your foolish decision at dusk. Please lay with me."

She hesitated before crawling into the bed where he held her tight.

Gianna closed her eyes and inhaled deeply. She'd remember feeling this kind of comfort in only his arms. But it was his words that would forever haunt her dreams. "My family is not complete without you. Don't leave me," he whispered as the blinds closed, plunging the room into darkness.

Tears pricked Gianna's eyes. Her heart was breaking. Never before had she prayed, hoped, or dreamed for anything. She made her own luck. But tonight, she implored any higher power willing to listen to her silent pleas.

*Dear gods, please don't make me choose. I love him and don't want to hurt him, much less want to leave him.*

***

Dusk arrived. Gianna rose and found Nicholas staring out the same window where she'd enjoyed a similar pictorial sunset. She almost gasped, in awe of his beauty as he gazed out at the calm sea. His eyes sparkled, revealing a hint of innocence and a crushing sadness. She swallowed past the lump in her throat. "Nicholas."

His eyes closed, wincing in pain from the sound of her voice, the sound he feared fading to soon. "Why? Why, Gianna?"

"You know why."

He remained silent as though allowing her answer to simmer in his mind. "Now I know how you felt when I left you the first time using the same excuse."

Speechless, Gianna lowered her head. What could she say? She wanted to crawl back into his bed and stay there forever, but she'd never broken her word and would remain true to Mattias so as long as he kept Nicholas safe along with the rest of their deal. "Nicholas, look at me."

"I can't."

"Nicholas, I'm so sorry it has to end this way."

He finally turned to face her. "I can keep myself safe Gianna. I'm not helpless! I could kill you in an instant. In fact, I should. I should do you that favor instead of granting you eternal damnation with a monster."

Nicholas grabbed hold of Gianna's throat, shedding a single tear. "I enjoyed my monotonous life! It was boring and predictable. Then you bring chaos into it, turning it upside down. You are spontaneous, dangerous, and passionate. I can't go back to that life, Gianna. I'd be lost without you."

She trembled in his grasp when he dropped her to the floor, his eyes fixed on the two marks on her neck.

"He bit you," he growled.

"Yes, he did bite, but it wasn't lethal and we're not bound. I agreed to go back with him as a sign of good faith to the coven. They believe that I'm willing to be like them once Mattias decides the right time. It could be tomorrow. It could be centuries from now. He wouldn't have to explain himself and no one would dare force his hand."

"I see," he said.

His brow pinched at the center, betrayed his obvious grief.

Watching him mourn over her loss snapped something inside her, breaking down all defenses. "I love you Nicholas. This is the only way I can truly love you. I would not want to know what it would feel like if you were no longer a part of my eternity. Please understand why I can't stay."

Gianna started for her luggage when Nicholas gripped her arm, stopping her from walking any farther. "Wait. You love me?"

She brought her eyes to his. "Yes."

He released her and pulled her into a heated kiss. Panting from emotion he begged, "I've waited for you to say it. Now that you have, I can't let you go. Please stay with me I will show you the meaning behind the words, Gianna. You'll never grow lonely and I will always want you."

"I'll feel the same, but you know what you're asking is impossible. Especially after—"

"What?"

She sat on his neatly made bed and ran her hand across the brown comforter in an effort to draw attention away from her melancholy disposition. "I owe Mattias more than I can say. I believed that my parents were dead, having met their end at his hand when in fact, they are alive."

"Let me guess...he's been protecting them."

"Yes. In addition to your pardon, he promised to take me to them upon arriving in London."

"How convenient."

"I need answers, Nicholas. I need to know where I came from and where I belong."

"You belong here...with me."

"Please don't make this harder than it is."

He raised his voice. "Don't make it any harder than it is? You're ripping my heart out with your bare hands!"

Gianna stood nervously and watched as Nicholas walked to the fireplace and lifted the poker from its holder. He handed it to Gianna, aiming it at his heart. "Please, I'd rather you do this than having to suffer the pain of watching you walk away." He begged for death over her departure.

She wanted to die. She wanted to give up everything to stay with him. How could she not? He'd give his life just to keep her at his side. She'd suffered physical wounds that would cause most humans to die, but this...this was the most excruciating pain that she had ever experienced. "I won't, Nicholas."

He tossed the poker to the floor angrily and in a moment of desperation, pressed his lips against the pulsating vein in her neck. His tongue touched her throbbing flesh.

Gianna begged. "Don't do it. Should I change or not, I will leave with Mattias."

He thought about it but reconsidered with a stern promise. "I will eventually turn you Gianna. I promise you that. And when I do, you will beg for it, welcome it and I want to see the relief in your eyes when you realize it's what you wanted all along."

Gianna hoped he'd have the opportunity to make good on his promise, but she felt this would be the last time she'd ever see Nicholas Sutton. She looked deep into his eyes, eyes that were beautiful even when filled with pain. "I'll miss your eyes Nicholas. I don't think I'll ever be able to look at the color green the same way."

He walked to a dresser on the opposite side of the room, and reached into a drawer. In his left hand, he held out a piece of jewelry. "I want you to have this. It belonged to my mother."

He placed a bracelet containing numerous emeralds on her wrist.

"I can't accept this Nicholas. You should give this to someone you truly care for, someone far more deserving of the honor, and keep it in your family."

"You are my family, Gianna. I want you to look at it and remember our time together. I'll be waiting for you always."

"Thank you. It's beautiful and I will treasure it."

One by one, Gianna packed her bags while Nicholas implored her once more. "Come to bed with me Gianna. You won't want to leave."

"Nicholas. I don't want to leave. You'll only make it more difficult for the both of us."

He kissed her harder than he ever had as though he wanted her to remember the passion that he felt for her. She wrapped her arms around his neck and he tried desperately to undress her. He deepened his kiss and ran his hands up her dress. She stopped him, took her luggage in her hands, and turned toward him. "I love you."

She descended the stairs and said meaningful goodbyes to the Sutton family. Bennett began the farewells. "Thank you Gianna. You are always welcome here anytime you wish to return."

"Thank you."

Gianna paused at Elizabeth. Her embrace was cold. She felt the tension, the anger Elizabeth held toward her for leaving Nicholas. "I'm sorry Elizabeth but I love him too much to stay and endanger the ones *he* loves most. If I stayed, Mattias's threat would always loom over this family and I can't have that. You are all free to go about your lives without ever having to look over your shoulders."

Elizabeth held Gianna tight. "I'll miss you my sister."

"Take care of your brother for me."

Elizabeth nodded. When Gianna looked up, away from Elizabeth, she saw Nicholas standing at the bottom of the stairs, watching her as if the moment was surreal.

*How does he do that?*

She finally made her way to Sofia, who spoke first. "Gianna, there's something I need to tell you. Something I think you should—"

"I already know, Sofia. Only I'm not sure I completely understand. You'll have to explain the rationale behind it one day."

"I'm so sorry, Gianna."

"Please, don't be. Everything will be fine," she promised.

Sofia held Gianna's hand tight. "You speak as if this is the end but I plan to continue assisting you no matter where your journeys lead. I will be back in London shortly to tie together a few loose ends and make sure you're settled wherever you are. I am also going to want to continue helping you keep your telekinesis under control. I hope your parents have answers regarding your ability and how to stabilize it."

"I'll be in touch soon," Gianna said.

"Good luck with your parents and with...Mattias. Please, don't ever forget what you left behind, waiting for your return."

"How could I? Take care of him for me."

"I will do my best but you'll soon learn that there is no bandage for a broken heart."

Sofia released Gianna. She approached the door that led away from the one place where she felt so welcomed and warm. She turned to look at a numb Nicholas who could barely make eye contact.

Bennett sensed the awkwardness of the situation. "We should give them a moment."

He led the group out of the room. Silence and restraint remained. So much was left unspoken. "I guess it's even pointless to try and ask again."

"I won't blame you if you curse my name for the rest of eternity. Just know this...my heart will always beat for you, Nicholas."

"And you will take with you a piece of my soul."

He gave her one last kiss that nearly stole her breath. "I love you."

"Do me a favor...don't. I don't deserve your love as much as I covet it."

"We both know it's too late for that, Gianna."

Two dark limousines pulled up to the house. Mattias stepped out and Gianna took that as her cue to leave. She lifted one foot over the threshold and felt dread with each footstep. She couldn't turn around, couldn't bear to see the pain. She hated herself for being such a coward, trading what could be with Nicholas for the family she never knew. No...she was saving him. Reuniting with her long lost parents played a small part in her decision making, bait that Mattias hoped she'd take. *Yeah, I'm a fucking idiot.*

She groaned with every step that took her closer to Mattias. He placed her luggage in the trunk and tried to help her walk to the car door. She looked back at Nicholas one last time as Mattias coaxed her into the vehicle and closed the door.

Gianna took note that it was only the two of them in the limo. No doubt, he wanted the ride to be intimately private. He caressed her leg in an upward motion, hoping to get a reaction as he kissed her neck. "Don't worry my love. I'll make you forget him."

"I hate you," she hissed vehemently.

"Keep telling yourself that, Gianna. Your pulse betrays you. The trembling heat of your body and your quick breaths tell another tale."

"Yes, that a part of me is still very human and even you can't change it." She touched the emeralds on her antique bracelet remembering the green of Nicholas's eyes.

"Time will tell."

Gianna wanted to hate him, wanted to rip his fucking heart out until he was reduced to apologetic cries. Those thoughts played out in her mind, bringing a smirk to her face until she caught the scent of warm chocolate. She succumbed to the sweetness that lingered in the air, calming her frazzled nerves and the more Mattias became aroused, the richer the aroma made her mouth water. She willed herself not to lick every inch of him. As much as she tried to convince herself that she loathed this man, she felt certain that she very well may lose herself to him.

***

Nicholas watched the car pull away as he dropped to his knees, defeated. When he finally placed himself back onto his feet, Bennett was there for support. Still standing with the door open and staring at the empty street that held Gianna's transportation moments ago, Bennett placed his hands on his son's shoulders. "She loves you, Nicholas. Far more than she even realized."

"What? I sacrificed too, Father. I didn't even have a choice. She sacrificed for both of us."

"I'm sorry you are hurting, son."

Nicholas breathed deeply for a few moments, regaining what remained of his sanity. "I've waited centuries for her and I'm not about to let this go."

"What do you intend to do?"

"I will give her some time to heal and then I will find her. I will fight for her, for eternity should it take that long, and to my end if need be. This is not over. It will never be over until I bring her home...permanently."

# 26

The ride to the airport wouldn't be short. In fact, it would last another forty minutes. What could Gianna do to pass the time? She could close her eyes and sleep the rest of the way, but then she'd run out of options during that dreaded eight hour flight back across the Atlantic. At that moment, she wished that she would've arranged for her own flight home. At least it would've given her some much welcomed peace. Peace would be a luxury she'd no longer have. She'd be at Mattias's every beck and call, he'd be relentless in his demands of both her mind and her body.

Mattias's hands seemed to be everywhere at once. It was both repulsive and arousing, a monumental conflict that allowed her conscious to break through her vocal chords. "Is this how you plan to spend the eight hour flight home?"

"Are you honestly going to pretend to not enjoy this?"

"I said nothing about enjoyment. It was a simple question."

"I took note of the connotation."

"Well?"

"I'm sorry, Gianna. I've wanted to touch you like this since the night we officially met. I'll always want you like this. It will be an effort to remain appropriate when necessary."

*Great. This is just how I envisioned my immortality. Please, decapitate me now and save me the anguish.*

His hands began to roam again. She looked him dead in the eye. "Can we have a serious conversation for a moment?"

Mattias withdrew with a sigh. He didn't particularly want to engage in conversation. He could think of far better ways to keep his mouth occupied. "What's troubling you, my love?"

"I have so many questions for you, Mattias," she said, her eyes searching his.

"I know."

"How old are you?"

"Five hundred seventy two years."

Gianna's jaw dropped so quickly, she swore she heard it smack against the floor of the limousine.

"What?"

"Yes. I know, it's quite a long time to have existed."

"I would've never...I mean—"

"You would've never expected me to be such an elder...that was my goal, Gianna. I had to adapt to most of the ways of the new world to be able to co-exist with the modernity of the age. Do you really think that I could lead a modern day coven, speaking ancient Latin?"

"I guess not...the things that you've seen, the experiences you've had. I can't begin to image the way of life."

"You don't want to. I've seen many things throughout my life, Gianna. Never have you lived easier than in this very century.

Still, you have war over the most mundane of things. If your feuding countries could see life five hundred years ago, your world would be at peace."

She took a moment to ponder what he just revealed. If he was as old as he claimed, could there be someone even older than Mattias? "Were you born a hybrid?"

"Yes. Our species cannot be a result of turning. We are born of a vampire and human union."

"Are there more like us?"

"There were. I've only ever come across a handful of hybrids in my existence. Some of them are not only vampire and human intermingling, but are a result of other species mating with humans."

"I imagine those were frightening."

"On the contrary, shape shifters or were species are actually quite attractive."

"Couldn't you have been besotted with one of them instead of me?"

Mattias was evidently wounded by her words. He looked to the floor in silence and for once during her time spent with him, Gianna felt remorseful for her verbiage. "I'm sorry, Mattias. I am honestly flattered that you would believe me to be worth the trouble. I just don't understand the fascination."

"First, let me address your last comment. Ever since your family came into my care, I have been watching you from afar. Do you know a female in existence that wouldn't take offense to that? Quite honestly, my significant other would always come second to you and that would be unacceptable. Not even I could do that to someone. Secondly, most females don't understand the magnetism, the gravitational pull that tugs at your entire being and screams until it's sated."

"So, I'm luring you?"

"No...it's an attraction that is unexplainable. I. Want. You...plain and simple. I won't accept any substitutes."

Gianna sighed before he spoke again.

"I would take your sigh as a wordless complaint. Is that what it is? Because last night, I didn't hear you—"

"Stop." She looked away.

"I know you enjoyed being with me. I can still smell desire emanating from your body. I can taste it in your pheromones hovering in the air. You want me just as badly as I want you. Only I'm not in denial."

"Is that what you believe? That I'm in denial? Don't pretend to know how I feel just because I don't advertise to the rest of the known universe."

"So you do want me?"

Gianna shifted the topic of conversation. "Why do we look like we're in our mid-twenties? Will we age?"

"See...denial. Oh, uh...age...right."

Gianna rolled her eyes.

"We won't age beyond twenty five years. It is the prime of our youth. From what I've gathered, anyone with an ability will arrive at full power as well."

"So, that's when it happened." Gianna had not intended to speak her thoughts.

"Gianna, do you have an ability?"

"Fuck," she muttered.

"You do. Oh please, do tell."

Gianna hesitated before answering, fearing that she would leave herself susceptible to attack. Hell, if she wanted to, she could cast him a great distance if he even dared.

"Gianna, confide in me." He placed his hand on her knee. "You can trust me."

"Can I?"

"I would never betray you."

She raised an eyebrow and somehow doubted his affirmation. One day he'd be put to the test. For reasons unknown, she felt safe revealing herself. She feared her uncontrollable ability more than she did Mattias.

"I do have an ability...telekinesis."

He sat back to absorb what she revealed. "That's amazing."

"Not from where I'm sitting."

"We'll need to discuss it further."

Mattias looked at Gianna as if his eyes bore the longing of the entire world. "Have you enough answers for one evening?"

"I'll never have enough answers."

"Fair enough. I have one small request...Can I have something genuine before we board the plane and resume our deception?"

She crossed her arms at her chest, hesitant of his petition. "What do you mean by genuine, exactly?"

He fell to his knees before her and placed one hand on each side of her, flat against the cool leather seat. She unfolded her arms in surprise. "Let me kiss you, Gianna...an honest one. I want you to close your eyes and let yourself feel what it is that you want to feel. You owe that to yourself. The torture at your own hand can only last but so long."

"I do not torture myself."

"So you say."

"What we shared last night was in fact, real."

"Yes, I am well aware of that. The difference is that now you know the truth for what it is. There are no secrets left between us...well, for my part." He smiled. "Close your eyes."

She did as he asked. He leaned into her, his hands still motionless as he pressed his lips lightly against hers, performing complete magic.

---

She melted at his touch before she pulled him against her to deepen what he started, permitting his hands to roam at will. She found her own wandering the width of his shoulders, which was far greater than her reach. She suddenly pushed herself away, breathless to speak against his lips. "I should hate you, Mattias."

"Should you?"

Mattias thought she should. He knew better than anyone that she had just cause to wish him every bit of harm that would befall him. He convinced both himself and her otherwise, but he knew the truth. If not for Gianna, he wouldn't have been so courteous to the Suttons, to her parents or anyone. She managed to keep him as humble as Mattias would allow and she had no idea the magnitude of power she held over him. Through a mere touch, she tamed the beast inside of him that was dying to claw its way to the surface. She alone was his Achilles heel.

Another thing he had to consider, no matter how much he didn't care to admit it, Nicholas Sutton was a worthy adversary. The vampire was a determined one, and if he was half as credible as Mattias deemed, he'd be back to challenge him for Gianna much sooner than he wanted. There'd be no way Mattias would let Gianna go without a fight. And what a fight it would be! Both would walk through the very fires of hell, barefoot and naked if she was the reward. Right now, she was all his and he relished the fact. He'd make her forget all about Nicholas Sutton, by God he would.

Gianna was lost in the taste of his lips in the touch of his hands. They were alone. The encounter was private, intimate, and heated. She willed herself away from Mattias's fondling, but fell short.

Damn, she couldn't deny that the man had a way with his hands. He could ease the tension from a rock and melt glass into puddles of sweet release. Still he moved like water, as his tongue continued to move in cadence with hers, his hands flowing expertly over her body, as though he knew what her skin craved better than she did.

Amused by her playful hindrance, he worked against her, breaking her will to resist. He lifted a hand to the back of her neck and pulled her close, breathing heavily into her ear. "Do you enjoy fighting me?"

"I'm not fighting you. It's a natural repulsion." Her eyes locked with his.

Mattias let out a soft laugh. "I find it interesting that my being repulsive takes you to a cliff's edge."

"Yes, I want nothing more than to hurl myself over the side. I hate it when you touch me."

"You say you hate when I touch you, but your body betrays you." His eyes fell to her nipples, hardened like pearls, straining against the fabric of her shirt.

Before she could answer, once more, he placed both hands beneath her hair, behind her ears, and claimed her lips. He smirked between lip smacking and exhales at the way she couldn't resist touching him in return, her hands stroking the muscular planes of his back.

Mattias himself, was lost in a reverie. But even more than the need to be with Gianna, was the need for attachment, to connect with her mind, body and soul on a level that transcended the normal methodic relationship. Somehow, he would reach that very part of her that spoke to him honestly and when he used his power to delve into her most private thoughts, he found exactly what he was looking for.

She buried her true feelings deep under a layer of darkness where she'd never be left emotionally naked but when he forced it to surface, the words were music to his ears as the thoughts slipped out vocally between her lips. "Touch me, Mattias. God, please don't stop touching me."

Surprised by her revelation she gasped, leaned into his ear while he laughed, proud of his defiance. "You insufferable bastard."

"Once again, I state the obvious. You are most definitely in denial. I cannot manipulate your thoughts, love. I can only force the truth of them, one you cannot possibly deny. Now, look into my eyes and tell me that you do not want me to touch you."

Gianna met his gaze and like a toddler desperate to prove a point. "I don't want you to touch me."

He reached out and cupped her face, causing her to release a soft exhale. He smiled at her attempt to cover her feelings while they both knew the facts. "Uh huh...and I would bet that if I ran my hands between your warm thighs, I would be rewarded with a slick treasure."

"If you are fond of your hand being attached to your wrist, I strongly advise against it."

He flashed that devilish grin that set her ablaze. She hated herself for reacting to him the way that she did. The wound of leaving Nicholas was still fresh and all that she could think about was resisting the urge to mount Mattias and riding him until they both dripped with sweat. *Damn it!* As he worked his lips to her neck, she tensed. Could he bite? No, he wouldn't....would he? Would he risk the coven seeing the mark and notice no change? It was daring, she gave him that.

Mattias licked her skin, the sweet berry essence that teased his senses and bared his fangs. Gently he pressed against her flesh, threatening penetration when she burst into what seemed like a thousand sparks, pushing her over that very cliff's edge to her own climax.

She tried to down play her obvious orgasm, forcing herself to stifle her screams when she dug her nails into his back so hard that if he were bare, he'd be bleeding.

Mattias was no fool. He was no stranger to the sight of a pleased woman. He laughed as he pulled away from her. Her look of surprise was worth a thousand words when he seated himself on the leather and addressed her reaction. "I asked for something genuine and I guess it doesn't get more genuine than that."

Still shuddering from her wave of ecstasy, her chest heaving, she wanted to scowl in protest but instead, she said the last thing she expected. "What can I do for you, Mattias?"

He smiled at her compliance. "Just sit where you are, against the seat looking as beautiful as I have ever seen you. You have just given me pleasure by fulfilling my request with minimal resistance. I will save my time with you for when we are in my bed and I have all the time that I desire to savor you slowly. For when I am through, there will not be an inch of you that I have not tasted."

She gulped at his statement. "Well, now that your ego is over-inflated and in dire need of a pinhole, what is the first order of business?"

"We shouldn't discuss these things while we're alone."

Mattias's wry look intended to inform her that business was the farthest thing from his mind. "Are you always about business first and pleasantries later?"

"Mattias."

"I suppose it would be foolish to overlook this superlative opportunity."

"My thoughts exactly."

"Well, I suppose we will board the flight and you should appear as you always do. Anything out of the ordinary will pique curiosity that neither of us can afford."

"Ok. I can do that."

"They may want to address replacing Lucas's and Kyle's positions in the coven. There is much to consider in filling the vacancy."

"Do my opinions count?"

"Well of course they do, my love. You are as much a part of the decision making as I am."

She smiled at his acknowledgement and acceptance into his world. He was willing to meet her as an equal for he knew that she was far too powerful to simply sit at his side. The realization touched her but she was careful to keep herself guarded. She wondered if there would be a time when she could open herself to Mattias. It was doubtful. Only one person was able to shatter the walls that she thought were indestructible and now he was free to live out eternity whichever way he chose. There were many people that she freed tonight. Sofia, Nicholas, and the rest of the Sutton coven. Hell, she was even able to free Mattias from the secret he had been keeping for over two hundred and fifty years. That was one hell of a burden to carry that he could never naturally take to his grave, and for that, she could sympathize.

Mattias watched as so many things played through her mind that resulted in the curving smile of her lips. "Careful, my love. You are appearing light-heartedly happy."

"Would you rather me sullen?"

"I would rather you naked."

"Ugh." She rolled her eyes.

"As you know, the flight to London will be a long one and the jet is private. You can feel free to sleep most of the flight if you do not wish to interact."

"We'll see how it goes."

"When we land, I'll take you home so that you can get yourself settled. I will then bring your parents to you. We will have to leave before sunrise due to the lethargy."

"I understand."

She looked out the window and wondered how it would happen, the first meeting with her parents in over two and a half centuries. Would they recognize themselves in her? Would they accept her for who she is, who she wants to be? Would they allow her to make her own decisions or would they immediately step into their respective parental roles complete with worry? Would they even like her? Yeah, she wanted to vomit over the thoughts. After centuries of wonder and sadness over the void, she grew terrified.

They were close to the airport. She secretly hoped that Nicholas would be there, a barricade of prevention, protesting her leave. In reality, she knew he'd respect her wishes, fighting everyone in his path until he came to his senses.

Mattias dropped a hand to her thigh as a reassuring gesture. "Do not trouble yourself with thoughts of hesitation. Your parents will adore you as I do. They have waited just as long as you have for this moment and they look forward to the meeting."

"They know?"

"Of course they do. I had to have them standing by in case this sort of situation arose. They await my contact."

"I swear, Mattias. If you are lying to me, I will—"

"Have my tongue, my head, in addition to my heart?"

"It's just a fair warning."

"One that is duly noted, I assure you."

The low flying aircraft above them signaled they were at the airport. Mattias confirmed. "We're here. In a few moments, we'll be just outside the jet."

Gianna saw the second limo waiting for them. Dante was pacing as if he anticipated something would go wrong. "Dante's nervous...and nervous, means dangerous. He will be on alert, looking for something...anything to be out of place. You don't want that."

Mattias looked equally panicked. "What do you suggest?"

She immediately regretted what she was about to do. "Take off your shirt."

"I like where this is going."

"Mattias, please."

He removed the dress shirt from his body. Even moving quickly, he never took his eyes from her, seducing her with speed. "Now what?"

She saw Dante watching the car, ready to approach when she removed her shirt as well, revealing a black satin bra. "Now let us see how good you really are at your own charade."

Before she lay back on the leather seat, Gianna pulled Mattias on top of her, his weight pressed against her bare abdomen. She locked her arms at the wrists around his neck and kissed him, her hottest yet. His hands traveled the length of her frame and reached beneath her skirt to caress the smooth thighs beneath when Dante opened the door. "Mattias are you—"

"Give me a fucking minute!"

311

Dante closed the door and Mattias resumed his travels of her body. She pulled away. "Mattias, I think he's gone. We're safe now."

"No. I can't leave. Not yet...not when I want you so badly."

"Mattias, we need to go."

"Gianna, I beg you, don't do this to me."

"Wasn't it you who said that you wanted to take your time? Well, in case you didn't notice, we have an audience."

"That fact escaped me."

Mattias rose slowly and composed himself as Gianna dressed.

*** 

Dante shook his head in a continued fit of anger. The sight of her beneath Mattias was distressing. He stared long enough to notice that soft, tawny skin was bare as it touched Mattias. Even more disturbing was the unnatural color of Mattias's burgundy eyes. They gave off a feral glare, a warning that she was his possession and if anyone dared to interrupt, they would endure great suffering at his hand.

*I don't know how much longer I can stand this.*

# 27

Mattias opened the limousine door and stepped out. All eyes of what remained of his coven members were on him as he reached into the limo, and extended his hand to help Gianna out. When she stepped out, the tension that loomed over the crowd began to subside. Cassius had a reason to lash out. He'd lost his best friend, his brother, and partner in all sorts of crimes. Instead, he smiled at Gianna. "It's lovely to see you again, Gianna."

"You too, Cassius."

Mattias walked past Dante, to the trunk of the limousine to remove Gianna's luggage. Dante began to apologize for his intrusion moments ago. "Mattias, I'm sorry that I was hasty. I did not mean to interrupt. I should have waited for—"

"Certainly you didn't intend to interrupt. Therefore, it's not an issue, Dante. Now, I am anxious to return to London. There are many things that need my attention. Is the plane ready for takeoff?"

"Yes."

"Good. Let us take our leave then."

Mattias walked to the plane with Gianna on his arm. He led her up the stairs and onto the aircraft. When she boarded, she looked around the lavish area that was so much more than she expected.

The transportation was evidently Mattias's own personal aircraft that he used when the need to conduct business abroad arose. The interior boasted neutral plush carpet, sofa-like seating, and numerous sections for privacy. He continued to walk through the plane until he came to a door after the main seating area. He pushed the door open and Gianna's eyes widened at the bedroom before her. It was gorgeous, a near exact replica of his room in London.

Once they stepping inside the room, he closed the door and turned to her. "This is my sanctuary away from home. I find my refuge here when long trips prevent me from being in London."

"It's definitely impressive."

"If you wish to separate yourself from the coven tonight, you may stay here for as long as you need. I will be in from time to time if that is what you choose."

"I'll consider it but I think I'll be fine with Dante and Cassius."

He reached for her arm, placing a soft kiss on the back of her hand. "Beautiful, brave and fierce."

"You have no idea."

"Don't I?"

She shook her head as he led her out of the room to the main seating area. Dante had a glass of Ouzo, an anise flavored drink comparable to Sambuca. Ouzo was Greek in origin. Mattias had it imported at Dante's request because it reminded him of home, growing up in Litochoro. He offered it to Gianna to sample. She accepted with the grace of a goddess and he watched as her eyes lit up, enjoying the sweetness of the liquid. "This is fantastic, Dante."

"I'm glad you enjoyed it. Can I get something for you? A beverage, perhaps? Are you hungry?"

"Thanks, Dante but I'll just have a glass of—"

"Grey Goose. It's her favorite." Mattias shrugged. "Why do you think I have the clubs stocked with it? I have nothing but the best available for my woman."

"That will be fine, Dante. Thank you."

Dante nodded and turned away, pained by what he was watching. Gianna seemed to be at ease in Mattias's company. Could she be coming around and considering the possibility of bonding with Mattias? He balled his hands into fists and pounded on the sink next to the bar, sending the glasses rattling to the ground, some of them breaking. Gianna, Mattias, and Cassius fell silent. "Is everything alright, Dante?" she asked.

"Yes, Gianna. Everything is fine."

She jumped from her seat and walked to Dante. "While I realize you're trying to be considerate, I am more than capable of preparing my own beverage."

Gianna flipped a glass to its base and dropped three ice cubes inside. She then took an unopened bottle of her vodka of choice and flipped it in the air once before cracking it open. Dante raised an eyebrow before she smiled and explained her toss. "For good luck."

"I see."

She cracked open the bottle and poured the equivalent of two shots before reaching into the refrigerator for tonic water and a lime to complete her cocktail. "Go sit down and relax. I have this covered."

Dante nodded and walked toward his seat.

Gianna reached for a glass and filled it with Jameson for Mattias before returning to sit by his side.

Mattias watched Gianna approach as he had hundreds of times before, but this was different.

They had an understanding and a certain camaraderie, being united for a common purpose. Holding that thought, his gaze began at the black heels on her feet, and traveled up her bare legs, muscular and toned.

She wore a black skirt that hugged her hips and flared out at the bottom. She wore a three-quarter-sleeved shirt with a plunging neckline, revealing an ample amount of cleavage.

He continued slowly up toward her neck where the skin was surprisingly dense, as if her vampire and human halves were indeed at war. It didn't stop him from sampling, it never would.

Her lips were plump and moist, wearing a hint of frosted gloss. Her nose was short and wide but was in perfect proportion with her rounded face. Although her eyes were round, they appeared pulled at the edges, like those of an exotic Egyptian and the warm chocolate hue that they bore was enough to seal his fate, whatever she decided. She wore her equally brown hair in flowing curls tonight, draping over her shoulders. He remembered how she had looked last night with those same curls draped over his hips, the silken feel of it. Dear gods, she was breathtaking.

*Mine.*

Gianna handed Mattias his glass and took her seat, crossing her legs. He placed a hand on her knee like a lover, and those around him watched. She had to admit that she didn't think Dante and Cassius would care enough to pay such close attention but she was wrong. They were indeed studying the chemistry between the two, looking for something out of sorts. Luckily, Mattias spoke, breaking the ice in the air around them. "Should we discuss the changes that need to take place once things settle?"

Dante nodded. "I think we need to form some sort of plan."

Cassius agreed. "We need to fill two seats in our house."

"All right, do you have any suggestions?"

Cassius suggested first. "What about the Anthony twins, Vexon and Vanner?"

"They are questionable. Vexon and Vanner are nearly as young as Kyle was and could prove to be more trouble than they are worth."

Dante added. "There is the matter of their nature. Rumor has it they're part incubus. But that little detail could be beneficial. They could serve a purpose."

"Dante, do we really need twin incubus issues?"

"I am just siding with Cassius as a possibility."

Mattias sat with his chin placed on his hand between his thumb and forefinger, deep in thought.

"I'm not sure if you want my opinion but what about Michael? Now he could serve a purpose," Gianna added.

Cassius's eyes widened. "Michael?"

Dante looked at both Cassius and Mattias. "Michael. He's an excellent candidate."

Mattias nodded in agreement. "Indeed. Do we offer him Lucas's seat?"

Cassius nodded. "Sure, why not?"

Uncomfortable silence followed. Gianna had just influenced the decision of the coven and they were all acutely aware. She didn't want to push things along too quickly and cause an uprising. Gianna stood to excuse herself. "Well, I don't want to ruin your fun. I'm sure you all have much to discuss. I am going to get some sleep before we land. Let me know if I am needed."

Cassius and Dante both bid her goodnight when Mattias stood to face her. She was unsure of what her actions should be.

Should she kiss him? Embrace him? Instead, she settled for a slight touch to the shoulder, and a seductive dragging of her hand away before she left them to their business.

"I'll be back soon, gentlemen. I want to be sure Gianna is settled comfortably," Mattias promised.

"I bet you do." Cassius laughed and nudged Dante.

The two vampires watched as Mattias left their company when Cassius spoke aloud. "I have a feeling that things are about to get real interesting."

Dante smirked. *You have no idea.*

Gianna shut the door behind her as she entered the bedroom. When she didn't hear the door catch, she turned quickly on her feet. Mattias stood at the entry in silence, staring before he walked inside, closing the door. His silence was disturbing and it was killing Gianna. She stood uneasy, waiting for a reaction. "Well? How are we doing?"

Mattias crossed the room and closed the distance between them. "Mattias, say something...please."

"Shh...keep it down. I don't want them to hear us."

"The silence is deafening."

He moved closer, pressing his hard body against hers. She could feel his cool breath against her skin. "You are amazing. Dante and Cassius are none the wiser. They still believe that you are human and nothing has changed, with the exception of your willingness to come home with me shows that you are open to becoming one of us...well one of them. You are much too convincing."

"I'm glad to hear it."

He leaned in to kiss her when she placed her hand against him in resistance. "Look, I think that maybe we should continue playing the part tonight. If we jump into things too quickly, it may trigger a warning sign."

"Gianna, you can't push me away for long. I thought we reached an understanding."

"I'm not pushing you away...well, I am but not for the reason you think."

She hoped that sounded convincing, too.

He signed in defeat. "Very well. I'll leave you to yourself until we land. If you change your mind I'll be right outside that door."

"I appreciate the privacy."

He nodded and left her alone in the room where she lay on the bed. She could barely hear the sound of the engine when she closed her eyes, desperate for pleasant dreams.

Her thoughts drifted to warm sand and a cool breeze beneath moonlight and a clear sky. She leaned her head back, feeling the wind as if she were sitting where she imagined. She could smell the salt of the ocean mingling with the air around her, giving her peace when she felt a touch that gave even more comfort. She looked to the source of the tenderness and saw Nicholas's face. He didn't speak. He sat motionless, staring at her, watching as the elements around them gave her vitality.

He moved closer, his eyes...those gorgeous, precious jewels meeting hers, their faces almost touching when he tilted his head toward her cheek and inhaled her scent like she did the sea air.

Gianna's fantasy was interrupted by a voice overhead.

*"Good evening, this is your captain speaking. If everyone would please take their seats, we will be taking off once the runway is clear. We expect clear skies this evening for a smooth flight to London."*

One thing was for sure, at least this horrid ordeal would be over and she could return to her life. Yeah, that was easier said than done. How could she return to her life when it was forever changed? How could she be with Mattias all the while wishing he was someone else? She would make it work as if none of it mattered. She would once again, numb herself to the feelings Nicholas dragged out of her. She cursed his name for what he managed to do while praying to the air.

*Hate me. Please hate me. Despise me so that you can move on with your life for both of our sakes. Otherwise, all of this will have been for nothing.*

Gianna felt the plane moving. They were approaching the runway leaving this country, bound for England. When she did step foot back on American soil, she would not head back to Cape May Point. If Nicholas did not try to contact her within six months time, she would consider that distance the confirmation she needed that their relationship was in fact, over. But she knew that he wouldn't ruin everything she set into motion to satisfy his own needs, even if they were hers as well.

It had only been moments since the captain's announcement but she already felt the aircraft gaining speed and once she felt that initial ascension, she knew they were in the air and there was no turning back.

***

Mattias took his seat next to Cassius and Dante as the plane made it climb to the necessary elevation. They watched as he sighed in relief. "Many thanks to you both for your cooperation. To show my appreciation for your dedication, I will offer the Anthony twins Kyle's position in our house."

Cassius straightened. "But there are only two seats available."

"Cassius, do not fret over the logistics. I have the room for a third position should I choose to grant one. Now, I'll leave it up to you to make the appointments with both Michael and the Anthony twins. I'll expect to handle this tomorrow evening. We don't want to leave ourselves shorthanded for long. We'll appear weakened, and we can't have that."

Dante nodded. "Agreed. What about Gianna?"

"What about her?"

"Is she alright? I mean, is she as dependable as she was before the situation with the Suttons?"

"I assure you, Gianna is far more dependable now than she was before she left London.

She won't be an issue. In fact, she'll prove to be a greater asset since I'm giving her more access to my dealings. She'll have more power and decision making than she had in the past. She has always served me well and we can only benefit from her knowledge."

The looks of concern from both Dante and Cassius were priceless. "No disrespect intended, Mattias, but are you sure that it's a wise idea?"

"Dante, if I did not think it to be a wise idea, I wouldn't have suggested it. Do you take me for a fool?"

"Not at all. I was just wondering if you were making it worth her while to come back with us and you offered her what you did to sweeten the deal."

"I didn't have to. It didn't take much convincing...but enough of that, back to the positions. I am being lenient with the offering to the Anthony twins. Should they prove to be a threat to our house, I won't hesitate to rescind my invitation. If your recommendation for them still stands, I will offer it."

Dante approved of the recommendation. Cassius concurred. For the first time in weeks, things seemed to be looking up.

Mattias was satisfied and although the thought was alien, he actually felt...human, poetic even, as he closed his eyes in relief that this chapter in his life was closing as the next one was opening. Only the Fates knew what the future held for him and he prayed for once, they'd be merciful.

Before he relaxed, he needed to be sure that Gianna was safe. It was one thing to be surrounded by vampires in a crowded nightclub in an overpopulated city but in a confined space thirty thousand feet above the ground was another matter. "Have you both fed before boarding?"

"We have."

"Good. I wouldn't want to have to kill either one of you for feeding from my human."

Mattias's statement brought up a good point that Cassius just had to address. "When will you be turning her anyway?"

"All in good time, Cassius. I see no need to rush things. I sort of enjoy her being human for now. It's rather dangerous situation with me being a vampire. It's like sampling the forbidden fruit."

"Well, if you know the Anthony twins as well as I do, the situation will prove to be more dangerous. They can't resist the temptation of taking a human...woman. Rumor has it that they are the product of a demon siring."

"Well, let that be a warning to them should they accept. Never, ever touch what belongs to me or they will meet a swift end."

Dante interrupted their conversation. "We really should relax. Things will be hectic upon our arrival when we relieve Michael."

"Yes. I will be tending to things upon our return as well."

"I will have transportation ready."

"It won't be necessary. I will be with Gianna tonight and I won't require your assistance, as much as it's appreciated."

# 28

Eight hours later and a trip through customs brought the vampire clan back to their familiar city. Cassius inhaled the air. "Ah...The sweet smell of London. Is there anything better?"

Gianna wanted to blurt out her answer but censored herself immediately.

Similar limousine transportation awaited them when they exited the airport with luggage in hand. Gianna recognized the drivers as Mattias's usual chauffeurs. They greeted him, took the luggage, and held the doors open for their entry. "Very nice to see you again, Mister Vitale."

"Likewise."

Once again, it was just she and Mattias alone in their vehicle while Cassius and Dante followed a short distance behind. She immediately questioned him. "So, how will this work?"

"Well, I'll drop you at your home and be back an hour later."

She remembered her Maserati being at the airport. "My car—"

"Has already been parked in your driveway."

"How did you know?"

"I told you. I know everything about you."

"So, I'm like an open book to you?"

"Not entirely. I use the word *everything* loosely."

"I'm pretty sure that what you've done could easily be considered stalking."

Mattias laughed. "I know what I need to know to ensure your safety. I also went a step further and I now know some trivial things that have become endearing to me."

"Interesting."

"I look forward to learning more of those things about you."

She yawned as she placed his hand on her knee. He smiled at the human reflex. "Are you tired?"

"No. I think it was just all of the commotion from the past few weeks that has me slightly off schedule."

"I understand."

They rode the next few minutes in silence, Gianna deep in thought as Mattias watched. They didn't speak again for the remainder of the ride. The car pulled up to Gianna's home, drove through the opening of the iron gate and stopped in the half-moon shaped driveway only steps from the front door.

She looked over to Mattias who was already outside the car. He walked to her door, opened it, and offered his hand. She took his offering and stepped outside the vehicle. Like a gentleman, he walked her to the door, luggage in hand.

He watched as she disarmed the security system and opened the front door. He carefully placed the luggage in the foyer so that she may do with it as she wished. Mattias gave Gianna one last glance before his departure.

"Thank you, Mattias."

"No love, thank you."

"I haven't done anything."

"You have done far more than you realize."

"So—"

"One hour. Give me one hour and I'll return with them. Please try not to be nervous."

Yeah, that was easy to say from where he was standing.

Gianna nodded as he reached for her hand and placed a soft kiss to the knuckles. "One hour."

"Got it."

He walked to the door and closed it behind him.

*Don't be nervous?*

*Don't be nervous!*

She paced through the house as if she could wear holes in the floor when she decided to shower and dress.

The hour seemed like days when finally, the doorbell rang. She tried not to sprint to the door when she heard the chimes but couldn't help herself. She opened it and there stood Mattias in front of a couple who appeared to be in their late thirties. The woman was petite. Her dark hair was pulled into an exquisite up-do hairstyle, allowing loose strands of long curls to flow to her shoulders. Her eyes were a piercing golden hazel. The man was tall. She would have guessed that he stood about six feet four inches in height. His hair was black and his eyes were hers, as though looking into a mirror.

She felt her gaze widen against her will and she held her breath, waiting for rejection, for criticism. Gianna's father raced past Mattias and swooped her off her feet, into the air, twirling her like a little girl.

"*Bambina!*" He'd yelled the Italian word for baby when the memory came back to her. She remembered how her father would often speak his native tongue so that he could teach her the language of their heritage.

His laughter caused Gianna's heart to soar, and when he released her gently to the ground, tears streamed down his face. She realized his pain had been just as great as hers. Her mother approached in a gentler, kinder fashion but was no less emotional. She was sobbing as if heartbroken, arms extended to embrace the daughter she'd given birth to over two centuries ago, the same daughter who was deceived to protect her existence. "My child. My sweet little girl. You are more beautiful than I could've thought possible."

"Mother?"

"Mother? Oh my darling daughter, please do not use formalities. Call me...Mom."

She reached out and hugged Gianna. They both exhaled sighs of relief. At long last, they were a family again.

Gianna pulled away from her parents and asked a question that she knew would sting Mattias, but she needed confirmation. "Did he treat you well? Have you been hurt?"

Mattias looked to the ground. His expression, tortured. Gianna's father, in his thick Mediterranean accent, defended the leader. "We owe so much to Mattias. If not for him, we would not want to know what your fate could have been. We were treated with reverence and could not have asked to be more accommodated."

Her mother agreed with her husband. "He was kind, sweetheart. He made sure that we were taken care of, and made certain that you were never left unattended."

Mattias interrupted. "Vincenzo, Grace, once again, it has been my pleasure to offer my assistance. I would do it again and have regretted nothing."

"Mattias, you are too humble. I have repeatedly requested that you call me Enzo."

"My apologies, Enzo. I come from a time where shortening a name was disrespectful."

Gianna's mother embraced Mattias and placed a gentle kiss on his cheek. "You are too kind, Mattias."

*What the fuck?* Gianna nearly fell on her ass in shock.

*No...he's using his fucking gift!*

"You bastard! I warned you. Release them or I swear to the gods, you'll regret it."

She growled low in her throat, a threat to Mattias as he marveled at her rage when she lost control, her eye color transforming to the violet that was her overruling anger. Before she had the opportunity to do any damage, her mother took hold of her arm with a feather-light touch. "Gianna Daniela Marino! Your anger is misplaced. He is not influencing us with his gift, child."

Having recognized her mother's voice, Gianna came to. Her eye color and erratic breathing returned to normal. Her mother embraced her before she fell to the ground, exhausted. "It's alright sweetheart. Mattias can help you with that, too."

Gianna looked to Mattias. "I'm sorry," she said with sincerity.

"I know."

Enzo stepped in, joining his wife in comforting their daughter. "Long, deep breaths, Gianna. You will be fine."

Moments later, Gianna stood when her father laughed. "You have your mother's temper."

Her mother laughed. "And her father's good looks. Now, Gianna, I am so very interested in hearing all about you, your interests and experiences. I'm sure you have been through so much these past few centuries."

Gianna led Enzo, Grace, and Mattias into a large living room decorated in cool earth tones. The walls were light and airy, lending a relaxing mood, which was once again, Sofia's idea. She offered her guests a seat on the blue-gray sofas, and served them refreshments of blood-laced wine while they chatted. When her parents talked amongst themselves, Gianna realized that Mattias was no longer in the room, and he hadn't spoken a word to her. She excused herself and walked toward the door, hoping to catch up with him.

She opened the front door and saw Mattias walking down the short cobblestone path, toward the crescent-shaped driveway where his custom, 2010 Black Dodge Challenger was parked. Yeah, Mattias was always into muscle cars and now that the new models resembled the older ones, he'd developed an expensive hobby similar to her own. Gods, she wanted to kick herself for what she was about to do. She must be losing her fucking mind. "Mattias, wait!"

Mattias froze in place and turned toward Gianna as she ran to greet him. "I'm sorry that I left without saying goodbye. I tried to slip away discreetly because I wanted to give you some privacy with your—"

Gianna interrupted him with a scorching hot kiss, one that made him tremble with need and left her aching with desire. Both would have to wait for a more appropriate setting. Mattias was tense at first, undoubtedly astounded by her intention, but relaxed almost as quickly, bringing his hands to her waist. His tongue assaulted hers, dueling for dominance. She pulled back to look at him. "Thank you," she said.

"It's the least I could do, love." He brushed a loose strand of hair away from her face to caress her cheek with the back of his hand. God, he loved her. "Just remember, I want you back at the club tonight as though nothing ever occurred," he instructed.

Damn her obligatory bargain. "Of course, same time and place as usual. I think I can pull off an acting gig pretty well, Mattias. No worries."

Mattias leaned close to Gianna, pressing himself against her puckered breasts while she felt his cool breath tease the fine hairs of her skin, and the tempting erection that nudged her hip.

"Absolutely nothing can appear out of the ordinary," he whispered.

"That's the plan."

"Every last detail."

She looked at him with an evil grin. "Everything including the indiscreet bedroom activity. Oh, wait! They'll think we still haven't been intimate. I guess we'll have to go back to that."

"Don't joke about that, Gianna. Touching you is no longer something I can live without."

"But you said, every detail must remain as it was."

"Well, I reserve the right to change a few rules as I see fit."

"You mean, so that you benefit."

"Well, I am the leader. And if you want to keep the leader happy..."

"Yeah, I think I understand."

"Go then, be with them. I'll see you tonight."

Gianna watched as she started the engine of his car, roaring to life like a wild beast. Dear god, he looked incredible, and that beautiful tattoo bulged and flexed as he gripped the wheel. He winked at her before he pulled away and she turned to walk back into the house where she kept her guests waiting.

After hours of conversation, and deciding they'd remain living in their spacious home, generously purchased by Mattias, Gianna's parents needed to rest.

They were vampires after all, and would become lethargic in the sunlight. She showed them to a room in the basement where she met a twinge of sadness. This was where Nicholas stayed. She hoped if she could disguise the sorrow with the now happy memories of her reuniting with her family she thought died long ago, then she could distract herself and redecorate the room with her new found happiness.

Gianna bid them farewell with loving embraces, and even though she knew they'd leave as soon as the sun set, she took comfort in the fact that she'd see them again, often, and always.

Gianna woke with renewed respect for Mattias Vitale and for the first time in centuries, she felt lighter, relived from the burden of her parents' death. Mattias— whom she once thought was incapable of such an act— had been the one who relieved her. It was now her turn to do the same for him by keeping her end of the bargain. Tonight she'd do something a little different, something to show her appreciation, and to show the rest of his coven, with the power that Mattias gave her, that she meant business.

Prior to preparing herself for Mattias's presence, she peeked into the room where she left her parents for the day. As she expected, they were gone and she stood in the empty room that took her back to Nicholas's stay. Before she had the chance to be engulfed by the moment, she turned quickly and walked out, hoping the memories wouldn't follow. She needed to forget him.

She strolled back to her bedroom and stared at the crumbled sheets that dressed her bed, remembering the first time she and Nicholas made love.

*Note to self, purchase new bed linens.*

With that thought, she rushed to the shower and dressed for her first night back at the Haven. Tonight, she drove and parked in plain sight. She stepped out of the car, walked toward the door, and met the new security guard who knew Gianna without introduction. "Miss Marino, welcome back. It's lovely to see you."

Gianna nodded and walked past the guard who turned his head for a second look once she passed. She walked the usual path through the club until she met Mattias's gaze. Yes, they had an accord, but his reaction was the same as usual.

Most females would relish the fact that they were wanted by a man of such power but not, Gianna. She wasn't swayed by position or impressed with popularity. Still, he'd done something for her that revealed a side of him that was unexpected and she was less than thrilled it appealed to her the way it had.

Mattias was seated with Dante, Cassius, Michael, and the Anthony twins. It was a pleasant sight.

*So, this is the new and improved Vitale Coven.*

Gianna inched closer to the group when she overheard the Anthony twins. "Holy shit, that has to be one of the hottest humans I've ever seen."

"Yeah, what I wouldn't give to sink my teeth into her and maybe have her birth my offspring."

"Couldn't you just picture those strong thighs on each side of you as she rode all night?"

"I'm going for it, Van."

"Like hell you are, Vex. I saw her first."

"We could share her. She may even like the idea."

Cassius spoke up in warning. "You may want to rethink that plan. She is off limits. Gianna is Mattias's exclusive human. That means, if you touch her, you die."

Mattias smiled in victory as Gianna strode in his direction. The coven males stood to greet her as Mattias reached out, wrapped his arms around her waist and kissed her deeply, a performance for the newly inducted brethren. The Anthony brothers licked their lips in unison and leaned in for a closer look.

Mattias released Gianna and introduced her to the new members. "Vanner and Vexon Anthony, this is Gianna Marino."

"Hey. I'm Vexon...he's Vanner. Vex and Van for short."

"It's nice to meet you, gentlemen."

Gianna took note that the twins were double-your-pleasure gorgeous. Two platinum blondes with hair that hung just to the shoulders and possessed unreal turquoise eyes, their bodies were both taut and their incubus ways left them aroused during her interaction with Mattias. Their pupils were dilated and their erections evident. When they filtered their pheromones through the air, she felt the tingle. It was the push she needed to end their round-table meeting.

She knew that due to the twins' incubus nature, they'd hoped to lure her in their direction to take turns torturing her in the most sensual of ways, but it worked against them, and in Mattias's favor. "Have they accepted their invitations, Mattias?"

"Yes. They've accepted and have been inducted as well."

"That's good to hear. Are you through?

"All major topics have been addressed."

"Good. Now we have business of our own to tend to."

Dante stood. "But we haven't finished our discussion."

"It can wait, Dante."

"No, Gianna. It can't."

"Dante, you can handle things for awhile. Minor details can wait until later."

"All right, Mattias...whatever you need."

Gianna took Mattias by the hand and led him to his bedroom while Dante scowled until they disappeared from his sight.

"Where are we going, Gianna?"

"I didn't think you would be complaining that I was stealing you away from business for a bit of playtime."

"Is that what you're doing?"

"I wanted to express my gratitude."

When they reached his bedroom they walked in and Gianna closed the door behind them.

\*\*\*

Dante was sure to bring a willing victim to his bedroom for the remainder of the evening. He needed to feed, to relieve the scorching frustration over the sight of Gianna and Mattias. It was a relief to see that she was back where she belonged and that she was safe but it was painful to be so close to her on a daily basis and not be able to touch her the way he wanted.

Gianna and Mattias weren't seen for hours since they disappeared claiming to be dealing with business of their own. Dante knew that they were probably panting, covered with sweat, and maybe even a little blood.

Suspicions were confirmed when he passed by Mattias's room with his female victim, and heard them both scream in pleasure.

*Yes, Mattias...harder. Harder!*

*Oh god, Gianna. You feel too good. I can't hold on any longer!*

*Come for me, Mattias. Fill me with everything you have.*

*You first.*

Their sensual taunts were followed by simultaneous orgasms that were loud enough that they may be heard by anyone who happened to pass by. Dante's victim laughed. "It sounds like someone's partying."

Dante turned to the woman. "Mmm...so it does."

He backed into a wall that overlooked the banister down to the nightclub. The wall was only a few feet from Mattias's bedroom door where Dante pulled the woman against him. He began kissing her hard and furiously. "Oh, Dante. Take me."

"Mmm...with pleasure."

Mattias's door came open and Gianna stepped out with the intent to go to the kitchen for a glass of water. It would've been a few minutes, there and back to Mattias's room. She eased the door closed and only walked a few feet when she came face to face with Dante and his female. She drew a soft gasp when Dante's eyes flew open, his fangs embedded into the woman's neck. Her back was facing Gianna and her moans were uncensored.

Dante stared at Gianna with curiosity when his pupils dilated, giving off an aura of lust. Lust meant for her. He moaned along with his victim, imagining the blood she was so willing to sacrifice was Gianna's.

Gianna wore nothing but Mattias's white dress shirt. Her legs and feet were bare and the first few buttons of the shirt remained open. The outline of her body was visible through the garment and Dante's eyes grew to complete darkness before removing his fangs from the woman's neck. A trail of blood flowed from her wound and Dante delivered one long, sensual lick and dropped his victim to the floor, his gaze still locked on the true object of his desire.

His chest heaving, lips and chin coated with fresh blood, he stared at her, licking away at what remained as he beckoned her in his direction. No words were spoken. They stood for what seemed like minutes, staring and breathing heavily. Lust lingered thick in the air around them and every move was made with utmost caution. His erection was evident and she wasn't disinterested.

Suddenly, Mattias's door opened, the coven leader leaned against one side of the frame. Gianna didn't give Mattias the opportunity to speak when she turned and shoved him back into the room, slamming the door behind them, surely resuming play. When they disappeared from sight, Dante sighed in both jealousy and relief before making a decision that would affect the future of the entire coven, and would set the stage for a drastic turn of events. Dante's time was coming.

# EPILOGUE

*Six months later...*

With the help of Gianna's mother, Sofia organized some things in Gianna's home. "Sofia, I cannot thank you enough for your assistance with Gianna. We couldn't have better friends."

"It's my pleasure."

Gianna rushed through the house, trying to make her way out the front door without being noticed when the two women in motherly fashion stopped her by calling her name in unison.

She froze where she stood and looked at the women. "Did I forget something Sofia? Mom?"

"Have you eaten?"

"It appears I *did* forget something."

"There is sushi on the table waiting for you. Please don't let it spoil." Sofia walked Gianna to the kitchen and continued their conversation.

"Thanks, Sofia. Oh, and please...go home. Your family needs you. Bennett must be worried sick without you."

"He's fine. He calls constantly, but he's fine."

"How are the others?"

"Everyone is well."

"How...umm...is—"

"He's managing. He's not happy, but he's managing. Every night is a new one. "

"I never meant to hurt him. I needed to call Mattias's bluff. I needed to know for sure. Mattias's would've killed him and would've never left you all alone, otherwise."

"I know and we are grateful. I am blissful, Gianna and I have you to thank for it."

"I'm sorry I haven't called. I wanted to give him space. We both needed time to heal."

"Have *you* healed, Gianna?"

She didn't answer. She couldn't. Instead, she stood and embraced Sofia. "Thank you so much for your continued hard work. I appreciate everything you do and I miss you in the house."

"It's the least I could do. Don't worry...I'll have the house filled with assistants in no time. Don't be a stranger. Come and visit sometime."

"I don't think I'll be doing that, Sofia, but I thank you for the invitation. Please give Bennett and the others my best."

Gianna left the kitchen, gave her mother a kiss on the cheek, and ran out the door. She walked to the garage and chose to drive the Hayabusa tonight. She needed to feel the kind of stress release that only driving her bike down the highway could give her. She started the engine, placed her helmet on her head, and was on her way.

Things had been hectic since Dante left the coven six months ago. It was sudden and no one saw it coming—no one except Gianna.

When Dante took a victim in front of her, all the while wishing it were her, she could see the hunger and the lust in his eyes. The restraint that he used by not fucking her where he'd dropped his victim was admirable, but she knew that it was his breaking point. To free herself of that awkward moment, she had screwed Mattias senseless and he was none the wiser for it.

Mattias's bed had been warm every night since their return from the United States and Gianna was every bit satisfied, never disappointed. Although she enjoyed their bed-sport, she felt she needed a night off that Mattias would never allow. She'd have to wait until he had business away from London. That is, if he decided not to take her along.

Something had the coven stirring lately and she couldn't place what it was but she had a feeling it was huge and was about to boil over. She had an even more disturbing feeling that during her ride to the Haven, someone or something was following her. She checked her mirrors and used every sense she possessed, but unless the tracker was blocking her sensitive perception, she was just plain paranoid.

When she arrived at the club, she parked her bike and peered into the darkness but nothing seemed out of the ordinary. She removed her helmet, shaking her curly brown hair free of its prison and removed her short leather jacket. When she stepped down off the bike and brushed her hand through her hair, she saw a flash of green that looked like a set of eyes—impossible in the dark of night.

She darted in the direction of the anomaly but found nothing but a line of would-be-clubbers waiting their entry into Mattias's building.

She shook the fog from her head. *It must have been the emeralds in the bracelet.* Yes, that, and it was six months since she last saw Nicholas Sutton. Six months was her confirmation that if he didn't try to make contact, it was the official end of their relationship. She was now convinced that what they shared was beautiful and now over. If that was the case, then why did she still hold his gift so close? It didn't matter. What's done, is done.

She gathered her things and walked into the club, toward Mattias who looked hot, as usual. She kissed him before she sat. "Mmm...I always look forward to that."

"I'm glad you haven't grown tired of me, Mattias."

"That will *never* happen, my love."

"What's going on? Why does everyone look so tense?"

"We need for you to sit down."

Gianna's eyes widened and she took her seat next to Mattias who opened the conversation among the coven. "We have been keeping a close eye on some suspicious activity reported from the Mediterranean area...Greece to be precise. Rumors have indicated that there have been vampire sightings and the air in Greece has an ancient practice stirring about."

Gianna was confused. "An ancient practice...as in?"

"I believe the modern world refers to the time of the ancient Greek gods and goddesses as Mythology but it is in fact, very real." Mattias looked to her as if about to speak in code. "As real as *you* and *I*."

She knew exactly what he meant—Mythic. "Who or what is the source?"

"Well, if the result is to summon the powers of the ancients, or the ancients themselves, it will take a powerful descendent to complete the  ritual."

Cassius motioned to speak. "Do we know of a descendent?"

"I can only think of one...Dante."

The twins spoke in unison. "Fuck."

Michael grew concerned. "What is your intention, Mattias?"

"My intention is to have someone investigate the site and if what we suspect is in fact, the case, we will need someone to infiltrate his operation."

Cassius volunteered. "I'll go."

"No. He will be too suspicious. We need someone he'll grow to trust or at least be too preoccupied with to see the truth. We'll need to send Gianna."

"Me? Why...me?"

"You know why, love. Do not fear, we'll be a phone call away. We would never risk your loss should something not go as planned."

"When do I leave?"

"As soon as possible. I'll take you to Greece myself."

*Great. This should be a real party.* She rubbed the tender area on the underside of her right wrist, concealed beneath a treasured emerald bracelet. The location bore a mark, black intertwining tribal branches on four sides, joined by a red circle in the center that appeared during the flight back to London, six months ago. The mark could only mean the one thing she refused to admit. She was bound to Mattias Vitale, and she prayed he'd never find out.

Meanwhile, outside where Gianna parked her street bike, a shadow approached, caressing where the hybrid sat moments earlier.

*I must be more careful. I underestimated the pain of seeing her again, but needed closure. Yet she still wears the bracelet, my gift to her, keeping me close, a sign that there is still...hope.*

The journey continues in book two of the Mythic Series...

# Blood Moon

The time of the mythological deities had ended. The world as we know it evolved, leaving little time to worship those whom were held with such esteemed regard. The influence once held by the gods and goddesses of Olympus had diminished and none of them were pleased with the outcome.

Ignorance of the modern world enabled would-be worshippers to turn their backs, weakening the beliefs and destroying the power of the Pantheon. The deities were vengeful and vowed to once again, influence the lands of Greece. The desire to be feared and respected was as great as ever and all that was needed was a catalyst of great power, a human descendent of the gods that could free them from silence and unbind them from solitude.

The great descendent was capable of invoking the powers of the Olympians by making offerings in their name. To obtain their abilities, the descendent must complete an intricate ritual during the time of the Blood Moon, when the celestial body was lowest in the sky above, holding a hue of deep crimson.

The astral event occurred once every thousand years. The anniversary was approaching and the descendent had been found. Soon, the wait would be over and the gods and goddesses of old would once again walk the earth while the descendent who released them would become the most powerful being to exist.

The descendent lived in the modern world, in the realm of human, earthly existence, a world among the non-believers, yet the chosen one knew of the truth, that there were far greater powers than of those which the foolish mortals were aware. Silently, he bided his time, waiting in shadow, hiding within the service of another, contented. Until the fateful moment when he made the decision to leave his service all because of the presence of a woman, one he ached to call his own.

To claim her was forbidden, for to do so would shame him, his people and his history. She would have to come to him with free will and accept what he would offer. Once the god powers were flowing through him, no woman would deny his touch and he only wanted one—Gianna Marino and she was claimed by another.

Only Dante Diakos was not the only descendent who was capable of unleashing the deities from confinement. The Diakos family had aristocracy flowing through their bloodlines. It was foretold that the son of Diakos would be the savior of the gods. The last of that bloodline produced two sons, each born to brothers, both of which still existed.

The fate of the world would depend on which of the Diakos sons would embrace their fate. If the gods were freed by a force of evil, the world would blacken and fall but if the gods of old were freed by a force of good, the world would flourish.

In addition to their release, the gods and goddesses still had the opportunity to refuse the descendent, objecting his birthright, to side with the other should they choose. This conflict would bring about a war among realms, one for which the modern world would not be prepared and only the strongest and most worthy would survive.

\*\*\*

*I don't want to do this,* she pondered over the idea of giving Dante exactly what he wanted. Angry over Mattias's instruction, devastated over sacrificing her happiness with the only man she'd ever loved because she felt indebted to Mattias, she straightened with renewal.

*Fuck it. I've been numb my entire life. I can be numb again. After all, it's part of the detail.*

She stood, dressed in a black chiton—a sheer dress worn by the Greek goddesses of old. Of course that's what he wanted her to wear. The thin garment barely concealed her body.

Gianna walked to the throne room.

*You can do this,* she thought.

Down the hall, she wandered to the place she knew she'd find him. Seated in a god's throne, an oversized seat made of solid gold, Dante sat with a long leg draped over the armrest. Two women knelt on either side of him and touched the self-proclaimed god with utter adoration.

She'd intended to walk to that place, to turn off all feeling, all emotion. Easier said than done when her breath caught in her throat. She didn't expect Dante to look so spectacular. It was about to throw a bit of difficulty into her plan.

# Author Bio

Jae Lynne Davies has been an avid fan of the paranormal since childhood, when her imagination began to take form in written word. Shortly after the birth of her second child, she began writing stories based on her ideas, and before she knew it, she'd created a world where the passion is hot, relationships are forbidden, and the constant struggle of power leaves readers feeling for the villain today, and the hero tomorrow.

When not playing in her fantasy world, Jae Lynne is a native of Philadelphia, Pennsylvania, and now resides in Southern New Jersey, is a wife to a wonderful and supportive husband, and the mother of two young children.

To learn more about the work of Jae Lynne Davies, please visit www.jaelynnedavies.com

Proof

19924070R00186

Made in the USA
Charleston, SC
18 June 2013